“Becaus[illegible] you abou[illegible] be for the better,” he explained.

“It just isn’t right. I-I-I care for you, yet these secrets between us are keeping me from…” She couldn’t say “trusting you,” but that’s how she felt. How could she allow herself deep feelings for a man who preferred to keep his identity anonymous?

He took her hand and pressed his warm lips to it, lingering and inhaling as if he wanted to commit her scent to memory. “Och, lass, I think it is for the best that our emotions do not run too deep.” Meeting her gaze with a hungry, almost predatory stare, he took a step closer. “A man could lose himself in those eyes of yours.”

Her mysterious Highland lord brushed his finger along Akira’s chin, sending gooseflesh down the length of her neck. “Let us enjoy the gathering this evening and forget our worries about things to come. For tonight you are a queen and I am a king. The world is ours…”

# THE HIGHLAND DUKE

*A Lords of the Highlands Novel*

AMY JARECKI



FOREVER
NEW YORK BOSTON

Cover design by Elizabeth Turner
Cover illustration by Craig White


Forever
Hachette Book Group
1290 Avenue of the Americas, New York, NY 10104
forever-romance.com
twitter.com/foreverromance

First Edition: March 2017

Forever is an imprint of Grand Central Publishing. The Forever name and logo are trademarks of Hachette Book Group, Inc.



ISBN: 978-1-4555-9780-2 (mass market), 978-1-4555-9782-6 (ebook)

Printed in the United States of America

OPM

10 9 8 7 6 5 4 3 2 1

*To my agent, Elaine Spencer, who rarely sugarcoats anything, but believes in me regardless of my flaws.*

*And to my talented editor, Caroline Acebo, who has a magical knack for bringing out artfulness.*

*I thank you both.*

# Chapter One

*Hoord Moor, Scotland. 21 August 1703.*

The dead Highland soldier stared vacantly at the thick, low-hanging clouds. Akira clutched her basket tight to her stomach. Concealed in the tall moorland grass, this man needed no healing. Now only the minister could offer help to redeem the hapless warrior's soul.

Death on the battlefield bore none of the heroics she'd heard from fireside tales. Death on the battlefield was cold and lonely, dismal like the mist muffling the shrill calls of the buzzards.

And for naught.

Gulping back her nausea, Akira turned away. A breeze rustled through the eerily tranquil lea as if putting to rest the violence that had occurred not more than an hour ago. She scanned the stark meadow, searching for men who might have need of a healer's attention. She cared not whether they were Government dragoons or clansmen from Highland regiments. Anyone suffering from battle wounds this day needed tending, regardless of politics.

A deep moan came from the forest beyond the tree line not ten paces away. She jolted, jostling the remedies in her basket. "Is s-someone there?"

When no answer came, she glanced over her shoulder. Her companions had moved on—women from the village of Dunkeld who had helped tend the wounded before red-coated soldiers marshaled the men into the back of a wagon. Where they would go from there, Akira hadn't asked, but she hoped they wouldn't be thrown in a prison pit, at least not before their wounds were healed.

The moan came again and, with it, a chilly gust that made her hackles stand on end.

Cautiously, Akira tiptoed into the trees, peering through the foliage to ensure she wasn't walking into a trap. A telltale path of blood skimmed over the ground, leading to two black boots beneath a clump of broom. Had the man dragged himself all the way from the battlefield to hide?

"Are you injured?" she asked warily, her perspiring palms slipping on the basket's handle. Could she trust he wouldn't leap up and attack?

"My leg," said a strained voice.

There was no disguising the pain in his tone. "Goodness gracious," she whispered, dropping to her knees in the thick moss and pulling away the branches and debris that covered his body.

Vivid hazel eyes stared up at her from beneath a layer of dirt. Wild as the Highlands and filled with agony, his gaze penetrated her defenses like a dagger. She'd never seen eyes that expressive—that intense. They made her so . . . so unnerved.

"What happened?" she asked.

He shuttered those eyes with a wince. "Shot."

Akira's gaze darted to his kilt, hitched up and exposing a well-muscled thigh covered with blood.

"You a healer?" he asked, his Adam's apple bobbing.

"Aye." She peered closer. Puckered skin. A round hole. "A musket ball?"

His trembling fingers slid to the puncture wound. "'Tis still in there. It needs to come out."

Care of musket wounds far exceeded her skill. "I-I'll fetch the physician."

Opening his eyes, the man clasped her arm in a powerful grip. The pressure of his huge hand hurt. Gasping, she tugged away, but his fingers clamped harder, and those eyes grew more determined.

"No," he said in an intense whisper. "You do it."

She shook her head. "Sir, I cannot."

He released her arm, then pulled a knife from his sleeve. "Use my wee dagger." The blade glistened, honed sharp and shiny clean against his mud-encrusted doublet.

She shied away from the weapon. "But you could die."

The mere thought of performing surgery after the loss of her last patient made her stomach turn over. And it had been Dr. Kennedy who'd carved out the musket ball in that unfortunate patient's knee, though she'd tended the lad through his painful decline and eventual death. Regardless of the physician's role, the man's passing had taken a toll on her resolve.

"Do it, I say." For a man on the brink of death, he spewed the command like a high-ranking officer. "I cannot risk being found. Do you understand?"

Licking her lips, she stared at the wound, then pressed her fingers against it. He was right; the ball needed to come out now, and if he refused to let her find a physician, Akira was the only healer in Dunkeld skilled enough to help him.

He hissed in pain.

"Apologies." She snapped her hand away. "I was feeling for the musket ball."

"Whisky."

She glanced to her basket. "I've only herbs and tinctures."

"In my sporran."

The leather pouch rested askew, held in place by a belt around his hips. Merciful mercy, it covered his unmentionables. Moreover, he was armed like an outlaw, with a dirk sheathed on one side of his belt, a flintlock pistol on the other, and a gargantuan sword slung in its scabbard beside him. Who knew what other deadly weapons this imposing Highlander hid on his person?

His shaking fingers fumbled with the thong that cinched the sporran closed.

She licked her lips. "You expect me to reach inside?" Goodness, her voice sounded shrill.

"Och," he groaned, his hands dropping. "Give a wounded du—ah—scrapper a bit o' help, would you now?"

Akira scraped her teeth over her bottom lip. The Highlander did need something to ease his pain. Praying she wouldn't be seen and accused of stealing, she braced herself, shoved her hand inside the hideous thing, and wrapped her fingers around a flask. She blinked twice as she pulled it out and held it up. *Silver?* Gracious, a flask like that could pay for Akira and her family to eat for a year or more.

She pulled the stopper and he raised his head, running his tongue across chapped lips. "Give me a good tot, lass."

His fingers trembled while he guided the flask in her hands, drank a healthy swig, and coughed.

"I'm ready," he said, his jaw muscles flexing as he bared his teeth—straight, white, contrasting with the dark stubble and dirt on his face. Dear Lord, such a man could pass for the devil.

The faster she worked, the less he'd suffer. With a featherlight touch, she swirled her fingers over the puncture and located the hard lump not far beneath the skin. Thank heavens the musket ball had stopped in his flesh and hadn't shattered the bone.

Though she'd never removed a musket ball before, she had removed an arrow. Steeling her nerves, she gripped the knife and willed her hand to steady. "Prepare yourself, sir." But still she hesitated.

He grasped her wrist and squeezed, staring into her eyes with determination and focus. "You can do this, lass."

Setting her jaw, she gave him a sharp nod. Then she returned her gaze to the wound, quickly slid the knife through the musket hole with one hand, and pushed against the ball with the other. The Highlander's entire body quaked. But no sound other than a strained grunt passed his lips.

Blood gushed from the wound and soaked Akira's fingers. Gritting her teeth, she applied more pressure, pushing the knife until she hit lead.

*I cannot fail. I will not let him die.*

She gritted her teeth and forced another flesh-carving twist of her wrist. The ball popped out. Blood flooded from the wound like an open spigot.

The man jerked, his leg thumping. Akira dove for her

basket and grabbed a cloth. Wadding it tight, she held the Highlander's leg down with her elbows while she shoved the compress against the puncture with all her might. Looking up, she stared at his eyes until he focused on her. "Hold on," she said. "The worst is over."

Though he never cried out, the Highlander panted, sweat streaming from his brow. Not blinking, he stared at her like a yellow-eyed wildcat. "Horse."

Akira pushed the cloth harder, the muscles in his thigh solid as steel. "The soldiers took all the horses."

"Damnation!" he swore through clenched teeth, his breathing still ragged. Then his stare intensified. "I will... purchase... yours."

The man could die with his next breath, yet he still issued orders as if in charge of an entire battalion of cavalry. His tone demanded she respond with instant agreement, but she could not.

"I can barely afford to feed my siblings. I have no horse. Not even a donkey—not that I'd let you have it if I did." There. She wasn't about to allow this Highlander to lord it over her as if he were the Marquis of Atholl.

His eyes rolled to the back of his head. "Buy one."

"I told you—"

"There is... coin... My sporran."

Akira glanced at the man's sporran again. She'd have to sink her fingers deeper this time. Though she might be poor, she was certainly no harlot. Fishing in there was as nerve-racking as carving a musket ball out of the man's thigh. With a grimace, she tried shifting his belt aside a wee bit. *Curses*—the sporran shifted not an inch.

And he was still bleeding like a stuck pig. "Even if I did purchase you a horse, you couldn't ride. I'd wager you'd travel no more than a mile afore you fell off and succumbed to your wound." Still holding the cloth in place, Akira reached for her basket. "Let me wrap this tight and I'll call the soldiers. They're helping the wounded into a cart."

"Absolutely not!" His eyes flashed wide as he gripped her wrist. The man's intense stare, combined with the hard line of his jaw, wasn't the look of a pleading man—it was the look of a man who would not be disobeyed. "Atholl's men must not know I'm here."

She gave him her most exasperated expression while she wrapped the bandage around his thigh. Asserting her authority as a healer, Akira squared her shoulders. She was in charge, not he. "You ken they can help you."

"The Government troops? They're murderers." He winced. "They'd slit my throat for certain."

Since the battle's end, she hadn't seen anyone slit a throat... but then she hadn't asked where the soldiers were taking the injured. She'd just assumed to the monastery to be tended by the monks. But the pure intensity of this man's cold stare told her to do as he said. Beyond that, she believed him.

The hairs on her nape stood on end as she twisted the bandage like a tourniquet and tied it while questions needled her mind. If this man was as important as he seemed, why had he been left alone? "Who are you?"

"Merely... merely a Highlander who needs to haste back to his lands"—he drew in a stuttering breath—"a-afore the ill-breeding curs burn me out."

She narrowed her gaze. *A man of property?* Akira wasn't daft—especially when her mother's larder was bare. "I'll fetch you a horse if you pay me a shilling."

"Done," he said, as if such coin meant nothing. "Make haste and tell no one I'm here."

Gulping, she glanced down to the sporran. She'd been in there once before. Besides, the Highlander was in no shape to do anything untoward. If it wasn't for the need to care for her mother and three sisters, she'd call over the dragoons and let them see to this man's need for a mount. But for a shilling? Ma would be so happy.

Akira's fingers trembled.

Taking a deep breath, she reached inside the sporran. Her hand stuck in the neck, forcing her to twist her wrist to push deeper. Something hard flexed against her fingers. She froze. *Holy hexes*, she was shoving against the rock-hard wall of his inner thigh. She had no choice but to look down.

*Dear Lord, please do not let anyone venture past us now.*

With her hand completely buried in the man's sporran, she looked like an alehouse harlot toying with his . . . unmentionables.

"Are ye having trouble, lass?" The man's deep burr lulled with a hint of mischief, practically stopping her heart.

"No." With a blink, she wrapped her fingers around a number of coins and forcefully drew her hand free.

Akira's tongue went dry. Three silver shillings and two ten-shilling pieces filled her palm. She'd never seen so much coin in her life. No, she should not feel badly about asking for payment. After dropping one shilling in her pocket and returning all but one of the other coins, she held up a ten-shilling piece. *This ought to be enough.*

Standing, she hesitated. "What is your name, sir?"

A deep crease formed between his brows. "'Tis no concern of yours."

He didn't trust her—not that she trusted him, either. The only man she'd ever trusted was Uncle Bruno. "I won't reveal it." She crossed herself. "I swear on my grandfather's grave."

His lips thinned. "You can call me Geordie. And you, miss?"

*Geordie is no given name I've ever heard. Odd.*

She curtsied. "You may call me Akira." Blast, she wasn't going to say "Akie." Only her sisters referred to her thus. And "Ayres" would make him suspicious for certain. Her family might be descendants of Gypsy stock, but they'd given up their heathen practices generations ago. If Mr. Geordie wanted to hide his identity, she certainly would hide hers.

* * *

After the healer left, George Gordon closed his eyes and prayed the woman had enough sense to keep her mouth shut. After Queen Anne had rejected the Scottish Parliament's proposed Act of Security, the entire country was in an uproar—and ready to strike against the Government at last. Yes, he'd agreed to stand by his cousin and challenge the Government troops. The queen's Act of Settlement was nothing but a sham, created to subvert the succession of the rightful Stuart line behind the guise of Protestantism.

Thank God he hadn't worn anything to reveal his true identity. He'd even kept to the rear beside his cousin William. After he was thrown from his horse, the skirmish had raged on and the clansmen had charged ahead across the moorland, leaving Geordie for dead.

Once he'd dragged himself into the brush, he must have lost consciousness until that wisp of a healer found him. He thanked the stars it had been she and not a redcoat. His lands would be forfeit if Queen Anne discovered he'd ridden against the English crown.

*James Stuart may be exiled, but he is the only king to whom I will pay fealty. I would take ten musket balls to the thigh if it assured his coronation.*

Geordie's leg throbbed—ached like someone had stabbed him with a firebrand. But through the pain, he must have dozed again, because it seemed that Akira returned in the blink of an eye.

He eyed her sternly, as he would a servant—an inexplicably bonny servant. "Did the stable master ask questions?" he demanded, forcing himself to sit up. God's teeth, everything spun. The sharp pain made his gut churn.

"Pardon?" she replied in a tone mirroring his own. Never in his life had he seen such a haughty expression come from a commoner. "'Tis a bit difficult to conceal a horse beneath my arisaid. Besides, I didn't *steal* the beast." She thrust a fist against her hip. "He asked where I came up with that kind of coin."

Gordon licked his lips with an arid tongue. "How did you reply?"

Akira's fist slid down to her side—a more respectful stance for a wee maid. "I told him I'd received handsome payment from His Lordship for tending his cousin."

"His Lordship?"

"The Marquis of Atholl, of course."

*Smart lass.* "Do you ken the marquis?" *Bloody hell*, he hoped not.

"If you call paying him fealty knowing him, then aye. So does everyone around these parts. He's lord of these lands."

*And he supports the Government troops, the bastard.*

Geordie needed to mount that damned horse and ride like hellfire. If anyone recognized him, he'd be shipped to the Tower of London, where they'd make a public mockery of his execution.

He leaned forward to stand. *Jesus Christ!* Stars darted through his vision. Stifling his urge to bellow, he gritted his teeth.

The lass caught his arm. "Allow me to help."

His insides clamped taut. Must she look at him with such innocent allure?

He gave a curt nod, hating to accept any help but knowing it was necessary. "My thanks."

Clenching his teeth, he slid his good foot beneath him. Akira tugged his arm while he pushed up with the other.

"Christ Almighty!" he bellowed from the depths of his gut before he had time to choke it back.

She slung his arm over her shoulder. *A lot of good that did. The lass might make a useful crutch for a lad of twelve.* "If they didn't ken you were here before, they do now."

"Ballocks!" he cursed, trying not to fall on top of the woman. Then he looked at the damned nag. "No saddle?"

She held out a few copper farthings. "There wasn't enough."

"Damnation."

The urchin narrowed her eyes at him. "I'll not be cursed at like a doormat whilst I'm merely trying to help you."

Geordie grumbled under his breath and removed his arm from her shoulder. He took quick note of the surroundings. They needed more cover for certain. He pointed deeper into the wood. "Lead the beast to the fallen tree, yonder."

She didn't budge. "Oh my," she said with a gasp. "Your leg is bleeding something awful."

He swayed on his feet. Good God, he couldn't lose his wits. Not until he had ridden to safety. "Can you stanch it?"

"Give me your belt."

He slid his hands to his buckle, when a twig snapped behind them.

"Who goes there?" demanded a stern voice.

Akira's eyes popped wide.

The beat of Geordie's heart spiked. With a wave of strength, he grabbed the lassie's waist and threw her atop the horse. Taking charge of the reins, he urged the beast into a run, steering it beside the fallen tree. Agonizing pain stabbed his thigh, but the pressing need to escape gave him herculean energy.

*Haste.*

In two leaps he landed astride the gelding, right behind the lass. Slapping the reins, he kicked his heels into the horse's barrel as he pointed the beast down a narrow path. Stabbing torture in his thigh punished his every move.

Musket fire cracked from behind.

Geordie leaned forward, demanding more speed. He pressed lips to Akira's ear. "Hold on, lass, for hell has just made chase."

# Chapter Two

After them!" roared Captain Roderick Weaver, leader of the Marquis of Atholl's regiment of Government troops. He dug in his spurs and whipped his reins. With a grunt, his steed pinned his ears and broke into a gallop, white foam leeching from his neck and withers. Roderick wasn't about to let another cowardly Jacobite escape into the Highlands.

"The horses are spent," yelled Corporal Snow from the rear. The beetle-brained halfwit forever bemoaned the comfort of the damned horses, though he never thrust his sword into the air and hollered for the men to follow him—unless he was heading for the mess tent.

"Onward!" Roderick boomed, ignoring the corporal's warning.

The horses were beasts of burden. If the animals fell, he'd sequester more from the locals. There was a reason Atholl hired Roddy from Yorkshire to quash the rebellion. A staunch supporter of Queen Anne, he'd relentlessly chase these traitors to the end of the earth. For a price.

True, Roderick's entire body ached with fatigue just like everyone else's did. The battle had been fierce and the cleaning up after was laborious. But they'd found a runner, someone the captain would like to use to make a statement. Show Jacobites throughout Scotland what would happen, not only if they crossed the queen, but worse, if they crossed him.

No one crossed Roderick Weaver. Not ever.

On and on he kicked his horse while the beast snorted louder and louder. The tree branches whipping past and stinging his face only served to heighten his ire.

"Captain..."

Roddy glanced over his shoulder. The corporal's shouts combined with the thundering hoofbeats, making him impossible to understand, though Roddy had definitely heard the word *lame*.

*Miserable bleeding heart.*

Returning his gaze to the path, he saw a fallen tree three paces away. No time to change course. Roddy slackened the reins, gave the horse his head, and prepared to jump. He leaned so far forward, his torso suspended over his mount's mane as together they soared.

*This old gelding can run all day.*

The front hooves hit the ground. But the hindquarters of the horse kept going.

"Woooooooah!"

Sailing through the air, Roderick curled into a ball, ready for impact. With a jarring thud, his hip slammed into the earth. Hard. Every muscle in his body tensed. Dammit, he hated looking like an arse in front of his men.

Corporal Snow hopped off his horse and dashed to Roddy's side. "Are you all right, sir?"

The captain jerked his fists away from his face. *Dear God!* Sharp pain shot from his hip down through his leg. "Of course I'm all right, you maggot. Quickly, we must continue after them."

The corporal gestured behind him. "Your horse is spent."

Roderick peered around thc coward. Blast, the beast was lame as well, and appeared to be limping on all fours. Sitting up, he pulled his pistol from his belt. "We'll have to shoot him." He waved the weapon at a pair of sentinels. "Muldoon and Grey, ride double. I'll take Grey's horse." That chestnut gelding was the most spirited of the lot.

"With all due respect, sir. Every last horse is finished. They need food and water, as do the men."

Snorting, their heads down, the horses looked like a mob of nags ready for the slaughter yard. "Bloody hell!" He jammed the pistol back into his belt. Damnation, there was no use whipping horses to gain a few miles only to have them all go lame. "But mark me, we ride at dawn. I want that bastard's neck swinging from Atholl's noose."

When they arrived at back at the clearing, Roderick dismounted, limping from being thrown by that miserable excuse for a horse. "I want to know the name of the bastard's accomplice."

Corporal Snow kneeled beside the bloodstained earth. "Looks like he's injured pretty bad."

"With that much blood lost, I doubt he'll make it through the night," said Grey.

"Good." Roddy grinned. "'Twill make our job on the morrow easier, though I'd prefer to find him on the brink of death rather than dead."

"What's this?" The corporal reached under a clump of broom and pulled out a silver flask.

"Give that to me." Roderick snatched it from Snow's hand and examined the engraving. "I'll be damned. If I'm not mistaken, 'tis the Duke of Gordon's coat of arms."

Snow stood and looked over Roderick's shoulder. "I'll wager that's worth a year's pay."

"Aye." Grey licked his lips. "But the duke's army didn't march against us—there was no Huntly pennant."

"His cousin, William Gordon of Strathdon, was here for certain," said Snow.

Roderick turned the flask in his palm. "The duke could have ridden with *them*."

"A duke ride without his army?" asked Sentinel Muldoon. "It would be far too risky for a man of Gordon's station to ride alone, especially into battle. His lands would be forfeit, not to mention his head."

Corporal Snow scratched his chin. "Right. Mayhap the flask was a gift?"

"A bloody generous one." Roddy had to agree with Muldoon. It was unlikely that the Duke of Gordon would have ridden into battle without his impressive clan of fighting Highlanders behind him. Regardless, whatever the culprit's clan, the runner wasn't long for this world.

Two more sentinels marched up and saluted. "Word is the woman was a healer from the village. She purchased a horse. Came up with the coin out of the blue, sir."

"Her name?"

"Akira Ayres—a thieving tinker."

Roderick snorted. "At least there's no need to worry about staging a rescue. The wench is as guilty as our mysterious, wealthy Highlander."

* * *

Racing through the forest so fast, everything passing in a blur, Akira hunched over the horse's neck as she dodged vines and sapling branches. The wind howled in her ears as if a tempest was brewing. Bless it, if Akira's heart would stop beating so fast, she might be able to think. She wove her fingers through the horse's mane and hung on for dear life, with the crazed Highlander leaning over her, demanding more speed with each kick of his heels. Every bone-jarring gallop made Akira's head hit the man's wall of a chest, while her seat slapped up and down behind the poor animal's withers.

"Stop leaning on me," she yelled. If only she had the nerve to let go and reach for the reins, she might be able to turn the beast around and head for home.

"Bit further," Geordie replied, his breathing ragged, his voice choked.

Akira chanced a backward glance. Oh no, his face looked as white as bleached linen. "Are you all right?" she hollered.

"Wha' ye think? Been shot."

Akira gulped and her palms perspired. She wasn't much of a horsewoman—hadn't had many chances in her life to ride. And now she was speeding into the Highlands on a mount with a bombastic wild man who spoke as if he were a commander in charge of the entire kingdom.

In a blink, the steed leapt a burn.

Her rear end soared off the horse. Akira closed her eyes and strengthened her grip lest she fall.

*I pray the fairies are with us.*

All three—horse and two riders—landed with a jolt. Her buttocks rebounded so high, the forward motion almost flung her over the horse's head. Stomach flying to her throat, Akira peered through the forest in terror. When would she fall, or worse, when would a branch smack her face and hurl her to her death?

A surge of courage pulsed through her fingers.

*It's me or him.*

Releasing one hand, she snatched a rein.

"No!" Geordie bellowed.

Ignoring him, she grabbed the other rein and bore down. "Whoa!"

Enormous fingers clamped over hers. "We need more distance, lass," he growled in her ear, his voice so deep it rumbled clear to her bones.

Her stomach squeezed. "You must be tended afore we both fall to our deaths running through the thick wood like a pair of lunatics."

"Outcropping." Overpowering her, he forced the reins to the right.

At first she had no clue what he was talking about, but as the horse turned, Akira saw it—a stony crag hidden in the trees. They hastened up the steep slope, rocks and gravel showering behind them. Halfway up, Geordie pulled the gelding to a stop, directly outside the mouth of a cave. She hadn't seen it from below, but there it stood, jagged and carved into the outcropping, with moss and leafy ferns draping over the opening, which was high enough for her to walk inside without stooping.

"Did you ken this was here?" Akira asked.

"Aye."

"Where are we?"

He dropped forward against her back. "Tay Forest. Not far enough from Hoord Moor, but you have to help me stop the bleeding."

She tried to push back with her elbow, but the man was too heavy. *Gracious, he must weigh at least sixteen stone.* "Are you feeling faint? B-because you keep leaning on me."

"I'm fine." Jerking up, he swung his uninjured leg over and slid from the horse. When his feet hit ground, he wobbled, all but collapsing.

Akira tried not to show her fear. Mercy, it seemed a long way down. Geordie grasped the bridle and placed a hand on her thigh—a very large and powerful hand for a man who'd lost so much blood. "Come, lass," he growled. "I'll help you."

"You can barely stand."

"Och, have a bit o' faith." He wrapped his arm around her waist and guided her to the ground, a strained grunt rumbling from his throat.

"See? You most likely made your wound bleed all the more." Though never so happy to be standing on her own two feet, she gave him a stern shake of her finger. "Look at you, you're half-dead."

"Inside," he grumbled, clearly not much for words, the commanding oaf. He draped his arm over her shoulders and leaned heavily, his face too white.

With no recourse but to wrap her arm around his waist, she threw a forlorn glance over her shoulder at the horse. She'd remove his bridle and hobble him later, but for now his reins were secured to a tree.

Together they staggered into the cave, its walls oozing with green algae. If she'd thought Mr. Geordie was heavy pushing against her on the horse, he now felt like four sacks of grain lumped across her shoulders. Worse, his breathing was labored.

Akira's fingers sank into banded muscle as she tried

to support him. Never had she tended a patient so solid. The Highlander couldn't have an ounce of fat covering his flesh.

They went deeper, serenaded by dripping water, the footing uneven and slick. A small stream ran through the middle of the rocks. The air was chilly, and gooseflesh spread across her skin like an eerie warning.

What if someone found her here with this strange man?

"I must return home," she announced. "I'll tend your leg, but then I must go."

He leaned against the stony wall, his head lolling. "I need your help. Stay a day until I regain my strength."

"Oh no." She shook her head. "My mother and sisters need me."

He closed his eyes. "I-I need you more." The words were soft, as if he hated to say them.

"No, I sai—"

"I will pay!" he boomed.

She sucked in a sharp breath. Hesitating, she looked him up and down. After Ma's accident, Akira couldn't trust strangers. Especially men. And there she stood, alone in a cave in the midst of the forest with a braw Highlander? But then, Mr. Geordie might grouse like an overbearing tyrant, but he was in no condition to do her harm.

She chewed her bottom lip. Few people in Dunkeld could afford to pay her much. Often her fee came in the form of food or the like.

*Payment? In coin?*

"How much?"

"Wha'ever ye—ah—need."

She glanced to his sporran, her tongue slipping to the corner of her mouth. "Ten shillings."

"Done."

She quashed her thundering heart with her hand. Never in her life had she been paid ten shillings for one task. She'd attended the man with the musket ball to the knee for a whole month and had only received sixpence.

Her eyes adjusting to the dim light, Akira watched the big Highlander slide down the wall and collapse onto a pile of musty old thresh left by the last occupant. Grunting, he hunched over, his head dropping to his chest.

"Sir?" When he didn't respond, she placed her hands on his shoulders and shook. "Geordie? Are you still alive?"

He took in a stuttered breath.

*Thank heavens.*

Tilting her head to the same angle as the man's, she examined his face. It was pleasant to look at, somewhat long and aristocratic, with bold eyebrows—but not too bold and definitely not bushy like her uncle's. The Highlander's hawkish nose suited his face, and dark stubble peppered his upper lip as well as his chin and jawline. Goodness, if Geordie were to grow a beard, it would be impressively full. But a beard wouldn't do at all, because it would cover the cleft in his chin—a very male cleft. Akira's tongue slipped across her bottom lip. A beard would also cover the wee mole on his right cheek. Aye, everyone needed to see that mole. It told anyone who regarded him that he wasn't perfect—his face, that is, wasn't quite perfect...but it was extraordinarily close to being so.

With another inhale, he snored a bit and his body jerked.

So did Akira.

His head lolled further to the side, and down with it

went his shoulders. He hit the cavern floor with a dull thud. Akira's fingers trembled as she held the back of her hand to his nose. Thank heavens, warm breath caressed her skin. As she ran her fingers through her hair, her gaze went to Geordie's leg, now covered by his blood-soaked kilt.

Wincing, she gingerly pushed the plaid up his leg until she exposed the bandage. A stream of blood leaked out and slid across his leg in a red stream. Quickly, she removed her apron and rolled it tight. Straining and grunting, she worked it under his enormous thigh, wrapped it around, and tied the linen taut.

With a deep sigh, she sat back and watched the blood seep through the cloth, fast at first, becoming slower. Thank heavens her mother had insisted she learn the art of healing. This man might actually live. If only she still had her medicine basket, food, candles, and the dozens of other things they needed.

She shuddered. What was she going to do with a patient in a cave?

*On all that is holy, I pledge that I shall not lose this one. Not this time.*

But she needed more than an apron for a bandage. How far had they traveled from Hoord Moor? She couldn't just disappear without letting her family know she was well. Besides, Ma and the lassies needed the shilling Geordie had given her.

And what about the dragoons who had made chase? Were they still following? By the angry shouts of the Government troops, Akira had no doubt they'd been keen to capture this Highlander. If she was found with him, they'd lock her in a pillory or the stocks for associating with a Jacobite.

She held her breath, listening for horses.

*I should leave him, deny having tried to help him.*

She glanced over her shoulder, out toward the wilderness. A hollow bubble spread through her chest.

*But I cannot. I wouldn't leave a dog to suffer alone. How could I abandon a man?*

She'd given her word, and if she could do nothing else in this world, she'd stand by her honor. Besides, she couldn't deny Ma and the lassies needed the coin he'd offered.

Making a decision, she dashed out of the cave, took a branch, and skittered down the hill. Running as far as she dared, she worked to hide their tracks just like her Uncle Bruno had taught her, raking dirt over hoofprints and covering the wet earth with leaves.

"*No self-respecting Gypsy can go through life without learning how to disappear.*" Ma's brother was the only member of the family who still practiced some of the old ways. But Akira might need to draw upon a few tricks he'd shown her. Now more than ever.

# Chapter Three

Though she had worked quickly, it took an hour or more to cover their tracks, and by the time she returned to the cave, the sun had moved behind the western mountains. Now that the smoke wouldn't give away their hiding place, she lit a small fire. As soon as she examined her patient, Akira's stomach dropped to her toes. The apron she'd tied around Geordie's thigh was completely saturated with blood.

*If he doesn't stop bleeding now, he'll die for certain.*

She shuddered at the task she must perform.

She placed her hand on his shoulder and squeezed. Gracious, every time she touched the man, she was reminded of his size—and his braw ruggedness. Together as a whole, he didn't seem so enormous, but when she examined his individual parts, every inch of the man was unusually large.

"Sir?" She gave him a shake, but he made no response whatsoever.

Chewing the corner of her mouth, she drew his dirk

from its scabbard and placed the tip in the fire. She busied herself by removing his bandages while she waited until the tip glowed red—just like it ought.

*By my oath, I will do everything in my power to ensure this Highlander stays alive.*

"Mr. Geordie?" She tried shaking him again, with the same lack of response.

*Might as well have it over with whilst he's still unconscious.*

She wrapped the dirk's handle in her skirt to keep from burning her fingers.

"Forgive me," she murmured.

Clenching her teeth, she slowly lowered the knife's tip. With the slightest touch, sizzling flesh burned and stank. She cringed while she pressed the scorching metal to the wound to cauterize it.

"Yeeeaaaaoooow!" Bucking a good foot off the ground, the Highlander hollered like a yearling in the castration pen. "Jesus Christ, holy hellfire, you vixen spawn of Satan!" Taking in deep gasps, he rolled on the ground, cradling his thigh. "Goddamn, ballocks, devil's dragons, and all the putrid, vile shite in Hades! Do not *ever* do that again!"

Smacked in the chest by his thrashing, Akira landed on her backside a good two feet away. She scooted back to the cave wall and stared, afraid he might wallop her again.

"If I kent you were going to curse at me like a joob from the alehouse, I would have gone home and left you to die!" She rolled to her hip and rubbed her backside.

He glared at her with horror, as if his angry stare could send her to hell's fire. "Damnation, you should have had the decency to rouse me first—allowed me to bite down on a stick. Bloody hell, woman, you're lucky I didn't bite my tongue off."

She clambered to her feet, still rubbing her behind. She took great risks to help this heathen, and he acted madder than a swarm of stinging bees. "I tried to rouse you, you bullheaded bear!"

He rolled to his back, air whooshing through his lips. "Well, you should have tried harder."

"Fine." She jammed her fists into her hips. "Next time I'll slap you across the face a few dozen times."

He draped his arm over his eyes. "There won't be a bloody next time."

"Agreed. There won't be." Akira stooped to retrieve the dirk. "I kent it would hurt. Had I let it go another hour, you would have bled to death. Not to mention you were far better off unconscious, you ungrateful varlet. And there you lie, blaming me."

She shook the dirk right at his face. "Well, I didn't tell you to ride into battle and get yourself shot. You did that all by yourself without my help, and now if I don't take care of you, you could die...and if you died, I'd never forgive myself."

Heat flushed through her body as she threw the accursed dirk against the cave wall. "Of all the ungrateful oafs I have ever met, you must be the most boorish. If you dare die in my care, I shall—I shall *kill* you!"

Without waiting for his reply, Akira dashed outside, a tear slipping down her cheek. She hated it when she cried. And she didn't want that pigheaded Highlander to see how much he'd upset her.

* * *

Dumbfounded and on the brink of losing his wits, Geordie watched the waif dash out of the cave.

*Die? It will take a lot more than a wee musket ball to send me to my grave.*

Devil's spit, Akira's bitter tongue rivaled the duchess's—the *former* duchess's. Though Elizabeth had gone to great lengths to force him to appeal to Parliament and endure a year of miserable divorce proceedings, the wicked shrew would always be a duchess. She had demanded her right to the title throughout the whole sordid affair.

Geordie watched Akira until she disappeared from sight. The poor lass didn't have an inkling how right she'd been when she'd called him a bullheaded bear and an ungrateful oaf. His mother had gifted him with a handsome face, and from his father, he'd inherited the lust of ten court suitors. From the age of fourteen, Geordie hadn't been able to keep his hands off any woman who struck his fancy. Worse, the more resistant the woman was, the more he enjoyed the chase. Aye, a resistant woman, once won, always proved to be more ardent in the bedchamber.

*But no more. Women are the devil's spawn—especially that blue-eyed, raven-haired vixen who just branded me within an inch of my life.*

Geordie winced at an onslaught of searing pain shooting through his thigh.

Bloody hell, the wound felt the size of a fist, like she'd carved out a cavern with the damned dirk. Hissing, he placed his palms either side of his thigh and examined the damage. Angry red, scalded flesh puckered, looking like singed raw meat and smelling of horehound.

Aye, he'd spewed a string of curses at the lass, but she should know better than to jam a red-hot knife into a man's leg without giving him fair warning. Regardless, Geordie knew many a man who would have struck out blindly given such a rude awakening.

He'd scared her, too. He could tell she was about to cry when she'd rattled on about trying to help him. And damnation, she was adorable, justifying her actions with such conviction. For a lass no more than five feet tall, Akira surely stood her ground like a badger. Either she thought he was too weak from pain to overpower her, or she was just plain determined. He reckoned it was the latter, else she would have robbed him blind, then left him in the cave to suffer alone.

He almost wished she had, until he again glanced down at his thigh. The bleeding had stopped. His head still spun like a top, but with a bit of rest, he'd be able to ride for certain.

Dear Lord, what a mess. He should be riding home by now with Willy and his cousin's regiment. But there he lay, George Gordon, the first Duke of Gordon, half-dead in a cave not but five or six miles from the disastrous Battle of Hoord Moor.

Aye, he supported King James III, the true king of Scotland, England, and Ireland recognized by Louis XIV after the death of James II two years past. Yet still the boy king continued to live exiled in France. A staunch royalist, George would support the true king until he took his dying breath. James Francis Edward Stuart's usurping and incompetent sister, Anne, had no right to the throne. The only heir born with the birthright to rule all of Britain was King James, but these were precarious times, and a man, especially a nobleman, had to be very careful to whom he proclaimed his allegiance, lest his head end up on a chopping block like the Earl of Argyll in 1685. Geordie shuddered. He'd rather die in a fight than be paraded up the scaffold to meet the headsman's ax.

No, he wasn't a coward. He'd fight for his king—he'd

give his life, especially if it guaranteed James's ascension to the throne. But he would be of better use to Scotland and *the cause* if he remained alive.

Bloody hell, ages ago, when Geordie had barely reached his majority, King James II had appointed him Governor of Edinburgh Castle and Geordie had held it against that imposter William of Orange for nearly a year. Even John Murray, the Marquis of Atholl, had stood by Geordie's side and fought against the rebels. But Atholl was like a bobbing buoy on the high seas. That man would kiss the arse of any usurper on the throne.

But not George Gordon. Geordie believed in the line of royal ancestry, in the right of birth, and in the laws that governed the Kingdom of Scotland.

As governor, he'd stood down only after he'd received a missive from James in France telling him to pass the keys to the Williamite government. Then they'd tried to lead him to the gallows, spewing a contrived list of misdeeds that had put him into more hot water with William of Orange, the *inglorious* usurper. Worse, now William's sister-in-law Queen Anne and her bumbling Dutch prince had ascended to the throne and proven even more inept.

With his next blink, a wave of pain made the bile in Geordie's stomach churn. Sweat streamed from his forehead and the chills started again. He curled into the musty thresh.

*I'll be ready to ride in a few hours.*

He chuckled. The lass had called him a joob from the alehouse—a Gypsy insult. Nonetheless, he'd seen many a young woman ruined by the whoring and abuse that went on in such establishments. But this lass didn't seem rough around the edges like a harlot. Perhaps healing was her way out of the gutter?

# Chapter Four

Geordie squinted in an attempt to open his eyes. How long had he been asleep? Blinding rays of sunlight glared through the vines that dangled from the cave entrance. He winced. Good Lord, his mouth was drier than sand. Chills skittered across his skin.

"Water," he croaked, sounding like a toad from the River Deveron behind Huntly Castle. His gaze shifted, searching for the wee lass, but dammit if he wasn't too weak to lift his head. A fire crackled, warming his right arm, but the rest of his body shivered with the cold.

"Water," he said, louder this time, praying the lass hadn't abandoned him.

Something rustled across the fire. Geordie's vision adjusted enough to see the raven-haired woman push up and sit. "You're awake?"

Licking his arid lips, he managed a nod.

"You thrashed throughout most of the night." Akira reached for a satchel and moved to his side.

Odd, Geordie didn't remember the satchel. "Where's your basket?"

"It fell by the wayside when we were fleeing from the soldiers."

"Hmm." He closed his eyes, recalling the battle, the field surgery, the horse, the chase. Good God, the bloody searing knife singeing his flesh. Moving his toes, he winced.

She pulled the cork from a water flask. "Are you in pain?"

"Bloody right I am." At least he could still feel his toes. That had to be a good sign.

"I'd best reapply the salve. 'Twill ease your suffering." Placing her palm under his head, she helped him sip.

When the cool water slid past his lips, he reached up and tilted the flask higher, guzzling greedily. By God's grace, he could pour the whole thing down his gullet and still have a thirst.

"Easy, Mr. Geordie," the woman cooed as if speaking to a wee bairn. "You'll end up with an awful ache in your stomach if you keep drinking like that."

Such an imperious warning only served to make him gulp faster, downing the water until he had emptied the flask. With a shudder, he again looked at the satchel. Truly, he didn't remember it.

"Are you cold?" she asked.

He nodded.

Unfastening the brooch at her neck, she removed her arisaid and draped it over him. The billowing motion blew a warm breeze of exotic fragrance—like jasmine oil from the Orient. The scent enlivened him, made tingles course over his skin. Better, the warmth calmed his chills.

He swallowed. "Where did the satchel come from?"

She reached inside it and pulled out a small pot. "'Tis mine."

He narrowed his gaze. Asking her if she'd been carrying it at the battle site mightn't give him the answer he sought. It would be too easy for the lass to say yes. "You said you had a basket in Hoord Moor—not a satchel." His heartbeat speeding, he tried to sit up but only managed to roll to his elbow. "Where in God's name did you get the bag?"

She studied him for a moment, eyebrows arching with intelligence, her teeth grazing her bottom lip. Devil's bones, those glistening, pert lips were too goddamned kissable.

Geordie clenched his jaw. The last thing on earth he should be thinking about was this woman's lips. She might be as pretty as a rose, but her ragged kirtle spoke volumes about her commoner status. "I slipped away home last eve. Collected a few supplies."

"You what?" His voice shot up and cracked. Christ, he almost wished she'd lied. "To bloody *Dunkeld*?"

She topped off her pout with a defiant little glare. "There's no need to start cursing—"

Damnation, did she have to purse those lips with her rebuke? "I'm not bloody cursing. Who saw you?"

"No one. Only my family."

He dropped to the thresh. "Jesus Christ."

"You needn't worry. The lassies won't say a thing, and my mother…" Akira's eyes shifted. "Well, she keeps to herself. Doesn't see anyone outside the cottage."

"Who are these lassies you speak of?"

"My three younger sisters. I-I am their main support. I had to take them the shilling you gave me and let them know I was all right." She flinched. "And…"

"What else?" he groaned, picturing a family gathering.

"Ma said dragoons came by the cottage looking for me. It appears I'm in trouble for associating with a fleeing Highlander."

"Good God, it grows worse. Did the redcoats see you?"

"Of course not. I know how to be a ghost. I waited until well past dark." She smiled as if she thought her skills were pretty damned good—though he sincerely doubted this wee lass knew a thing about being a spy. She'd be more likely to wave a red flag when she entered the village.

Geordie snorted and shoved himself up, his head spinning and threatening to rob him of consciousness. "You may think they didn't see you, but I'll wager they were watching the cottage."

"They were not—and I rode the horse through the burn so they wouldn't see my tracks." She shifted his plaid aside and gently rubbed in her salve. "I used a twig to cover our tracks just like Uncle Bruno taught me."

Geordie tried not to wince. Her deft fingers were ever so gentle, but nonetheless, pain shot clear up through his hip like she'd just stabbed him. "And whereabouts is this uncle?" he asked, his voice clipped and straining. "Did you have a family gathering whilst you slipped into the village?"

"No, silly. He lives on the borders—only comes to see us at Yuletide."

"Thank goodness for small mercies." Geordie shoved the arisaid aside and grunted at the shooting agony his movement caused. "Give me a hand. I need to be on my way afore the bloody dragoons find us."

"Now, sir?"

He held out his palm. "Why not now?"

"'Tis midday. Would you not be less conspicuous traveling at night?" Ignoring his hand, she let her gaze slide down to his thigh. "Are you certain you're well enough to travel?"

"Of course I'm well enough to travel." Bracing himself, he pushed with all his might. He gnashed his teeth, and a deep bellow strained his voice. He blinked in rapid succession as stars crossed his vision. His leg wouldn't work worth a damn. "Devil's fire, what's in that salve? Bloody sheep's piss?"

"Well, actually, 'tis goat—but not much," she said with the sweet tenor of an angel rather than the tones of the vexing nymph she was. "It has avens oil and houseleek and a number of other herbs. The concoction has been handed down through the family for generations."

Geordie propped himself against the craggy wall, his chin dropping to his chest. Holy hellfire, he was tired. The maid might be young and inexperienced, but she was also right about traveling at night. This close to Hoord Moor, in daylight they'd be spotted by scouts for certain.

"I brought some sausages to cook over the fire. Why don't you set back down and rest that leg whilst I prepare them?"

His stomach growled. Perhaps she was right. He ground his back molars and gingerly slid down to his pallet. "Och, very well then."

Akira had already skewered two links on a pair of sticks. Turning away, she bent down and set them in the flames. Without the arisaid draped around her back, the lassie's kirtle skirts clung to her hips—quite shapely hips. The corners of his mouth turned up. He doubted she wore more than one petticoat beneath.

Geordie rubbed his fingers, aching to reach out and raise her hem ever so slightly just to prove himself right. Then his head swooned and lolled to the side. For the love of God, he'd never been this close to death, and there he sat contemplating a woman's petticoats? Could he not give his lustful urges a rest?

He picked up a bit of her arisaid and held it to his nose. *It must be the damned jasmine fragrance addling my mind.*

The lass straightened and brushed her hands as she regarded him. "You look awfully pale. Perhaps you should lie down."

There she went, trying to tell him what to do—and without her command being followed by a bloody *Your Grace*. With a groan, he cast his highborn difference aside. "Would you fill the flask with a bit more water? I still have a thirst."

"Very well." She held up a slender finger. "But you must promise not to guzzle it this time. You'll end up with a bellyache for certain."

"Och, my stomach is hewn of iron." Geordie swiped his hand across his forehead and watched Akira pick up the flagon and retreat. She certainly posed a sight for a miserable patient, a sweet diversion to take his mind off the bloody throbbing in his thigh.

Groaning, he forced himself to look away.

A few bites to eat and a few tots of whisky, and he'd be well enough to ride. She could return to her family, and he could return to Huntly. The sooner he made it home, the sooner he'd be free from suspicion by Government troops.

Licking his lips, he slipped his trembling fingers into his sporran and froze. He shifted his hand from side to side just to be sure. Jesus Christ, the silver flask bearing the family crest was still on the battlefield.

"Mr. Geordie?" The lassie's voice sounded anxious as her footsteps pattered into the cave.

He shifted his gaze her way. "Aye?"

"There are a dozen dragoons heading up the crag."

# Chapter Five

Jolting upright, Geordie cast the arisaid aside. "How much time do we have?" he asked through clenched teeth, trying to steady the spinning in his skull.

Akira collected the pot of salve and quickly slipped it into her satchel. "Five minutes. Mayhap less."

"Christ." Pushing to his knees, he stifled his urge to bellow. "Is the horse saddled?"

"We don't have a saddle, remember?" She reached for her arisaid and swung it over her shoulders. "If we hurry we can escape down the other side."

After shoving his dirk into its scabbard, Geordie swallowed against the bile churning in his gut and shoved himself to his feet. "I'd best go it alone from here."

"Are you certain?" She hastened to kick sand over the fire. "Do you think the dragoons will lock me in the pillory once I return home?"

"They could, but 'tis not you they're after. My guess is

any punishment they might issue will be akin to a slap on the wrist. I'm certain of it."

"I don't like that they came to my ma's cottage looking for me." Her voice was filled with uncertainty as she held out her satchel. "If you're sure you don't need me, take this. There's food, a flint, and salve inside."

"My thanks... ah, for everything." Agonizing pain like knives stabbing his leg tortured him when he took the bag. As fast as he could, he limped toward the cave entrance.

She rushed alongside him. "I don't think it is a good idea to send you out on your own—especially when you're in terrible pain."

He didn't have time to argue. "If you ride with me, you could be hurt."

"You're in no condition to ride." Ignoring him, she cupped her fingers over her sleeve and brushed it across his forehead. The cloth came away damp with his sweat.

He jerked his head away, the motion making his head swim and his gut squelch. "I'll be fine."

She slipped his arm over her shoulders and insisted on helping him outside. "What will you do if they catch you?"

"I'll not allow it." Geordie fought against the pain as he collected the horse's reins and led the gelding to a boulder. Any other day he could hop on an unsaddled pony without a mounting block. But not when his thigh sported a hole the diameter of an iron cattle prod.

"You must apply the salve every hour until the wound scabs over," Akira instructed. "Do not put undue stress on your leg, else it will start bleeding again."

He almost vomited as he flopped onto the horse stomach first and struggled to slip his good leg over.

"Goodness, you're whiter than snow."

Those words were the last he heard.

* * *

"Mr. Geordie?" Akira frantically shook the Highlander's hand, trying to rouse him.

"I think you were right, corporal. Someone's been here for certain," said a deep voice down below. The voice didn't sound friendly at all; it sounded dark and nasally and full of venom. A man with a voice like that would never be lenient on a poor lass who tried to help a wounded Jacobite Highlander.

A cold shudder coursed up the back of Akira's arms.

*Dear Lord, they'll hang him without blinking an eye.*

"Hold steady, ye wee beastie," she whispered, grasping the reins and climbing onto the big boulder. Her hands shook like saplings in a gale. She'd ridden the horse to Dunkeld without issue—at a walk, of course. Without another moment to think, she mounted behind the Highlander, reached around him, and gave the reins a hearty slap. Where they were headed, who knew? Akira focused on one goal—run in any direction the soldiers were not.

She hadn't been to the far side of the outcropping, and now she knew why. The horse's footing stuttered on the uneven and rocky ground. Devoid of trees, the crag plunged downward, far steeper than anything she'd ever traversed. Tightening her fists, Akira tugged on the reins to keep the horse at a walk, but rocks and debris showered down the sheer slope with their every step. The horse stumbled, moving his legs faster and faster. Her palms grew sweaty and the reins slipped, her breathing sped with the quickened cadence of the hoofbeats, while the unconscious man swayed in front of her.

Merciful Moses, picking her way through the burn for a few miles was a lot different than slipping away from soldiers and running for her life. If she'd known this slope was so steep, she might have opted for another path.

"Easy, laddie," she urged, but her words were futile.

Pinning his ears back, the horse jostled, then slipped and skidded toward an abrupt ledge.

Squeezing with her legs, Akira tugged on the reins. The horse reared, shaking its head from side to side.

"No," she squeaked, trying not to shout.

"There they are!" a dragoon yelled from above.

Squeezing her legs tighter, Akira slapped the reins as hard as she could and ducked her head against Geordie's back. "Haste, ye wee beastie!"

A musket blasted.

Akira's entire body jolted.

Geordie shifted.

The horse broke into a full-on gallop—straight for the edge of a cliff. With nowhere to run, Akira closed her eyes, held on for dear life, and waited for death.

Her stomach flew to her throat as the horse leapt. Akira prayed for her family and curled tight against Geordie's back.

The horse's front hooves hit the ground with a jarring thud. His hindquarters absorbed the shock, and they sprang forward again and again. She kicked her heels, demanding a gallop faster than she'd ever ridden in her life. Only a miracle could explain how the gelding stayed on his feet while he continued to race down the sheer precipice.

Frozen with fear, Akira managed to keep hold of the

reins, her arms around Geordie while she clamped as tight as she could with her knees. Where were they headed? She stole a bobbing upward glance—west into the Highlands, country so rugged nary a soul in Dunkeld would dare to cross some of its peaks.

* * *

After the pair of Jacobites plunged down the mountainside on their suicidal quest, Captain Roderick Weaver pulled his horse to a stop at the precipice of the cliff with his men in his wake.

"Did you have a look at that?" asked Corporal Snow.

Sentinel Grey pointed his misfiring musket down the slope. "She's a bloody sorceress, that one."

"Magic runs through her veins for certain," said Sentinel Muldoon. "I'll wager she's a witch."

Roderick had seen a lot of foolhardy displays of horsemanship in his day, but never one as reckless as what he'd just witnessed. How the lot of them didn't end up with their necks broken was beyond him. "She's either a witch or she's crazier than a featherbrained hen without a roost."

"So, what do we do, sir? Is the Highlander worth our time?"

"Bloody oath, I want that bastard's head." Roddy shifted his gaze to the corporal. "Those two embody all the ills of miserable Scotland." He pulled his coat tighter at the collar. "'Tis bloody August and there's a chill."

"Aye, it looks like rain," said Grey.

"That's all we need." Roddy returned his gaze to the undulating and rocky mountains to the west—nothing but barren cliffs and forested hillsides as far as the eye could see.

"The marquis is expecting the regiment in Perth, sir."

"Yes, Corporal Snow, I'm well aware of our orders." Making a decision, Roddy pointed. "Muldoon and Grey, you'll ride with me. You, too, corporal. The rest of you head to Blair Atholl. Report to the marquis and tell him I'm chasing an escapee—someone I sense will be of great interest to the crown."

"Do you think it's the duke?" asked Grey.

"Mayhap. And if 'tis not he, I'll reckon it is someone close to the duke—someone who, with enough convincing, would testify that the Duke of Gordon is a Jacobite loyalist."

Snow pointed down the path the fugitives had taken. "Are we following them up the mountains, captain?"

Roddy chuckled. "I'm not insane. We'd be risking our necks for naught riding up into the Highlands even if it is summer." He reined his horse toward the safer path. "We'll ride around, catch them coming out of the western pass—if they survive."

# Chapter Six

While his body rocked back and forth, Geordie fought to open his eyes, but his eyelids were too heavy. His limbs were weak. Lithe arms surrounded him as he hunched over a horse's mane. His head throbbed, he shivered with chills, and, goddammit, his thigh felt like a stonemason had drilled a hole straight through to bone.

Hoofbeats pummeled the ground, making his head pound all the more. The horse blew repeated snorts as if from overexertion.

High-pitched gasps came from behind—very close behind—squeaking with every thud against his back. If he weren't so sick to his stomach, he'd stop this nonsense this very minute. But his head ached so much, he couldn't move. He prayed for the misery to end.

"Mr. Geordie?" Akira's voice came from behind, sounding panicked.

He squeezed his eyes. Hadn't she returned to Dunkeld? Damnation, his head hurt so badly, he couldn't think straight.

"Are you awake?"

"Mm," he moaned.

"I-I cannot get the horse to stop."

Just as he opened his eyes, a branch came at his head with the speed of an arrow. He ducked and the thing grazed the top of his hair. "Pull on the reins!" he bellowed.

"I have been." Her slender arms tightened around his waist, her fingers tugging the reins in front of him.

Glancing back, he caught sight of a bare knee, squeezing just above the horse's flank. Dear God, it was a wonder they hadn't been thrown. "Ease up on your seat."

"What?" she shrieked.

"Don't clamp your legs around the bloody beast. It makes him go faster." Sycamore branches whipped past as Geordie reached for the reins. White foam leached from the horse's neck and withers, and his snorts were labored. "Whoa, fella." He pulled back on the reins, cuing the horse from a gallop to a walk within a matter of steps.

Akira's head plopped against his back as she panted. "You make it look so easy."

Too weak to hold up his hands, Geordie dropped them to the horse's withers. "I thought you rode the horse into Dunkeld."

"Aye, but at a walk." She wrapped her arms around Geordie's waist. Bloody hell, if only his head would clear, he might enjoy being the lassie's protector. She had to be frightened. Her voice even carried a tremor. "This was life or death. The redcoats came after us—fired a musket at us, too—and this big fella ran as if being chased by the devil."

Geordie patted the gelding's neck, the movement making his head swim. "This big fella hasn't got much left. How long has he been running like hellfire?"

"I don't know. I was s-s-so scared, all I could do was keep hold of the reins and pray we wouldn't fall to our deaths."

He rubbed his forehead in the crook of his arm and glanced back at her wide eyes and blanched face. "You should have gone home to your ma."

"So now you're full of bullheaded advice? You didn't give me much choice when you collapsed over your horse." She thumped him on the shoulder, making his head hurt all the more. "Do you lose consciousness every time you're on the back of one of these wee beasties?"

"Only when I've been bled to within an inch of my life." The corner of his mouth twitched. So she'd stayed with him to ensure he escaped the redcoats?

*She has gumption, for certain.*

Against every aching fiber in his body, Geordie scanned their surroundings. They were still climbing up a hill. Trees provided a canopy above, while dark clouds hung low overhead, making it impossible for him to determine his orientation. "Where are we?"

"I... ah... the horse... well, he leapt off a cliff—"

"He what?"

A cry squeaked from her throat. "It was a bit frightening when he did that. For a moment, I prepared to meet my end."

Geordie rolled his gaze to the clouds. "Dear God."

"And then he ran for the mountains—north or west, I think."

"Which was it?" He gulped down his bile and forced himself to focus.

"North. Mayhap northwest." One thing he knew for certain. The lass lacked a keen sense of direction.

When the forest opened to a slope covered with rubble,

Geordie spotted a conical peak, green with mountain grass—though high enough to be covered with snow throughout the winter months. He pointed. "We'll be able to find our bearings up there." Thank goodness the summit was rounded and looked fairly easy to climb on horseback.

When they reached the top, he pulled the horse to a stop and looked full circle. Though ominous clouds hung above, he made out the setting sun by the glow on the horizon. To the north there was nothing but mountains, growing ever higher until they disappeared into the veil of a thunderhead. Indeed, they'd traveled northwest.

The good part? There wasn't an enemy coat in sight.

Akira peered around his shoulder. "I don't think they followed us."

"Probably not up this way." Most likely they were taking a more direct route to Huntly, or heading them off from the western pass.

"Have you been here afore?"

"Not on this very peak."

"So you ken where we are?"

Geordie looked west—more mountains. "We're in the southern range, I'd reckon."

"Is that close to your home? We are in the Highlands, are we not?"

"Aye, we're in the Highlands." Regardless of the pounding of his head, a smile still spread across his lips. "And nay, we're not close to my home, but I've allies to the west. Men who can see you home." More than likely, the redcoats had found his flask. That's why they'd bothered to chase after one man. If a redcoat officer brought in a duke, he might earn title and lands for himself, the bastard.

But the farther they traveled from Hoord Moor, the better Geordie's chances of proving his innocence. Even if the Government troops had found his flask and paid a visit to Huntly, they still had no proof of his whereabouts. Just because he wasn't presently on his lands didn't mean he'd been a part of the rising. Hell, with his role in Parliament and endless court business, he was hardly ever home anyway. And before he returned to Huntly, he needed to find a way to return Akira home to her family.

Heading west made the most sense. A Highlander born and raised, no city-dwelling redcoat could best him in the crags and glens that provided both haven and fortress. Indeed, George Gordon survived best in the Highlands, no matter the range. And once they crossed the Highlands, they could catch up with the MacDonells of Keppoch or the Stuarts of Appin. He hadn't seen either clan's colors in the battle, and they would provide him with an alibi for certain. He'd be able to arrange for Akira's safe transport and make his way home via a more circuitous route. With luck he'd avoid meeting any more Government troops—especially if they were heading north to Huntly.

The only problem with his plan was the miserable ache in his thigh. The horse sidestepped and wobbled a bit.

Akira jostled behind him. "I think this wee beastie needs a rest."

Geordie shrugged. "If we take it slow, we can ride a while longer."

"How is your leg?"

"Bloody hurts."

"Do you think you'll swoon again?"

He scowled over his shoulder. "Men do not swoon."

"All right," she said with a resolute stare. "You are my

employer, so I will not argue that point. If men do not swoon, they simply drop into unconsciousness."

Damnation, those almond-shaped eyes staring at him were bluer than the loch in summer. They were damned distracting, especially when she was being so maddening. He didn't intend to swoon—ah—pass into unconsciousness again.

She blinked at him. Christ.

"Are you feeling dizzy, like you might topple over?" she asked.

"Dear Lord, you are persistent." He shook his head, looking anywhere but at her face. *I will not allow a pair of bonny indigo eyes to affect me in any way.*

She patted his shoulder. "Just trying to prevent a fall. Only heaven kens how you stayed on the horse this far."

A smile almost stretched his chapped lips. "My mother used to say I was born on the back of a horse."

"Truly?"

"Well, she said it anyway, but I was born in Hunt—ah—in a bed."

Good God, he'd almost said "Huntly Castle." If the lass learned he was the Duke of Gordon and ended up being captured, the redcoats would beat his true identity out of her. Geordie grimaced. If any filthy soldier placed his hands on Akira, he'd explode in a rage. The lass had already taken a great risk to save his life. And now, when she should be sitting beside home's hearth, she was up in only God knew where, sharing a horse.

She drew in a stuttered breath.

He again glanced at her exposed thigh nestled just outside his hip. Did she even know he could see her skin? Skin that looked like burnished satin—not creamy white but with an olive tint, as if kissed by the sun.

"Are you cold?" he asked in a throaty whisper.

"Aye, and hungry."

With the sun going down, it would grow colder for certain.

A bolt of lightning streaked through the sky above, followed immediately by a deafening crack of thunder.

Akira squealed and threw her arms around him. In an instant, Geordie didn't feel quite so miserable. He wanted to reach around behind and pull her in front of him so he could protect her between his arms. But he didn't trust his strength. Not yet.

With another blinding flash, the clouds opened. "Mayhap 'tis time to find a shelter."

Akira squeezed her arms tighter. "I hate thunder."

"Not to worry, lass," he said. Geordie didn't care for it much himself, especially with the clouds being so low overhead he could practically touch them. "I spotted a shelf on the journey up. We can take shelter beneath it until the storm passes."

The horse pinned his ears back and started down the mountain like there was a deerhound nipping at his heels.

"Whoa, laddie." Geordie tugged the reins downward, making the gelding lower his head, which brought him under control.

Rain pelted them in sheets and the footing grew slippery. Lightning flashed in forked streaks across the sky. Thunder boomed so loud the ground shook. Akira clutched her arms around Geordie's midriff. Heavenly stars, soft breasts molded into his back. He blinked and imagined what she might look like naked. Pert breasts, a slender waist, wicked hips. The corner of his mouth turned up as he shifted his seat forward to negotiate the rocky slope. No better elixir could there be than a woman who needed him—a bonny woman who needed a strong man to protect her.

He rather enjoyed being anonymous for a change. Elizabeth had wanted him only for his title. The first daughter of a duke couldn't bear to marry beneath her station.

"Hold on," he shouted over his shoulder. "I see the shelf yonder."

Akira squeezed him tighter. "Why must it rain today of all days?"

Geordie could conjure a hundred replies, but none of them would do a lick of good to change the weather. If he told the lass that having her arms around him eased his pain more than any healing salve ever invented, she'd probably release him and give him a good thwack. So he just bit his tongue and urged the horse to a trot.

Once they'd traversed the crag, he helped Akira slide down, then swung his good leg over and gingerly dismounted. The gelding had been trained well, standing there like a soldier. A green horse would skitter sideways—might even try to rear.

Regardless, the movement caused a surge of blinding pain, and Geordie had to balance himself against the horse until his head stopped spinning.

"I should hobble him," Akira said, pulling a length of rope from her satchel.

Geordie reached for it as rain streaked into his eyes. "I'll do it."

"But you're on death's door."

He scowled. "No woman will do a man's work whilst I'm still breathing."

"I hobbled him at the cave."

"That was different. I'm conscious now, and no gentleman worth his salt would allow a lass to do his work." He waved her beneath the stony shelf. "Go on, get out of the rain."

It nearly killed him to crouch down to tie the horse's front legs so he couldn't move but at a walk. Nonetheless, in no way would he allow himself to appear like a weakling in front of a woman. His hands shook as he knotted the rope, and then he glanced over his shoulder. Ballocks, Akira watched him like a mother hen.

Garnering all his strength, he bore down and stood, sucking in his urge to bellow. He ran a hand across his eyes to clear the rain—and the tears, though he'd never in his life admit to the latter.

Once the worst of the pain passed, he patted the animal's shoulder. "You're a good fella. Sturdy, too. I'd like to find a place for you in my stables."

Walking the few steps to join Akira nearly brought him to his knees, but he ground his back molars and endured the pain. Ducking his head, he stumbled beneath the shelf, spinning and sliding down the rock face to his bum. "Arragh!" Jesus Christ, the last jolt of agony forced the groan from his throat.

"I'm sorry you're in so much pain." Akira's teeth chattered, and she clutched her sopping arisaid tighter around her shoulders.

"I'll be fine with a bit of rest." It was too wet to start a fire, so he placed his arm over her shoulder. "Come, I'll warm you." He hoped. Just listening to her teeth made him shiver.

She drew away, a look of distrust pulling down the corners of her mouth. "But 'tisn't proper."

Good Lord, Geordie had endured a lifetime of propriety, drilled into him by everyone from his mother to his former duchess. "I'm in no condition to do anything untoward, and there's nary a soul for miles." He pulled her closer.

Akira rubbed the outside of her arm and leaned in, releasing a long breath. "I'll allow it this once, but you must give me your word you will not breathe a word of this to anyone."

"You have my solemn vow, m'lady," he said, his noble breeding rising to the surface. But only for a moment. Aside from running for his life with a hole in his leg, he was enjoying his role as Geordie, a mere Highlander. The tension in his shoulders eased. Her softness molded into him and soothed away the chill. He closed his eyes and inhaled her scent—jasmine kissed by rain. He could lose himself in such a fragrance.

A nicker drew him from his moment of calm. The horse hovered over them, his head bent beneath the shelf. Geordie shooed the beast with a flick of his wrist. "Can you not find some grass to eat? There's a wee meadow but twenty paces down."

Akira shifted, nestling closer. "I don't think he likes the rain, either."

"Well, he'll not be sharing our meager shelter." Geordie thumped the gelding's chest. "Go on and graze, lest you'll not be fit to carry us on the morrow."

The mule-brained varlet shook his head and snorted.

Akira laughed. "I do not think he likes your idea."

Groaning, Geordie leaned his head against the rock. If he didn't have the hole in his leg he'd lead the damned beast down to the lea himself, but the mere thought of putting more stress on his injury made his head spin.

"Why not let him stay?" Akira asked. "He's blocking the wind."

With a frown, Geordie considered her suggestion. "That he is," he mumbled without conviction. "If he could light a fire, I'd be happier about it, though."

Her body shook with a chuckle. "You are funny."

He knit his brow. Him? Funny? No one ever made such a comment about the Duke of Gordon. "Why do you say that?"

"Because you talk like you're heartless, but I do not think you are."

"You hardly know me." *And she certainly has no idea who I am.*

"I think I've witnessed enough. I've seen men in Dunkeld whip horses for less. You merely gave the old fella a wee push."

"Aye?" Geordie stretched his leg out in a futile attempt to find comfort. "Well, I'm not quite myself."

She drew her knees up beneath her skirts as if growing a tad more comfortable. "Then if that's the case, I hope you stay injured."

Drawing his eyebrows together, he gave her an exasperated look. "I beg your pardon?"

She smiled, and her grin was radiant enough to make the clouds part. Her teeth were white and healthy, one on the top right slightly crooked, but that gave her character. Those indigo eyes shone vividly, encircled by black feathery lashes and dark eyebrows. Then her lips pursed as if in thought. Red as rubies, her mouth formed a bow—a full and ever so kissable bow.

She winced. Her eyes turned dark and filled with anger—or distrust. "If you were to turn into a blackguard and tried to hurt me, I'd—I'd—I'd...Well, I'd take the horse and ride away from here as fast as I could."

Geordie blinked. Honestly, that was the most sensible

thing she'd said since he regained consciousness. But what had she said at first? His brow furrowed. "Have you been...ah...hurt?" He flexed his fingers. He'd kill anyone who tried to take advantage of the wee lass.

"Not me, but I've seen terrible things. Remember, I'm a healer." Shaking her head, Akira swiped a hand across her mouth like she was holding more inside.

"Aye, I can imagine." With a sigh of relief, Geordie squeezed Akira's shoulder. "You have no need to worry about me."

"I ken." She lowered her hands and regarded him with a hint of a smile playing on her bonny lips.

But he had no business thinking about the lassie's lips, or any other part of her body for that matter. They might be safe for the time being, but he could not forget for one minute that a mob of bloodthirsty dragoons was on their tail. Allowing himself to give in to amorous ideas would only see him dead. He inclined his head to her satchel. "You mentioned you were hungry. Do you have anything to eat in there?"

"A bit of cheese and bread." Her hands trembled as she fished inside and held up a leather-wrapped parcel. "I'm sorry. I've eaten most of it. Here. You need your strength."

He rubbed the outside of her arm. "I only have a thirst. Seems being shot in the leg saps a man's hunger as well as his strength."

"Do you still have whisky?" Unwrapping the parcel, she glanced at his sporran and gasped. "Oh dear, your flask."

"'Tis lost." He shrugged, though he was anything but unconcerned. That damned lump of silver could lead the redcoats straight to his castle gates.

She bit off some cheese. "But it was fine enough to be an heirloom. You'll miss it for certain."

*I'd miss it a lot less if I kent it was still buried under the clump of broom.* "'Twas just a trinket." Downplaying the importance of the gift from his father, he pointed to the satchel. "Do you mind if I help myself to the water?"

She nudged it toward him. "Sorry, yes," she said with her mouth full of bread. "Are you sure you don't want to eat?"

"You have it, lass." He took a long drink, the cold water giving him unwanted shivers.

After nipping off one more bite of cheese, she wrapped the remaining morsels in the piece of leather. "I'd best ration it. When do you think we'll meet up with those friends of yours?"

"A day, mayhap two." He looked at the rain dripping from the shelf and streaming down the horse's back. "Depends on the weather, I'd reckon."

"Oh my goodness, we'll starve."

"Nay." Closing his eyes, he couldn't help but incline his nose to her hair. "Not in the Highlands."

If he wasn't careful, he could succumb to charms such as hers. Deep blue eyes, a scent to ignite a fire in his ballocks, and thick waves of black hair. Holy hellfire, Akira was a recipe for disaster.

# Chapter Seven

Curled under Geordie's arm, Akira actually stopped shivering. All around them rain splashed. Everything was soaked and their little alcove smelled of horse—not a horrid smell, but not one she'd choose for her boudoir either. If she had a boudoir.

She chose to ignore the voice in the back of her head telling her it wasn't proper to allow a strange man to put his arm around her shoulders and offer her warmth. Besides, he'd been right when he said no one would see them. She also believed she was completely safe. If she didn't, she would have already fled—would have left him in the cave. But there was something in the way Geordie looked at her that made her feel all warm inside and, moreover, protected. Aye, he'd been in a great deal of pain—was still in great pain—but since he roused from his last bout of unconsciousness, he'd behaved admirably. He'd brought the horse under control, figured out where they were, and formed a plan to take them to someone he could trust to provide her with an escort home.

With darkness, the air grew colder. Clutching her fists under her chin, Akira curled into Geordie's heat. Indeed, the man could suffice for a brazier. He smoothed his palm along her outer arm, his touch soothing.

When he turned his lips toward her, his warm breath skimmed across her forehead. "Try to sleep." The gentle burr of his voice imparted all the more comfort.

But she couldn't get too comfortable; she must do her duty. He was still her patient—a patient who promised payment. She tugged at her collar and cleared her throat. "I'm the healer. I should be telling you to do the same."

"No need to worry about me. I only wish this rain would let up so we could start a fire."

"That would make this night near perfect."

His hazel gaze drifted to her mouth, and he grinned.

With a quick gasp, Akira covered her mouth. He must think her a harlot.

Then he grazed his bottom lip with his teeth. Swarms of butterflies flitted around her stomach. How did he do that to her? With just a look, and in the cold? She should be as wretched as a stray dog.

Akira quickly leaned forward and picked up her satchel. "Your wound needs another application of salve."

"Very well." He pulled his arm away, but not before running his fingers across her back. Blessed tingles spread over her skin as if she'd been caressed by feathers. Oh, heaven help her, his touch was unbelievably sublime. If only she could ask him to run his fingers back and forth again—just one more time.

She reached for the hem of his kilt, then quickly snapped her fingers away. What had she been thinking?

True, she'd applied the salve before, but that was when he was mostly unconscious and definitely before he'd put his arm around her shoulder and smiled at her like a…like a…brawny Highlander.

"Have you gone shy, lass?" he asked with a hint of humor in his deep brogue.

She peeked at his face. He was smiling, his teeth white and shining through the darkness, as did his eyes, making him look devilish—too much so. Akira clutched her hands around her middle to stop the butterflies fluttering about. "I—ah…"

He dipped his chin. "Did our mad dash on the horse give you too much of a fright?"

"No." She glanced back to his hem. "For some unknown reason, I've become somewhat bashful. If only your wound were a wee bit lower…"

"But 'tis not." His lilting voice grew huskier.

"No." She looked up again. By the gooseflesh spreading across her skin, she knew she shouldn't have done that. "Would you mind exposing your wound? I-I mean, afore, you were unable, but now…"

"Now?" He leaned toward her, his lips but a hand's breadth from hers.

If she didn't know better, she'd swear he was about to kiss her. "N-now you are entirely able to do it yourself, and it would be improper for me to—ah—touch you—ah—I mean touch your kilt."

With a shrug, he turned those tempting lips away, slid the wool up, and exposed his thigh. Akira tried not to notice the muscle surrounding it, or the chestnut-colored hair peppering his thigh—hair she wanted to run her fingers over to see if it was as downy soft as it looked.

Squaring her shoulders, she remembered her duty,

leaned forward, and sniffed. In the dark, it was almost impossible to determine how well he was healing. "It smells like wet horse."

His entire body shook with his laugh. "You do have a sense of humor."

Akira glanced at the gelding. He'd been standing like a statue for hours. "Mayhap he'll go down and graze after we fall asleep."

"I'm sure he will." Geordie patted her shoulder. "Are you aiming to apply that salve or hover over my leg for the rest of the night?"

"Sorry." She pulled the stopper off the pot and scooped a healthy bit with her fingers. "I hope this doesn't sting."

By his hiss, she reckoned it did. "Sorry," she said again.

"Devil's piss," he cursed through clenched teeth.

She blew on the wound to cool the burn, then stoppered the pot. "My ma says 'tis a good sign of healing if it stings."

Geordie closed his eyes. "Och aye? What else does your mother say?"

*Never allow yourself to be alone with a man. Always be demure. Always insist on payment afore you provide healing services.*

The list of her errors could go on all night.

"Ah, she says to keep it clean—says 'tisn't as likely to fester if you keep the dirt away."

"Really? I'll have to tell my physician about that."

"You have a physician?"

"Uh, the family physician comes to the ca—ah—house when needed."

"Just like Doctor Kennedy in Dunkeld, I'd reckon."

"Mm hmm."

Akira replaced the pot in the satchel and sat back, trying not to curl into Geordie as she'd done before. She clasped her arms across her body to stave off the cold. "I wish my clothes were dry."

He rubbed her arisaid between his fingers. "'Tis almost dry." He opened his arm. "Come. You'll catch your death if you stay over there."

"I mustn't. As you said, I'm nearly dry." *And being so utterly close to you, I can scarcely think straight.*

"Very well." He scooted toward her with a grunt. "If you refuse to move toward me, you give me no choice but to slide toward you so I don't catch my death."

She bit her bottom lip, allowing him to drape his arm across her shoulders. "Forgive me. I must have sounded awfully insensitive."

He jostled until they fit together like a mold. "There's nothing to forgive."

"It's just—" She shouldn't say it.

"What?" His fingers massaged her shoulder.

Oh, did his touch have to feel so good? Her eyes fluttered back and she gave a wee moan. Akira couldn't help but melt into the powerful warmth surrounding her. "I-I've never been so close to a man afore."

Geordie's warm breath skimmed her forehead. "Not your father?"

"I never knew my father." She covered her mouth. Her sisters were sired by her stepfather, and then he'd left, too.

"Forgive me. I didn't mean to pry." He took her hand in his palm, his fingers rough and ever so much larger and more powerful than hers. Slowly he raised her hand to his lips, his gaze locked with hers. Then, as he closed his eyes, soft, pliant lips kissed the back of her hand. Not a quick peck, but a lingering kiss full of tenderness, reverence, and meaning, as if he knew his gesture spoke more than mere words—words that would be inappropriate given the brevity of their acquaintance.

Akira's breathing quickened, and her heart thrummed a rhythm so fierce she feared the thundering beat might make him release her. But instead he drew her hand to his face and gently rubbed it across his stubbled cheek.

"Mayhap we should try to sleep," he said, his voice deeper than before—and with a trace of hoarseness to it. And that voice made yearning swell inside her. An intense tug pulled on her heart, a sensation she'd never before experienced.

Sighing, Akira agreed, wondering how on earth she'd ever be able to close her eyes as long as Mr. Geordie was near.

* * *

Slumped to his side, Geordie awoke to the smell of wood smoke. A crackling fire warmed him. The only problem? Every muscle in his body was stiff as an iron rod. He pushed himself up and grunted at the needling pain in his leg. Would it never end? As he scrubbed the heels of his hands over his eyes, his neck stabbed him with a twinge. Nothing like sleeping on a bed of rock to make a man feel more tortured than Job.

He rubbed his neck, taking in a deep breath. Sunrays shone through the alcove. Akira had built a good fire, but she was nowhere in sight. Geordie leaned forward. Down below, the horse grazed like he hadn't a care. A hunger pang rumbled in Geordie's stomach for the first time since he'd been shot.

He pulled his kilt up high enough to examine the

wound. His skin was red and mottled around a half-inch hole filled with greasy ointment. Though the flesh was warm to the touch, he didn't see any pus. Bloody hell, it couldn't heal fast enough. Stranded in the mountains, he'd need his wits for certain. If nothing else, Akira needed him to see her to safety. Of course, if he didn't make it home soon, Oliver, his chief lieutenant and man-at-arms, would send out a search party. Then all of Scotland would be alerted that something was amiss. Christ, if the duchess caught wind of his disappearance, she'd probably cross the channel from Flanders while celebrating her good fortune.

*It would be like Elizabeth to toast to my death afore they find my body.*

"You're awake." Holding the water flask, Akira climbed under the shelf and kneeled beside him. "There's a burn down below. The water is fresh."

"My thanks." He took a healthy drink and set it down.

Her black tresses swung forward and brushed his leg as she peered at his thigh. "How is your wound?"

Jesus, the tingling from the caress of her hair told him he could forget any amount of pain. "A bit better, I reckon."

She fished in her satchel. "The locals say Ma's ointment has magic." Then she scoffed. "'Tis the only good thing they say about us."

Geordie couldn't imagine anyone saying a bad word about Akira. "Why is that?"

An adorable blush blossomed in her cheeks and she averted her eyes. "'Tis on account of our ancestry."

He brushed the hair away from her face. "Gypsy ancestry?" He as much as anyone knew it was a dangerous question for her to answer. Gypsies and beggars had been outlawed for near a hundred years.

"No... er, aye." She glanced up, anguish pulling on her lovely features. "You must swear not to tell anyone. Ma raised me to be a proper Scottish lass—no thieving, no trickery, and definitely no begging. But people are still afraid of us."

"You and your mother?"

"Aye, and my younger sisters." She applied the salve. "We keep to ourselves, and people leave us alone for the most part. Except..."

Geordie flexed his thigh against the sting. "Except?"

She turned her face away. "Och, it doesn't matter. I shouldn't be telling you these things, else you'll think me a tinker." Then her back went ramrod straight as she snapped around and eyed him with a defiant stare. "And I'm not. I'm a respectable healer. People come from Perth to Pitlochry for my tinctures."

Geordie's heart squeezed as he brushed a finger over her cheek—silken like a newborn kitten. "I'm certain they do. You're doing a fine job of healing me." He could only imagine the hardship this lass had endured. She mightn't know he was a duke, but he'd never felt so guilty about his life of privilege. Elizabeth's words rattled in his head: "*You cannot feed the world, George. Our lot in life is to increase our family's wealth, not dole out coin to vagrants.*"

Akira shrugged, pulling a bandage from the satchel. "I thank you. Honestly, hearing you say so means a great deal."

He bent his knee slightly to allow her to wind the wrap beneath his leg. "And I owe you for my life," he whispered.

"I prayed you would live." She kept unraveling, not meeting his gaze. "I lost a patient to a musket ball wound not too long ago. But that injury shattered his knee and the physician couldn't get the ball out."

"How awful."

"It was." She tied the bandage. "That ought to do. Can you eat? We have the last of the bread and cheese."

"You eat it, lass. I'm not hungry." His stomach growled. Loudly.

"I think your stomach disagrees." She grinned, her smile lighting up the alcove as if the sun radiated around them.

In the end, he capitulated and they shared the last of her meager morsels while Geordie tried to cast his gaze anywhere but at Akira.

Dear God, he felt like a fraud. His skin tingled every time she looked at him.

*The lass may have been born in the gutter, but she has tenacity. And she's bonnier than any woman I've ever seen in all my years at court.*

Perhaps he could find a match for her—find a good man who wasn't blinded by his prejudices. Geordie snorted. *Such a task might be easier said than done.*

The thought of finding her a match didn't sit well—made his blood boil and his gut churn.

She tied his bandage in place. "You look deep in thought."

He blinked. Dear God, did she have to look so ravishing when she smiled like that? "Just thinking about our route out of these mountains."

She brushed off her hands. "Right. I'll fetch the horse and we can be on our way."

Geordie rolled to his knee. "No, I should—"

"I won't be but a minute."

Slinging her satchel over her shoulder, Akira headed

down the hill. Geordie watched her retreat. Sturdy shoulders tapered to a slender waist. Hips flaring into a delectable heart shape. In a blink, she disappeared down the slope.

Almost at once, a shriek filled the air.

His heart flying to his throat, Geordie sprang to his feet, ignoring the stabbing in his leg. Holy hellfire, a mudslide had ripped from the side of the hill, taking the lass tumbling downward in a deluge of rocks and debris.

Over and over she plummeted with the oozing mud.

"Akira!" He ran as fast as his injured thigh would allow.

# Chapter Eight

Akira finally stopped falling when she hit the grassy lea. She lay there on her side for a minute, sucking in gasps of air. What hurt? Moreover, what didn't? She wriggled her fingers and toes without any sharp jabs of pain.

Nearby, the horse continued grazing as if nothing had happened.

"Akira!" Geordie called for the second time.

She pushed to her elbow. Oh dear, the man was hobbling down the hill, putting far too much stress on his wounded leg.

Before she could tell him to slow down, he dropped beside her with a grunt. "Are you all right?" He pulled her into his arms, crushing her head to his chest. "Please tell me you are unharmed."

"I think I am well." She again flexed her toes. Everything hurt, but no sharp pains jabbed her. "Mayhap a bit bruised."

He smoothed his hand over her crown. "I never want to see you fall like that again."

Closing her eyes, she allowed herself a moment to enjoy his succor. Melted into it as blessed warmth spread through her body. If only he would touch her like that again and again. She would never grow tired of such comfort, such a sense of security. Goodness, his gentle touch almost felt like a caress, didn't it? Yet *he* was the patient, not she. Forcing herself to push away from his embrace, Akira regarded her kirtle. "Oh no, I'm entirely covered with mud—and there's a wee tear over the knee." Even her hair was smattered with dirt.

When a bit of blood dropped on her skirts, Geordie took her hand and turned it over. "You've grazed your palm."

She hissed. "I guess I did."

"Do you have another length of bandage in your satchel?"

"Mm hmm." Somehow the bag had stayed with her the whole ungraceful romp down the hillside.

He reached in and pulled out the bandage, tearing off a length and replacing the rest of the clean roll.

"This could use some of your salve."

"'Tis in the satchel as well."

Akira watched while he tended her as if she were a delicate flower. Using his fourth finger, he rubbed in the salve with a featherlight touch. "Does it sting?"

"Aye."

He blew on it to cool the burn, just as she'd done to him countless times.

This Highlander seemed such a quandary. They'd spent so much time together, but she knew nothing about him. "Where do you hail from in the north?"

Frowning, he wrapped the bandage around her hand. "The region of Aberdeen."

"Ah," she said as if she knew where it was. Of course, she'd heard of the town, but the mountain where they were sitting just might have been the farthest she'd ever been away from Dunkeld. In fact, she was quite certain of it.

He turned her palm downward, tied the bandage, and gave her a wee pat. "Now let's see if you can stand."

Akira could tell he tried not to grimace when he pushed up to help her, and by the color flooding from his face, she knew he was hurting. She leaned forward and braced herself. "I can stand on my own."

"I forbid it," he said, as if in command of every living creature.

"I beg your pardon?"

He cleared his throat, straightening on his boots. "Ah... It would be ungentlemanly of me not to help you stand, given the magnitude of your fall."

Baffled, she regarded him with a pinch to her brow. First he boomed an order like the Marquis of Atholl, then he took on a polite tone, the likes of which she'd never heard in her life.

He offered his hand. "M'lady."

She took it and allowed him to pull her to a stand. "Who are you?"

He shifted his gaze away. "Just a misguided Scot who needs to go home."

"Aye? You've said that afore, but by your speech, I reckon you're a man with a great deal of property."

"I do hold property," he said, stepping back but keeping ahold of her hand. "Now take a step toward me."

She did.

"How did that feel?" Craning his neck, he peered down to her feet. "Are you unsteady at all?"

"I think everything is still in working order." Her knee hurt when it rubbed against her skirts. She imagined it was a bit grazed, but the idea of having Mr. Geordie push up her skirts and rub his rugged palms along her calf mortified her to no end.

"Very well," he said, his tone growing gruff again. "Let us hope we can remain unscathed from here on out."

* * *

Once the excitement of Akira's fall abated, Geordie's thigh decided it was time to punish him for his attempt at heroics. He hadn't even thought about the pain when he bounded down the hill and took her into his arms. The horrible sight of Akira falling, with the ground giving way beneath her, had nearly stopped his heart. Every time he closed his eyes, he shuddered. What if she'd been seriously injured?

Not that he had grown affectionate toward the lass. That wasn't it at all. As a man and a duke, he had a duty to protect women in general. True, he'd been a bit rakish in his past, but now he'd been gifted with the opportunity to show what a true gentleman he could be—to be a true hero. Not a man who fought a battle and received medals of valor, but a man respected in the eyes of a bonny young maid who had no notion of his standing in society.

Akira broke the silence. "'Tis a relief to enjoy the sunshine," she said, sitting the horse aside like a proper lady. Except she was wedged between his legs—yet another challenge to his lustful Gordon urges. Thank God for the hole in his thigh, else he mightn't have made it this far without attempting to ravish the lass... or at least starting the chase.

She turned her face up, allowing the sun's rays to wash over her. Most women he knew would have been too concerned about age spots to risk exposing their delicate porcelain skin so. Taking in a deep inhale, she smiled up at him. "Do you like sunshine, Mr. Geordie?"

"Indeed, I do." He chuckled, humored by the way she oft added *Mr.* to his nickname. As a matter of fact, it was refreshing not to be referred to as "Your Grace."

"And it is ever so much warmer than yesterday." She shifted her seat, the soft flare of her hip nudging his loins.

A deep moan rumbled from his throat before he could stifle it. Dear Lord, the mere shift of her buttocks between his legs was enough to bring him undone. And when she moved, his cock shot to rigid, not just a wee *rush* but a full-fledged erection. He rolled his eyes and tried to focus on his pain. He dipped his chin and inhaled. Ah yes, lovely jasmine, mixed with wild woman. *Dear God. Stop.*

"Do you have any family?" she asked.

"A son and a daughter." He mightn't be free to tell her the specifics, but he could mention his children. At least they hadn't left him.

"You have children?" She sounded surprised.

"Aye, many men of three and thirty have children."

"Sorry, I just didn't take you as a family man. You haven't mentioned anything about your wife—or your bairns."

Every day, he blocked his mind from thinking of his dragon of a former wife—but never in a million years would he forget his children. He cleared his throat. "Elizabeth left me to join a convent."

Akira touched her dainty fingers to her lips. "She left you alone with two young children?"

*Aye, and near two hundred servants.* Geordie's gut twisted. He didn't want to talk about the duchess. "Aye."

"What kind of woman would do something so heartless?"

"A very selfish one."

"With two bairns at home, how could you leave your children and ride into battle? You could have been killed—*were* almost killed, actually."

"Duty to country must come before family." Sometimes he hated being a nobleman—the pressure, the expectations, the pomp. It was a breath of fresh air to be just a man for once in his life.

"You believe that?" She slapped a hand through the air. "I spit on any cause that harms my family. Why, I would protect my sisters with my life—even Annis, who is the most vainglorious lass I've ever met."

Geordie almost laughed. How could any waif be vainglorious? "I doubt you've met the du—um—many noblewomen."

"Well, no, I haven't had much of a chance to." She thumped his chest with her pointer finger. "But you should be home with your wee bairns."

"Not to worry, they are being well cared for by their governess."

"Governess? Goodness, you must be well off." She turned away and ran her fingers through the horse's mane. "Pray tell, what are your children's ages?"

"Alexander is eleven and Jane seven."

She sighed. "And they're learning to read and write? You must be very proud."

"I am."

"I wish someone had taught me to read." A blush filled her cheeks as she bit her lip and looked down.

Bloody hell, this lass could tug on his heartstrings like no one he'd ever met. "Mayhap that's something we can remedy once we return to civilization."

"Ha, as if a poor woman like me could afford a tutor."

"One never kens." He clamped his lips shut. Once he handed Akira's care over to an escort, he doubted he'd ever see her again. And he wasn't about to start making empty promises to the lass.

They rode in silence for a time—Akira's hip still nestled firmly against his groin. Though his mind ran the gamut, Geordie's confidence in his ability to resist her charms grew.

After cresting one of the numerous hills, he pulled the horse to a stop. The scene below looked as if it could only be from an artist's rendering.

Gasping, Akira drew her hand to her chest. "How indescribably beautiful. 'Tis almost as if it is magical."

Geordie had to agree. "Magnificent."

A waterfall cascaded in four tiers, fingering wider as the water splashed down to an inviting pool of cobalt blue. Trees draped with moss surrounded the oasis, and had he not pulled the horse up in that very spot, he might have missed the exquisite view. Gradually, he walked the horse into the ravine.

"Do you think we might have time for me to rinse out my kirtle?" She shook her skirts, a bit of caked mud dropping from the wool. "I feel ever so dirty."

Geordie looked to the waterfall and licked his lips. If only they could go for a swim—together. "Aye. We may as well stop here for the night. I'm sure with a tempting pool like that, there ought to be plenty of wildlife about. Besides, we can't go much further without a meal."

"Mm, I'm hungry, too."

"My appetite is returning as well." Pulling the horse to a stop, he slid off. "Let me help you dismount."

"I can do it."

He looked at her with a stern eye. "I'm sure you are able, but I would be no gentleman if I didn't give you a lift. And you haven't tried to walk since falling this morn. Your legs could be a wee bit unsteady."

Brushing a bit more dirt from her kirtle, she nodded, blushing again.

She placed her hands on Geordie's shoulders as his fingers closed around her waist. Ignoring the pain in his thigh, he lifted her, fully intending to set her on her feet with finesse, but the mule-brained horse swung his hindquarters around and struck Akira's back. With a high-pitched squeal, she plunged straight into him. Soft, delectable, round, and sumptuous breasts crushed against his chest. Her arms whipped around his neck. His hands slipped to her back, embracing her tightly.

Stunned, he stood motionless with his arms wrapped around her luscious waist, looking into those fathomless blue eyes fanned by long black lashes most women would give their right arm to possess. "You have such beautiful eyes." His voice rumbled with a raspy growl.

She turned a lovely shade of rose and lowered her gaze. "Have I hurt you?"

"Not at all," he whispered. Dear Lord in heaven, how could she do anything to hurt him? So enamored with the softness of her breasts pressed against his chest, he could hardly feel the throbbing pain in his leg. If his hands weren't full of her already, he'd tip up her chin and incline those ruby lips high enough to capture them in a kiss.

"Geordie—I—what—we—"

"'Tis all right. No one is here."

She drew in another wee gasp, but still did not meet his gaze. "Ah . . . you can set me down now."

He glanced to the ground, then back to her bonny face. His knees wobbled. Och aye, powerful knees built for battle had actually wobbled. He hadn't realized she was still dangling in his arms. No wonder his wounded leg felt like it was about to give out. "Of course," he said hoarsely.

Good God, he was in trouble.

# Chapter Nine

Against Akira's advice, Geordie took his flintlock pistol and set out to find food. They could have set a rabbit snare, but he insisted the only way for his leg to heal was to stop cosseting it.

She could fault him for nothing, however. Gracious, for a moment she thought he might kiss her. What would she have done? She almost wanted him to try it. His body had felt so inexplicably hard pressed against hers. Thank heavens she'd stopped him, else she never would have been able to look him in the eye again. And she was his healer. She had to look him in the eye, lest her ten shillings be forfeit.

No wonder Ma forever warned Akira and her sisters against the charms of men. Geordie might speak assertively like an army captain, but the more she grew to know him, the more she realized he was a man of honor, a man who would cast aside his own pain to help her when she fell.

Akira hadn't met many men and trusted fewer. True, as a healer, she'd helped numerous people, and some were men, but they all eyed her with guarded expressions. No one outside of her family spoke to her overmuch—and aye, she'd heard rumblings through the walls about "bringing a tinker into the house" more than once when she'd sat beside a sickbed for hours on end.

But if Geordie thought badly of her, he hadn't let on. Though they'd known each other only a few days, it was in the most peculiar circumstances. They'd been thrown together amidst a life-and-death situation. They'd run for their lives. And somewhere out there, dragoons might still be searching for them. But given a choice between overbearing redcoats and Geordie, she'd pick the braw Highlander every time.

*I trust him.*

He had proved himself to be chivalrous like no one she'd ever met. Nonetheless, it was her duty to care for Geordie's leg, not to gaze into his hazel eyes and wish for a wee kiss.

Akira knew what came after kissing, and it included a swelling of the belly, then a bairn in an unwed lassie's arms. No, no, no. Ma would die if Akira got with child afore she was wed. Besides, she didn't want to end up like her mother, plundered by some blackguard in the alehouse.

And she would be fooling herself to think someone like Geordie would fall in love with the likes of her.

Mr. Geordie was a man of substance. Everything about him spoke of wealth, from the coin in his sporran to the fine tailoring of his velvet doublet and lace cravat. He even spoke like a nobleman. Perhaps he was the second son of a baron or the like. A man of property like Geordie would never give a poor lass a second look.

One day Akira would find a nice man who didn't look at her with wary eyes like the townsfolk in Dunkeld. She'd make a good wife if someone would give her a chance.

After starting a fire, Akira removed her kirtle and petticoat. Goodness, she could hardly tell the gown was blue it was so dirty. She held out her shift and pointed her toe to the side. The linen was nearly as filthy as her dress, caked with mud clear up to her knees. And by the saints, the waterfall looked enticing.

She looked up the hill.

*Geordie should be away for an hour or more.*

She fished out a wee bar of soap she'd thrown into the satchel and headed to the far side of the pool.

* * *

Flintlock pistol in hand, Geordie rode the horse into a copse of trees. He'd have better chances hunting in the wood. With luck he'd happen on a herd of deer. Hell, he was so hungry, a rabbit or two would do as well.

Through the course of the day, the pain in his leg had ebbed a little, or he was growing accustomed to it. Damn it all, he hated being an invalid. He was born of rugged Gordon stock and would not allow a shot to the leg to get the better of him. It was time to buck up and bear down, to cast the pain and agony aside. Pain made a man tougher, stronger, and he would channel it into determination. God knew he couldn't hide out in the mountains much longer. Sooner or later the redcoats would pick up his trail. He needed to send the healer on her way and make haste to Huntly.

Thank the Almighty he hadn't succumbed to a bloody fever.

He shuddered, blocking such a notion from his mind. A true Gordon to his core, Geordie had never taken to his bed due to illness—a fact on which he prided himself.

Akira seemed a healthy sort as well. Where on earth she inherited such resilience, he couldn't fathom. But then, her kind had to be tough to live like tinkers. Oh yes, Geordie liked her strength. It added to her allure. Her olive skin was as vibrant as the setting sun, and her eyes clear and more expressive than those of any noble lass he'd ever met. And then there was her hair. Bless the saints, her tresses shone with a luminous black like a raven in sunshine—a sure sign of good health.

Blinking, he cleared his throat. Of course, as he'd told himself a dozen times, he couldn't lust after the lass.

*She will make someone a good wife.*

Again he shuddered.

He had almost kissed the temptress. Why in God's name did he have to grow so lustful whenever he was near a beautiful woman? Why could he not be impervious to their allure, their scent, the softness of their hair, their feminine curves? Lord forgive him, how he adored the shape of the female form. It mattered not if a woman were buxom or slender, with pert breasts like Akira's. He derived undue enjoyment from watching women, especially when they danced. Their skirts would billow and sway, helping him form an image of their figures beneath. And if he happened to be blessed that eve, he might even spirit a lovely above stairs and discover if his imaginings were right.

He clamped his fingers around his pistol. Damnation, he should not be thinking about women dancing. He should be thinking about how in God's name he was going to arrange Akira's transport home, then avoid being stopped by redcoat patrols on his journey to Huntly Castle. He should be hunting for the next meal so he'd survive to see Jane and Alexander again.

He glanced up at the sky. Without a cloud sailing overhead, the color reminded him of Akira's eyes. Aye, he'd grown to enjoy looking into those eyes in the past few days. Those eyes could hypnotize a man and make him forget himself. Geordie could attest to such a fact. She'd seduced him with a look more than once, and the last time she'd almost persuaded him to kiss her.

Ahead, a rabbit disappeared beneath a fern. Geordie steered the horse toward the quarry, his eyes darting from side to side. The rabbit dashed through the scrub. Geordie took aim. The rascal disappeared beneath a patch of gorse.

He lowered his weapon.

*No use wasting gunpowder.*

Squaring himself on the horse's slippery back, he wished Akira would have taken enough coin to purchase a saddle. Though riding double was probably more comfortable bareback.

A grin spread across his lips and warmth swelled in his chest.

He'd been quite content when she rode seated aside in front of him. With every inhale, the scent of her hair made a restless desire swirl deep in his loins. The curve of her hip resting between his legs provided an everpresent reminder that she was oh, so delectably female. Their closeness, combined with their unintended touches, made him want to surround her with his arms and ply her with kisses.

Holy hellfire, he wanted to give her a lot more than kisses. Hot, passionate, crazed plundering came to mind and made his heart pound.

Geordie growled.

No wonder he'd all but thrown himself at the lass when he'd helped her dismount. He'd been bottling up his urges for hours—convincing himself that he could never take advantage of the wee healer, which he couldn't.

*Absolutely not.*

He could not prove Elizabeth right by allowing his cock to take charge of his actions. No matter how much he desired Akira, he must feign indifference.

He couldn't entertain a relationship with the lass. For the love of God, he was a bloody duke. His miserable divorce had already dragged him through the mire with his peers. He could scarcely show his face in Parliament as it was. What would they think if he showed up with a commoner on his arm?

He almost laughed out loud. The absurd image of him greeting Queen Anne and introducing Akira Ayres, descendant of Romany blood, was almost tempting. He could even make up some fictitious Romany royalty just for a good jape.

He hated the hypocrisy that came with being a duke.

And he could never put Akira into any situation that might cause her embarrassment.

They couldn't possibly have a future together.

And a brief liaison was out of the question.

Was it not?

*Yes, God damn my wayward mind.*

Dear God, she was the sweetest, kindest wisp of a woman he'd ever met. He must not think of showering her with affection, only to break her heart in the end. Besides, if anyone discovered them, she'd be ruined.

*I am a duke. I am ten years her senior, and it is up to me to control myself.*

On the morrow, this journey would be over. He planned to pay Akira her due and that had to be the end of it.

Geordie's ears pricked at the sound of a snort, then another. Cocking his weapon, he crouched and peered through the foliage. A mob of foraging feral pigs headed straight for him. Holding his breath, he eased his seat, telling the horse to stand fast. As the pigs neared, Geordie's mouth watered. What he wouldn't do for a scrumptious bite of roast pork and applesauce right this minute.

He set his sights on a healthy sow and pulled the trigger.

The horse skittered with a sidestep. The copse erupted in a maelstrom of squeals as the mob scattered and scampered for the protection of the underbrush. When the smoke cleared, the sow lay on her side, a hole between the eyes. Geordie couldn't have hoped for a cleaner shot. He dismounted and led the horse to the beast.

When he squatted down to shove his hands under the sow, tears welled in his eyes at the pain shooting through his thigh when he hefted the pig into his arms. His damned knee buckled and collapsed beneath him. He fell back and the dead pig landed on his chest like a keg of ale.

Gasping, he gaped at the sky. "Ballocks!"

Thank God Akira hadn't witnessed that feat of weakness.

He clenched his teeth and shoved the animal aside, the throbbing in his leg causing stars to cross his vision as he stood. Damnation, no self-respecting Gordon would allow an injury to prevent him from enjoying the spoils of the hunt.

"You will not get the better of me, you colossal beast. A miniscule hole in the thigh cannot stop George Gordon."

Steeling his mind to the pain, he planted his feet wide, braced himself, and heaved the pig across the horse's withers. He slapped the pig's rump, determined to haul his quarry back to the pool regardless. In Gordon territory he owned vast forests in which he'd led many a hunt, gracing his table with venison for weeks.

He mounted behind the pig and headed for camp, sitting a bit prouder. He chuckled, anticipating Akira's response—the look on her face, the appreciation in her eyes. As hungry as he, she would be elated, smacking those sumptuous lips. He would fashion a spit and they'd eat roast pork until their bellies were so full neither one of them would be able to take another bite.

Trotting the gelding all the way, it wasn't long until they stood at the top of the crag across from the waterfall.

Suddenly, all the wonderfully mouthwatering thoughts about food completely fled from Geordie's mind. Moreover, every thought he'd ever had melted into oblivion—except one.

*Perfection.*

Bless the stars above, a pure goddess had replaced the Gypsy nymph, and in her place stood the most beautiful woman he'd ever cast his gaze upon. Completely naked, Akira waded in water up to her thighs. Standing before the waterfall, her movement as graceful as a swan, she cupped her hand under the cascade. She raised her chin and encouraged a stream to shower her skin, making her flesh glisten like pure amber.

He'd never seen a profile so alluring, so flawless. When she turned, a deep yearning clamped deep and low, and he leaned forward for a better glimpse. God's bones, the woman's breasts were fuller than he'd imagined, rounded and tipped with tantalizing rosebuds—

flowers he wanted to caress between his fingers and suckle. His gaze trailing lower, he recalled how he could touch his thumbs when he placed his hands around her slender waist.

Aye, he wanted his hands there now.

Dear God, no woman should be endowed with such a delectable splay of feminine hips.

He rubbed his fingers together, imagining how soft her skin would be to his touch.

No wonder he'd been so impassioned by the curve of her hip pushing against his cock. His fingers flexed, itching to sink into her soft, rounded flesh and inhale the jasmine fragrance of her sex. Another stuttered exhale escaped his lips as he regarded that black triangle of curls at her apex.

*An invitation wrapped in black silk.*

Good God, he was hard. He could race the horse into the ravine and in seconds, he'd have her in his arms, strip off his clothes, and make love to her beneath the waterfall, feel those hot thighs wrap around his waist as he lifted her up and buried himself deep inside her sleek core.

Geordie shifted his seat and licked his parched lips.

Akira raised one arm and rubbed it with a slim bar of soap, the motion so lithe, so delightfully tempting, Geordie's balls ached with a searing fire. The woman's wet, raven tresses plastered to the sides of her hips while she cleansed the other arm, then her neck and shoulders, her breasts, and oh, for the love of everything holy, between her legs. Water sprayed around her like a fountain as she turned her back to him.

Dear Moses, it was as heavenly as the front! Her long, glistening tresses hung past her waist, clinging to the enticing flare of her hips. Then she pulled her hair aside and allowed the water to shower her, revealing the length of her feminine neck, the curve of her back, the perfection of her form.

Geordie inched the horse toward the trail.

Looking up the hill for the first time, Akira dropped into the water, submersing her hips.

Blinking himself from his trance, Geordie smiled and held up a hand in greeting.

"Eeep!" A high-pitched squeal echoed and swirled through the ravine. Crossing her arms over her breasts, Akira sank clear up to her neck.

Geordie tapped his heels into the horse's barrel and walked the gelding down the incline. He couldn't shift his gaze from the lass. His hands shook, his damned cock was harder than the steel rod of a smithy's hammer. Och aye, he wanted her.

"I'll be done in a minute," she said, her eyes fearful, her voice too shrill.

Something clicked at the back of Geordie's mind.

*Take control of yourself.*

She glanced to her clothing, spread across the bushes in the sun. "I-I didn't think you'd return so soon."

"Just arrived," he croaked, hardly able to find his voice. "We'll be dining on roast pork this eve."

"Such good news...but"—she bit her bottom lip—"can you wait a wee bit longer? I-I-I've nothing to wear."

Geordie forced himself to drag his gaze away. By the looks of her clothes, held secure by the thorns of a yellow gorse, they would be wet for hours. "You could wear my shirt whilst your things dry."

"Will you not be c-cold?"

"Nowhere near as cold as you are now." He visualized

the erect tips of her breasts and his cock pulsed, leaking seed. He slid off the horse and untied his cravat. "Sorry I haven't a clean shirt to offer, but mine will cover you whilst we roast the pig." He couldn't help staring at her lovely face, her enormous blue eyes framed by black eyelashes. Her face, the color of honey, glistened with water droplets reflecting the afternoon sunglow.

After removing his doublet and pulling the shirt over his head, Geordie's hand shook as he waded into the water and held the garment out to her. Devil's bones, he stood so near—with one more step he could cast the blasted shirt aside and pull her into his embrace. Wrap his arms around her and enjoy the thrill when her wet breasts molded into his chest—skin to skin. Dear God, the temptation ripped through him like a bolt of lightning shooting from his chest and out the tip of his cock.

She tightened her arms across her chest, making the mounds of her breasts push together—swells of pure bliss.

She met his gaze with a defiant stare. "Turn your back."

He froze for an instant. She would deprive him of feasting his eyes on a goddess? Then he gulped. *Of course, ye daft duke.* "Ah..." He offered a nod and did as she asked, holding the shirt out behind while trying to focus on the chill of the water. Perhaps it might serve to cool his lust.

* * *

Akira shivered, with gooseflesh rippling across her skin as she watched Geordie turn away and hold the shirt out. She shook so violently, she hesitated to reach for it. How on earth had he caught her bathing? He hadn't been gone for very long. And why hadn't she kept her shift on? She could have waded into the water to wash the hem.

Overcoming her mortification, she hastily stood, snatched the garment, and pulled it over her head. As she tugged the linen down, the material clung to her wet skin. With every tug, her teeth chattered. What an embarrassing state of affairs.

If only he'd been away a bit longer, she would have slipped her wet shift back over her head and stood in front of the fire.

And the man had brought back a pig? *A pig, for goodness' sakes!* She'd hoped for a rabbit or a grouse at best. Holy fairies, Geordie had been knocking on death's door for two days.

"Do you intend to make me stand here forever?" Geordie asked over his shoulder with a hint of mischief in his voice. "I've a spit to prepare and a sow to clean."

With two last tugs, the shirt managed to cover her thighs but left her calves bare. She shot a panicked glance to her arisaid. There was no way she could reach it without him seeing. "I'm afraid this isn't long enough. Please avert your eyes whilst I pass."

"I wa..." Geordie turned, his voice trailing off, his jaw dropping. Those hazel eyes grew as dark as coal as his gaze drifted downward. Akira's skin warmed when he paused at her breasts, then slowly swept his stare lower until he stopped at her exposed legs. His Adam's apple bobbed and his face reddened. "Ah..."

Her hand slid over her heart. Dear Lord, she'd never imagined he'd look so...ah...so deliciously braw without his shirt. His arms were thick and sculpted with muscle, his chest, too, like carved marble, and then his abdominals...Oh, heaven save her. Akira's fingers practically grew a mind of their own, reaching out, craving to rub across the undulating bands of muscle.

In a blink, she snatched her hands away and crossed her arms over her breasts.

Still staring at her legs, Geordie raked his fingers through his wavy chestnut tresses. "Apologies."

If nothing else, Akira was sorrier. She never should have agreed to don his miserable shirt. Gracious, it even smelled of spicy male, and the scent made her insides ridiculously queasy. She swiped her wet hair away from her face. "I must look a fright."

His gaze meandered back up to her face, his eyebrows slanting outward, the corners of his mouth twisting up. "Not exactly how I would have worded it."

Akira glanced down, ankle deep in water—he'd seen her knees now. But that was the least of her woes. Heaven's stars, the linen clung to her body like a second skin. She tugged it out and gave it a good shake. "I didn't ken the fabric would be so...so...so sheer."

His eyes grew even darker, like a starved man staring at a platter of roast mutton that was just beyond his reach. The hunger in his eyes made shivers course across her skin. One part of her begged for her to drop her arms and walk toward him. Begged for her to give in to all the wanton feelings of desire that had spiked through her body over the past few days.

But she couldn't. She barely knew this man and, furthermore, could have no possible future with him. How many times must she remind herself she was the healer and he the patient?

She swallowed and forced herself to pull her gaze away.

She gave him a wide berth as she headed for the shore. "I think my clothes have started to dry. I'll just take them behind a clump of broom."

"Let them dry, else you'll catch your death," Geordie grumbled behind her, his footsteps splashing through the water. "Forgive me. I'll try to keep from ogling you."

Akira stole a glance at him over the brush. In the time it took Geordie to limp out of the water, his expression had gone from desirous to irritated. He hauled the pig from the horse with a grimace. "You could make yourself useful by stoking the fire and finding a pair of branches sturdy enough to use for a spit."

Akira slipped her feet into her shoes. "Yes, of course." Goodness, he sounded so upset, yet at first he'd appeared almost enraptured. Had she disappointed him? Truly she was mortified to her toes when she realized he'd seen her naked, but his reaction was a complete quandary.

Had she misread his initial expression? Why hadn't he called down from the top of the hill and given her a warning? She could have donned her shift and wrapped her wet arisaid around her shoulders. They would have dried soon enough.

She wrung out the water collected at the bottom of her arisaid and tied the wet woolen garment around her waist for a bit more cover. She wandered away a bit, hiding behind the brush while she collected branches for the fire. Dear Lord, if only she could hide for the rest of her life. But aside from having a duty to perform as a healer, she was starving and lost, with no place to run.

Once out of sight, she squared her shoulders and took a deep breath.

*I am a good healer. I ken my trade, and I refuse to wallow in shame. I have done nothing wrong. Nothing.*

# Chapter Ten

Thus far, Geordie had kept himself busy rotating the spit and making a pallet of ferns and grass on the sandy bank. Since turning around and seeing Akira wearing nothing but his shirt clinging to her damp body, he'd worked like a badger to do anything to keep from looking at her.

A lot of good that did.

He could no sooner erase those images from his mind than he could forget to breathe. She had the shapeliest calves, and her thighs—oh God, those thighs clearly visible through the linen were what brought him undone. And now, with her arisaid tied around her waist, every now and again he caught a glimpse of a sleek, slender leg. He didn't dare mention it, lest she traipse behind the broom and don her wet kirtle. Not only would that deprive him of those wee peeks, she might catch her death.

His balls ached every time she moved. And every time, he'd catch himself ogling her like a hungry dog, wishing her leg would slip out just a bit farther. If only he could steal another look at her thighs, or be blessed with a peek at quim. He lengthened at the mere memory of seeing the triangle of black curls that guarded her...

*Damnation.* He turned the spit faster. He hadn't come in his breeches since he was a wet-eared lad, and he wasn't about to do so now.

Och, he was a lecherous beast. But what red-blooded man wouldn't be drooling for a glimpse at such treasure? He'd swiped his hand across his mouth about fifty times to ensure he wasn't slavering.

When, finally, the meat was cooked, she sat on the pallet with her legs tucked under and completely covered by the plaid, thank God. Geordie cut off two slices of roast and sat beside her. "'Tis not served up like a feast, but if you're as hungry as I am, it'll taste the same."

She grinned, her blue eyes catching the evening's firelight. "'Tis a feast to me. My sisters and I rarely have the pleasure of eating meat." She bit down and ripped into the pork with her teeth.

Although his stomach was growling, Geordie paused and watched her. Must she make everything look sensual? Even the bit of juice running from the corner of her mouth was alluring, as the grease made her lips shine, begging for a kiss. Her eyes rolled back. "Mm."

Geordie stared. *I'm either in heaven or in purgatory.*

She glanced his way and stopped mid-chew. "Are you not eating?"

Unable to drag his eyes from her lips, he bit into his portion. A burst of meaty flavor made his mouth water. "Good," he managed to say. His mind possessed by a myriad of stimulations, he feasted like a starved fox and Akira joined him.

Licking her fingers, she reached for the flask. "I'll wager you'd prefer ale or wine."

He nodded, stuffing his face and rubbing the grease off his hands. "Or whisky."

She took a drink, her chin tilting up, exposing her long, slender neck. Black hair cascaded in waves down her back. Wiping her mouth with the back of her hand, she gave him a look. How everything happened as if a maestro were slowing the tempo, Geordie had no idea, but he savored every moment. The firelight danced across her face with amber tones. If only he could devour her now.

Akira handed him the flask. "Ever since you returned from the hunt, you've been looking at me with the most peculiar glint in your eye."

"Have I?" He took the flask and drank, yet did not shift his gaze. "Apologies."

"Thank you for lending me your shirt." Her gaze dipped to his chest and stayed there.

"'Twas the least I could do." His heart throbbed with the heat of her eyes upon him. Mayhap she liked him, too—not because he was a duke, but she liked him for Geordie, the man he wanted to be.

"You're not angry with me?"

"Why would I be angry?"

"Ah..." Her tongue tapped her top lip as her gaze drifted up and met his. "You seemed a bit agitated."

Och aye, he was agitated, all the way down to his aching balls. "Not at all." He leaned closer, those moist lips beckoning him.

Blushing, Akira glanced down. "Truly, I thought you would be gone longer. I shouldn't have tried to bathe. But the pool was so inviting."

A lock of her hair flicked up with the breeze. He

couldn't help but catch it and twist the silkiness around his finger. "No apology needed, lass."

With a shy smile, she regarded his mouth, her lips parting with a wee gasp. How could a man resist such an invitation? As if pulled by a force outside his body, he scooted closer and cupped her cheek.

Her tongue slipped out and tapped her top lip.

Geordie couldn't stop his gasp. "I want to kiss you, lass."

Her chin inched up ever so slightly.

His hand moved back and cradled her head while his mouth inclined toward her rose-petal lips, then lightly brushed his mouth over the most delectable lips in all the world.

Her wee moan made a fire hotter than the flames of Hades burn deep and low inside him. Gradually lowering her to the earth, he reverently savored her. Every fiber of his body stirred to life, the blaze in his loins raging like a fire gone wild.

Dear God, he had to keep himself under control, hold his lust at bay. But all that consumed his mind was kissing Akira while her supple breasts caressed him. Drawing a ragged breath, he groaned and tasted her, threading his fingers through her black tresses. Luxurious hair he'd been longing to rake his fingers through since he'd first laid eyes on her. Hair so soft, it could be mistaken for spun silk. Every beat of his heart hammered, begging him to devour her.

But the woman in his arms was the young maid who'd saved him. The lass who'd cast aside her doubts to help a wounded man she hardly knew flee from a mob of redcoats. Moreover, the lass cared not an iota about Government or Jacobite agendas. She cared about her family and finding the next meal. Akira wasn't to be taken like a harlot, but to be cherished and savored. He tenderly spread her lips with his tongue, stroking her with soft, unhurried licks, showing her how to kiss a man.

For a moment he opened his eyes and watched her melt, giving way to his kisses, shedding her maidenly unease. Aye, he hadn't been mistaken. She desired him as much as he wanted her. Sighing, she met him swirl for swirl, little suck for little suck. Clutching him tighter, she kneaded her fingers into the muscles at his nape.

Easing the kiss, he nibbled along her jaw and down her neck while his hand slid over and cupped the supplest breast on earth.

"Stop," she said with a gasp, her fists shoving up between them. "Why is it I have so much difficulty resisting you?"

"Believe me, lass, I am the one who has been rendered utterly powerless."

He hoped she would laugh and fling her arms around him, going for another kiss. But not Akira. She eased out from under him and pushed herself to her feet, tugging her damned arisaid closed.

She gave him a pursed-lipped sideways glance. "You mustn't ever do that again. I'm a healer. Not a harlot."

He lumbered to his feet. "Of course you're no harlot. You're bonny and irresistible."

Had he misread her? The sensual flick of her tongue, the allure in her eyes?

*God's teeth. She's an innocent, and I'm a damned cur.*

Geordie picked up a rock and threw it into the pond, watching the circle of waves expand.

*I mustn't kiss her. I'm about to explode and still I cannot forget my station.*

Under the evening sky, frogs carried on like a pack of windless pipers.

"See, you're acting angry again."

He crossed his arms. "I'm not bloody angry."

Akira moved beside him and threw her own rock into the pool.

Geordie looked her way just at the wrong time. Her arisaid billowed out, giving him the glimpse of sleek calf he'd been aching to see all evening. His heart banged against his chest, making it difficult to breathe.

She faced him, her hands on her hips. "Ma says to stay away from men like you."

"Like me?"

"Aye. You've not given me your real name, nor have you told me where you're from—even I am educated enough to ken the region of Aberdeen is a vast place, and you could be far more specific. I-I don't think you trust me at all."

"'Tis not you who is untrustworthy."

She tapped her cheeky little foot. "Oh?"

"If the Government troops got hold of you, it would be best if you didn't know my name or where I'm from."

"Why? Are you someone important?"

"When you put it like that, aye. I'm someone who should have kent better than to ride into battle with a regiment of Jacobites. It's just—"

"What?"

He threw his hands to his sides. "After Queen Anne scoffed at Scotland's Act of Security, I could no longer sit on my laurels. I've had a gutful of English superiority, but to protect my children, I had to act anonymously."

"I wouldn't ken much about that. 'Tis hard enough worrying about keeping food in my belly and ensuring there's wood for the fire."

Geordie couldn't help his smirk. "Then you are blessed."

"Indeed I am." She touched his arm, making goose-flesh spread clear up the back of his neck. "I understand you may not want to give me your family name, but what is your given name—the one your friends call you?"

"Honestly, my closest friends call me Geordie—even my sisters." He sighed. "If you must know, my name is George, but the only person besides my mother who called me by it was my former wife."

"Your wife who went to the convent?" she asked.

"Aye, she forced me to pursue divorce proceedings and then set sail for the nunnery in Flanders."

"How utterly awful. I do not ken of anyone who has obtained a divorce."

Geordie kicked a rock. "'Tis a rite of humiliation reserved for the upper classes."

An uncomfortable pause followed until Akira glanced up and twisted her mouth. "To tell the truth, George is nice, but I think Geordie suits you better."

"My thanks." His tone sounded gruffer than he intended.

"I still think you're angry about something." She wandered over to her clothing and rubbed the corner of her shift between her fingers. "I think this is dry enough to don."

"Thank God for small mercies." Geordie didn't know how much more he could resist of Akira's bare legs tantalizing him through the gap in her plaid.

* * *

Looking up, she glared at the Highlander. "I beg your pardon? You are the one who gave me the shirt."

He rolled his eyes. "I didn't mean it that way."

"Truly?" She clutched the arisaid closed around her legs, trying to look anywhere but at Geordie's well-muscled bare chest. "If you'll kindly turn your back, my clothes are near enough to dry. I can return your shirt."

After a long, heated stare, he shrugged and did as she asked.

She plucked her garments from the thorns on the gorse and headed behind the brush, keeping the firelight in view. Goodness, it was dark away from the fire.

She whipped the shirt over her head, pulled on her shift—at least that was dry. She tied her stays loosely in the front, then shrugged into her damp kirtle. It had dried when they'd been caught in the downpour; there was no reason she couldn't withstand a wee chill while it dried now.

"Is everything all right over there?" Geordie's voice resounded from the direction of the fire.

She tugged the laces on her kirtle. "Everything is nearly back in order." Why on earth had she agreed to take his shirt in the first place? Ever since she pulled the blasted thing over her head, she'd been flummoxed. It smelled too much of Geordie—made her think too much of his kiss, made her crave another... and another.

*Absolutely not.*

She'd been acting irresponsibly and it was time to stand up straight and behave like a healer ought. He was her patient. She was there to help him regain his strength, and if he kept improving, her services wouldn't be needed by the time they found his allies on the morrow.

*This is the last night, and then I shall return home and everything will be back to normal.*

She sighed at the thought of home. What she wouldn't

do to be sitting in front of home's fire, or curled into the box bed she shared with her sisters. Funny, she had always longed for her own bed up until now, but after two nights with very little sleep, she'd pay a whole penny to claim her little corner of the bed.

Besides, Ma was probably growing worried.

After pulling her hair out from under her kirtle and wrapping the arisaid around her shoulders, she picked up Geordie's shirt and strode back to the fire. The Highlander reclined, his muscles even more defined by the flicker of the fire. She covered her eyes, trying not to stare.

Stubbing her toe, she tripped and nearly fell atop the man. Thank goodness, she caught herself in time. Lord only knew what he would have thought of her if she'd fallen on him. "Here. Thank you for lending this to me."

When he reached for it, he caught her hand. "I'm sorry for taking liberties. I overstepped my bounds."

She gave him a nod. "We both faltered. Now that is done, it mustn't happen again." Her gaze trailed to their joined hands. "I only..."

"Yes?"

She couldn't tell him how much she'd enjoyed her first kiss, how much she wanted him to kiss her again. That would be admitting the same hot Gypsy blood coursed through her veins as it had in her family for generations. Ma had warned her, blast it all. "Ah... I'm looking forward to going home."

His face fell. He released her hand and tugged the shirt over his head.

Akira's fingers tingled, but a hollow chasm spread through her chest. Why did he constantly make her feel as if she'd said the wrong thing? Twisting her lips, she sat on the opposite side of the fire.

Geordie pulled on his doublet. "Now the sun has set, 'tis growing cold."

"Another reason why I needed to return your shirt."

He nodded, reclining on his elbow and staring at her across the flames. He could have passed for a statue of a Roman god, his head resting in his palm, bottom knee bent, top leg straight.

She glanced to the wounded thigh. "How is your injury?"

"Still there." Goodness, how he could unnerve her, staring from across the fire. Did the man ever blink?

"Better?" she asked, trying to calm the butterflies dancing around her stomach.

A single eyebrow arched. "Coming good, I reckon."

Akira rubbed her eyes. "I think 'tis time for sleep. I'm so tired I can't see straight."

*Mayhap once I've rested, I won't feel so out of sorts.*

He patted the ground beside him. "Then you'd best come lie on the pallet I've fashioned. The sand and ferns have made it quite comfortable."

She bit her lip. "No, I think I'm content to stay here."

Looking a wee bit forlorn, Geordie furrowed his brow with a twitch to his stubbled jaw. "As you wish."

# Chapter Eleven

With morning came a heavy mist, reminding Geordie of the direness of his situation. The more they tarried in the Highlands, the better chance he gave the redcoats of riding around and setting an ambush.

He was a far cry from safety, and if the Government soldiers had found his flask, the Marquis of Atholl would be out for blood. Och aye, John Murray and his army of dragoons would jump at a chance to elevate his status in the eyes of Queen Anne.

*The bastard.*

Akira's arm brushed his chest as it had so many times on this journey. And yes, every wee touch made his heart quicken, but this morrow, he would take her to Spean Bridge and ask Clan MacDonell to take her home. His heart squeezed. He might miss the lass, but she'd be far better off back home with her family, and Lord knew, he had a host of dealings awaiting him at Huntly.

She swept the back of her hand across his forehead. "I think you might be a wee bit fevered."

He took in a shivering breath. He didn't have time for a damned fever. "'Tis nothing a good swig of whisky will not heal."

"And I need to make you some willow bark tea at our very next opportunity."

He looked beyond her, steering the horse around an enormous boulder. Picking their way through the fog wasn't just tricky in the Highlands, it could be lethal. "I'd prefer whisky."

"Aye, spoken like a true Highlander, but you hired me as your healer. And if you want to heal quickly, I suggest you do my bidding."

"Och aye, I'd almost forgotten." The fog grew thicker with every descending step. "Ten shillings, is it?"

She gave him an assured nod. "That was our agreement."

"Not to worry, lass. I honor my debts, like a true Gord—ah—honorable merchant."

As they continued their descent of the western Highlands, sweat beaded Geordie's brow. Though he wouldn't admit it to Akira, he *was* a bit fevered. The past few days had sapped his strength—they would have taken their toll on any man with a musket shot to the leg. He shoved his hand through his hair. He'd weather this ailment like a true Gordon. A wee musket ball couldn't take the wind out of his sails—at least not for long.

Sound asleep against his chest, Akira sighed. Heaven help him, she looked almost as beautiful sleeping as she did when awake. Though she was peaceful in sleep, he preferred gazing into her indigo eyes, even when she was a bit angry. Mayhap *especially* when she was angry.

And she'd had every right to be irritated with him last

eve. Like an idiot, he'd fashioned the pallet anticipating a night sleeping beside her.

*Bloody lecherous cur I am.*

Who knew what would have happened if she hadn't donned her clothing and insisted upon sleeping on the other side of the campfire? He was unlikely to have been able to control himself throughout the night—especially in the wee hours.

At least Akira had a sensible streak. And thank God good sense had escaped her when she'd opted to bathe in the pool. Truly, she wouldn't have done something so rash had she known of Geordie's reputation. But now he'd seen her nude, nothing else would do.

Soon they'd climb down from these mountains and the dream would be gone.

Movement through the haze drew him from his thoughts. Tugging on the reins, Geordie slowed the horse and peered down the slope.

His gut leapt to his throat.

*Redcoats.*

A musket fired, the blast resounding between the hills.

Akira snapped up with a gasp. "Wha—?"

"Wheesht!" Geordie hushed her, slamming his heels into the horse's barrel.

With a cry, Akira threw her arms around his waist as the horse spun northwest, heading back into the mist. Ahead, more shots came.

"Surrounded?" Geordie whispered, looking left then right. *Damn.* His only choice was to run from whence they came.

"*Ghàidhealtachd*," a deep voice growled, the Gaelic word for the Highlands. The sound came from a ravine—a perfect place for an ambush.

Against every military lesson he'd ever been taught, Geordie made a snap decision and reined the horse toward the sound. Musket fire cracked overhead. He crouched over Akira, shielding her with his body. "Keep your head down!"

The horse raced through the rocky ravine, kicking stones and blowing snorts of air through his nose.

"*Lean*," growled the voice giving a command to follow.

Straining his eyes, he caught a glimpse of a brown pony swishing its tail. Geordie trailed after it, staying close enough to keep the tail in sight.

As they galloped downward, the mist cleared enough for him to make out a burly Highlander crouched atop a garron pony. The sound of horses pummeled the ground, running in the opposite direction. Through the mist above, he made out the ghostly outlines of an entire Highland regiment mounting a charge, cutting them off from the bloodthirsty dragoons. Muskets blasted behind them as Geordie reined his horse behind the Highlander, barely able to keep the man's shadowy form in sight.

"What's happening?" Akira asked in a sharp whisper.

"I think we've found a mob of friends."

The musket fire grew distant as Geordie followed the Highland soldier for miles until he led them into a dense forest and stopped outside the gaping entrance to a cave. A dozen questions came to the tip of Geordie's tongue as he pulled his mount alongside the big man. "I owe you a debt of gratitude. You arrived just at the right time."

The man looked up and removed his cap, his eyes flashing wide. "Your Gra—"

"Sir Coll of Keppoch?" Geordie boomed, loud enough to drown out a squawking rooster. Thank God he'd finally happened upon an ally, but he didn't want anyone knowing his identity, especially with the enemy on his heels. "How in God's name did you ken we'd be traveling through?"

"Ah—word was, the redcoats were setting an ambush for a wounded—ah—man and a healer." Coll's gaze flashed to Akira. "I've a great deal to tell you."

"I'm certain you have." He helped Akira down and introduced her. "Is there anyone inside who can offer the lass a meal and a comfortable seat?"

"Freddy!" he hollered as he dismounted. "We have company."

A lad no older than twelve stepped outside. "Yes, sir." He took one look at Akira and his mouth dropped open. "H-h-hello."

Geordie slid off his mount and winced at the pain.

Coll eyed him with concern furrowing his brow, but motioned to his man. "Take Miss Akira inside and see she eats a bellyful."

Akira curtsied. "Thank you, sir."

The chieftain gave her a lopsided grin. "God's teeth, the report didn't say anything about the healer being so bonny."

Geordie's gut clenched, along with his fists. At one and twenty, the young chieftain had best keep his hands and his eyes to himself. "Watch yourself, MacDonell. Anyone who lays a finger on the lass will answer to me."

"She's yours, then?" asked Coll.

"Aye." What else could he say? He certainly wasn't going to let on that she was an unmarried maid. She'd have an entire clan of MacDonell Highlanders trying to woo her.

Akira's bewildered stare shifted between the two men. "I beg your pardon?"

"Will you be all right, miss?" Geordie asked, manners

drilled into him since the cradle materializing out of nowhere.

She blushed like a rose in full bloom, while bewilderment reflected in her eyes. "Of course I will. The question is, will *you* be all right?"

He squared his shoulders, pretending nothing was amiss. "Give me a moment with Sir Coll and I'll join you forthwith."

Drawing her eyebrows together, she stared at him as if he'd just flown down from the moon. "Ah—very well."

Once the lass followed Freddy, Geordie beckoned Coll with a wave of his hand. "Come. Let us walk." *Or limp, as the case may be.*

"I cannot tell you how surprised I am to see you, Your Grace."

Slicing his hand through the air, Geordie glanced over his shoulder. "'Tis best if no one kens I'm a duke. If the redcoats catch wind of it, they'll crucify me for certain."

"Yes, Your Grace... I mean... sir?"

"Sir is fine."

"It just seems wrong." Coll scratched his full head of red hair. "I should at least say 'm'lord.'"

"Nay." Geordie stumbled, pain shooting up his thigh.

"Are you injured, Your—ah—m'lor—ah—sir?"

"Damnation." He grasped Coll's shoulder to regain his balance. "I took a musket ball to the thigh."

"Dear God. You should be abed."

"Aye, if only there were one handy." Geordie beckoned him to continue on. "But I haven't time for that now. Did you ride into Hoord Moor?"

"Nay. I'm still feuding with the bloody MacIntoshes."

"And how is that proceeding? Are you in need of reinforcements?"

"Nay. I'll beat them back to the Hebrides for certain." Coll slapped the hilt of the sword at his hip. "We'll be ready for the next Jacobite rising."

"Good lad. But 'tis a fortunate thing you stayed home—you can give me an alibi if needed." Geordie wiped his brow with his sleeve. Good Lord, he was weak.

"Bloody Christmas, are you all right, sir? You've turned white as bed linen."

With a shake of his head, Geordie slapped a dismissive hand through the air. "That's why I've brought the healer. I reckon she's kept me alive." It wasn't the entire truth, but close enough.

"'Tis a good thing indeed." Coll looked back toward the cave and a half-cocked grin spread across his ruddy face. "She certainly is bonny."

"Aye, and she's not for you."

"Oh?"

"Give it a rest, MacDonell."

Coll's lips thinned. "Ah yes, I've heard word of the duchess leaving for Flanders."

"How dare you question me?"

"I thought I wasn't supposed to treat you like a duke, *Your Grace*." The ginger-haired scoundrel bowed. "Beg your pardon. I meant to say, 'sir.' "

"Ungrateful whelp." Geordie cuffed the back of his head. "The healer is under my protection and that is all." He looked to the trees rustling with the wind above. "I need to arrange an escort to safely take her back to Dunkeld."

"Are you jesting?" A snort shot through Coll's nose. "No Jacobite in his right mind would venture anywhere near Dunkeld or Hoord Moor at the moment—even a royalist suspected of being a Jacobite would be a stretch."

"Blast!" Geordie balled his fist. "Nonetheless, you didn't show your colors on the battlefield, and I need someone to take her away home."

"Och, I've a miserable parcel of my own problems." Coll's face blurred as he threw up his hands. "Bloody Christmas, of course I'll take her home if need be. Ye ken I'd do anything for you, but not afore you've healed a bit more, Your Gra—ah—sir."

"Thank you." Leaning forward and resting his hands on his knees, Geordie took in a few reviving breaths. "You must remember to call me sir. Who else was with you at court that might recognize me now?"

"Just Glen and my brother, Angus."

"Make sure nary a one uses my courtesy."

"I'll catch them as soon as the men return."

"Good." Geordie straightened and turned full circle. "Where the devil are we?"

"In the hills above Loch Laggan. I had no idea it was you on the run from the redcoats, else I would have taken you straight to Glen Spean."

"Och, you did the right thing—MacDonell womenfolk and bairns should be your priority."

"Thank you, sir."

"I'm a wee bit concerned for Miss Akira, though. I don't want anyone getting the wrong idea about her."

"I'll tell the men she's under your protection."

"Then they'll want to ken why I'm so goddamned important—you'd best tell them she's under *your* protection."

The corners of Coll's mouth turned up. Geordie knew full well what the laird was thinking—the varlet. Christ, any man merely had to glimpse Akira and he'd want to bed her.

"Very well," Coll agreed. "And as soon as 'tis safe I'll take the pair of you down to Glen Spean. You can have use of my house until you're well enough for the journey home."

"Not to worry about me. I'm a Gordon. I could fight a hundred battles if need be."

"Och aye?" The overgrown lad arched an eyebrow. "With all due respect, sir, you're as pale as a snow owl in winter."

Worse, Geordie's limbs ached, making him bloody weak. "Perhaps a night's rest on a real bed will remedy that."

# Chapter Twelve

Akira had heard tales of ferocious Highland chieftains and how nary a soul was safe in their clutches. Living like wild men, they preyed upon women and children and attacked their neighbors with fire and sword. But at this very moment, she could prove every naysayer wrong. Sir Coll, who she discovered was the sixteenth chieftain of Clan MacDonell of Keppoch, had been nothing but gracious, albeit in a cavalier sort of way.

His manse was enormous, with nooks and crannies everywhere she looked—and she'd only been introduced to her chamber and the dining hall thus far. Goodness, her chamber was nearly as large as the shieling she shared with Ma and her sisters. And it had a four-poster bed that she wouldn't even need to share.

Aye, there were a few nice homes in Dunkeld, but she'd never been inside them. Amazingly, Sir Coll seemed to have a servant for everything—cooks and servers and chambermaids, grooms and valets—the list went on.

Seated at an enormous dining table, she could practically see her reflection in the sheen of the wood, and her chair had upholstered cushions as well as arms.

She picked up the miniature spoon in the silver saltcellar and watched as the salt sprinkled from it, forming a tiny mountain of white granules.

"My word, Akira, you act as if you've never seen salt on the table afore."

She dropped the spoon into the cellar and met Geordie's irritated stare. "Sorry." It would be too embarrassing to admit she was too poor to afford a commodity as dear as salt.

"Not to worry," said Sir Coll, grinning with a wink. Though there were lines etched in the corners of his eyes, he had a youthful face and a mop of wild auburn curls. He wasn't a typical ginger with freckles and pasty skin. His face had a slightly amber glow to it, which made his cornflower-blue eyes sparkle like the sun on a loch. "We'll serve up a good meal to the pair of you, and after a night's rest, I'll wager you'll both be fighting fit come morn."

Geordie speared a bite of meat with his eating knife. "Would you mind sending up a tub of hot water? I'm in sore need of a bath."

"Consider it done." Coll threw his thumb over his shoulder. "Would you be needing a wee lass to wash your back, sir?"

The hackles on the back of Akira's neck stood on end. "I beg your pardon?" And why did a man as important as a Highland chieftain keep calling Geordie sir?

The hall rumbled with Coll's laugh while he pounded his knuckles on the table. "I reckoned that might light a fire under you, miss."

Across the table, Geordie glowered at their host. "*Haud yer wheesht!* My skirt-chasing days have long since passed."

"Forgive me, sir." Coll's big grin was immediately replaced with a more somber expression. Pity, for Akira liked the smile better.

She gave Geordie a quizzical look. "You were a what?" Did she hear him right? Had he been a rake?

Her mysterious traveling partner raised his tankard of ale to his lips. "Apologies, miss. I made errors of judgment as a younger lad, and unfortunately my reputation is tarnished for the rest of my days."

She looked to Coll. "Is that right?"

The chieftain waved a dismissive hand. "Bah, no one cares overmuch about the past."

Akira stewed over Sir Coll's words for a moment. Geordie had a questionable reputation? Aside from their fleeting kiss, he had behaved respectfully toward her. "I think once a reputation is earned, it is very difficult to change. Though I must admit my patient has proved to be as gentlemanly as any of the other people I've tended."

The two men looked at her, Coll in mid-chew, Geordie lowering his tankard. Then he grinned. "See, MacDonell, I told you she was a rare blossom."

"Indeed."

Heat flooding to her cheeks, Akira studied her plate and swirled a bite of roast lamb in gravy. Roast lamb. She could count on her fingers the number of times she'd had such a lavish feast.

When she looked up again, Geordie's face had grown ashen, with a damp sheen.

"Are you not feeling well, sir?" she asked, figuring if Sir Coll was referring to Geordie as "sir," she should as well.

"Just overtired, I reckon." He pushed back his chair and stood. "I think I'll turn in for the night."

Coll scooted his chair back and hopped to his feet. "I'll send up a bath and some Speyside whisky. That'll set you to rights."

Akira stood as well. "I should dress your wound after your bath."

Leaning on the chair, Geordie frowned and shook his head. "You need to sleep as well."

"Aye, I will, right after I've tended you. After all, you're paying me to heal you. I'd best do a good job of it."

* * *

"Is there anything else you need, sir?" asked the valet, placing a glass of whisky and a drying cloth on the table beside the wooden tub filled with steaming water.

Geordie looked at the bath and licked his lips. His entire body ached along with the endless throbbing of his thigh. Why was it injuries had to worsen before they healed? "Please send the healer in with her satchel."

The servant bowed. "Straightaway, sir. And I'll have your doublet brushed and shirt washed and returned by morning."

"Thank you."

After the valet left, Geordie removed his borrowed robe and sank into the water. "Sssss." Damnation, his thigh stung as it met the warm water. Clenching his teeth, he reclined and closed his eyes until the sting abated. Good Lord, it felt good to be back in civilization.

But still, the redcoats had come too damned close. On the morrow, he must head north and leave Akira in Coll's capable hands. Unfortunately, the thought of leaving her didn't sit well. He'd grown attached to the wee imp. But she'd be completely flummoxed once she discovered he was a duke. And that would spoil everything.

A soft rap sounded at the door as Geordie reached for his whisky. "Come."

Akira peered inside with a wee gasp. "Apologies, sir. I was told you sent for me."

He beckoned her. "I did. Close the door."

Clutching the satchel over her shoulder, she stepped inside. "Perhaps I should come back after your bath."

He watched her from behind the glass as he took a long drink of whisky. This very well could be the last evening he'd spend with the bonny lass. Aye, he'd respect her as he had this entire journey, but that didn't mean he couldn't enjoy a wee bit of fun. "I hoped you might have a healing essence for my bath water."

Taking in a sharp breath, she nodded and moved toward him. "Aye, I've a tincture of avens oil and mallow." She dug inside her satchel and pulled out a vial. "Here it is."

He beckoned her closer. "Would you add it to the basin?"

A worried look furrowed her brow. "All you need do is sprinkle a bit into the bath and then soak until the water cools."

The corner of his mouth twitched. "My guess is you're nervous about doing it yourself."

"Aye." Her gaze dipped to the water. "'Tisn't proper."

"But I'm paying you to be my healer. I think it would be best if you tended me."

Clearing her throat, she snapped her gaze back to his face and gave him a more self-assured nod. "Very well."

Geordie almost forgot his fever as she neared. Aye, the

ache in his head was replaced by a much more urgent ache in his loins.

Akira stood over him, poured in the tincture, and shoved the stopper back into the vial. "If you'd like, I'll return after your soak and apply the salve."

He took another sip of whisky and placed the glass on the table. "Would you sit with me?"

Her gaze strayed to the water, her lips parting with her sharp inhale.

His erection lurked beneath, and it was all he could do not to stroke himself and show her exactly what she did to him. Dear God, the game of abstinence was practically more erotic than any he'd ever played.

If only she weren't an innocent...

He licked his lips. "Am I making you nervous?"

"Aye." She picked up a cloth, dipped it in the water, and wrung it out. Her gaze met his with a crackle of energy. "I think you're toying with me."

"Perhaps." He grasped her wrists. "But I like it when you're near." And he didn't want young Coll of Keppoch making advances toward the lass, either.

After a moment's hesitation—a moment where their unblinking stares held as if in a battle of wills—she pulled her hand away and wiped his brow. "I like you as well, sir, but you confuse me."

"Oh? Why? And why have you all of the sudden started calling me sir?"

"Sir Coll refers to you as such, and as my employer, I figured I must pay you your due respect as well."

Dear God, he should just have out with it and reveal his true identity.

She scrubbed the cloth down his chest—a bit heavy-handed about it, too. "Why does the chieftain call you sir?"

"His clan pays fealty to my clan."

"So then, you are a chieftain as well?"

"Yes, I am." That was no lie. His line had been the chieftains of Clan Gordon for centuries.

"Then that explains it." The swirls of her cloth grew softer, though her hand trembled a bit. "And I'll reckon you're afraid you'll lose your lands if the Government troops discover you rode against them at Hoord Moor."

"Right you are." He caught her hand and pressed his lips to her fingers. "'Tis time I sent you home."

She nodded with a gulp.

"I wish it didn't have to be thus."

"Me, too," she whispered, the firelight picking up a tear in the corner of her eye. "I-I'd like to see you recovered afore I take my leave."

"I'll come good, thanks to you and your ma's salve."

"But I'm worried about fever. You need rest. Will you stay on here for a time?"

"I cannot. If I ride hard, I'll be home in two or three days."

"Oh." She drew her hand away and busied herself by hanging the cloth on the side of the tub. "Is there someone near your home to tend you?"

He chuckled. "Too many people, to be honest."

"And I suppose the chieftain has his pick of any lass he wants."

Hot blood thrummed beneath his skin. The way she looked at him, combined with the soft allure of her voice, gave rise to a deep-seated desire. She liked him. He could swear she wanted him to kiss her, and that made him even harder. Geordie again caught her hand and lightly rubbed his fingers around her palm. "Nay." Blast it all, he couldn't make her empty promises—not

Akira—not this lass who had all but sacrificed her life for him.

A tear dribbled from her eye as her lips neared and caressed his forehead. "I am but a poor maid. I ken my place, sir."

When she pulled away, Geordie kept a firm grasp on her hand. Before he could think, he was on his feet, embracing her against his wet, naked body. Aye, with Akira in his arms he could ignore the pain in his leg—he could ignore the whole goddamn world.

She opened her mouth to protest, but he didn't give her reproach a chance to meet the air. He slid a hand to her slender jaw and claimed her mouth for himself. The time had passed for teaching the woman about kissing a man, the time had come to show her the power she had over him—the power she could have over any man of her choosing. And, by God, Geordie wanted the object of her desire to be him and only him.

Her hand pushed between them, but her mouth opened, welcoming the deep plunging of his tongue.

He swirled his fingers into her back, hoping, praying she could feel his hardness pressed against her. Hoping, praying she wanted him as much as he craved her—with his very life. He'd wanted her since he'd first gazed into those indigo eyes. God, regardless of the gaping hole in his thigh, his cock had been hard for four long days.

Gradually, he moved his hands downward until he cupped her buttocks. Oh God, yes. He held her hips flush against his body and ground his erection into her. Akira matched the fervent demands of his tongue, dancing with him in a maelstrom of sensual fervor.

The devil be damned, how erotic to be making love to a woman when completely naked while she remained clothed. And by her mewls, he knew he was wearing down Akira's resistance, chipping away at that stoic shroud she hid behind. The anticipation of touching her damp core drove him to the brink of madness.

What was he doing standing in the middle of the floor when the bed was only paces away? Hell, he mightn't make it to the bed.

With one deep moan, he forced himself to pull away far enough to pick her up and gather her into his arms. "I want you, lass," he growled, ignoring the twinge of pain in his leg.

"I... want..." She watched him with half-lidded eyes, looking more wanton than anything he'd ever seen. When he set her on the bed, her gaze dropped to his cock. He could come just having her eyes on him.

But she drew her fists beneath her chin and scooted her back against the headboard. "Geordie, I can't."

"What? Why?"

Springing to her feet, she held up her palms. "You are a wealthy landowner. And if Clan MacDonell pays you fealty, I can only imagine that your house must be even grander than this manse." She began inching toward the door, her mouth drawn as if in a panic. "I-I am but a poor healer born of Gypsy parents, with a father to whom my mother was not married. That makes me a *bastard*." She uttered the word as if it were the vilest thing on earth. "And the only thing I have of value in this world is my virtue. I cannot throw it away on one night of passion."

He reached out a hand, his tongue twisting as he searched for the right words. "But—"

Turning, she picked up her satchel and fled for the door.

# Chapter Thirteen

Akira awoke in a complete daze. She had no idea when she'd finally fallen asleep—she'd been awake half the night replaying the events in Geordie's chamber over and over again. It had taken every ounce of will she could muster to spring to her feet and make haste for the door. And now she knew exactly how weak her own flesh could be. If she'd remained on that bed for a moment longer, she never would have been able to resist him.

Every time she closed her eyes, she saw him naked and oh, so very virile. Ma had never told her how beautiful a man could be, stripped bare. Akira clutched her hands over her heart. She doubted there were many men who would look as strapping as Geordie—a highborn clan chieftain from the region of Aberdeen. Goodness, he possessed muscles everywhere.

She'd been shamelessly breathless when he was submerged in the bath—bare naked of all things, inviting her into his chamber. Oh, how easy it would be to surrender to his temptation.

Thank the stars she would be heading back to Dunkeld this day. She missed her family, and she missed the safety of the shieling, no matter how shabby. At home with her sisters there was no one to tempt her like Sir Geordie—or George, chieftain of Clan Mysterious.

Sir Coll had said Geordie was a rake, and the man didn't deny it—just said he was irresponsible when he was younger. But could men change their nature? Was she merely a target, another of the great man's conquests? Had she been playing into his hands all along?

But he'd been in sore need of a healer.

Clapping her hands to her head, she squeezed her eyes shut.

*I am only a simple lass. I must tread carefully around him. He's so much wiser in the ways of the world—and older.*

But none of her worries mattered. They would say their good-byes this morn, their paths never to cross again.

"Miss Akira?" said a deep voice from the passageway, followed by a knock.

She sat bolt upright, clutching the bedclothes beneath her chin. "Aye?"

"Sir Geordie is fevered. Are you up?" It was Sir Coll for certain. "Ah—I could summon the MacDonell healer if you're still abed."

She hopped up, stepping into her kirtle and hastily tying the laces. "No, I'll tend him." Shoving her feet into her shoes, she opened the door. "Did I oversleep?"

"Aye, you both did. 'Tis almost ten. And when I decided to check on the d—I mean his lor—I mean Sir Geordie, he didn't rouse. His forehead is afire."

"Oh dear, that's what I was afraid of when he turned pale at the table last eve." She grabbed her satchel and headed across the passageway.

Sir Coll followed. "Sir Geordie is fortunate to have you."

"'Twas a good thing I found him afore the dragoons did."

The big chieftain opened the door and ushered her inside.

Akira hastened to the bed. Lying flat on his back, Geordie seemed to be sleeping peacefully, but his dark hair was thick with sweat. She gave his shoulder a shake. "Sir Geordie, 'tis time to break your fast."

A deep moan rumbled from his throat. Moving her hand to his forehead, she checked for a fever. "'Tisn't good." This was what happened to the soldier she'd nursed with the musket shot to the knee—though that man had been in a sorry state from the outset.

A furrow formed between Sir Coll's brows. "Can you help him?"

She clenched her fists tight. Just as she had vowed at the cave, she would not lose him. Not now. Not ever. She would prove her worth for all to see, and Geordie would ride north to join his clan just as he'd planned.

Akira dashed for the bowl and ewer. "We must try to cool him down. Can you lower the bedclothes to his waist while I moisten a cloth?"

"Of course."

She heaved a sigh. It was far more proper for Sir Coll to manage the bedclothes.

Returning with a damp cloth, she patted it over Geordie's forehead and then up and down his chest. He gave a shiver, and his teeth chattered.

Sir Coll leaned over the patient with a frown. "I think

he's overcold." He grasped the edge of the bedcover. "Let me cover him up again."

"No." Akira grasped the chieftain's wrist. "The chills are expected. They help him heal."

"But he's freezing."

"Ma says a fevered patient feels cold because their skin is overwarm. Covering him up will only serve to make his fever worse."

"How do you ken this?"

"I've been healing folk since the age of twelve."

"And how old are you now?"

"Three and twenty." Turning her back to him, she dipped the cloth in the bowl. "And you, sir?"

"One and twenty."

"'Tis young for a laird."

"Aye, my father only recently passed."

"I'm sorry."

"It couldn't be helped." Sir Coll crossed his arms and regarded her. "I'm afraid we cannot escort you home this day. My men and I are in the midst of a feud with the MacIntosh clan, and I've had a report they're mounting a raid."

"How awful. D-do you think they'll attack here?"

"I rather doubt it. We aim to head them off long before they reach Glen Spean. Will you be all right remaining here for a while longer?"

"Aye." She faced him, putting on a determined expression. "I cannot possibly leave Sir Geordie's side until I ken he's well enough to start his journey home."

"You're a good lass." The big man grinned. "I'll send up a tray for you. Is there anything else you need, miss?"

She drummed her fingers against her lips. "Could the cook prepare a tankard of willow bark tea?"

"I'll have a pot of it sent up and then I'll take my leave."

Akira grasped his elbow. "Be careful. I do not need any more Highlanders to look after."

He bowed. "Not to worry, miss. Just help His Lordship come back to rights."

Before Akira could ask him to repeat those words, Sir Coll slipped out the door. She wrung the cloth and placed it on Geordie's forehead. "Your Lordship?"

*Unbelievable.* She'd kissed a lord? Geordie must be a nobleman, a peer, a titled baron...or only heaven knew what else.

Her hands shook. *What if he perishes in my care? I would be blamed. I could end up thrown in the stocks, or worse, hanged from the gallows.*

She doused a second cloth and spread it across his chest. "Geordie, can you hear me?"

*Should I continue to refer to him as "Geordie"?* That's what he asked of her. And knowing him, he'd be upset if he discovered she knew he was a lord.

Akira plucked the cloth from his forehead and dunked it in the bowl. Nonetheless, there was so much more she did not know about him—like his family name.

She smoothed the cool cloth over his forehead and face. Why was she fretting about what to call him? He needed her to help him now as much as ever. It tore her up on the inside to watch him shiver, but the only way to bring the fever down was by way of cool compresses and willow bark tea.

When the kettle arrived, she quickly poured a cup and began spooning small drops into his mouth. "Drink."

His Adam's apple bobbed.

Her heart skipped a beat. "Can you hear me?"

It didn't dissuade her when he gave no reply. She continued to spoon the tincture into his mouth. "This will set you to rights."

All day, she continued her vigil, cooling him down with cloths and spooning tea into his mouth. She only left his side to refill the ewer with water and request more tea. Geordie had done so well in the mountains, she refused to allow herself to consider that he mightn't pull through.

As evening came, she ran the cloth over his chest, talking all the while. "Come morn, you will rise from this bed and haste away home. I'll wager your children will be ever so happy to see you. Indeed, you are a lucky man to have two bonny children. A lad and a lass, did you not say?"

"Mm," he moaned.

She stilled her hands and regarded his face. Though he remained in a deep sleep, she was certain he could hear her on some level. She talked about everything she could think of: about her sisters and her mother and the fact that Ma used a cane. Akira confessed that although she'd learned not to be overly trusting of men, she felt she could trust Geordie—though she didn't know if she could trust *herself* on the occasions when he looked at her with fervent passion.

After the witching hour, Geordie began thrashing his head from side to side. "I refuse to surrender the castle to a usurper!"

Akira clutched her hands beneath her chin, her gaze shooting to his face. His eyes were still closed.

"What castle?" she asked.

"Edinburgh, you damned fool."

She gaped at him. "I thought you lived in Aberdeen."

He thrashed some more, pushing the cloth from his head.

Picking it up, Akira shook her head. The fever was making him rave nonsensically.

She busied herself by changing his bandage and applying more salve.

As the night wore on, Geordie continued with his ramblings. "Och, Elizabeth, you would sell your soul for a parcel of land."

Akira's ears piqued. "Elizabeth? That's the wife who left you, aye?"

"You would abandon your children?" he growled, while his breathing grew unsteady. "I've never met a woman so fickle and self-absorbed." His head whipped from side to side. "So this is all my doing, is it? Bloody hell..." He continued with a string of indecipherable mutterings that sounded more like curses and insults than anything.

Rubbing his temples, Akira blew on his face to cool the burn. "Calm yourself, m'lord. That woman can hurt you no more. I'm here now, and you have my word I will care for you until you no longer need me."

* * *

Geordie opened his eyes, trying to remember why he was in a strange bed feeling as if he'd just trudged through purgatory. "Where am I?" His throat felt like he'd swallowed a rasp.

Something rustled. "Are you awake?"

He knew the voice—it belonged to Akira, the bonny woman who'd already threaded her tendrils through his heart. His gaze shifted, but he only spied the outline of her black hair. Rubbing his eyes, he asked again, "Where are we?"

"Sir Coll MacDonell's manse."

Ah yes. It all came flooding back. "I feel like I've been fighting a tempest and lost."

"Perhaps you have." Her face became clearer. "You've been out of sorts for three days."

"No." Geordie tried to sit up, but the pounding in his skull sapped him. "That long?"

"Aye." Akira removed a wet cloth from his forehead and proceeded to feel his head with the back of her hand, then slid her soft palm to his cheek "Thank heavens, I believe your fever has broken."

He scrubbed his knuckles into his face, meeting with a growth of itchy beard. "Dear God, I must look frightful."

"I haven't attempted to shave you for the thrashing."

"I beg your pardon?" Bloody oath, his head felt like a spider had spent three days filling it with a sticky web.

"You've been rambling and thrashing quite a lot."

Geordie closed his eyes, clapping a hand over them. Good God, no self-respecting duke would want to be caught rambling deliriously for three days. *What has the lass overheard?* He had so many secrets. He could have given away the kingdom—or his heart—or any number of self-incriminating exploits. He spread his fingers and regarded her through the gap.

She smiled, concern reflected in her eyes. "How are you feeling now?"

"Like I've run a hundred-mile footrace." He stretched his legs, his thigh annoying but not hurting as much as before. "I'm thirsty."

"That's a good sign. I've some willow bark tea."

"Nothing a bit more potent?"

She eyed him like any healer would a bedridden patient. "How about we start slow? If you can manage the tea, I'll allow a pint of weak ale."

Geordie groaned, shoving his hands into the mattress and pushing himself up. The effort exhausted him.

"Let me help." Akira levered his shoulders forward and stuffed a pillow behind. "How's that?"

"Better," he groused.

Akira collected a tankard and spoon and sat in a chair beside the bed. "I've been trying to ladle this into you a wee drop at a time. It will be so much easier now you're awake." She held the spoon to his lips.

He flicked her hand away. "For crying out loud, woman, I'm not an invalid." He reached for the tankard, and tea sloshed across the bedclothes.

Akira pursed her lips, picked up a cloth, and set it beside him. "Shall I prepare a shaving kit, m'lord?"

"Aye, thank you." He gulped down the remains of the tea, then froze.

*She just referred to me as "m'lord." What else does she ken?*

He set the tankard on the bedside table and dabbed the spillage with the cloth.

*Not everything, or else she would have said "Your Grace."*

She set the razor and soap beside the bowl on the table. "Shall I shave you, or would you prefer to do that yourself as well, m'lord?"

His hands were so unsteady, he'd probably slit his own throat—a fact that might make a great many people overjoyed. "You'd best do it, thank you, *m'lady*."

She snorted, but still didn't explain herself.

He held up his chin and allowed her to soap up a lather. "How much have you slept?"

"Some." She wiped her hands on a cloth.

Geordie eyed a pallet on the far side of the bed.

"Who else has tended me during the three days of my illness?"

"Just me, sir."

*Now a sir? Is she testing the water?* "Where is Sir Coll?"

She picked up the razor. "Still away, feuding with the MacIntosh clan."

"God's teeth, if he doesn't have enough to worry about."

She regarded him with a critical eye and a wee pucker to her lips. They hadn't grown any less kissable while he'd been dancing with the devil.

Geordie started to reach for a lock of raven hair when Akira leaned in with the razor. He forced his hand to still while she took the first stroke and wiped the blade clean just like a barber would do. "You've done this before."

Her warm breath caressed his cheek like a summer's breeze. "Aye. I've cared for a number of bedridden patients."

His gut squeezed. That didn't sit well with Geordie. First, he didn't like being referred to as bedridden, and second, having Akira touch anyone—or any man except for him—well, it was just wrong. A twitch flickered in his jaw with her next scrape. "I'm not bedridden."

She pushed up his nose and shaved above his upper lip with quick flicks, those indigo eyes focusing with intensity. "I'd like to see you up by the morrow."

He ground his teeth. "I can spring from this bed this very instant."

"Perhaps you should try sitting up a bit straighter first." She gave him a knowing smile—one far exceeding her years and her innocence. "No man returns from Satan's fire ready to dance a reel."

"Then I shall surprise you. Send for a plate of meat and bread and a tankard of ale."

She swiped his face with the cloth and regarded her handiwork. "I'll go fetch some broth. If you can keep that down, then bread, then meat, then ale."

He slapped the mattress. "You're the devil's vixen."

"Oh? If you want to rise from that bed and charm me with some fancy dance steps, then I suggest you pay heed to my advice. I may not be a noblewoman, but I ken how to heal even the most cantankerous of patients."

"Cantankerous?" he griped as she headed for the door. "I'm not bloody cantankerous!"

# Chapter Fourteen

Sitting on a wooden bench, Akira watched Geordie address the post with his sword. His fever broke two days past, and against her better judgment, the big Highlander insisted on heading outside to rebuild his strength.

He'd quickly dismissed Akira's idea of going for a stroll in the gardens and headed for the sparring courtyard. "If I cannot wield a sword I may as well be dead, what with all the redcoats peppering the highways and byways."

She couldn't fault him there. And she knew neither of them could stay in Glen Spean much longer. Sooner or later, Sir Coll would return and want his house back. But thinking about it did nothing to cheer Akira's spirits. She'd been over it a thousand times in her mind. Her liaison with Geordie would soon end. All the things she wondered about him didn't matter, because she had no chance of ever setting eyes on him once they returned to their lives. Their circumstances were just too different.

*Simply enjoy the moments we have together.*

The sun brought out rich auburn highlights in his chestnut hair as he lunged and attacked the post, grunting with his every movement. Clearly he was testing the limits of his injured thigh as he stressed it more and more.

Then his body lurched as if his leg had given out. Dropping his sword, he stumbled and caught himself on the post.

Akira held in her gasp and resisted the urge to run to his side.

"Damnation," he growled under his breath.

"You're looking impressive." She patted the bench. "Why not take a rest and sit beside me for a moment."

He stood up straight and shook his head. "I cannot stop."

Trying another tack, Akira retrieved his sword and handed it to him. "I think September is my favorite month."

He tapped the post with the blade. "Why is that?"

"'Tis when the purple heather blankets the Highlands. And the days are the sunniest in September, but still, there's something in the air, a warning that a change is coming." She brushed an errant lock of hair from her face. "What's your favorite month?"

He looked up at the blue sky, taking a deep breath. "Perhaps May. There's no more snow and the leaves are coming out. By the end of the month everything is colorful again." Wiping his brow with his forearm, he gave her a nod. "Now you'd best step back, because I aim to take out my ire on this beastly post."

"If you must." She threw her thumb over her shoulder. "I'll fetch us a ewer of ale."

He grinned—an accursed smile that could make her forget her place. "Now there's a good lass."

Akira hoped once she came back from the brewhouse,

Geordie would have worked up a thirst. But when she returned, he'd removed his shirt and had all but chopped the post in two, and it wasn't a small post—it had to be as thick as her waist.

The ewer and two tankards nearly slipped from her grasp.

The muscles in Geordie's back flexed and bulged with each move, glistening in the sunlight. But he'd gained a rhythm that hadn't been there before. He moved with deadly precision, the post not standing a chance. Shoulder-length chestnut locks had fallen from their ribbon, curling and brushing his shoulders as he worked.

Wearing his kilt belted low on his hips, he turned enough for Akira to glimpse the cut of muscle in his abdomen—banded, looking hard as forged steel. With his next lunge, his calf stretched, displaying power, strength, and downright rugged maleness.

Geordie raised the big sword over his head, and with a bellow that boomed across the courtyard, he spun and lopped the post in half. He glared down at the fallen chunk of wood. "Die, you turncoat bastard."

Akira might have laughed if not for the menacing tone with which he cursed his opponent. Surely, she would never want to be on the receiving end of such ire. Instead, a gasp slipped through her throat.

He spun around, a scowl darkening his features. But faster than a snap of the fingers, his countenance brightened. "Ah, just in time. I've quite a thirst." He sheathed his sword and gestured to the bench. "Shall we?"

Akira's gaze swept to his bare chest, still heaving from his exertion. "Uh-huh."

He chuckled and reached for his shirt. "Forgive my impropriety."

Remembering how to use her legs, she strode to the bench. "'Tis nothing I haven't seen before."

"My exact thoughts." He used the shirt to wipe off his perspiration, but he didn't don it.

Trying not to smile, Akira poured for them both. "I must say I am quite impressed with your recovery, m'lord."

"Thank you, m'lady."

She hid her grin behind her ale. Though neither one of them had tried to correct the other, she almost burst out with laughter every time he referred to her as "m'lady." Never in her life had she been referred to thus, and she doubted she ever would be again. Why not enjoy her circumstances?

But for how much longer?

As she took a long sip, another thought worried her. Now confidently on the path to recovery, Geordie no longer needed her services. If only she could be bold enough to throw her arms around His Lordship and ask him to take her to Aberdeen with him.

But that would be folly. She had too many responsibilities at home.

No. She couldn't turn her back on her family even if Geordie wanted her for more than a passing fancy.

* * *

A fortnight had passed since Geordie's fever broke, and he held the basket while Akira stooped to examine the leaves of a weed sprouting from the moss on the fringe of a trickling burn.

"This is water avens for certain."

Though a note of excitement rang in her voice, Geordie preferred the view of her backside prone to him, albeit covered with skirts. "How can you tell?"

"'Tis stouter than common avens. And see the downy stems? Though it flowers in spring, the leaves form a rosette." She carefully cradled the leaves in her palm and gestured to the weed as if it were fine lace. "See?"

"'Tis a relief you ken what to look for."

"Aye, now hand me the spade, please."

He kneeled beside her. "Why not allow me to do the dirty work?"

She snatched the spade from the basket. "Because you might bruise the root—and that is what we need to boil to leech out the oil."

"Ah, of course." He rocked to his bum and watched her painstakingly dig around the plant and lever it up from the dirt. "A couple more of these and I'll be able to replenish my supply of avens oil—mayhap make a vial for you to carry on your journey home."

Geordie's throat thickened as her gaze met his for a fleeting moment. In that exchange, he sensed her sadness, just as he, himself, regretted their fast-approaching goodbye. "'Tis very thoughtful of you."

She glanced away. "What kind of healer would I be if I didn't provide you with prevention for relapse?"

He placed a hand on her shoulder. "I do believe you are the finest healer I've ever encountered."

"Do you mean that?"

"Aye. I wouldn't have said it if I did not."

"Thank you." She squeezed his hand. "Such encouragement means a great deal to me."

He pursed his lips. He didn't care to think of her home situation, sharing some dirty one-room hovel with her sisters and mother. "Akira, I—"

"There you are." Sir Coll bounded through the wood with a pair of slobbering deerhounds in his wake.

A rock sank to the pit of Geordie's stomach as he stood and shook the young laird's hand. "'Tis good to see you've returned in one piece."

Coll flexed his fingers, a look of surprise brightening his ruddy features. "And you've recovered remarkably."

Geordie gestured to the lass. "I owe my good health to Miss Akira."

She grinned at them from her heap of dirt as the deerhounds pattered to her side, shoving their noses into her work. "His Lordship pushes himself overmuch."

"I would expect nothing less." Coll snapped his fingers. "Come behind, ye mangy hounds."

Geordie chuckled as the dogs tucked their tails and skulked behind their master. "How did the meeting with the MacIntoshes go?"

"Bloody as usual—though most of the blood spilled was theirs." Coll's gaze shot to Akira. "Aside from reiving a few head of cattle, we felled a doe on the journey home. We're to have a gathering this eve."

She stood, grasping the basket between her hands. "A gathering? Oh, how exciting!"

Geordie regarded the dirt staining her apron and inclined his head toward the manse. "You'd best haste back to your chamber and ready yourself."

Glancing down, she grimaced. "Och, I'm afraid there's not much that can be done with these rags with only a moment's notice." She grasped one of the dogs by the collar. "Come, big fellas, I'll take you past the kitchen to see if Cook has a morsel for you."

Together, Geordie and Coll watched her move down

the path, a breeze picking up her black tresses and dancing with them.

"She's lovely," said Coll.

Geordie's eyebrows slanted inward as he regarded the man's googly eyes. "You'd best close your mouth afore a fly takes up residence in it."

"I wasn't ogling."

"I daresay you were."

"As were you, Your Grace."

Geordie thwacked the young man on the back. "I beg your pardon? I thought we had an agreement."

"Even in the wood, sir?"

"Even here." Geordie gestured to the path leading away from the manse. "You said the fighting grew ugly."

"Aye—and the bastards enlisted a number of Government troops as well, say they have the inherited rights to Glen Spean."

Such galling talk made Geordie shudder. "Didn't you rightfully inherit the land?"

"I did—built onto Da's house—but as you ken, our forefathers fought over the land, and it has changed hands many a time since the years when the MacDonalds ruled as Lords of the Isles."

Geordie bent down and inspected the leaves of a weed. *Not avens.* "So they're trying to make a case for ancestral rights?"

"Aye."

He brushed off his hands. "I'll see what I can do from my end once I return to Huntly."

"My thanks." The chieftain dragged his fingers through his mop of ginger hair.

"'Tis the least I can do after you've given me a place to recover."

Coll kicked a rock into the burn. "And when do you think you'll be well enough to start your journey home?"

Geordie didn't want to think about it—home he'd welcome, but leaving Akira was a different matter altogether. "A day, mayhap two."

"You don't have to be so hasty about it on account of me."

"I ken, but my clan and kin will be carving my effigy if I do not soon darken Huntly Castle's halls."

"All right," Coll agreed. "And the lass? Do you still need my men to accompany her back to Dunkeld?"

"Aye. 'Tis her home." Ambling along the pathway, Geordie plucked a leaf and twirled it in his fingers. *Akira would be able to tell me what plant this is from.* He paused, letting the leaf twirl to the ground. "Do you think someone might be able to fit Miss Akira with a new gown for the gathering?"

Coll scratched his growth of ginger beard. "Not certain—we haven't much time."

"I'd like to do something for the lass."

"Perhaps if I spoke to the tailor, he'd be able to alter one of my mother's gowns. They've been packed away for years."

"That's a marvelous idea. I'll pay him handsomely, of course."

Coll turned on his heel. "Let's see it done. Even I would like to see the look on Miss Akira's face when she peers into the looking glass dressed in red silk."

"Red?"

"I think red would suit her."

"Pink or blue." Akira might look like a goddess from the sun in red, but Geordie sure as hell didn't want Coll MacDonell gaping at the woman in a red frock. He didn't want anyone except him feasting his gaze upon her this eve.

# Chapter Fifteen

Her hair wrapped in rags to make ringlets, Akira stood with one arm held out while the tailor tied a bow and stitched it in place just above her forearm. The gown Sir Coll had sent to her chamber was the most gorgeous work of art she'd ever seen. Simply the sleeves possessed a multitude of intricate detail—capped slashed sleeves in brocade, showing the ivory satin underdress beneath, and from her forearm, lace cuffs loosely draped from the narrow blue ribbon he so fastidiously secured in place.

"I think this was my favorite of Her Ladyship's gowns," said the tailor's wife from her perch across the chamber.

"I can see why." Akira glanced down at the brocade stomacher and bodice that gave way to billowing light-blue skirts. "I doubt I've seen such fine workmanship."

The tailor looked up from beneath his spectacles and grinned. "I thank you."

"Hurry along, Hamish." Mrs. Tailor rose, picking up

the brush from the chest and shaking it. "'Tis time to take the rags out, else the lassie will not be down in time for the gathering."

"A moment longer," mumbled the man with pins hanging out the side of his mouth.

Akira didn't know what to think. They'd brought the gown in hours ago, telling her the laird had ordered them to alter it for her, and she'd been poked and probed ever since. Sir Coll didn't fancy her, did he?

*Of course not. He was there when I said I couldn't do anything with my ratty old kirtle. Lord kens I need a new kirtle and arisaid, not some impractical gown like this with taffeta skirts. Why, if I dare spill anything on it, I'll simply die.*

By the time her hair was done and Mrs. Tailor had padded the satin shoes with a bit of wool so they wouldn't fall off her feet, Akira stood in front of the mirror and didn't even recognize herself. She turned full circle staring at the woman in the looking glass. "'Tis a miracle."

Mrs. Tailor moved in behind Akira and regarded her reflection. "You are as bonny as a picture. No wonder Sir Coll wanted to see you dressed to the teeth."

Akira emitted a nervous laugh. "Most likely he felt sorry for me."

The woman smiled. "With a face and figure as bonny as yours, no one has any business feeling sorry for you."

"You are very kind."

Mr. Tailor picked up his sewing kit. "My wife and I are simply speaking the truth."

When Akira opened the door to show them out, Geordie almost fell into her. He quickly straightened up and tugged on his doublet sleeves. "Ho-ly hell-fire!" he said, exaggerating each syllable while his eyes grew wide.

"I beg your pardon?" asked Mrs. Tailor.

Taking in a deep inhale, Geordie didn't even acknowledge the woman. He grasped Akira's hands and held them wide, his gaze drifting from the top of her head down to her shoes and back up again. "You look more radiant than a queen."

"Aye, she does, and 'tis a good thing you appreciate it," said Mr. Tailor. "Else I'd have words with Sir Coll."

"That shan't be necessary." Geordie offered his elbow. "Shall we, miss?"

"Thank you." Goodness, the nobleman looked as dapper as the Marquis of Atholl when he paraded through the town square. Mayhap even more so. Geordie's kilt had been pressed, and he wore a new starched shirt and cravat beneath a doublet made of fine quilted silk. "You clean up nicely as well, sir."

He gave her a sly wink and bade the Tailors good day. Akira could have floated as Geordie escorted her all the way to the fence-lined paddock where the clan had gathered around an enormous bonfire. She stopped in the shadow of a trellis of grapevines that spanned the walkway. Beyond, the clansmen and clanswomen wore common garb of kilts and kirtles. Not a single lass had donned a gown as fine as hers. "Goodness, I would have fit in better wearing my old kirtle and arisaid."

He faced her, flicking one of her ringlets. "Nonsense. You are my guest, and as such, you should be dressed in finery whether we are in a castle built by man or one provided by God."

"What did you mean by 'as such'? Do you admit to being a nobleman?"

"Och, ye ken it to be so. You've been calling me

m'lord since I roused from my fever. I reckon Sir Coll let something out of the bag."

"And why can you not trust me with your true identity?"

"Because when you return home, they'll try to question you about it, and if you do not ken my clan name, it will be for the better."

"It just isn't right. I-I-I care for you, yet these secrets between us are keeping me from..." She couldn't say "trusting you," but that's how she felt. How could she allow herself deep feelings for a man who preferred to keep his identity anonymous?

He took her hand and pressed his warm lips to it, lingering and inhaling as if he wanted to commit her scent to memory. "Och, lass, I think it is for the best that our emotions do not run too deep." Meeting her gaze with a hungry, almost predatory stare, he took a step closer. "A man could lose himself in those eyes of yours."

"Sir Geordie," Coll called from across the bonfire. "Come and share my plaid."

Her mysterious Highland lord brushed his finger along Akira's chin, sending gooseflesh down the length of her neck. "Let us enjoy the gathering this evening and forget our worries about things to come. For tonight you are a queen and I am a king. The world is ours."

She squared her shoulders. "You are right. I've never even seen a gown this grand, let alone worn one. I shall put my doubts on the shelf and enjoy the fun."

"Now that's a good lass," he said with a wink.

Akira smacked his arm. "Queen."

He grinned, white teeth reflecting the flickering of the fire. "Och aye."

Ahead, dozens of families were gathered, sitting on

plaids, talking loudly, and laughing even more loudly. Parents and elders watched wee children run and tumble, while a group of lads competed in a game of shinty.

As they neared, the aroma of the meat cooking on the spit grew stronger. "Are you hungry?" Geordie asked.

She smoothed her hand down her stomacher. "I'm laced so tight I do not think I can eat a thing."

He slipped his hand to her back and tugged on her laces. "That can be remedied."

"You wouldn't dare?"

"Mayhap not until I enjoy a few drams of whisky."

Akira laughed, covering her mouth and glancing away. Then her stomach squeezed as everyone stopped what they were doing and stared at them. Geordie didn't miss a step. He acted like they were alone in a dining hall and led her straight to Sir Coll.

The big chieftain raised his tankard. "I was wondering if you would arrive afore the food. You've missed the games."

"Apologies." Akira sat, tucked her legs under, and smoothed her skirts. "I was trapped above stairs for hours."

Waggling his brows, Sir Coll grinned like a devious lad. "It looks as if Mr. Tailor did you well, miss."

Akira felt both thrilled by and out of sorts with all the attention. "He did, and Mrs. Tailor styled my hair and took care of so many things."

The chieftain poured a tot of whisky into Geordie's tankard. "'Tis good to hear."

"Well, I thank you for your hospitality." She bowed her head. "'Tisn't often my kind are treated graciously."

"And what kind might that be?" asked Sir Coll as a servant placed a trencher of meat and bread in front of him.

"Did Sir Geordie not tell you?" She looked between the men.

Geordie spread his palms and shrugged. "It makes no difference to me." He leaned to Coll and whispered something in his ear.

"Well, that just goes to show all tinkers are not bad—though I'd wager my father just rolled over in his grave for that remark."

Laughing, the two men clanked their pewter tankards and drank heartily. Then Coll stood and spread his arms wide. "Clan MacDonell, join me in welcoming my friends from the north and east. Let us extend to them our Highland hospitality and share in this grand feast. May God look kindly upon our kin and give us great bounty, amen."

The crowd responded with a boisterous amen and everyone turned their attention to the food before them. Everyone but Akira. Too many stimulating things were going on around her. Because of that—and her stays being bound almost to the point of making her swoon—she nibbled politely while trying to take it all in.

Such a happy crowd of clansmen and clanswomen gathered around the bonfire. And who wouldn't be cheerful with so much abundance and children running about, laughing and chattering? Geordie was right when he said they should enjoy the evening. The sun would rise on the morrow and her destiny would unfold whether she worried about it or not. For once in her life, she would focus on the present.

A fiddler tuned his instrument while a drummer and piper joined him, and within two blinks of an eye, lads and lassies were making room for a reel.

"Do you fancy a dance, Miss Akira?" asked Sir Coll.

She clapped her hands. "I'd love to dance."

When Geordie cleared his throat, she bit her lip. "That is, if it meets with your approval, m'lord? After all, you are still my employer."

He flicked his wrist toward the merriment, though he was scowling. "Go on with you."

Dancing a Highland reel made her throw her head back and laugh as Sir Coll swung her about the elbow to the whoops and hollers of the crowd. And the fiddler seemed to increase the tempo with every verse. At each opportunity, Akira stole a glance at Geordie. He watched her, sipping his whisky—his dark stare looking as dangerous as the devil.

The most disturbing part? Akira liked the wickedness of it, liked that he raked his gaze over her, stopping at the swells just above her bodice. Her skin sizzled with the heat from his look. It was as if a fire burned behind his eyes.

"Miss Akira?"

She startled and looked to her dance partner. "Aye?"

Sir Coll bowed and then offered his elbow. "I thank you for the dance."

"It is I who should be thanking you, especially for lending me this gown. 'Tis absolutely stunning."

"'Tisn't a lend. 'Tis a gift."

"But, sir, 'tis too much—"

Stopping, Sir Coll held up his palm. "You'll have to take that up with Sir George over there. He's the responsible party—he just asked me to do his footwork." He leaned closer to her ear. "He's trying to remain anonymous, ye ken."

"Aye, I do ken, and the ruse is growing ever so annoying."

Coll chuckled. "I have to admit I'm enjoying the

green looks of envy from the du—I mean His Lordship—this eve."

"Envy?"

The ruddy chieftain snorted. "You've not noticed? I reckon he's as smitten as a bull in a paddock of heifers in spring."

Drawing her hand to her chest, Akira couldn't help but look Sir Geordie's way. "He's staring at us."

"He's staring at you, miss. Hasn't been able to take his eyes off you since you arrived in Glen Spean."

She giggled. "Except when he was unconscious."

"Aye, well, I suppose you can forgive him for that."

She thumped the big jester on the arm. "You're insufferable."

"I'm honest is all…Let's have a bit of sport, shall we?" He gave her a wink and accompanied her to the plaid. "I hope that leg of yours will hold up, sir, else every young buck in my clan will be asking for a turn with this bonny lassie."

Geordie scowled. "You'd best bloody bet your life my leg can hold up to an entire night of dancing."

"Is that so?" Coll crossed his arms and tapped his foot. "What say you to a sword dance?"

His Lordship's gaze narrowed and then shifted to Akira. Thinning his lips, Geordie lumbered to his feet. "I can outleap you even with a hole in my bloody thigh, ye mongrel."

Akira grasped his arm. "Are you certain? I wouldn't want you to have a relapse now you've come so far."

He jerked his arm away, but then caught her chin in the crook of his finger. "'Tis but a display of brawn, lass. When 'tis over, you'll save the rest of your dances for me." Before she could object, he sealed his command with a kiss on her lips right in front of everyone. "Come, young MacDonell, let us see how high you can leap."

*Mm—wood smoke and whisky. I wouldn't mind another wee taste with a kiss as potent as the last.*

Akira licked her lips as she watched the men each place two swords on the ground, making square X's.

The music began and the two combatants bowed to each other to cheers from the crowd. Of course, everyone cheered for Coll. Akira clutched her hands to her lips and prayed Geordie would survive. For heaven's sake, he still had a pronounced limp to his gait. Not that they were going to pick up their swords and duel, but his leg might give out, or he might have a sharp pain.

Together the Highlanders leapt from side to side, dancing in a square around their swords, never once touching them. With every leap, they jumped higher, their kilts swishing in tune to the music, revealing enticing flashes of muscular legs.

The contest was too close to call—Sir Coll's toe nudged his sword, though the younger, uninjured man jumped a bit higher. When the music ended, the crowd overwhelmingly chose their leader. The big redhead strutted around the circle, puffing out his chest.

"What must he do?" asked a woman, clapping her hands.

"Make him swim the river," a clansman bellowed.

Sir Coll shook his head and his hands together. "Nay, nay, nay. Sir Geordie is my guest, and therefore I shall offer him a dram of Speyside whisky. Bring me a bottle of the 1672."

Geordie bowed. "My thanks to the host."

A man dashed into the circle with a bottle and cup. "'Tis our finest."

Coll poured and handed Geordie the cup. "Drink it down—one tilt of the cup and not a drop to be spilled."

Akira applauded with the others while Geordie swigged the whisky. Taking a breath of air, he turned the cup over to prove he'd accomplished the task, then wiped his mouth on his sleeve.

He beckoned Akira with a flick of his fingers. "Come here, bonny lass, and do me the pleasure of a dance."

The fiddler blessed them with a slower strathspey, and Akira took up her place in line across from Geordie. If anything, his exertion, combined with the whisky, made him appear even more dangerous. A pressure deep within her churned—some deep, feral impulse that made her movements more pronounced, perhaps even more seductive. Was it the Gypsy in her blood boiling to the surface? Was it the music stirring her soul?

While she danced, her cheeks burned, but she was having too much fun to stop. Though every eye watched, the attention made Akira accentuate every step all the more. The man dancing forward and touching his palm to hers commanded her attention as if they were the only two people at the gathering, serenaded by music that could send her to heaven.

Ending in a curtsy, Akira smiled as Geordie stepped forward and took her hand. "I hope you're not tired, because I intend to keep you on my arm until the music stops."

# Chapter Sixteen

As the evening progressed, Geordie's restraint waned. From the moment he'd stepped into Akira's chamber, he'd been completely and utterly enchanted. Dear God in heaven, since the day he opened his eyes to her bonny face, he'd been under her spell, but now he had no chance. And it had been his bloody idea to outfit her with a gown.

If only he'd known how rapturous she'd look.

Placing his hand in the small of Akira's back as he escorted her to her chamber, he chuckled to himself. He had to admit he'd wanted to see her dressed as a queen. Akira should be dressed in finery every day, with her own keep to command. Aye, she was uneducated, yet she had common sense no man could learn from a book. And she'd learned the healing arts far better than some physicians Geordie had met.

Entering the passageway, he let the lass walk a wee bit in front of him. The intoxicating scent of pure woman laced with wild jasmine made his head swim. Of course, his state of consciousness had nothing to do with the whisky he'd swilled earlier.

Akira had bewitched him body and soul, and she tempted his lust this eve—tempted it to the brink of self-control. His breath grew shallow as they approached the door to her chamber, and his skin tingled with anticipation.

When they stopped, she turned and faced him, her back to the door. "I must thank you for the gown and for the marvelous evening. I feel like a princess from a fairy story."

He watched her ruby red lips as she spoke.

"I'm glad." He placed his hand on the doorjamb and let his gaze slip lower. Every inhale made her creamy breasts press against the plunging neckline of her bodice. Christ, his fingers longed to run across her flesh.

She caught his cravat in her hand and tugged until she released the knot. Holy hellfire, did she have any idea how hard that wee tug made him? His breath catching, he met her heavy-lidded gaze. And before he could have another thought, his mouth crushed over hers and his arms wrapped around her, burying those delectable breasts against his chest.

His tongue plunged inside her mouth and swirled with hers as if they were dancing again, but this time, the most seductive, intoxicating flirtation of their lives. With her gasp, his cock lengthened, and he ground himself into her.

His fingers slipped to the door's latch and together they stumbled inside the dim chamber. The door closed behind them.

Akira stiffened and backed from his arms. "George, we mustn't."

He blinked. She'd called him by his given name—the

same one that rolled off Elizabeth's tongue like the shrew had swallowed a bitter tonic. "Please, I prefer Geordie," he said, sauntering after his newfound rose.

Akira backed into the room, her lips swollen and redder than before. "And you prefer lowborn lassies to women of nobility?" Lord, she was baiting him.

He adored the chase, he adored Akira, and this time there'd be no stopping.

He grabbed her hand and tugged her into his aching body. "I prefer *you*, lass. Your parentage matters not to me. All that matters is you... and me." His last words came out with a growl, warning her not to trifle with him. "Let me show you how much you've come to mean to me."

Muffling her rebuke with a kiss, he showed her how much he desired her, how much his body needed her. Slipping his fingers to the top of her bodice, he moaned into her mouth when he finally swirled his fingers across her silken flesh. Dear God, since he'd escorted her to the gathering, he'd wanted to cup her breasts and run his lips across them. Suckle them and brush his aching chest across them skin to skin.

Panting, Akira drew her lips away. "I do not ken what's come over me. I feel like I'm floating." She reached to her back. "Mayhap my stays are too tight."

He ran his hand down her spine and found a lace—one of many he would enjoy removing.

She touched her hand to his chest as if she thought she might reject his advances. "But you mustn't."

"Allow me this once." He tried to focus on her eyes instead of the way her breasts heaved up and down with her breathing. "I promise I will not take your innocence."

For the first time in his life, he meant those words.

Akira needed to be molded and loved, adored and bedded like the queen she was.

*And all I have is this night.*

No, Geordie wouldn't defile the lass and leave her without a chance at a better life, but he would show her pleasure.

Trust filled her eyes before she turned and presented her back to him. As he unlaced her, visions of the nymph bathing at the waterfall attacked him. Drawing out the anticipation, he pulled the laces through one loop at a time until her bodice sailed to the floor. He did the same to the stays, and after her petticoats fell away, he slid his hands to the front of her shift and cupped her breasts. Blessed taut nipples bore through the thin fabric, revealing how much Akira responded to his advances.

Pushing her black curls aside, he trailed kisses along her neck. "You are so fine to me."

"Mm, heaven help me," she pleaded, resting her back against his chest. "I am too weak to resist you, m'lord."

"Geordie," he rasped, tasting clean skin infused with the erotic fragrance that had been driving him mad for sennights.

His fingers slipped to her skirts, slowly drawing them higher.

She leaned her head against his chest and closed her eyes. "You mu—You mu . . . Oh, Lord."

He grinned. This time she didn't ask him to stop.

With one more tug of her skirts, his hand slipped beneath the hem and found her thigh. With deft fingers, he kneaded until his fingers toyed with the nest of curls hiding her treasure.

Gasping, Akira pushed her back against him, her hips swirling, moving as only a woman could. "Noooooooooo."

"Och, but you want me to," he growled, sliding his finger into hot, moist folds. "And I promise to show you a wee bit of heaven."

"But—"

"Ride the wave of passion, lass. 'Tis a gift I want to give." He pressed his lips to her ear and whispered, "Do you trust me?"

She nodded, turning her head up to him, her eyelids fluttering open long enough to look into his eyes.

He found her tiny button, hot, wet, and slick, and used her moisture to tease her, to rub and swirl while his cock pressed flush against her buttocks. God, if only he could turn her around and take her against the wall. Thrust deep inside her tight quim and take his pleasure.

But dammit, he'd promised.

Her breathing sped while her hips gyrated against his aching cock.

Crying out, Akira went limp in his arms as her body shuddered and swayed with the sensuous movement of his fingertips. When at last she drew in a deep gasp, Geordie covered her cry with his mouth. She whimpered with quick licks of her tongue, and he turned her in to his embrace. He squeezed his eyes closed, memorizing the feel of her body molded to his, memorizing her scent, for he wanted her memory to stay with him through the years until he took his dying breath.

# *Chapter Seventeen*

Geordie awoke to a pounding. Not certain if the sound came from inside his head or the door, he opened his eyes. At least he'd managed to make it to his own chamber last eve.

Holy hell, if the pounding would only stop.

The door flung open and Coll marched inside. "A retinue of miserable, bleeding, bloody redcoats are burning cottages, bellowing your name. Can you tell me what that's about... *m'lord*?"

Springing to his feet, Geordie wrapped his plaid around his hips and grabbed his belt. "They must have found my flask, dammit."

"You left your flask?"

"Aye, fleeing from the battlefield right after Akira carved a musket ball out of my thigh."

"Christ Almighty, just the thought of it makes my gut turn over." The redheaded chieftain winced. "You must move quickly. The MacDonells are preparing to stop them."

Geordie shook his head. "I started this. I must end it."

"Are you mad? They have nothing on us—we didn't ride into Hoord Moor. I'll deal with them, but you must go. Take the escape route to the stables. I've sent Freddy to saddle horses for you."

Geordie shoved his feet into his boots. "How much time?"

"Not long. Ten minutes at the most."

Pressing the heels of his hands against his temples, he couldn't forget his promise to his Gypsy rose. "You must take Akira back to Dunkeld."

Coll guffawed. "Are you daft? If the redcoats find her in Glen Spean, they'll ken you've been here for certain."

"I'll stand and fight, damn it all."

"And then what? What of your children, what of the bonny lass who has cared for you? Are you planning to break her heart as well?" Coll shoved Geordie in the shoulder. "I don't care if you're a duke, you're not going to die on my lands."

He caught the younger man's wrist and squeezed. Blast it all, he knew Coll was right. His children had already been abandoned by their mother, and if Coll refused to do it, someone needed to spirit Akira away. A tic twitched his jaw. "I will ride, but I am no coward."

"I never said you were, m'lord."

"If this doesn't end, send word and I'll dispatch five hundred men of Clan Gordon to your aid."

"It will end. I'll see to it." Coll thrust his finger at the door. "Now go."

"Bloody hell." Geordie strapped on his sword, shoved his pistol and dirk in his belt, then dashed across the passageway and pounded on the door. "Akira! Make haste." He burst into the chamber as she shot upright, clutching the bedclothes beneath her chin. "Don your kirtle. Gather only what you can carry."

"What—?"

"They've found us, the bastards."

With one forlorn look at the blue taffeta strewn over the chair, Akira pulled her kirtle from the peg on the wall. "Give me a moment."

"I'll collect your things." Geordie grabbed the satchel and stuffed her herbs and tinctures inside. She took it from him and shoved in something white and frilly.

"What the blazes is that?"

"There is no chance I'll leave a new set of stays behind."

He shook his head and ushered her out the door. "Women."

"This way." Coll took the lead. At the end of the passageway, he pulled a panel from the wall. "This takes you straight to the stables."

Geordie peered through the darkness. "Do you use this often?"

"'Tis a safeguard from MacIntosh attack—and now Government troops as well."

Clasping the chieftain's hand, Geordie gave it a firm shake. "I will never forget this."

"I'll send word if it escalates." Coll cuffed his shoulder. "Now go, m'lord, and do not turn back."

* * *

Akira placed a hand on the pommel and another on the saddle and frowned.

Geordie bent beside her and cupped his hands. "Let me give you a leg up."

"Riding astride?"

"Quickly." As soon as she bent her knee, he hoisted her up. He grasped her ankle and slid her foot into one of the iron stirrups. "Do you need me to use a lead line?"

She tugged her skirts down on either side as far as they would go. "I think I can manage."

He patted her thigh. "I'll bring a rope just in case. The riding will be strenuous, and there was no spare sidesaddle."

Freddy strode forward and handed Geordie a water skin. "There's a bit of bully beef inside the roll of blankets attached to your saddles. Sorry, there was no time to ready a packhorse, sir."

Geordie climbed on the gelding Akira had purchased in Dunkeld. "My thanks, lad. You've done quite enough, and I look forward to returning the favor one day."

"Thank you, sir." He pointed out the back. "The trail along the River Spean will take you through the wood skirting Loch Laggan."

"Aye, I ken it well. A hundred miles and I'll be sitting before home's hearth."

"Go with God."

"And you." Geordie tapped his heels and beckoned to Akira. "We've no time to waste."

Before they left the barn, the snare drum from the Government troops sounded in the distance.

Her stomach squeezed as she tapped her heels and the pony beneath her took off with a jolt, his gait nowhere near as smooth as the gelding's had been. Within minutes, Geordie had pulled so far ahead, she feared she might lose him. She couldn't yell for him to stop—not with the dragoons so close behind.

She slapped her reins and kicked her heels. "Come,

you big mule, go faster." Sidestepping, the pony didn't seem to appreciate her candor.

She kicked harder and tightened her reins.

The horse reared.

A squeal erupted from her lips as she squeezed her knees to hold on. Snorting, the pony thrashed his head from side to side as if he knew an inexperienced rider controlled the reins.

Horse hooves pummeled the ground as Geordie circled back. "I kent I should have tied on a lead line."

He clipped the rope onto the side of her bridle and headed off at a canter. Flopping in the saddle, the inside of her thighs rubbed and chafed, Akira held on as best she could. "How long will we keep up this pace?"

"We need to put a good distance between us and the redcoats." He glanced over his shoulder. "Push your heels down and rock your hips with the movement of the horse."

She gathered a bit of mane with her reins and bore down on her heels. Watching Geordie, she rocked as he did. The ride was bumpy at first, but she soon caught on. Moving with the horse's gait made the ride fluid, almost exhilarating. She smirked. She might even have enjoyed following on a lead line if they hadn't been running for their lives.

"How long will the journey take?" she asked.

"Two to three days, near enough."

Akira cringed, imagining that by the end of three days, her legs would be rubbed as raw as a plucked chicken.

"There's a river crossing ahead. Hold tight."

Every muscle in her body tensed as the horses plunged into the water. Before she could catch her breath, the pony sank to his shoulders. Everything from Akira's hips down dragged under the water. She screeched when a splash from Geordie's horse hit her face. The water crept higher. The horse seemed to lose his footing and drifted down with the current.

Geordie tugged the line close to his body. "Just a moment longer!" he hollered.

Akira squeezed her eyes shut and prayed. *Hold on, ye wee beastie.* As her lips mouthed the words, the pony regained his footing and hastened beside Geordie's larger mount.

After the river crossing, Geordie slowed the horses to a fast trot and showed her how to post up and down—he said a horse could travel at that pace for hours.

The only problem was, how long could she hold out? Her legs already ached from sitting astride, not to mention the fact that she hadn't yet broken her fast. But now was not the time to complain.

Akira had been so consumed with fear it wasn't until much later that the significance of Geordie's comment about home's hearth dawned on her. "Holy Moses!"

"What?"

"We're heading to your lands."

# Chapter Eighteen

Captain Roderick Weaver led his battalion into Glen Spean. At last he had the bastard trapped, and by God, he'd arrest a duke this day.

As they rounded the bend, a regiment of Highland troops stood behind the stone walls of Coll of Keppoch's lands, their muskets trained on the dragoons.

Roddy raised his hand and gave the command to halt. He looked across the faces of the Jacobite traitors. "Who dares challenge the Queen's Army?"

"Who puts innocent women and children under fire and sword?" An enormous man clad in a red-and-blue plaid marched forward with two henchmen in his wake. "I'm Coll MacDonell, chieftain of these lands, and I've word you've set fire to the homes under my care at Spean Bridge."

"How dare you question one of the queen's officers with such disrespect?" demanded Corporal Snow.

"I am Captain Weaver. No one else will be harmed if

you comply." Roddy sliced his hand through the air. "I've come to arrest the Duke of Gordon for taking up arms against the queen at Hoord Moor."

"Who?" Coll smirked, looking between his men. "Have either of you seen a duke in Glen Spean in the past fortnight?"

"No, sir," said one, shaking his head.

"I'm looking for an injured man riding a gelding with a healer. Word has it they passed through this way." Roddy narrowed his gaze. "And my guess is you've been harboring them right here in Glen Spean."

"Has anyone harbored a fugitive duke on MacDonell lands?" Coll hollered, loud enough to be heard in Fort William.

No one said a word.

"I think you're lying." Roddy leaned forward.

The redheaded chieftain's eyes filled with hate, and his fingers twitched. "I beg your pardon, captain, but no one calls Coll MacDonell a liar."

"Then you will submit to a search?"

"And allow your dragoons to plunder *my* home?"

Roderick eyed his corporal. He didn't care much for the odds with the Jacobites facing them locked and loaded. God knew, at least two of them had their sights trained on him. Besides, he wanted inside. There wasn't a need to ransack the man's house. At least not yet. "Allow me and my corporal to walk through—you can give us the grand tour. That's all I ask." He looked to the fire pit and added, "While they're waiting, I'll need a meal for my men."

Coll grinned. "I'll permit only *you* inside, Captain Weaver. And the others can eat their fill of bread and cold meat whilst they wait. Let no officer say he wasn't treated well at the hand of Coll MacDonell of Keppoch."

Pulling the Duke of Gordon's silver flask from his lapel pocket and taking a sip of fine whisky, Roderick caught a slight shift of the chieftain's eyes.

*The man is lying. Just what I'd expect from a false-hearted Highlander. Damn their misplaced code of hospitality.*

Word must have preceded him. Perhaps Roddy had been a bit cavalier setting the crofts along the River Spean to fire and sword. But he'd find the duke. Christ, he could smell the bastard.

* * *

Dusk had turned the sky violet and pink by the time they rode into the village of Newtonmore. It was the seat of the MacPherson clan, and Geordie said they would be friendly. Akira's thighs burned from chafing and her stomach growled with hunger. They hadn't stopped for their nooning. In fact, they hadn't stopped at all. The horses were spent and so was she.

They dismounted outside the stable yard. Geordie dug in his sporran, pulled out a handful of copper coins, and dropped them in her palm. "I'll trade the horses for fresh mounts. Go to the alehouse and order us a meal."

"Fresh mounts?" The idea made her ache all the more. "You mean we're going to keep riding?"

"'Tis not safe to stay in town—we'll need to ride on a bit further at least. Only a bit longer, I promise." He pointed across the muddy street. "Now go buy us some food. I'll be there directly."

Akira stood in front of the alehouse doors for a moment. She hadn't been inside such an establishment since she was young. But Geordie was right, it was the only place she'd seen where they could order a meal.

A man pushed outside, causing her to stumble backward. Catching himself on a post, he swayed in place for a moment, giving her a wide-eyed, inebriated stare. Then a lecherous grin played across his lips. "Are ye looking for a tumble, lassie? 'Cause I ken of a fresh pile of hay but a quick jaunt from here."

If it wouldn't cause a stir, she'd slap the man for his vulgarity. "No." She folded her arms tight across her body and hastened inside.

Raucous voices filled the hall. Dirty thresh covered the floor, and above, an enormous chandelier encrusted with layers of melted candles dripped wax. The sound ebbed to a hum as all eyes shifted her way. A burly man behind the bar crossed his arms. "Och, lass, I suggest you run along home afore ye find more trouble than ye can handle."

She forced herself to move toward him. "My—um—*employer*," she said in a low tone, "will be here anon. He sent me to order two meals, please." She slid a penny in front of the man. "And two pints of ale."

"That'll be two and a half."

Feeling like a hundred pairs of eyes were boring into her back, she decided not to barter, though two pennies should have been plenty. "You drive a hard bargain." She slid another penny and two farthings forward, then glanced over her shoulder. Dear Lord, every man in the room was staring—and there weren't any womenfolk to be seen.

She caught sight of an empty table near the back, but Akira didn't dare walk through the maze of oglers. She drummed her fingers. "I'll wait here."

"Suit yourself." The barman snatched the coins. "Helga, two plates full!" he hollered.

"Two plates," came a cackling reply from a passageway at the side of the bar.

"Thank you." Akira smiled, trying to be pleasant, but her skin prickled and her ears rang as the men resumed their conversations. The door opened and slammed closed again. She resisted an overwhelming urge to turn around.

The barman placed two pewter tankards of ale in front of her. She grasped the handle of one and raised it to her lips with a trembling hand. Good heavens, her fingers were shaking from hunger before she entered the place, and now she had to clamp her muscles taut to keep from spilling her drink for nerves.

Footsteps crunched the thresh spread across the floorboards.

Akira lowered her tankard, turning her head enough to peer out the corner of her eye. Blast, the vile man from the street moved in beside her. "You're none too friendly for a tinker."

Heat spread across the back of her neck. Since she'd been traveling with Geordie, nary a soul had made a belittling comment regarding her heritage. Until now. The man licked his lips like a pig and smelled worse than a pickled sewer.

She inched away, trying to ignore him.

He grabbed her arm and bared a row of crooked, yellow teeth. "Come, lassie, there's a table in the back ye can buy me a pint."

She jerked back, but his fingers gripped tighter. "Please, leave me be. My employer will be here soo—"

"Employer?" He threw his head back with a crowing laugh. "What are you, a poor man's whore?"

She straightened her spine. "I am a healer."

"Aye, and I'd like a wee kiss to heal me ails." He yanked her into a crushing embrace. "Give us a peck on the cheek, lass."

Shoving her fists into his chest, she fought to break away. "Let me go!"

His breath smelled foul and pickled. "Just one kiss."

As she leaned her face away from the stench, her hips rocked forward and her mons brushed him. Ice pulsed through her veins. The drunk trapped her against the bar and pressed his slobbering lips to her cheek. "See? That wasn't so bad."

The hall erupted with boisterous claps and shouts, egging him on.

"Stop this!" She pushed him away, but as she started to run, he caught her arm.

"I still have a taste for a pint, lass. Surely you can spare a penny."

The door slammed.

Thunderous footsteps thudded their way.

The shouting stopped.

Something clicked. "Step away. Now."

The drunkard's eyes shifted. "Mind your own affairs, I'm just having a bit o' fun."

Over the man's shoulder, Geordie's eyes blacker than coal, his mouth in a hard line. He pressed a pistol into the man's temple, looking like he could pull the trigger without a bit of remorse. "I said step away." His voice rolled with a low growl. "If you want to live."

The man shifted his eyes. "What is the wench to you?"

"That is no concern of yours." He pressed the weapon so hard the blackguard was forced to bend his neck clear to his shoulder. "Release her arm now or meet the devil."

Dropping his hand, the man backed away.

Akira clutched her fists beneath her chin and slid beside Geordie.

He swept his pistol across the gaping faces. "If any man tries to stop me, he'll be the first to take a musket ball to the gut." He reached for a tankard and guzzled the ale, never taking his eyes or his weapon off the crowd. He slammed the cup onto the board. "Grab my dirk, lass. We're walking out of here."

She unsheathed the weapon and pointed it at the drunkard.

The cur shrank.

Geordie tugged her arm. "Now."

Together they backed to the door. "Anyone who tries to follow will be the first to die," Geordie growled, turning the latch and pulling her through.

Akira stumbled after him, running for the waiting horses. "It was about time you arrived."

"Aye?" He hoisted her into the saddle. "You'd think ordering a plate of food wouldn't cause such a stir, God bless it."

Her chafed thighs burned as she dug in her heels, pointing her mount north. "It wasn't my fault."

"Next time, we stay together." He cantered off, tossing a look over his shoulder: "Haste, afore the whisky makes some bastard think he's a hero."

Akira managed to keep up this time. Why the blazes did Geordie blame her? He was the one who'd told her to enter an alehouse unescorted.

*Curses.*

* * *

Geordie's blood pulsed hot beneath the skin. Every time he blinked he saw that ill-breeding swine with his dirty fingers wrapped around Akira's arm. For Christ's sake, how could he have been such a buffoon, telling her to go into an alehouse alone for the purpose of saving time?

Though she looked sultrier than sin on Sunday, she was an innocent—a lass who carried around a basket of remedies and did what she could to help people in need. Akira was dear and beautiful and made sunshine radiate in his chest when she smiled. Goddammit, he'd murder any blackguard who dared to touch her.

Aye, she may have been Gypsy born, but there wasn't a lass in the Highlands who could match her genuine beauty, her sincere kindness, her tenderness.

By God, he'd scribe a missive to the chieftain of Clan MacPherson and tell him exactly what he thought of the town under his jurisdiction, and if he didn't receive an apology in due course, he'd put the whole bloody village to fire and sword.

Geordie glanced over his shoulder to ensure Akira had managed to keep pace. A few yards back, she kicked her heels, her eyes wide, a grimace on her face. Christ, the lass had to be the worst horsewoman he'd ever seen.

He tugged his reins and slowed a bit for her sake.

How on earth was she supposed to learn horsemanship? She'd said she was the sole support for her family. How many of Scotland's children could not afford horses or shoes? How many wore ill-fitting clothes and went hungry at night? Bless it, according to Geordie's former wife, such worries were too frivolous for a duke.

But he worried.

And Akira's poverty, her happiness, her acceptance of life and the myriad of situations thrown her way, made him realize exactly how pompous and privileged his entire life had been. Akira had cared for him, fled from soldiers with him, and kept his secrets when she'd had no reason to do so except for the kindness in her heart.

And she'd just suffered at the hand of a slobbering swine.

*Thank God I arrived when I did.*

Geordie remained in the lead, listening to make sure Akira didn't fall behind. For miles and miles, he berated himself for being such a goddamn louse.

As night fell, the path lit only by moonlight, he drove the horses up into the shelter of the mountains—a journey with which he was familiar. When they reached a clearing far enough away from Newtonmore, Geordie finally slowed his mount and stopped. Akira didn't ride in beside him. She pulled up short at the edge of the trees, her face downcast.

"Why on earth are you keeping to the shadows?" Dismounting, he strode toward her. She sniffled. "Are you injured?"

"No." Her voice warbled.

"Well, you're safe now." When he grasped her horse's bridle, she looked up. Tears glistened on her cheeks.

His heart squeezed in his chest. Och, would he ever stop acting like a fool? "Jesus bloody Christ, I'm sorry." He reached up. "Come, I'll help you down."

She shook her head. "No. I don't want to."

"Please, Akira. I acted like a bull-brained oaf." He grasped her waist and pulled her down.

"I-I told him to leave me be." She buried her face in his shoulder. "But he was inebriated and vile."

Closing his eyes, Geordie held her tight, plying her crown with tender kisses. "There, there, lass. I wanted to lodge a musket ball in the bastard's brain when I saw him heckling you. I wouldn't have hesitated if not for your safety."

She rocked against him. "I *never* ever want to enter an alehouse again."

His insides ripped apart. "I should have had you wait until I could go inside with you. I am sorry."

"B-but, but I thought you were upset with me."

Jesus Christ, she was the one accosted, and she thought he was angry with *her*? "Nay, *mo leannan*." He'd never used the Gaelic endearment for *sweetheart* with any woman, but for Akira it rolled off his tongue like sweet cream. "I could never be upset with you. I am angry with myself. You are but an innocent rose among the thorns of men."

She drew in a series of deep breaths, clearly trying to regain control.

Geordie smoothed his hand up and down her back, whispering, "Easy, lass, I'm to blame, not you," over and over again.

When her breathing finally became steady, he raised her chin with the crook of his finger. "Did ye ken you're the kindest, most selfless woman I've ever met?"

She shook her head slowly. "I'm not."

"Ah, but you are." Ever so slowly, he lowered his mouth while he studied Akira's features in the moonlight. Her eyes more vivid, her lips a darker shade of ruby, her skin luminous. His entire being craved her. He couldn't back away now if someone held a musket to *his* head. Unable to close his eyes, he brushed his lips over hers with feathery strokes. No, he couldn't pledge undying love to this woman, but together they could share the passion that flowed between them every time their lips met, every time their gazes locked, and every time flesh caressed flesh.

Sighing into his mouth, Akira slid her hands around his waist and pressed her body flush against his. Soft, unbound breasts molded to him as if they'd been destined to be joined.

Of all the women he'd had, no one had suited him as Akira, in both body and spirit. She had not a care for titles or airs. She saw him as a man who could protect her, a man with honor. Yet this wisp of a lass could stand up to him, and if she wanted, she could bring him to his knees. Finally closing his eyes, he kissed her. This was no plundering of the mouth; it served as an offering from his very soul.

His head clouded. Nothing around them mattered. The rustling of the trees sang a song of love, the soft neigh of the horses gave a blessing to the unique bond that had grown between them in such a short period of time.

Savoring her sweet taste, he pressed his forehead against hers. "Can you ever forgive me, lass?"

"As long as you stay with me next time," she whispered. "Thank heavens you came when you did, else I might have bit the blackguard's nose right off."

"Now that's a sight I would have enjoyed." Chuckling, he stepped toward his mount and slid his hand inside the roll of blankets. "I spoiled a warm meal for you as well, did I not?"

She rubbed her belly. "'Twasn't your fault, though I'm hungry."

He offered her the parcel of dried meat. "You take it, lass." After untying the thong, she held up the meager meal. "There's plenty. We can share."

"Perhaps I'll have some after you've eaten your fill." He took her hand and led her to a log where they could sit. "I fear after our hasty departure, word of our passing through Newtonmore may have already alerted the Government troops. If they are following, they'll have added incentive to make chase."

She crossed her ankles with a grimace, then rubbed her thigh with a pained exhale.

Geordie furrowed his brow. He hated to ask her to keep going when she was obviously exhausted. "How are your legs holding up?"

"Still sore."

He looked to the night sky. "If you can weather it, I reckon there's about another eight hours' ride to Glenlivet. If we ride steady, it should put us there in the wee hours afore dawn. I've kin there. They'll shelter us and feed us, and fight for us if need be." He brushed her tresses away from her face to better see her eyes. "Are you up to riding all night?"

She blessed him with a beautifully brave smile. "If it means we'll be safe, then my legs will have to bear it for a bit longer."

# *Chapter Nineteen*

Akira startled when Geordie pulled her from the horse into his arms. "What happened?"

"You fell asleep." He chuckled as he marched toward a tower, his limp somewhat pronounced. The stone walls glistened blue with the moonlight. "You've been draped over the horse's withers for the past few hours."

She leaned her head against his chest. "Why did you not wake me?"

"No need. I clipped on the lead line and the horse ambled along steadily enough."

She peered up at the enormous tower. "Where are we?"

"Glenlivet, the border of Gordon country." He continued walking as if she weighed nothing.

"That's a good thing?"

"A very good thing." He grinned, his white teeth catching the moonlight. "It means we're only thirty miles from Huntly."

"Your home?" Goodness, she was still so sleepy her head felt like it was full of cobwebs.

"Aye." He kicked the door. "Guard!"

A deep voice grumbled inside. "Who the bloody hell is pounding on the door in the wee hours?" Footsteps shuffled, and with a loud creak, a viewing panel opened. "This better be goo—" The whites of the guard's eyes grew as round as silver sovereigns. "Your Grace?" His voice shot up like an adolescent lad.

"Aye. Let us in." Geordie inclined his head toward Akira. "We've been riding all night and the lass can go no further."

She blinked and dropped her jaw. *Your Grace?* Lord Almighty, such words could mean only one thing.

The door swung open, revealing a gateway with a torch on the wall. "I'll awake the governor."

"Nay," Geordie said. "Let him sleep."

"But he's in your chamber, Your Grace."

Geordie faced the guard with a pinch to his brow. "Is the red chamber occupied?"

"Nay."

"That will suffice for the night." Geordie set Akira on her feet and took the torch from the wall. "Tell no one of my presence here."

The guard bowed. "Of course. Is there anything else you need?"

"Bring up some cheese and fruit straightaway, and a ewer of ale." Geordie stopped. "You do it, and do not let on to a soul for whom you're fetching the food."

"Aye, Your Grace. I'll follow you directly."

Geordie proceeded into the stairwell, with Akira close on his heels. Her every step burned her inner thighs, but she forced herself to stay close while he climbed, holding the torch high. Biting her tongue, she'd wait to confront him about his identity until they were behind closed doors.

Three flights up, Geordie stepped into a chilly passageway and opened the first door on the right. "I'll set to lighting the fire."

Rubbing her hands, Akira moved inside while Geordie headed for the hearth. "You're a duke? Royalty, no less?" Prickles spread across her skin. No wonder he'd been so secretive. If the Marquis of Atholl's dragoons had discovered a duke wounded on the battlefield, they would have done everything to see him ruined. Though she didn't know much of nobility, she had no doubt he would have lost his lands, and worse, his life.

Geordie hardly acknowledged her question as he stacked kindling like a commoner and held the torch to it. As the fire crackled to life, the glow illuminated the chamber—tapestries on the wall, a large bed with a red canopy and curtains.

Needles and pins still prickled her skin as Akira gazed around the chamber. *Such opulence.*

This room was spacious, with a gilded table and two chairs standing before the hearth. An enormous bed with thick and ornately carved wooden posts supported a red canopy and curtains. Two benches padded with red silk adorned the window embrasure. Akira was chilled by the night air and by the realization of how deeply over her head she'd become—and unknowingly, like a silly fool. Who was she to harbor amorous feelings for any noble, let alone a man as lofty as a duke?

What was she supposed to do now? She'd kissed a duke, been angry with a duke, allowed a duke to carry her, seen a duke completely naked, tended a duke's wounds—well, at least the last one was more believable. She couldn't stay there. She couldn't fancy herself infatuated with him. For all that was holy, she should be groveling at his feet. How on earth could she have been so foolish, so taken in?

Her chest became a hollow void.

Keeping his back to her, His Grace placed a log on the fire.

She balled her fists and stiffened her spine. "If Your Grace would be so kind as to point me in the direction of the servants' quarters, I shall make up a pallet for the night."

He doused the torch, then stood and faced her. "I beg your pardon?"

Surely he'd heard her. She dipped into a deep curtsy, one expected when in the company of royalty. "Please, m'lord, where are the servants' quarters?"

In two strides he crossed the floor and tugged her to her feet. "What the devil has come over you?"

She blinked in disbelief. "Of course, after meeting Sir Coll, I suspected you were more than a wounded Highland chieftain, but never in my wildest imaginings did I think you might possibly be a duke. For the love of God, you're but steps removed from the throne."

"Several more steps away, now the true king is in exile." He snorted, unlike a duke but like the Geordie she knew. Then his gaze softened and he fingered a lock of her hair. "I rather enjoyed not being a duke when I was alone with you."

Had she heard him correctly? Did he intend to keep up his charade indefinitely? "I am no man's fool." She stamped her foot, ready to blow steam from her nose. "How can you not face your birthright and pretend to be someone else?"

A tic twitched his jaw as if she'd delivered a slap.

"Believe me, never for one minute have I forgotten my station. I've been more myself with you than I have been in years. To you I was Geordie—a name used only by my mother and my closest friends, a name used only by people I trust."

"That may be all well and good, but you cannot run from who you are, just as I cannot." She pushed back her tresses, making the lock abruptly fall from his fingertips. "I'm the duchess of nothing. I'm so lowborn, even commoners spit upon me and my kin."

He reached for her hand. "To me you are—"

"No!" She snapped it away. "You're like all the other men in Christendom. What do you plan to do when you tire of me? Beat me and leave me for dead like they did to my ma?"

"I beg your pardon? What has come over you? I would *never* harm you." His hands dropped to his sides and hurt flashed through his eyes. "What the devil happened to your mother?"

Akira hid her face in her hands. This was it, the brutal truth that followed her everywhere. "'Twas awful. She didn't leave the cottage for years—still doesn't venture out much."

"Tell me." The tone in his voice was one of an all-commanding duke. She should have known.

Spreading her fingers, Akira was almost afraid of what she'd see. He stared at her with such intensity, she wanted to crumple and melt. But now they were baring their souls, she might as well tell him everything. The sooner she did, the sooner he'd point her toward the servants' quarters. "After my stepfather left us, Ma worked as a barmaid at the alehouse. A drunkard broke her arm and took a knife to her face."

"My God."

"They brought her home on a stretcher." Akira slid the heels of her hands to her temples and pressed to ease the throbbing in her head. "She lay abed for three months. Taught me how to make salve from her pallet. I was twelve."

"Christ," he swore. "And you have three sisters? How did you survive?"

"We begged some. Sold my salve, too. Then people started paying me to tend the sick." Akira hung her head. "'Tis why the ten-shilling piece is so important. I made a vow that my sisters would never have to take to the streets begging again."

"Good Lord." He dragged a hand over his hair. "I never imagined... You've been responsible for your family since the age of twelve?"

She nodded, unable to look him in the eye. "The merchants in Dunkeld treat us like urchins." Clenching her teeth, she willed herself not to cry. "We *are* urchins."

"No." He lowered his chin, giving her one of his dark stares. "That isn't right."

"But that's how it is." She stepped back. "And once people ken I have Gypsy blood, they treat me worse than thresh on the floor. They fear me, suspect me of stealing, though I've never stolen anything in my life—except a loaf of bread when we'd gone a whole day without anything to eat. I felt so badly, I swore I'd never again do anything the like."

Geordie moved toward her. She shuffled backward until her spine pressed against the wall. But he didn't stop. His tempting lips moved ever so close. Why did he have to look so delectable? His eyes had grown darker, a lock of chestnut hair slipped from his ribbon and dangled over one eye.

"It angers me that people would be so disrespectful of you. You're honest and thoughtful, and not one of those mongrels deserves to kiss your feet." He placed his hands on the wall, either side of her head, his gaze boring into her soul. "You should be loved and respected."

He leaned so close, his breath tickled her cheek. "I want to look after you."

Akira closed her eyes. His words played like a harp in her ears. Yes, she wanted to believe him—wanted to believe he would be hers for all time. All she needed to do was slip her hands around his waist and cling to him. Wasn't it? So much had changed in the past few minutes, she couldn't think straight. "But you're a duke. You cannot look after the likes of me."

He smoothed his fingers along her cheek and around to her neck. "I believe as a duke I have the right to say whom I do and do not look after."

"But—"

"There are no buts, lass." When he lowered his gaze to her lips, Akira's heartbeat hammered an erratic rhythm. How could she argue when the spiciness of his scent, the hard male body pressed against hers, turned her entire body into a boneless heap of rapturous nerves?

A knock came at the door. "Your tray, Your Grace."

In a moment of sanity, Akira slipped aside and wiped a hand over her lips—lips that craved to kiss him, to feel him kiss her like a man who desired her as much as she did him.

"Of all the bloody bad timing," Geordie growled. "Leave it."

Akira reached for the latch. "I'll fetch it."

Geordie's hand swiftly caught hers. "I have more urgent matters to attend to first."

She met his gaze, while awareness tingled across her skin. She'd been hungry only moments ago, but now she wouldn't be able to eat a thing. Her mouth went completely dry, and all she could do was nod. That single hazel-eyed look spoke volumes about the depth of his desire. No words were necessary to express what passed between them. The passion was as jolting as a bolt of lightning.

Sweeping her into his braw arms, he carried her to the bed and rested her atop the most gloriously soft mattress—even softer than her bed at Glen Spean had been.

"Ah," she sighed as the tension drained from her limbs.

"You like it?" Geordie asked, kneeling over her and trailing kisses along her neck.

"'Tis gloriously comfortable." Drunk with exhaustion, she abandoned her fight. She could no sooner resist him than cease to breathe.

As his lips wove magic across her skin, his fingers coaxed her up. He unlaced her kirtle and then her stays. Pulling away the layers, he continued to ply her flesh with kisses while he kneaded her breasts through the thin linen. Heavier and heavier they grew, as desire surged to her center. She needed to see him bare again, yearned for his touch, yearned for all of him.

Fumbling with his doublet's buttons, Akira managed to push the jacket from his shoulders. Geordie rocked back on his haunches, released his belt, and cast it aside. He unfastened the brooch at his shoulder, letting the folds of his kilt cascade around his knees.

"Are you bare beneath that linen shirt?" she asked wantonly.

A single eyebrow arched as Geordie's eyes darkened—

devilish and desirable beyond all measure. "Aye," he rasped, "and I want you to take it off me now, lass."

Such words made her hunger for something more. He could no more stop her from discovering what lay beneath the fabric than she could stop herself from doing so. A hot swirling pulse of awareness thrummed through her blood as she rose to her knees and slowly raised the linen up and over his head. Her entire body quivered. Gazing upon him warmed every inch of her flesh, made her wild with desire, made her want to lay with him, made her crave the rough pads of his fingertips upon her flesh.

Taking a stuttered breath, she drank him in. His sculpted chest, the rippled muscles in his abdomen that tapered to sturdy, masculine hips. Akira's tongue swept across her top lip. Her breathing stopped when she stared at the dark curls surrounding his erect manhood. A flood of heat surged between her legs. If only she could reach out and wrap her fingers around that velvet-tipped column of flesh and guide it to the place on her body aching for him.

With a deep chuckle, he lifted her chin with his pointer finger. "If you keep looking at me like that, I'll come undone."

Holding her gaze, he fingered her shift's bow and untied it. She remained motionless while he slid it from her shoulders, though her breath came in short bursts. Aware of what she was doing, Akira didn't fear the consequences for the first time since she'd run away with him. Geordie pushed the cloth from her breasts and then past her hips.

A feral growl rumbled from his throat as his eyes raked down her body just as she'd done to him. "God help me, you are the bonniest woman I've ever laid eyes upon."

The flickering candlelight made the world spin like a dream. With a low moan, Geordie cupped her breast and joined his mouth with hers. His hand worked magic, as if he knew exactly what she wanted as he teased her nipple. Akira kissed him back with all the passion thrumming through her blood. But she needed more—needed closeness, needed all of him joined with her. This time, she moved toward him, pressed her body against his, showing him how much she wanted him to make love to her.

With a deep chuckle, Geordie guided her down to the mattress. He kneeled over her, kissing her neck, trailing down to her breasts. Akira gasped when his tongue circled the tip of her nipple. The smoldering flame deep inside ignited as if fed by a gusty breeze. Akira threw back her head and moaned as he kneaded her and suckled her, plying her sensitive skin with his tongue.

"What are you doing to me?" she said, the words coming in a ragged, breathless whisper.

"'Tis only the start of the magic to come." He raised his lids and met her gaze with a wicked glint in his eyes.

Akira shuddered and watched him, so virile, so masculine, so incredibly desirable—and he wanted to care for her. How on earth had this happened to her? Her? Akira Ayres. Her tongue slipped through her lips. "Show me how a man makes love to a woman."

He grinned—this smile even more devilish than the last. "Och, lass, you've no idea the pleasure that waits, and I'll not deny you." From her breasts, his kisses continued downward. Gooseflesh rose across her skin when he swirled his tongue in her navel. Then he again glanced up at her, his white teeth glowing through the dim light.

With a rumbling growl, he swirled his fingers through the curls at her apex. "I've dreamed of kissing you here."

"W-what...?" Her thighs quivered at his naughty wink. The memory of his finger teasing her to the brink of madness made her desire stir like wildfire.

"Spread your knees for me, lass." He grazed his teeth over his bottom lip, looking like sin and temptation served at once. Inhaling deeply, he coaxed her legs wider with his shoulders.

Mercy, with one lap of his tongue the passion inside her grew almost to the point of bursting. A shrill gasp tore from her throat. Again he licked. Akira's hips rocked and swayed. She tossed her head from side to side. He slid his finger to her opening and circled it—yet another action that sent her mind into a maelstrom of hot, driving need. His finger slid in and out while his tongue performed pure magic. With uncontrollable shuddering, her voice made high-pitched noises as she succumbed to his touch. Higher and higher her passion soared, when all at once her entire body went taut, hanging upon the precipice of pure ecstasy. A cry caught in the back of her throat. With her next gasp, the entire world shattered into pulsing bursts of euphoria.

When finally she regained her senses, Akira reached down and urged him atop her. "Why is it you turn me into such a wanton woman?"

He nuzzled into her hair, his thick member pressing between her legs. "You do the same to me, *mo leannan*."

She moved her hips, his manhood sliding between her wet thighs, rekindling the hot craving at her very core. "How can I bring you pleasure?"

* * *

When Akira uttered the words, a spike of desire hit Geordie so hard, his ballocks squeezed taut, almost making him lose his seed. Needing to slow his fervor, he rolled beside her and gazed into her eyes. "Are you certain?"

She nodded, her gaze drifting to his manhood. "More certain than I've been in a long time."

He ran his finger around her nipple, aching to be inside her. "I want it to be good for you."

She kissed him, her lithe fingers reaching down. "It will be. I ken it."

Geordie sucked in a ragged breath when her fingers lightly brushed the tip of his cock.

She gasped and slid her hand around him. "Did I hurt you?"

"Nay," he managed to utter. Dear God, how could he think with Akira milking his cock? With a feral growl, he rolled atop her, kneeling between her legs. He slid his member up the crux of her legs, his thighs trembling when hot moisture spilled over him.

Her hips arched up and caught the tip of his cock at her entrance. Geordie held his breath. Wet woman brimmed around him. God, he could come right now, but he wanted to make this the most memorable night of her life. Show her exactly what she'd been missing. "I'll try to be gentle."

She nodded, her hips continuing their seductive, swirling rhythm. Christ, he was supposed to be the one seducing Akira, but without a lick of schooling she'd proven to be an expert. Slowly, he pushed inside.

She sucked in a gasp.

Geordie froze. "Am I hurting you?" His hips rocked back. "If you want to stop..."

Her fingers clamped into his bum. “No.” With a firm tug, she urged him deeper. God, he adored this woman. Ever so slowly, he slid into the length of her, and when he reached a wall he gazed into her sultry eyes. Even in the dim light the dark blue of her eyes bewitched him.

Geordie blinked. “Are you all right?”

She rocked her hips beneath him. “Oh yes.”

With her words, Geordie’s ballocks clamped so taut, he had to suck in deep breaths to keep from spilling before he began to thrust. Casting all gentleness aside, he gave in to the frenzy of passion that claimed his mind. Heaven and earth, with Akira’s deft fingers kneading his backside, he lost all control. Her breath was coming faster. Her wild scent ensnared him. Stars flashed across his vision.

Faster and faster he thrust. Akira cried out, clinging to him for dear life. And now she’d reached her peak, he was free to drive hard and fast. Out of control, his breathing sped, his heart hammered, and all at once the surge of rapture flooded through his blood. His body quivered with strain. Crying “Akira!” he swelled within her. With one last deep thrust, he crashed into the wave of glorious release.

He held himself over her, his head dropping forward as he fought to catch his breath. “Lord have mercy,” he growled, while his heart began to steady.

Pushing up on his elbows, he raised himself high enough to regard the temptress’s face beneath the shadow of the canopy. Her lips swollen and slightly parted, her heavy-lidded gaze, black hair sprawling in a mass of tangles, framing her beauty. God save him, she defined rapture. Akira bewitched him mind and soul, and he would fight heaven and hell to make her his.

With a satiated moan, he trailed kisses down her neck. "Was it good for you, lass?"

She moved her hips beneath him, stirring the passion again. "Astonishingly good—so good, there are no words."

"You are the world to me." Breathing deeply to catch his breath, he rolled to his back and pulled Akira atop him. "You ken I adore you."

She rested her head on his chest. "And I you."

He ran his fingers through her hair and cherished the silkiness of it. The woman in his arms made his chest swell with pride—made him want to be a better man. In Akira's arms he was a man, not a duke, nothing but a man who adored a woman to the depths of his soul. He could lay there all night with his rose entwined with his limbs. And he fully intended to lose himself in her wiles until the sun rose on the morrow.

# Chapter Twenty

Geordie opened his eyes when a servant entered and began to stir the fire.

Morning had arrived far too soon. If only he could pretend to be invisible and make love to Akira all day.

Curled into his arm, the lass looked up with a smile, her sleepy blue eyes as bonny as ever. Her mussed hair, wild and wanton, made him want to take her that very moment. He gave her a reassuring peck on the temple before she retreated beneath the coverlet.

"Good morrow," he said to the chambermaid, sitting up.

The servant dropped her stick of wood and whipped around. "G-good morrow, m'lord."

Geordie cleared his throat, toying with Akira's hair beneath the bedclothes. "Tell my cousin I will attend him within the hour."

"Is that Sir Malcolm, m'lord?"

"Aye." The guard must have done his job, keeping

mum about Geordie's identity. "And please bring in the cheese and fruit on your way out."

She curtsied. "Straightaway, m'lord."

Closing his eyes, Geordie waited until they were alone before he lifted the linens. "'Tis safe to come out now."

"How could you sound so unruffled?" Akira grinned at him as she scooted up. She swirled her fingers through his chest hair. "I feel like I've been shamelessly naughty."

He shrugged. "She's a servant. 'Tis her burden to go about her duties no matter what she might see."

"I beg your pardon? Do you look upon all servants as mere pawns to serve you whilst remaining unbiased? Do you think nothing of their feelings?"

He flinched. She made him sound as callous as Elizabeth. Moreover, she was right. "Forgive me. That did sound rather harsh." Geordie slid his arm around her shoulders and squeezed, breathing in the scent of jasmine mixed with passion—mixed with more than mere words could express.

He pulled a plaid from the end of the bed and wrapped it around her shoulders. "Come, let us break our fast."

"I'm starved." When Akira moved, she hissed and pressed her hands to her thighs.

Geordie's gut twisted when he glimpsed the wince of pain on her face. He smoothed his hand atop hers. "Did I hurt you?"

She shook her head. "Nay. 'Tis from riding."

Bloody hell, even when he had the best of intentions, he'd behaved like a damned rake. She'd complained yesterday, but he'd not paid a bit of attention to her discomfort while he made love to her. He fingered the plaid. "Allow me to have a wee peek."

Tugging the plaid tighter across her body, she shied

from him. "Not to worry, the chafing will ease within a sennight."

Since last eve, the lass had grown inordinately bashful.

"Akira." He gave her a pointed look, one that never failed. "Now is not the time to be shy. Show me."

Groaning, she opened the plaid.

Dear Lord, chafing didn't even begin to describe the red-raw flesh on the inside of her thighs. He ventured to touch the outer edge of the rash. "Why didn't you tell me how bad this was?" And why the hell hadn't he noticed it when he was making love to her? Though it had been dark, he should have noticed—at least asked about her soreness from the saddle.

"I mentioned it yesterday in the clearing, and then when we arrived last eve..." Her gaze trailed aside, while a red blush flooded her cheeks. "Weeeeell, I reckon we were too enraptured to worry overmuch about the state of my thighs."

"Blast it all. I kent you were hurting. I should have insisted I have a look first before..."

"Afore you ravished me?" She giggled. "I think we were both a bit distracted. Besides, 'twas too dark to see."

Geordie managed to frown, though he had to force the corners of his mouth downward against a tickling urge to grin. "Mayhap, but that doesn't alter the fact you need to be tended. I'll fetch the salve."

Bare naked, he retrieved the pot from her satchel. And when he returned, Akira's gaze focused on his manhood.

Holy hell, he immediately lengthened.

She gasped.

"Never mind me," he rasped. "You need to be tended."

"Very well, Your Grace." Holding the blanket over her body, she moved over as he sat beside her.

"There's no need for formalities between us." He scooped a bit of salve, pushed the blanket from her thighs, and nudged her legs open.

He used gentle strokes to spread the salve on her inner thighs. It was all he could do to ignore the fire rekindling in his loins while her black nest of curls teased him. "You'll not be able to ride with this abrasion." He stoppered the pot and set it on the bedside table.

"I'll be fine. I managed to make it this far." Her gaze trailed to his loins, sending him instantly erect.

"I'd planned to eat, and then pay my cousin a visit afore we set out." He lowered his gaze to her lips while his hand slipped just below her breast.

She smoothed her hand up between his thighs, stopping her fingers right before she touched his erection. "But eating seems so unnecessary at the moment."

He didn't move. "No, lass. You need your strength. And I cannot take advantage whilst you're injured." With a wicked giggle, she stroked him.

Geordie's eyes rolled with his moan, while ecstasy shimmered through his entire body. He grasped her hand and stilled it. "Are you certain you are not too sore?"

She climbed onto his lap and straddled him. "Not too sore to mate with you."

"Good God, your charms are enough to lead any man to the edge of madness."

She seductively rocked her hips forward. "Is that a good thing?"

"'Tis better than good." He raised her hips and slipped inside her liquid core. "'Tis incredible."

* * *

He hadn't intended to make love to Akira this morn, but Geordie should have known he couldn't gaze upon a goddess's naked flesh or be anywhere in her vicinity without losing his mind—at least until his lust had been satiated. After, he'd made quick work of cleaning up and reviving himself with a bit of food before descending the stairs to his cousin's solar. In fact, the solar belonged to the Duke of Gordon, as did the tower house in which they'd slept, but he'd appointed Malcolm governor of his lands in Glenlivet, and thus, Malcolm slept in the great bedchamber and ran the affairs of the county from the solar on the second floor.

When Geordie opened the door, Malcolm pushed back his chair and hastily stood. "Cousin, you're among the living, I see." Only a year younger than Geordie, Malcolm was a stout man with dark Gordon features.

"You kent I was here?" After closing the door, Geordie moved farther inside. "I told the guard to keep my presence silent."

Malcolm snorted. "Aye, that was until I threatened to emasculate him when the stable boy reported two new horses and kits of tack this morn."

Geordie chuckled and slid into a chair. "What the devil? You've stooped to threatening to cut off your guard's cods?"

"Only after he told me you didn't want to be named. I had to somehow remind him who was governor of this castle." Shrugging, he gestured to the sideboard. "Would you like a cup of cider?"

"My thanks." Geordie crossed his legs, making himself comfortable. "Who else kens I'm here?"

"Only me. Even Eleanor is unaware as of yet." Malcolm placed two tankards on the table.

"Good, then let us keep it that way." Geordie sipped, and the tang of sour apples tickled the corners of his jaw.

"Oh? 'Tis not like you to lay low—ah..." Malcolm waggled his shoulders with a lecherous smirk. "Not even when you've a wench in tow."

Geordie dearly loved his cousin, but within a click of the mantel clock a bolt of heat flared up his spine. He snatched the errant man's wrist and squeezed. Hard. "Akira is no wench," he seethed.

Turning red, Malcolm gulped. "Aye?"

"Never forget it." Having made his point, Geordie released his grip.

Malcolm rubbed his wrist, then took a healthy swig of cider. "I've never seen you so defensive about a woman. She must be something to behold."

"The lass is no concern of yours." Geordie rocked his chair back. The time for sniveling small talk was over. "I'm being pursued by an army of redcoats. Should they come this way, I trust you will discourage them from traveling further into Gordon lands."

"Trust a Gordon to play with fire." He grinned. "Should we expect a fight?"

Geordie took another drink. "When it comes to Government troops? Always prepare to defend yourself."

"Talk first?" Malcolm picked his teeth with his thumbnail.

"Aye, 'twould be a fair bit less messy. And you haven't seen hide nor hair of me since the gathering last May."

"Understood."

"We'll need to be on our way soon." Geordie shoved his chair back. "Please have a coach ready at the main gate within the hour."

Malcolm snorted with a salacious grin. "A coach? Are you growing soft, old man?"

Spreading his palms wide, Geordie scoffed. "Who are you calling old? My traveling companion is experiencing some chafing."

"Damnation, you arc an insatiable dog even if you are a duke."

"Pull your mind from the sewer. The lass is sore from the saddle, and that is all."

Malcolm shook his head. "Och aye, now you're Lord George the merciful?"

Geordie stood. Devil's bones, if Malcolm wasn't his cousin, he might give him a good hiding. "Shut your gob and order the bloody coach."

# Chapter Twenty-One

Everything inside the coach was sumptuous, from the salmon-red walls to the matching pillows at each end of the cushioned seats.

Akira smoothed her hand across the black velvet upholstery. "I never imagined a coach would be so grand inside. 'Tis like a small parlor." She pushed aside the silk drapes and opened the wooden shutter in the door. The scenery passed by as if they were riding through a dream.

She laughed when the breeze tickled her face. Never before had she felt so alive. So many new experiences showered her every day. When would the fairy tale end? Plopping back to the seat, she pointed. "Look out the window. 'Tis amazing."

Geordie laced his fingers through hers and peered outside. "What do you find so intriguing? Does it not look the same whether you're riding in a carriage or on a horse?"

"No, silly." She made a large square with her hands.

"The window makes the passing scenery look like a painting—except it's constantly moving."

He slung his arm over her shoulder and kissed her temple. "Och, it does. And that's another thing I find so endearing about you."

"What?"

"You see the world as magical—a special place. Such small things give you joy."

"A coach is not a small thing."

"Mayhap not to you, but I have ridden in coaches all my life."

"You are lucky."

"Most of the time, though I cannot deny I was born into comfort. I sometimes do not appreciate luxuries as I should."

She returned her gaze to the window, listening to the creaks of the wheels. "How long will our journey take?"

"We should be at Huntly in time for the evening meal." Geordie frowned, while a tic twitched in his jaw.

"What is it?"

"Nothing."

"No." She leaned closer. "I saw that look. Something is bothering you."

"When we arrive, we will be inundated with people and I will need to attend to urgent missives and a host of other matters." The corners of his mouth turned up. "Alexander and Jane will be there, too."

"Your children?"

"Aye."

Akira clutched her hands against the flitting in her stomach. "Do you think they'll like me?"

"Of course they will. You're as endearing as a kitten."

She snorted. "Hardly."

He waggled his brows and slipped his hand to the back of her neck. "I disagree. You are impossible not to embrace. Though only I will do this..."

Och, how she loved it when his gaze dipped to her lips and he lowered his mouth to hers. Joining in a long, slow kiss consumed her mind, making her need for him flare through her insides like wildfire.

"Forget the children. I want you for myself," he growled, taking in a deep breath. "And do not worry about Alex and Jane. They will warm to you, I'm certain of it."

"I'm excited to meet them."

"I borrowed this from my cousin's library." He held up a book. "Shall I read to you to help pass the time?"

"What is it about?"

"'Tis a play by William Shakespeare."

"*Romeo and Juliet*?" She peered at the cover, looking for a drawing, but found only a jumble of words. "I hope so, because I saw the play by the tinkers when they visited Dunkeld."

He arched an eyebrow. "Did you now?"

"Aye."

"Did you enjoy it?"

"Very much."

"Well then." He turned the book over in his hands. "This is not *Romeo and Juliet*, but a comedy, *Much Ado About Nothing*."

"Nothing?" She puzzled. "That seems a bit nonsensical."

"And that's precisely the theme. Would you like to hear it?"

"Oh yes, indeed." She wrapped her hands around his arm and nestled against him. "Tell me this story of nothing."

* * *

Akira concentrated on Geordie's every word, completely enchanted by the tenor of his voice. She laughed often, but could listen to him recite the Bible and derive enjoyment from it. The coach stopped twice to feed and water the horses, while she and Geordie ate a small meal packed by the cook in Glenlivet. Goodness, she could grow accustomed to a life of privilege if she didn't watch herself. But she didn't want to ever forget her roots, ever forget the common folk who worked the land. No, she vowed to help those less fortunate.

The sun had begun to set when he closed the book. "So what did you think of the story?"

"Silly, funny—but it makes me think."

"Oh? How, would you say?"

She drummed her fingers for a moment. "I think the moral is honesty. Deception should never be used, even if someone has the best intentions."

"Well thought, my dear." He nuzzled into her hair. "What else did you like about it?"

"I liked that everything was sorted out in the end. But I didn't like it when Claudio was tricked into rejecting Hero at the altar."

"Agreed. I think that was the worst deception of all."

Akira rested her head against Geordie's shoulder. "I don't want there to be any more deceptions between us."

"Nor do I." Humming, he smoothed his hand along the outside of her arm. Oh, how marvelous to be wanted. "In fact, I should tell you what I've been thinking."

"Oh?"

He fingered a lock of her hair. "I cannot abide for you and your family to live in such deplorable hardship. I've decided you, your ma, and sisters should move into the dower house on the Huntly estate."

"*You've* decided?" She rubbed her finger along the velvet collar of his doublet, mulling over his words, while prickles at her nape needled her. "Dower house?"

"It's a manor house—seven bedchambers above stairs, servants' quarters. Honestly, the home is big enough for a large family."

A lump the size of her fist caught in her throat. She hadn't thought much beyond Geordie's declaration to care for her. What, exactly, did he mean? He was now making decisions on her behalf? Would they marry? Would the dower house be for her and her family until the wedding? Akira bit her bottom lip. Perhaps now wasn't the time to ask. Things were already happening too fast.

Her face grew hot. Of course he would marry her. Wouldn't he? She glanced up at him.

Grinning with the excitement of a lad, he rubbed his hands. "I want only the best for my Gypsy rose—gowns and horses and coaches at your disposal. We'll need a tutor for your sisters. Why, they can even attend lessons with Jane and Alexander."

She clapped a hand over her heart. "They'll learn to read?"

"Aye." He pulled her into an embrace. "And you, too, if you'd like. I'd like nothing better than to teach you to read myself."

"Do you not think I'm too old?"

"Nay, you're never too old to learn."

"Not in my wildest dreams did I believe I would gain an education. Just think, I will be able to read and write, just like a refined lady."

"Indeed you will, and do not let anyone tell you you're

not refined. You have more thoughtfulness in your heart than any noblewoman I have ever met."

"That is very kind of you to say." Truly, she was excited beyond all measure, but the whole arrangement with the dower house still played on her mind. Looking away, she twisted the corner of her mouth.

Geordie brushed her tresses aside. "Are you worried, *mo leannan*?"

"Perhaps a little."

"You must know I will do everything to ensure you are welcomed by my clan. They will simply adore you."

"A-and . . . ah . . . how long will I reside in the dower house?" There, she'd said it without using the word *marriage*.

His eyes widened with his deep inhale. "Of course, I'll expect you to stay in the castle with me most of the time, but you'll need your own accommodations to keep up appearances with the outside world."

Suddenly Akira couldn't breathe. It was as if a pile of stones had just fallen on her chest. "Appearances?" She covered her nose and mouth with her hands, pressing her fingers to the inner corners of her eyes, willing herself not to burst into tears. "Do I embarrass you, m'lord?"

"Embarrass me?" He rubbed his hand across her shoulders. His touch suddenly didn't feel soothing, but brash. "Of course not, but a duke cannot have a mistress living under his roof."

A tear dribbled down her finger. "Mistress?" she squeaked. Oh God, what would Ma say? Being a mistress was akin to being a whore, was it not? A kept woman? Someone to be toyed with but hidden from society like a leper?

Geordie's hand stilled. "Och, I cannot marry you, *mo*

*leannan*. You ken I'm divorced. The bishop would never grant me leave to marry again. Besides…"

She stiffened.

He cleared his throat but didn't finish his comment. "Do not misunderstand my intentions. All great men are forced into arranged marriages. The fortunate ones learn to love their wives, but most, like me, find themselves incompatible with the women with whom they are united for the sole purpose of maintaining a noble bloodline." He kissed her temple. "I will deny you nothing. You will live in wealth and be respected by all society."

A snort blew through her nose. "Aye? But what about respecting myself?"

He groaned. "I'm making a muddle of this, am I not?"

She turned her face and pulled out from under his arm.

When he touched her back, she slid farther away. She didn't want his touch right now. How could he do this to her? Did he not love her? Did he not want marriage and a family?

"Please, Akira," he pleaded. "We can work this out. My only desire is to see to your happiness. Let us take one thing at a time."

With a stuttering exhale, she hid her face with her hand. Dear God, if ever she needed her mother's counsel, it was now. But how could Akira tell Ma how stupid she'd been? She'd trusted Geordie, believed him to be pure of heart, believed he would treasure her as much as she treasured him.

Is that why he read her the play about deception?

And what did he mean, they could work it out? What was there to work out?

"Akira?"

She said not a word.

"Please, look at me," he deplored, as if she was hurting him, not the other way around.

Wiping her eyes, she complied with his request.

Blast it, the sparkle in his eyes made her want to trust him. "I promise I will always care for you. Never again will you want for anything."

"But—"

"Huntly Castle, m'lord," the coachman shouted.

* * *

Of all the rotten timing. Just when he'd stuck his boot in his mouth, the damned coach had to pass through Huntly's gates, proceeding with haste along the tree-lined drive. In minutes they would stop in the castle's courtyard. How could he have been such an idiot? Akira was uneducated in the ways of the aristocracy. Why didn't he realize the lass wouldn't immediately warm to the idea of being a mistress?

Because he was a dolt. Every other peer he knew kept a mistress. He'd entertained more than one himself, though not recently.

In no way could they arrive at Huntly with this misunderstanding separating them.

Akira shrank low in the seat. "Perhaps 'tis time for me to return to Dunkeld."

Geordie grasped her hand and held it over his heart. "Please don't leave."

"You expect me to stay here and forget that you insulted me to my very core? Just because I'm a poor healer doesn't mean I have no pride." She moved away from him and crossed her arms. "And there you sit, making decisions for me? How dare you!"

Geordie glanced out the window as the coach proceeded along the drive far too fast for him to beg, plead, and grovel for mercy. "You are right. I am a complete and utter nitwit. Clearly I haven't thought this through."

"No, you have not."

"I cannot bear to have you angry. Please, all I ask is that you give me some time to set my affairs in order. If after a fortnight you still wish to return to Dunkeld, I shall accompany you home myself."

When he reached for her hand, she snapped it away. "Is there not someone else who can take me?"

He reached for her hand again and squeezed it between his palms. "I would trust your care to no one else. A fortnight. That's all I ask."

She shook her head.

"Please. Before the driver reins the horses to a halt. I must have your word."

She pursed her lips and gave him a heated glare, snatching her hand away again. "A fortnight, but you will promise not to ravish me again."

Throughout the duration of the carriage ride, all Geordie had been able to think about was locking the door to his chamber and making sweet love to Akira hour after hour. It would kill him to abstain.

"You must agree, or I'll have to insist you order an escort to take me back to Dunkeld with haste."

God, he adored her. No woman he'd ever met in his life would have been able to command him so—but he could deny Akira nothing. She might even turn him into a decent man—if such a thing were possible. "Agreed." Watching her eyes, he plucked a lock of her hair and plied it with a kiss. "I am yours to command, *mo leannan*."

Before Geordie had a chance to compose himself, the coach came to a halt. Geordie's gut clamped like a fist.

*Damnation!*

Dogs barked, Jane's and Alexander's high-pitched laughs carried through the window, while the servants clapped, shouting welcomes as they always did after he returned from a long journey. The coach door swung open.

"Your Grace!" A big grin spread across Oliver's pock-marked visage. "Praises be, you live."

"Was there any doubt?"

The man-at-arms stepped aside, allowing Geordie to alight. "Lord William said you disappeared after the first attack."

"I was shot in the leg. Left alone to drag myself under a patch of broom." Geordie motioned for Akira to take his hand. "If it weren't for this healer, I would have perished for certain."

Oliver bowed. "Pleased to meet you, miss."

"Ayres," she said. "Akira Ayres."

Geordie blinked. He'd never heard her utter her last name before—a Gypsy name for certain.

"Da! Da!" Jane and Alexander dashed down from the entry steps.

Ignoring the twinge of pain in his thigh, he hefted seven-year-old Jane onto one hip and clutched eleven-year-old Alexander around the shoulders. "There you are, my beautiful children. What mischief have you been doing whilst I've been away?"

"Mostly worrying about you," said Jane, tweaking his nose.

"Aye, even Mother returned from France." Alexander rolled his eyes. "Said I needed to be readied to take my place as the next duke, but I told her you weren't dead. I kent it right down to my toes."

Tongue-tied, Geordie shot a panicked glance toward Akira.

With a pronounced start, the lass clapped her hand to her chest, then scanned the courtyard—looking for a duchess, no doubt. Or was it she was overwhelmed by the fifty or so servants who'd come to greet him?

The fist in his gut sank to his toes. Dear God, could things grow worse?

Geordie set the children down and introduced them. "Please show Miss Akira to the suite of rooms in the east tower." He snapped his fingers at Byron, the valet. "Send a chambermaid to help Miss Akira settle in."

"East tower?" Jane complained. "But that's miles away."

*Thank God.* He gave his daughter a stern look. "Do it, I say—you, too, Alexander."

"But why can she not stay with me?" Jane asked.

"Because my word is law." Geordie clasped Akira's shoulder and turned his lips to her ear. "Remember what I said: Things will seem hectic at first, but pay it no mind. I will visit you in your chamber anon."

She eyed him with a wary glare while Jane tugged her arm.

The lass took her hand without hesitation, and skipped along at her side. "Come. I think you'll like the east tower. I'd stay there if Da would let me."

Geordie watched his Gypsy rose follow the children, admiring the sway of her backside as she climbed the entry steps. But one upward glance instantly cooled his lust. Elizabeth stood in the window of an upper chamber with her hands on her hips, glowering straight at him. The witch.

Holy hellfire, the last thing he needed was to face that dragon.

# Chapter Twenty-Two

Walking through the labyrinth of passageways and up and down the tower's spiral stairs, Akira was completely lost. Not to mention completely staggered by her exchange with Geordie in the carriage. If only there had been more time to discuss this ridiculous state of affairs, she might feel a bit more confident, but presently, she followed the duke's children with trepidation.

Lithe as a dancer, with taffeta skirts swishing around her long legs, Jane ran ahead, chattering like a finch while Alexander, a bit older, trailed behind with a very serious expression on his face—looking not unlike his father. Jane was fairer in complexion, with tawny tresses, whereas Alexander's hair was dark. Neither one of them had Geordie's eyes. Jane's were blue as the sky and Alex had brooding gray eyes.

As they proceeded, Akira caught glimpses of opulence. Alcoves sporting ornate vases and furniture too lavish to sit upon. Some walls were lined with rich silk tapestries, and others paneled with dark wood, displaying portraits of richly dressed men and women.

*Merciful fairies, Geordie must be as wealthy as a king.*

The deeper into the castle they walked, the more Akira's insides churned. What on earth was she doing there? Worse, it hadn't passed her notice that a woman stood in a second-floor window looking very angry. And Akira had no doubt it was the children's mother—*a duchess*.

"How on earth does one venture outside?" she asked. Mayhap she'd need to steal away, run far from Huntly so His Grace could never find her. Dear Lord, she was so lost, she wouldn't be able to make her way to Dunkeld if she tried, blast it all.

"There are plenty of doors everywhere," said Alexander from behind, speaking for the first time.

"Well, I'm impressed you children can find your way around so easily."

Jane glanced over her shoulder. "We go exploring all the time."

"Aye, we thought we'd lost Jane once. Unfortunately, Da found her in the turret of the west tower."

"Goodness, how awful to be lost in one's own home."

"I wasn't lost." Jane scrunched her nose at her brother and stuck out her tongue.

He gave her shoulder a playful shove. "Yes, you were."

With a snort, Jane proceeded with her nose in the air. "You only thought I was lost. I was having a tea party with the pigeons."

Before Alexander could come back with a testy remark, Jane opened a door and ushered them into a brilliant chamber.

Unable to breathe, Akira stopped inside the doorway.

"Do you not like it?" asked the heiress.

What was there not to like? The chamber shone as if lit by sunlight. The walls were painted white, with reliefs of birds and flowers in the arches near the ceiling, and white silk curtains framed a large bed. There was a marble hearth, two chairs, a table, a dresser painted white, an elegant settee, and more.

"'Tis amazing." Akira wandered between the furnishings and traced her finger along a brass candlestick, polished to such a sheen it seemed to glow.

"Ma's chamber is fancier," said Alexander, who hadn't moved from the doorway.

Akira's face grew hot. Was the heir upset about his parents' separation?

*Poor lad. I'm sure the tragedy affected him a great deal.*

She pressed her fingers to her lips and smiled. "I thank you and your parents for allowing me to stay for a wee while. And I'm happy to say your father's injury is healing nicely."

"What happened to him?" asked Jane.

"He was shot in battle. Took a musket ball to the thigh."

The door closed behind Alexander as he moved forward, his expression taking on a hint of interest. "Did it hurt?"

"My oath, it did." Akira sat on the settee and patted the cushions either side of her. "After the fighting ended, I ventured onto the battlefield with my healer's basket and heard your da moan—found him half-conscious under a clump of broom."

Eager to learn more, both children sat beside her and listened while Akira spun a tale of her battlefield surgery and their flight from the redcoats. She was careful to focus on her role as a healer and Geordie's recovery, and the pair seemed to warm to her.

Jane jumped up and twirled across the floor. "You must be the best healer in the whole world."

The lad puffed out his chest. "And Da took a shot to the leg whilst he fought off the bloody dragoons."

Jane stopped and jammed her fists into her hips. "Alex, I'm going to tell Mrs. Finch you were swearing."

Akira laughed. "I don't think His Lordship's curse was all that bad. After all, I would expect you pair to be terribly worried about your da."

Jane skipped back to Akira. "Oh, we were." She nodded at her brother. "We were, were we not?"

Alexander sniffed, his mouth forming a hard line. "Aye, and I'm angry with Ma for saying 'twas time to claim my inheritance." He shook his head vehemently. "I'm not ready to bury my father yet. I want him to live forever."

Akira patted the lad's shoulder. "Of course you do, m'lord." Sensing the need to change the subject, she leaned back and crossed her ankles. "So what do you like to do best?"

"I like drawing and riding my pony." Jane swayed from side to side, looking ever so much like Akira's youngest sister, Kynda. "Da gave me a bay garron for my birthday."

"You are a lucky lass, indeed." Akira turned her attention to the lad. "And you, Lord Alexander?"

He shrugged. "I've been learning swordplay from Master Oliver. He says I show promise. If I'm to be the next Duke of Gordon, I'd best ken how to defend my lands."

Akira regarded the stoic future duke. The lad spoke too much like an adult. "I'd like to watch your lesson sometime. I'm sure you're quite practiced."

"I am."

"Hello?" A chambermaid entered and curtsied. "I'm Fiona. His Grace has appointed me to your care."

Standing, Akira greeted the lass. "I hope we can become good friends."

"Och, you do not make friends with the servants," said Jane.

"And whyever not?" Akira didn't like that one bit. "Servants are God's children, placed on this earth just like you, lass. Take note of what I say. 'Tis important to treat everyone with respect, no matter their station."

"Even a beggar?" asked Alexander.

Akira gave him a stern eye. "Especially a beggar—for they have been met with the most unfortunate circumstances of all."

Jane twirled in a circle. "I've never thought of it that way afore."

Alexander sprang from the settee and yanked his sister's arm, practically knocking her off kilter. "Aye, and do not mention a word of it to Ma, else she'll become hysterical—ye ken how she flies off."

Jane rolled her eyes. "I ken."

Fiona pulled a bit of measuring ribbon from her apron pocket. "M'lord and m'lady, you'd best return to your lessons."

"Curses. Always lessons." Jane twisted her hands behind her back and focused her enormous blue eyes on Akira. "Will you watch me ride my pony later?"

"Certainly, I'd enjoy that."

After the children took their leave, Akira heaved a

sigh. Though endearing, they were both spoiled beyond imagination.

Fiona held up the ribbon. "His Grace has ordered a dozen gowns for you with all the trimmings."

"I beg your pardon?"

"'Tis what he said, and when the duke orders something, everyone must act swiftly, or there will be hell to pay."

Blinking, Akira regarded the chambermaid. *Does Geordie rule his castle with an iron fist?* "Is that so?"

Fiona ran the measure along the outside of Akira's arm. "Aye, no one ever crosses the Duke of Gordon, at least not in these parts."

Akira drummed her fingers against her lips. "Is that because there is hell to pay or because he is a generous man?"

"A bit of both, I'd reckon. Now, put your arms to your sides, please, so I can collect your measurements."

Akira did as asked, watching the lass. "Aren't you going to write them down?"

"Nay. I keep them in my head."

"Do you write?"

Fiona shook her head, a hint of shame in her eyes.

"Neither do I." Akira covered her giggle with her palm.

"Honestly?" Fiona bit her lip and grinned. "Do you mind if I say something familiar, miss?"

"Not at all—as I said, I hope we can become friends."

"What you said to the children about respecting folk—I trust you meant it. Do not take me wrong: Lady Jane and Lord Alexander are lovely children, but living in this grand castle, they cannot possibly understand how it is to be a... a commoner."

Akira nodded. "I thought so myself."

"Well, 'twas what they needed to hear and I'm glad you said it."

"Thank you." Akira sighed. Her mind in a total muddle, she was anything but glad about being at Huntly Castle. "You wouldn't know how long the duchess will be here?"

"No, miss. Except, now the duke has returned, I'd reckon not long."

Though she'd guessed the answer, she had to ask. "Why do you say that?"

"Did you ken they are divorced?" The maid spewed the word *divorced* like it was a curse.

"Aye."

"Well, when she left, the duchess said she couldn't even live on the same island as His Lordship." Fiona shook her head. "They used to argue something awful, too. And Her Ladyship oft grew so enraged she threw things. Nay, 'tis best if she returns to Flanders with haste."

* * *

Finally alone, Geordie removed his sword belt and weapons and slung them across his bed. Devil's spit, he was bone weary. He hadn't paid much attention to the wound in his thigh, but arriving home reminded him it still hadn't completely healed. A stack of missives awaited him on the table before the hearth. He sank into his overstuffed chair and reached for the first, sliding his thumb under the wax seal.

"I wish I could say it is good to see you, George." He could never mistake the loathed woman's English accent.

Geordie's skin crawled as if a rat had just skittered across the back of his neck. Elizabeth stepped out from the window embrasure—where she'd been lying in wait, no doubt.

He tossed the missive back on the table. "What the devil are you doing here?"

She smirked. "When word arrived that you were missing, and possibly killed in that vile Jacobite uprising, I had no recourse but to join my children."

He crossed his legs and arms. "Och, so you care about them when you think I'm dead."

She sniffed. "I always care about them."

"If only your actions stated the same."

"Good heavens. You're stirring that up again? Are you turning my children against me because I cannot tolerate your whoring?"

Christ, the woman could raise his ire like none other. "The children will always respect you as their mother. If there is any discord between you, it is on account of your own doing."

"My doing?" She flung her finger toward the window. "I see our despicable divorce did nothing to change your ways. You're still fornicating with any harlot who catches your fancy."

"Akira is a healer, damn you. She saved my life."

"I'm sure she did. In more ways than one." Elizabeth paced. "How could you allow your children to see you come back from the dead with a wench on your arm?"

"That wench to whom you just referred kept me from meeting my end on the battlefield." He sprang to his feet, throwing up his hands. "God on the cross, why am I bloody trying to explain this to you? Think what you like and leave my chamber."

With a cough, she drew a hand to her chest. "You are a barbarian, just like all Scots."

"Aye? Well, you are a self-absorbed prude." Geordie strode to the sideboard.

"Well, I've never—"

He removed the silver lid from a flagon. "What? Why don't you go back to Surrey and keep company with your father?"

"I prefer the convent. It seems, though I may be a duchess, I have no tolerance for mingling with dukes."

"That would be right." He poured himself a dram of whisky. "One prude cannot bear another."

"Stop!" She stamped her foot. "You are insufferable, and I refuse to tolerate another moment in your presence."

Geordie bowed and gestured toward the door. "Last I checked, this was my chamber. As a matter of fact, this is my castle. You are free to take your leave, Your Grace."

With a deep inhale, she thrust her nose in the air. "I've never been so insulted."

Geordie picked up his glass and saluted her. "I find that difficult to believe."

Elizabeth moved to the door, but stopped with her back to him. "I was hoping to propose a truce—to stay in the dower house—for our children. But I see that will not work. No. I shall return to Flanders."

Slamming the glass on the board, he gestured eastward. "Shall I arrange a coach to take you to the port?"

"A ship sails a fortnight hence." She regarded him over her shoulder.

"Very well, then." Geordie made an exaggerated bow and waited while Elizabeth flounced out the door.

*Good Lord, I must endure the dragon's presence for a fortnight?*

He quickly poured another tot and downed it in one gulp.

# Chapter Twenty-Three

The following day, wearing a new kirtle and arisaid that Fiona had laid out, Akira applauded as Jane jumped her garron pony over a small log. Honestly, the lass had far more skill with a riding crop than Akira, who had only her forced experience on the back of a horse. Jane expertly sat sidesaddle, too. Akira rubbed her thighs, still sore from their flight from Glen Spean. If only she'd had a sidesaddle, she mightn't be so sore. And she was nearly out of salve.

The groomsman beckoned the young lady and gave her some instruction. Akira leaned forward to better hear. Lord knew, when it came to horses, she could use every bit of advice she could find.

"There you are," came a deep voice from behind, a voice she'd never in her life be able to forget.

When she turned, however, she hardly recognized Geordie.

He looked every bit a duke, and nothing like the man

who'd accompanied her through the Highlands for the past fortnight.

Hopping to her feet, Akira dipped into a curtsy. "Your Grace, I was just watching Lady Jane demonstrate her horsemanship."

"Ah, she's reeled you in, has she?" The man grinned like Geordie, had shiny hazel eyes like Geordie, but he wore a brown velvet doublet over his shirt and sported an ornate cravat and cuffs of lace. Worse, atop his head he wore a periwig. Aye, all the gentry wore periwigs, but Akira never imagined Geordie in one. At least his kilt and hose were somewhat recognizable.

"Da!" Jane hollered, cantering in a circle. "Watch me jump the log."

His gaze swept to his daughter as a proud smile spread across his face. "Let us see how much you've progressed."

With a renewed look of determination, Jane jumped the log for the umpteenth time.

"Well done, lassie." Geordie strode forward and grasped the horse's bridle. "I am duly impressed."

The little girl beamed. "Thank you."

Geordie gestured to the groom. "When do you think she'll be ready for a higher jump?"

"Her Ladyship is ready, Your Grace. I just didn't want to make such a change before gaining your approval."

Akira's head swam. How on earth would she remember so many formalities? How stiff everything seemed. She far preferred her Geordie over the Duke of Gordon. It was as if the Highlander had transformed into a stiff marionette with his every action rehearsed. Even his stance appeared stiff and practiced.

Geordie patted the garron's hindquarters. "Very well,

you have my permission to raise the jump another six inches."

"Aw, but I'm ready to jump a whole fence, Da."

"You'll be ready when I say you're ready."

Jane jutted out her bottom lip, while the groom grasped the bridle and continued with the lesson.

As if remembering why he'd made an appearance on the grounds, Geordie held up his finger and grinned at Akira. Wee butterflies tickled her insides. Aye, that grin was more like the Highlander she knew. "I have something to show you."

"Oh? What is it?"

"Something I think you'll like. Come along." He offered his arm and they strolled across the pathway as if they were dancing an allemande—except for Geordie's limp. They walked toward a stone manse, every bit as large as Coll of Keppoch's home. "The servants haven't opened it yet, but I wanted to show you the dower house."

Her mouth dropped open. "That's the dower house?"

As they climbed the porch steps, a hundred thoughts popped into her head.

*Ma would be in shock. My sisters could gain so much from tutors, learning to ride, living away from the filth of Dunkeld...*

But something needled at Akira. "Why doesn't the duchess live here?"

He smirked, placing his hand on the latch. "Lady Elizabeth detests the sight of me. She'd rather cloister herself in a convent in Flanders—cannot even bear to stand on the same soil."

"But why? You are not only a duke, you have a kind heart. I just saw you with your daughter—you were kind and gracious like a father ought to be, and in turn, Lady Jane adores you."

"Unfortunately, I made too many mistakes when it came to Elizabeth. She's the daughter of the Duke of Norfolk. Her expectations were...Let's just say her expectations exceeded that which even the Almighty could have delivered." With a sigh, he opened the door.

Stepping inside, Akira nearly swooned. "Holy fairy feathers!" she mumbled, her gaze sweeping up to an enormous chandelier in the entry. Encrusted with innumerous crystals, it sparkled even without the candles lit. That piece alone must have cost an untold fortune. And on the floor, an oriental silk carpet in muted blue tones made the entry truly welcoming.

Geordie ushered her toward an open door. "To the west is the tapestry drawing room. When she was alive, my mother had it renovated in the French style." He pulled off a sheet of linen covering a chair embroidered in ivory with a leaf-and-rose pattern in the center and around the edges. "It will look a mite better once the dust covers are removed."

Akira didn't know what to say. The drawing room was every bit as opulent as any chamber she'd seen in the castle. And the tapestries were incredibly intricate, depicting scenes of lords and ladies picnicking, with trees and birds and oh, so many flowers.

"Do you like it?" Geordie asked.

"'Tis..." What should she say? She regarded his face—his eyes hopeful, his stance relaxed. Indeed, without anyone else around, he behaved more like Geordie and less like the pompous duke who'd appeared on the castle foregrounds. But Akira's spine wound tighter than a spring and her chest tensed. "I do like it. 'Tis fancier than anything I've ever dreamed of. However—" She turned away, clutching her hands over her heart.

When he moved behind her, the heat of his body radiated against her back. "However?" He placed his hands on her shoulders, big, strong hands that could wield a sword and fight for her freedom. Warm hands that had been tender with her and shown her love.

How could she deny him when he offered so much?

*I must.*

"This"—she gestured to the chamber—"doesn't feel right."

A deep cavern pinched between his eyebrows. "No? Whatever is bothering you, I can fix it. Is it this chamber? Is it too French? Is there not enough light? It will look so much better when the linens are removed, I promise."

"No." She whipped around and faced him. "This." She flung her arms to her sides. "Can you not see? I am but a poor maid. I live in a one-room shieling with my mother and three sisters. It has one small fire pit, one wooden table with two benches, and a dirt floor. I share a bed with my sisters—all four of us in one bed, whilst Ma sleeps on a pallet near the fire."

He blinked, as if trying to comprehend. "And you do not want to improve their lot in life?"

"Of course I want such comforts for them, and mayhap I'm being selfish, but I feel out of sorts. You're wearing a pompous periwig, a-and outside you were so inordinately stiff, I wanted to pinch you to see if you were the real Geordie." Akira clapped her hands to her head. "And since I've uttered your name, pray tell: How should I address you now we're in Huntly and you're the Duke of Gordon?"

"You—"

She cut him off with a slice of her hand. "I feel awkward. Fiona, my chambermaid, lives better than I do in Dunkeld. I should be fortunate to be employed as a servant carrying your slops." Tears burned behind her eyes and threatened to burst forth. "I'm a simple maid. A healer."

"I ken all that," he replied, ever so softly. "And those are the reasons I love you."

She covered her mouth with her hand, every nerve in her body firing at once. Her head spun. "Please, do not say it. How can a man like you love me?"

He clasped her hands between his warm palms. "Because you were kind to me when you didn't know who I was. You were gracious to *me*, not to a duke, and not because it was something I ordered but because you have a kind heart."

She closed her eyes and shook her head, a tear streaming down her cheek. "I would show such kindness to any man who needed my help."

"And that is what makes you so endearing." He pulled her into his embrace and pressed his lips to her forehead. "People have behaved respectfully to me all my life because I was born into an affluent family. It pains me to admit it, but women have fallen at my feet because I have the means to give them nice things—women who are as hollow as a gourd. But all those women left me soulless. Until..."

Inhaling deeply, he clutched her tighter against him. "Until I found you."

Unable to push away, Akira dropped her head against his chest. Must he be so warm, his arms so inviting, so soothing? *Curses.* Why did such action bring her so much solace at a time when she needed to be firm? "But you offered me payment to care for your wounds. You employed me."

"I did." With a gentle touch of his finger, he raised her chin. "And I need to make good on my debt."

"Aye," Akira agreed. No matter what happened, her family would need those ten shillings. "And you must take me home to my family." Stepping away, she covered her eyes with her hand, forcing herself not to cry. Regardless of how much she loved him, she didn't fit in at Huntly Castle—and in no way did she want to be looked down upon by the servants for being His Grace's mistress.

"I will take you home, and I aim to meet your family and bring them to Huntly, no matter how long it takes me to convince you to open your heart to me. And, remember, you promised me a fortnight."

Dear Lord, didn't he know the depth of her torture every moment she spent in his presence? "It is unduly awkward knowing the duchess is here."

"Aye, but she will keep to her rooms just like she has for years."

Akira wrung her hands. "What should I do if our paths cross?"

"I doubt they will, but perhaps I should have the dower house prepared now."

"You mean for me to stay in this enormous house alone?"

He waggled his eyebrows. "I'd be more than happy to sleep outside your door, m'lady."

She scoffed. "I could never ask you to do that."

Rolling his hand, Geordie bowed. "Or inside your chamber—ah—if it please m'lady."

*Goodness, now he's teasing me.*

"I am not a highborn lady, Your Grace."

"You are to me." He pulled her into his arms. "And,

please, when we are alone together, call me Geordie. It sounds best rolling off your tongue."

Akira's knees turned to butter as he gradually lowered his lips to hers and claimed her mouth. Restless desire pooled in her loins. Merciful heavens, how did she end up in this situation? She craved Geordie more than food, more than the flowers and butterflies or the air she breathed. Heaven's stars, keeping this man at bay would pose far more of a challenge than she'd first imagined. She'd allow him time as he'd asked, but then she must return to her family.

* * *

Geordie's blood boiled when he read a missive from the Privy Council condemning the Jacobite action in Hoord Moor as treason. The redcoats had attacked them, not the other way around. For the love of God, had all the gentry in Scotland gone soft?

"Your Grace." Oliver stepped inside the solar. "Forgive my intrusion, but a most interesting caller has arrived."

"Oh?" Tension flared up the back of Geordie's neck. It was odd to see his man-at-arms announcing a caller. Such a task was usually handled by his valet, Byron, unless the visit was of a tactical nature. "Who is it?"

"Captain Roderick Weaver of the Marquis of Atholl's Thirty-Second Dragoons."

To mask the sudden quickening of his heartbeat, Geordie calmly folded his missive and tucked it away inside his doublet. *Christ, the devil wasted no time.* "Did he state his business?"

"Was a bit aloof, I'd reckon. He said he had something to discuss only with you."

"Has he questioned anyone?"

"Not that I'm aware of, and I've been with him since he dismounted in the courtyard. He asked me if you've been away."

Willing his inner calm, the duke smoothed his hands over the table. "What did you tell him?"

"Exactly as we discussed. That you recently returned from a visit to your estate in Inverness."

"Very good." Geordie rapped his knuckles. "Bring Captain Weaver in and let us hear what he has to say."

"Straightaway, Your Grace."

Geordie held up a finger. "But do not allow anyone else in the household to speak to him—and make bloody certain Miss Akira remains out of sight."

"I'll see it done."

Standing, Geordie moved in front of the mirror and straightened his cravat. Then he regarded his periwig. It was a daft mass of curled horsehair, and he hated the damnable thing, even more so since Akira had drawn attention to it. Perhaps he would do away with wigs. He'd spent far too much of his life worrying about his appearance and not enough worrying about the people under his care. He chuckled to himself. How ironic that it took a wee healer to show him the error of his ways.

When the familiar sound of footsteps echoed in the passageway, George Gordon, the Duke of Gordon, took his seat and assumed his most haughty expression.

He'd certainly need it.

The door opened, and Oliver introduced the captain, then remained standing at ease near the door—though the Highland soldier's sword was at the ready.

The captain bowed. "Your Grace, 'tis reassuring to see you in good health this afternoon."

"Good health? I am but three and thirty. Why would my health be otherwise?" Dear God, he was well practiced at being an imperious aristocrat.

The captain tugged at his collar and stretched his neck. "Would you mind if I sat?"

"If your business will take more than a minute, then by all means." He gestured to the seat.

"Thank you. I am rather parched. I've been riding for days."

Geordie opted not to offer a refreshment. "Days? What on earth brings you to Huntly?"

The captain reached inside a satchel at his hip and pulled out Geordie's flask. "Did you lose this recently?"

"Ah." Reaching for it, he turned the gift from his father over in his hand. "My word, I thought this was gone forever. Where did you find it?"

Frowning, Captain Weaver crossed his arms. "In Hoord Moor on the battlefield—immediately following the skirmish where we cut off a mob of angry Jacobites. It seems Highlanders were not impressed with the queen's response to the Scottish Parliament's Act of Security."

"Indeed. Just this day I received a missive from the Privy Council regarding the upstarts."

Weaver pointed to the flask. "That's an expensive piece—one I'd think even a duke would cherish."

Geordie eyed the man with distrust. "I daresay, I agree." He rested the flask on the table.

"How did you lose it?" The bastard was digging.

But Geordie had concocted an iron-clad alibi. "'Tis embarrassing to admit, but I lost the flask at cards in Inverness. I had a slip of judgment and made a wager with the damnable thing. Whisky will do that to a man."

"You are aware your cousin William showed his colors at Hoord Moor?"

"I'd heard."

"Did you ride into battle with him, Your Grace?" The man asked the question as if he were asking if the sun rose that morning.

"Believe me, if I had ridden with my cousin, you would have kent about it afore the first shot was fired."

"Hmm." The captain scratched his chin. "I tracked one of the traitors from Hoord Moor all the way to Huntly."

Now Geordie knew the dragoon was fishing. He doubted very seriously Captain Weaver would have been able to track anything from Glenlivet onward. He feigned boredom. "That's quite a distance to follow a man. No wonder you have a thirst."

"Indeed. And the traitor has an injury."

Sniffing, Geordie leaned back with an aghast expression. "You mean to say you tracked an injured man near a hundred miles and were unable to catch up with him?"

Captain Weaver licked his lips. "'Twas a great deal more than a hundred miles—went over the mountains and up through Newtonmore. And he had an accomplice—some tinker lass."

Geordie's gut twisted. If this weasel intended to lay a hand on Akira, he would die a most painful death. He gripped his armrests and dug in his fingers. "I can assure you there have been no injured soldiers accompanied by tinkers or healers come through Huntly. Not in the past fortnight, not in the past month, not whilst I've been the Duke of Gordon."

The captain leaned forward. "May I make a request, Your Grace?"

"And what, pray tell, is that?" Geordie drew in an impatient breath, meeting the man's steely glare with one of his own. "Mind you, you are very near overstepping your station."

"Will you stand and walk to the door and back."

Feigning a fit of rage, the duke slammed his fist on the table. "Have you lost your mind? Asking a duke to parade around like a commoner? What the devil are you on about?"

"I think the injured man—the man who lost that flask—is you, m'lord."

Geordie shoved back his chair and stood, crushing his knuckles into the table. "How dare you come into my home and accuse me of raising the Gordon flag against Government troops. You, sir, have lost your quarry and have found no recourse but to blame the innocent." He gestured to his legs. "As you see, I am uninjured."

The man's eyes shifted, as if he was considering his next jibe.

Before the dragoon could spout another incriminating word, Geordie thrust his finger toward the door. "I must ask you to leave, sir."

The captain rose to his feet and bowed his head. "Forgive me, Your Grace."

Geordie took a couple of very sure steps to prove his point. "Lieutenant, please escort Captain Weaver off Huntly grounds."

"Straightaway, Your Grace."

The captain shoved his hat on his head and strode to the door. Before moving through, he stopped and regarded the duke over his shoulder. "Oh, there's one more thing."

Geordie raised his chin.

"If this traitor is you, I'll see to your beheading."

Narrowing his eyes, the duke took on a tone of deadly calm. "And I will have words with your superior officer regarding your insolence and outrageous accusations. Men have hanged for less."

Geordie stood his ground and waited until the footsteps faded down the passageway before he collapsed in his chair. Atholl's Captain Weaver was a damned bloodhound, no doubt out for fame and fortune. Worse? Geordie doubted this was the last he'd seen of the bastard.

# Chapter Twenty-Four

Wearing another new gown, this one of muted plaid, Akira took one last bite of porridge when a knock sounded at the door.

"Come—"

Not waiting for her to respond, the lord of the castle pushed inside. "Why are you not breaking your fast in the dining hall with the family?"

She glanced at her empty bowl. "I didn't want to intrude, Your Grace." Akira had taken a number of meals in the dining hall, but it was so stuffy, she'd needed a respite this morn.

"Of course 'tisn't an intrusion. Jane inquired after you, as did Alexander. The children are already enamored with you."

"But what of their mother?"

"I've told you, Lady Elizabeth will remain in her rooms."

"I find that quite odd, especially for Lady Jane and Lord Alexander."

"Bah, they are accustomed to their mother's reclusiveness. Besides, they're spending their afternoons with her." Geordie strode forward with a pronounced limp and pulled Akira up. "Anyway, that's not why I came."

"No?"

"My leg is needling me. I think you'd best have a look."

Was this the best excuse he had for visiting her chamber? Goodness, she applied the salve only last eve.

"Of course." Akira moved to the bedside table and picked up the pot. "I think 'tis time for me to pay a visit to the castle's herb garden. I left the avens roots I found in Glen Spean behind."

"You ken the formula?"

"I ken what Ma has taught me." She pulled off the stopper. "Tell me, do you have a healer at Huntly?"

"An old crow who uses far too much houseleek if you ask me."

Akira gestured to the chair. "Then I must prepare a batch of salve afore I return to Dunkeld."

He sat and held out his hand. "Before I forget, this is for you." A ten-shilling piece dropped in her palm. "We did have an agreement."

She closed her fingers around the coin and slid it into her pocket. "Yes, we did, and I thank you for remembering." The coin mightn't be important to him, but it was of utmost importance to Akira.

"And my valet tells me the dower house will be ready for you to move in on the morrow."

"Honestly, you shouldn't—"

He grasped her elbow. "'Tis already done. You'll have a host of servants and needn't worry about being alone."

A knot in her stomach churned. No matter what, she

could not continue living a lie. If she stayed, she'd never be able to regard herself in a looking glass without feeling shame. "Have you forgotten I'm returning to Dunkeld?"

"And have you forgotten I aim to convince you to bring your entire family back to Huntly?" He stretched out his leg and raised the hem of his plaid until he exposed the wound.

Licking her lips, Akira did her best to remain unmoved. Regardless, a memory of that muscular thigh rubbing against her own flesh made her pulse race. She glanced higher, all too aware of what lay hidden beneath the folds of wool. She busied herself with scooping her fingers around the inside of the pot. "It looks better today."

"It itches something awful."

"Ma always says that's a good sign—but you must take care. A musket ball to the leg might heal on the outside, but you mustn't push yourself. It will be at least six months before your limp completely goes away—and it could be far longer."

"Och, I'm hardly limping. I pulled the wool over the dragoon's eyes a few days ago. He had no idea I'd taken a shot to the leg."

She stilled her hand. "You didn't tell me a dragoon had been here."

"It wasn't worth mentioning. I threw the bastard out." He looked her in the eye and arched his brows.

"Did he suspect you?" Akira's heart skipped a beat.

"Aye, found my flask."

"What did you tell him?"

"That I'd lost the blasted thing in a wager in Inverness." He chuckled. "At least my flask has been returned. Da gave it to me when I reached my majority."

"The piece was dear, indeed." Akira gave his knee a pat and stoppered the pot. "Lady Jane has invited me to attend her writing lesson this morn."

"She has?" He chuckled. "Och, Jane is an affable lass. How do you feel about learning alongside a wee one?"

Akira shrugged. "I'd like to learn to read—even a little."

"Excellent." He rubbed his hand along her backside.

She shifted her gaze, trying to conceal the passion that might reflect in her eyes as a rush of desire pooled low in her belly. "The lesson starts soon. I was planning to head to the nursery after I finished breaking my fast."

"Then you'd best go." He glanced to the bed. "Else, I might have difficulty making good on my promise."

Goodness, Akira didn't have to ask him what he'd meant. For the past few days, simply having the big Highlander sitting in her chamber made tingles skitter across her skin.

Geordie stood and took her hand, his face growing dark, as if a shadow had passed over. He stroked his thumb along her bottom lip—so rough, but soft at the same time. Akira's insides trembled as she looked to the bed. Backing away, she willed her inner strength.

But the duke didn't give her a moment's respite. Staring into her eyes with a heavy-lidded hazel gaze, he followed, slipping his hands to her waist. A feral growl rumbled in his chest. "I ken I must wait until you invite me to your bed, but that does not mean I cannot kiss you, lass."

If a person could melt, Akira would have ended up a pile of mush, but Geordie pinned her against the tapestry, his powerful frame flush against hers. He placed one hand against the wall, the other slipping behind her neck. Then he lowered his lips and claimed her mouth in a bone-melting declaration of passion. Taking his time, he kissed her with domination and expertise, his body molding to her every curve, revealing the hard length of his desire.

Akira's head felt faint as he fluttered kisses along her neck and around her bodice. Somehow she regained a thread of strength and clasped his face between her hands. Breathing so deeply she was practically panting, she rose on her toes and gave him one last, long, luxurious kiss.

"You're going to bring me undone if you keep kissing me like that," she moaned, trying to keep her wits.

"Me?" Dear Lord, if only he knew how close she was to raising her skirts, they'd be on the bed in the blink of an eye. "I fully intend to, *mo leannan*."

His hand slid to the latch and, with a devilish chuckle, he slipped out the door.

Akira took a moment for her hot blood to cool, then patted the curls so expertly pinned by Fiona and headed for the nursery. Finding her way around the castle was becoming easier—at least she knew where to find her chamber, the dining hall, and the nursery. And at the moment that was enough.

At the end of the east passageway, a door closed behind her.

Heat prickled the back of her neck.

"If it is not the poor tinker who has stolen the duke's heart. I wondered when our paths would cross."

Akira stopped and turned, immediately dipping into a curtsy as was required when meeting a duchess face-to-face. "Your Grace."

The woman pursed her lips, looking every bit as haughty as Akira imagined a duchess would be. Her hawkish gaze swept from Akira's head to her toes. "You are pretty for a tinker."

"I beg your pardon?"

"Not to worry." The woman dismissed Akira's question with a flick of her wrist. "Lord Gordon will soon tire of you. He always tires of his whores."

Akira gulped as her ribs squeezed inward. How dare this woman insult her thus? "I am a healer."

"Oh, honestly, you are daft. Do you think a wee musket ball can do much damage to that bullheaded duke?"

"He was quite ill for—"

"A ruse to get you into his bed." With another wave of her hand, the duchess smirked. "George has a heart encased in iron. No lead musket ball to the leg could damage such a wretched soul. Mark me, he'd need a direct shot to the heart—and with an arrow tipped by nightshade."

Goodness gracious, the woman sounded as bitter as wormwood. "How awful. How can you say that about the father of your children?"

"My, you are young and naïve, are you not? 'Tis unfortunate the world is full of an endless queue of young women willing to give their innocence to that man for the promise of riches." Lady Elizabeth circled Akira as if she were assessing a slave on the auction block. "Tell me, how much did he pay you? Did he give you coin—or a ruby brooch like the last harlot?"

The ten-shilling piece in Akira's pocket practically burned a hole to her hip. "He paid me only for my healing service."

The duchess stopped. "So you admit to bedding him?"

"With all due respect, that is none of your concern."

"Never mind. No wench can resist the bastard. You are but an idler, a covetous tinker. I spotted your ruse from my chamber window the first time I laid eyes on you."

"I am not. I—"

"You cannot fool me." The woman tossed her head. "You have brought your immoral character into this house, and you are poorly influencing my children."

Akira squared her shoulders—she mightn't be as tall as this shrew, but she wouldn't be browbeaten by her. "I have done nothing of which I am ashamed."

The woman scoffed. "George just left your chamber with a grin on his face."

Stepping in, Akira met the duchess's accusations with a sneer of her own. "Mayhap because he has found happiness."

"No, because he's found another bit of quim for his cock." Folding her arms, Lady Elizabeth sniffed loudly. "Go back from whence you came, and leave my family in peace."

Completely ignoring decorum, Akira blinked back tears as she whisked past the duchess and dashed for her chamber door.

"You do not belong here," the woman shouted after her.

Pushing inside, she turned the lock, then dashed across the room and flung herself onto the bed. Before allowing herself to wail, she shoved her face into a pillow, and then let loose a silent scream that grated and burned her throat.

Akira had met rude and obnoxious people before, but Lady Elizabeth was the absolute worst, most hideous, nastiest person in all of Scotland. How could a woman who had brought children into the world be so evil?

Rocking back and forth and clutching the pillow over her mouth, Akira sobbed, her tears blinding. Aye, she was a simple lass, but she was a person with feelings. She always tried to help and show kindness to others. Even if the duchess wanted to warn Akira about Geordie, she could have been nicer about it. With her next thought, Akira's stomach twisted. She had heard only the duke's side of the story. Was he responsible for turning that woman into a shrew? Lady Elizabeth was born into privilege. Could have anything she wanted. A woman of her stature should be gracious and kind, yet she'd become bitter as hops. Was there a side to George Gordon that Akira had not yet seen?

She curled into a ball. What was she doing in Huntly? Geordie—the *duke*—no longer needed her. He said he had a healer and a physician, too. His wound was well on the way to recovery and free from fear of worsening.

She'd told Geordie she didn't fit in, that she felt awkward, and he'd ignored her.

Sir Coll had alluded to Geordie's philandering, and Geordie himself had said he'd been akin to a libertine. But she hadn't imagined he'd entertained many mistresses.

Her throat closed.

*How many women?*

And he asked Akira to be his mistress? Asked her to live near him so she could be his lover? And Lady Elizabeth freely admitted he has never been faithful. How long would it be before he grew weary of her and cast her aside like her stepfather did to her mother?

*Dear God, what am I doing?*

Akira wiped her eyes on her sleeve and struggled to steady her breathing.

*I cannot remain here for another minute.*

Springing from the bed, she grabbed her satchel and stuffed the bread from her meal inside. After pinning her arisaid around her shoulders, she ran for the stables.

# Chapter Twenty-Five

Geordie stood with Oliver in Huntly's courtyard, watching the guard spar. "What news from this morn's scout of the grounds?"

Oliver threw his thumb over his shoulder. "Deer spotted to the north."

"No redcoats?"

"You would have been the first to hear about it if any had been seen, Your Grace."

Heaving a sigh, Geordie felt his shoulders relax. He'd been so bloody tense. The captain's visit was enough to rile anyone. Add that to the tension of seeing, smelling, kissing Akira and holding her in his arms, yet forcing himself to abstain from carrying her to a bed...or the floor...or the wall. Indeed, he'd not slept well for all the delicious thoughts of how he could have her. Oh yes, when she finally made up her mind to move her family into the dower house, they would enjoy every position he could imagine.

"Is your leg still ailing you, Your Grace?"

Geordie blinked, snapping himself from his wayward thoughts. "'Tis coming good. Why?"

"By the look on your face, I reckon something isn't sitting well."

"There are a number of things on my mind." Geordie looked up as Elizabeth came into sight across the courtyard. She walked toward them, a haughty smirk on her face. "Right there is one of them," he mumbled under his breath.

Oliver chuckled. Bless him, the soldier had stood beside Geordie through the roughest of times.

"George, I'm surprised you're not out there sweating with your men-at-arms. You're not one to hide your brawn." The woman didn't try to hide her contempt, either, not even in front of his man-at-arms.

He'd been continuing to spar with a wooden post until he completely healed. In no way did he want to appear weak in front of his men, especially since they all knew him to be deadly with a blade. Forcing a smile, he bowed his head. "After seeing you this afternoon, Elizabeth, I just might go a few rounds with Oliver."

She glanced at the lieutenant. "You'd best not push him too hard. The wench tells me George is still weak from his injury."

Oliver bowed. "I assure you, the duke can hold his own, Your Grace."

She grimaced. "I'd guessed no less."

A cold sweat broke out across Geordie's skin. The witch had spoken to Akira? "What have you been up to?"

"Nothing untoward." She batted her eyelashes. "Perhaps clearing the castle of vermin."

"If I discover you've—"

"Save your breath, George. Your threats are useless

with me." With a swish of her skirts, the nasty excuse for a duchess flounced into the castle.

Geordie shifted his gaze to Oliver. "Do you ken what she's on about?"

The man-at-arms held up his palms. "Nay—and I'll not venture near that woman. Ye ken my opinion, Your Grace. The castle was far better off the day she left for the convent."

Clenching his fists, Geordie turned toward the east tower. Jane's writing lesson should have ended hours ago. "What are the children up to?"

"I'm not their governess. 'Haps you should ask Mrs. Finch."

His gut clamped into a hard ball. The hairs on the back of Geordie's neck stood on end. "And where's Akira?"

"That, too, Your Grace. I suspect you'd ken the lassie's whereabouts better than I."

"Jesus Christ, the ship to Flanders cannot sail soon enough." He thrust his finger toward the men. "Spread out. Search the grounds for Miss Akira." He pulled his pocket watch from his doublet. "I'll meet you back here in a half hour."

A furrow creased Oliver's brow. "Ye think the lass has gone missing?"

"I have an ill feeling, and I hope to God I'm wrong."

* * *

After finding Akira's chamber empty and discovering she had not attended Jane's lesson, Geordie could have jumped out of his skin. It was still too early for the men to have returned from their perimeter search, so he raced to the stables.

The groom, Fionn, poked his head out of a stall. "Are you looking to ride, Your Grace?"

"Aye. Have you seen Miss Akira?"

"She took one of the garron ponies out this morn. Said she longed to feel the wind in her hair."

"Are you mad?" Geordie stomped his booted foot. "Miss Akira is no horsewoman. Why was I not informed?"

Fionn spread his palms, with a daft, dumbfounded look on his face. "Apologies. I didn't ken you wanted me to watch her so closely, Your Grace."

"In which direction did she ride? Did she seem upset? Was she crying? Were her eyes red?" He slammed his fist against the wall. "Answer me, man."

"Ah—ah, now you mention it, I reckon she might have been a wee bit upset." The idiot's head bobbed like a puppet. "Aye, her hands were shaking when I handed her the reins."

"Bloody hell!" Geordie kicked a pile of straw. "Saddle my horse immediately and take him to the courtyard. I need a blanket and food supplies for a dozen men, and I need them in the courtyard faster than you can blink."

"Straightaway, Your Grace."

"Do not stop to breathe." He shook his finger. "I mean it. We ride at once."

Geordie scanned the grounds as he hastened toward the courtyard. Oliver and the search parties were galloping back to the castle. At least the man-at-arms understood the need for urgency. But Geordie could have sworn someone had stacked a load of bricks on his chest. Akira wasn't with them.

*Damn that evil duchess to hell!*

Oliver rode in the lead and Geordie met him at the

gates. "Gather your gear and a retinue of twelve men. We're riding after her." He pointed to his sergeant-at-arms. "Mr. Wallis, take the duchess to Aberdeen and lock her in a chamber at the Boar's Inn until the bloody ship sails."

"The duchess, Your Grace?"

"I hereby place that woman under arrest. We're divorced, and she's trespassing on my lands. Guard her until she sets sail for Flanders." He thrust his hand in the direction of Elizabeth's window. Doubtless the wretched vixen lurked in the shadows, enjoying Geordie's fury. "Now go and do my bidding. And make certain Mrs. Finch is overseeing the children. Dear God, one of you will pay if anyone else I love goes missing."

# Chapter Twenty-Six

Akira's thighs already chafed. She had told the stable hand to give her a standard saddle, because she'd gained a certain amount of confidence riding astride. And this would be a long journey. During idle talk, Fiona had said it was a hundred miles to Dunkeld.

The problem?

She had no idea where she was headed. All she knew was to travel south, and she turned down the southward road at the end of the Huntly drive.

As the afternoon wore on, howling wind swept through the trees, and dark clouds formed overhead. It turned cold, as autumn afternoons often did, and Akira had pinned her arisaid tight around her shoulders.

Without another soul in sight, every rustle through the trees made her jump. She tugged the reins too tight and the horse slowed. When she gave him a tap of her heels, he sidestepped. Remembering Geordie's instruction, she loosened the reins and her seat. The pony dropped his head and his movement grew smoother, as it had been when they'd first set out—when she'd been more certain of what she was doing.

Gradually, the sky grew darker and doubts shot through her mind. Perhaps she should have talked to Geordie first. But then he would have showered her with declarations proclaiming his philandering ways were over. Doubtless, his heavy-lidded gaze and his deep voice would have turned her insides to warm honey, and she wouldn't have been able to think straight.

It was difficult to believe all the horrid things the duchess had said about him.

*Geordie couldn't be that awful, could he?*

But then, he'd kept his identity hidden from her for so long. What was she to think of his ruse? Was he a liar? Heaven's stars, Akira hadn't encountered enough men to know what to believe. Her heart told her Geordie was a good man, but the man who hurt Ma was supposed to be good, too.

Akira needed her family, needed Ma's wisdom, needed the security of the shieling. It might be shabby, but it was home. There she was loved. There she knew her place.

A streak of lightning flashed through the sky. Every muscle in Akira's body tensed. The horse skittered. Akira cowered at a booming roll of thunder. The wind blew harder and the trees rustled and popped. With the next bolt of lightning, the sky opened, sending sheets of rain pouring down.

*Boom!*

The thunder pealed like God had spoken. The garron reared and broke into a gallop.

Akira flopped in the saddle, her feet slipping out of the stirrups. "Whoa!" she shouted, tugging on the reins, but the pony ran as if they were being chased by Satan himself. Light burst around them over and over again, while rain pelted Akira's face and soaked through the weave of her woolens.

"Stop!" she screamed, her feet fumbling blindly for the stirrups.

Ahead, something dark sprang from the forest straight into their path.

Akira clutched her fingers around the reins.

The horse's croup dipped low.

She leaned forward to keep her balance.

Skidding, the gelding whinnied and reared.

Squeezing her knees, Akira closed her eyes, willing herself to stay on. The wet, slick saddle proved too slippery. Her grip failed and her body soared backward through the air as her mouth opened, releasing a bloodcurdling shriek.

She hit mud, and water splashed around her.

A deep voice cackled with a hideous laugh. "Och, we've found a wee lassie." A big ugly brute with hairy legs sauntered toward her, flanked by a pair of scraggly thugs grinning like they were looking at warm Christmas pudding, while the rain plastered their hair to their heads.

Ice pulsed through her blood as Akira scooted backward. "Leave me be." She might need a guide, but every jumping nerve in her body told her these men were up to no good.

The leader narrowed his gaze. "What are you doing out here in this squall?"

"And alone?" asked another.

Akira eyed her horse, standing beneath a sycamore not ten feet away.

The men stepped closer.

Bearing down with all her weight, she sprang to her feet, dashing for the garron.

Curses, her wet skirts were heavier than armor. Clenching her teeth, she forced her legs to pump harder.

Brutal arms wrapped around her, tackling her to the ground. "Och, that's my horse now, wench," a vile voice growled.

Akira's chin hit hard. Twisting and kicking, she fought to free herself from the man's grasp, but the more she struggled, the tighter his arms clamped around her body. Shrieking, she rolled and slapped him across the face.

"Bitch!" The thug hit her back.

Her teeth rattled as stinging pain seared across her cheek. The iron taste of blood filled her mouth. "Get off me!" She bucked, fighting futilely.

Lying atop her back, he groped her body with one hand, shoving his fingers into her pocket. He flipped her over and held the coin in front of her face. "What have we here?" He gave her a black-toothed grin—breath that stank of moldy mutton. "Where did you come by this?"

"'Tis my payment from the Duke of Gordon." She prayed that using Geordie's title would put some fear in the scoundrel's heart. Wrenching a hand free, she reached for it, but he was faster. "Please. I need that coin for my family."

"I reckon I need it, too." A sickly grin spread across his lips as his eyes bore into hers while crushing her with his chest. Then the blackguard tugged her skirts. "And you're too bonny not to poke."

The men laughed. Black, ugly cackles. "I'm next," one said.

*No, no!*

Akira kicked and gasped for air. Rain stung her eyes.

He lowered his gruesome, bearded face and licked her mouth as he yanked her skirts higher. Thrashing her head from side to side, she wouldn't give up the fight. "No! No! No! No! The duke will kill you for this!"

"Aye? Where is his army?" asked one of the braggarts.

Cold air blew over her inner thighs and up where it never should be. Dear God, why did she race away alone?

The brute seized her wrists with one hand and pinned them above her head. With the other, he reached down and grasped himself.

A musket fired, making her ears ring. One of the highwaymen fell.

In a blink, the thug atop her sprang to his feet, dagger at the ready.

Another blast, and the awful man clutched his chest, dropping gape-mouthed beside her.

Howling, the third man ran into the wood.

Too terrified to move, Akira curled into a ball, clutching her arms over her head. "Please do not kill me."

A pair of black boots stepped up to her. "Well, well. Let me guess. You're Akira Ayres from Dunkeld." She remembered hearing this man's voice once before. Below the outcropping. He had an English accent, filled with menace.

Her hands trembling like the saplings in the storm, Akira regarded the dead felon beside her, then shifted her gaze to the red-coated dragoon, slapping a riding crop in his palm. "Who are you?" she asked.

He tapped his hat with the crop. "Captain Roderick Weaver, and I've been following your trail for weeks."

She shook her head, hiding her face in her palms while praying for a miracle. Anything she might say could incriminate Geordie.

The rain slowed to a drizzle, but she was bone cold. Out of the corner of her eye, a bit of metal flashed. Her coin rested a few feet away.

"Answer me, wench."

She edged toward the coin. "W-why have you been following me?"

He laughed—an evil cackle as menacing as the felon. "Playing dumb, are you? Well, it won't work with me."

Nearly close enough to reach the coin, she stretched for it, but her fingers filled with nothing but mud. "I would think a captain would have far better things to do than traipse after a healer."

"Keep your hands where I can see them."

Quickly drawing her fingers back, she held up her palms with a forlorn backward glance. "Why? Do you think I can outsmart an officer?"

He pointed to one of his men. "Slap a set of manacles on her wrists." Then he smirked at her. "You're under arrest."

"What for?"

"Aiding a fugitive."

"I did no such thing. I'm merely a healer." Cold iron closed around her wrists, locking closed.

The officer pulled her to her feet. "Do you admit to helping the Duke of Gordon escape?"

Goodness gracious, what should she say? "I have no idea who that is, sir."

"I didn't think you'd squeal easily." He thrust his finger toward the garron. "Sentinel Grey, help the prisoner mount." He pointed to two other dragoons. "You pair, shove those bodies off the path and cover them with broom."

Pulled by the sentinel, Akira stopped and yanked her wrists away. "You're not planning to bury them?"

"We've no time for that." The captain marched to his horse and mounted. "We ride."

The dragoon grasped her elbow, led her to the horse, and gave her a leg up. "Where are you taking me?"

Running his reins through his palm, the captain sneered. "To stand trial in Inverness."

*Merciful Father, no.* "For being a healer?"

"Shut it," sniped Grey.

As they rode away, the captain's horse trampled over the glistening silver coin.

# Chapter Twenty-Seven

Geordie's gut turned over when they found two dead men shoved under a clump of broom alongside the road. Though he'd seen his share of death and brutality, coming upon the evidence of murder was an ugly state of affairs, and he prayed to the Almighty they had misread Akira's tracks.

He held up his hand, stopping his men well away from the soupy pandemonium of footprints. "Halt."

After dismounting, Geordie and Oliver examined the corpses.

"Shot at close range, I'd reckon," said the lieutenant, pointing to the blood-soaked clothing.

"Aye, and from their ragged clothes and the stench, I suspect this pair of highwaymen attacked the wrong pigeon."

Oliver scratched his head. "Or set of pigeons. There's tracks everywhere."

"Why would a pair of bedraggled thieves attack a group of riders?"

"Must have been desperate, Your Grace."

No more than five paces away, a coin caught Geordie's eye. He stooped to pick it up. "I'll be damned."

Oliver peered over his shoulder. "What is it?"

"I gave a ten-shilling piece just like this to Akira just this morn."

"Do you think it's hers?"

"God, I hope not." He looked down the pathway. "I hope she traveled through before all this occurred."

Oliver moved around the stretch of road, studying the tracks. "Bloody hell, these prints are so soupy it's near impossible to discern a thing." He walked up the fork in the road leading northeast, and pointed. "Och, I'd reckon the men who killed these sorry souls headed toward Inverness."

A lead ball sank to Geordie's toes. "What about Miss Akira?"

Oliver shook his head. "Lord only kens."

"Beg your pardon, Your Grace," said an obsequious voice from nowhere. A disheveled beggar stepped from behind a sycamore, hunched over in a bow as if he were addressing the queen.

"Who the devil are you?" Geordie asked.

Oliver pulled his dirk and stood between the duke and the wastrel. "Take one more step and you'll end up in hell with your mates."

The man held up his palms, his eyes shifting. "The wench said she'd earned that coin from the Duke of Gordon. I reckon that would be you, m'lord."

A rush filled Geordie's ears and his pulse raced. Shoving past Oliver, he grabbed the tinker by the throat, his fingers digging into flesh like iron teeth. "Where is she, goddamn you?"

Spittle bubbled from the man's lips as he struggled to speak, his face turning red.

"Ye might want to ease your grip a bit, Your Grace," Oliver said from behind.

Snatching the man's arm, Geordie wheeled him around and wrenched his wrist up his back. "Where is she?"

The cur licked his lips, squirming futilely. "I reckon I need payment afore I say another word."

"You're in no position to negotiate." Clenching his teeth, Geordie wanted nothing better than to slam his knuckles into that scraggly-bearded jaw. He forced the arm higher. "If you value your life, you'll not waste another breath before you tell me what happened."

The man scrabbled his feet with no effect. "We didn't mean nothing."

"Spill your guts, you flea-bitten sheep-swiving maggot." Shifting his hold, Geordie snatched his dirk and held it to the man's throat. "I'll ask you once more. Where. Is. The lass?"

"We just wanted her coin...but Illiam was aiming to give her a good poke when a mob of rutting dragoons shot him. Shot my brother, Clach, too."

Geordie pushed the dirk hard enough to draw blood. "You violated her?"

"Nnnnnn-no, Your Grace. They shot Illiam afore he could give it to her."

Geordie's stomach turned over with revulsion. "I ought to slit your pitiful throat and rid the world of your stench."

The man shied. "But I c-c-can tell you more, Your Grace."

Geordie tightened his grip, holding his dirk firm. "I'm listening."

"It was them redcoats. They tried to make her confess

about helping you." He licked his lips and glanced downward. "Then they slapped a set of manacles on her and took her with them."

A cannonball sank from Geordie's gut down to his toes. *Captain bloody Weaver.* "Where are they headed?"

"The officer said Inverness to stand trial."

*Good God.* Geordie looked to Oliver. "We have to stop them before they reach the city."

"Aye." Oliver inclined his head toward the prisoner. "What do we do with him?"

Releasing his grip, Geordie shoved the man to the mud. "Let him go."

The beggar bumbled to his feet. "Please. Give a poor man a shilling for his good deed."

Geordie jammed his dirk in its scabbard. Never in his life had he wanted to kill a man in cold blood, but if decency hadn't been drilled into him since birth, he'd have run his blade across this varlet's throat. For the love of God, the man had been all too ready to violate the love of his life. He abhorred such cowards.

Tipping up his chin, he regarded the beggar, his blood near boiling. "You've received ample payment this day." He sauntered forward and gripped the man's cods, squeezing them in his fist. The ruffian squealed like an adolescent lad, and that only made Geordie squeeze harder. "If you ever even think of violating another woman again, I will hear of it," he growled through clenched teeth. "And I will not rest until your ballocks are sliced off and shoved down your throat afore I drain your life's blood from your miserable body."

Again he shoved the cur away.

"Come, men. We ride!"

# Chapter Twenty-Eight

Akira opened her eyes to an eerie mist shrouding the clearing. Curled in a ball, she'd done her best to stay warm throughout the night, but her efforts had been futile and sleep fleeting. Now, her stomach roiled, and an uneasy prickling of her scalp hinted at impending danger. Was someone watching her? She glanced at the muted outlines of the sleeping dragoons, still snoring as if they hadn't a care. Even the captain's chest rose and fell with his steady breathing.

The remains of the fire smoldered.

Something snapped.

Akira gasped, her gaze darting through the fog, squinting as she tried to make out figures in the shadowy brush. Everything looked alive. Everything rustled and moved with the wind. Her heart pounded in her ears like the steady beat of a distant drum. The breeze swept a strand of hair across her face. Brushing it aside, she saw movement.

She clapped her hand over her mouth, stifling an urge to scream.

The mist hadn't played a trick on her this time. An enormous man crouched but ten feet away.

Gooseflesh rippled across Akira's skin. Had her prayers been answered? Or was this a band of outlaws come to finish her off for the murder of their kin?

A gust of wind caused the mist to lift a bit.

*Dear God!* Her heart fluttering, Akira rose to her elbow.

Geordie held his finger to his lips, then panned his hand across the perimeter of the camp.

Holy Moses, the Gordon guard had them surrounded. Highlanders dressed in dark plaid with navy bonnets pulled low over their brows crouched among the trees like ghosts, ready for battle.

Nodding her understanding, Akira curled into a tighter ball.

Geordie sliced his hand through the air.

A deafening war cry boomed through the clearing and Clan Gordon burst through the mist, brandishing their weapons.

Jolted from slumber, the dragoons hastened to their feet, grabbing for their swords.

High-pitched screams shrieked.

The wind picked up, while the clearing erupted in a frenzy of fighting. Steel scraped, and muskets fired with blinding flashes of light.

The captain ran for the horses, disappearing into the fog.

Bellowing like a madman, Geordie barreled after him. "You'll not slink away like a coward!"

Akira scrambled to her feet, hugging her shackled wrists against her chest, as a gust swept the mist away.

Ahead, two men circled, crouching low, swords drawn and ready to strike.

The captain lunged, stabbing with his saber.

Akira screamed.

Fast as lightning, Geordie dodged the blade and countered with a kick.

The captain's arms sprawled out as he stumbled straight toward her.

Before she could run, he snatched her arm and spun her into his body, pressing the sharp point of his sword to her neck.

She twisted against his powerful hold, but the tip of the sword sliced into her flesh. With a hiss, she bared her teeth, leaning back, her head stopped by an unyielding shoulder.

The blackguard tugged her backward toward the horses. "Stop struggling," he growled. "Unless you want your throat cut."

Geordie followed, his eyes blacker than coal. "You're far outnumbered. Let the lass go and I'll spare you."

"Not on your life," the captain hissed. "This filly is my ticket to lands and riches, and now that you've attacked me, I have proof that you were the bastard who lost the flask at Hoord Moor."

His lips curling, Geordie stepped nearer. "You can prove nothing."

Akira flexed her fingers, waiting for her chance to break free.

Roderick's body shook against her back as he cackled. "I can, and the Marquis of Atholl will see to it the queen grants me title and lands."

Geordie's gaze turned deadly. "Miserable, bleating gold-digger."

A click sounded.

Akira glanced up, shifting only her eyes lest her throat be sliced open.

Oliver held a pistol to the captain's head. "Take one more step and it will be your last."

With a sideways strike, Geordie snatched the saber's hilt from the officer's grasp, shoving it away from Akira's throat.

Gasping, Akira dashed to Geordie's side, and clung to his arm.

Not taking his eyes off his quarry, the duke inclined his head toward her. "Are you all right, lass?"

"Aye," she said, trembling and only able to utter a single word.

With a low growl, Geordie pressed his lips against her forehead, then nudged her behind him. He moved to within a hand's breadth of the officer, towering over him.

"I don't give a shite if you are a duke, you're a rutting Jacobite."

Springing forward, the duke slammed his fist into the captain's jaw. "Someone tie up this bastard afore I lose my temper and carve out his tongue."

One of the Highlanders bound the captain's wrists, patted him down, and removed his weapons. All around the clearing, Gordon clansmen held the dragoons at bay by the points of their swords and bayonets.

"How does it feel to ken I hold your life in my hand?" Geordie paced around his quarry, whipping the saber through the air. "You'll swear never to plague me or my kin ever again."

The man spat. "You're a disgrace to the gentry."

Snarling, Geordie grabbed the back of the captain's neck and shoved the saber against the side of his mouth.

"Swear it, or I'll string you up by your neck and make you watch as your men die!"

Gasping, Akira clapped her hands to her cheeks. She'd never heard Geordie sound so utterly terrifying.

Captain Roderick Weaver bared his teeth. "Spare my men."

"Swear to me now, you cur. Unless you want to witness each of your men's butchering, you will sign a proclamation stating that I was visiting my lands in Inverness during the time of the Hoord Moor rising and that you are satisfied with my testimony and the witnesses' account of my whereabouts."

The man hesitated.

Geordie pointed to one of his Highlanders. "Dirk the first!"

Akira's stomach turned over. *Geordie, no!*

"Jesus Christ, captain. Sign the bloody note!" shouted a dragoon as a Highland dirk leveled at his throat.

"Stop!" The captain held up his bound wrists. "I'll sign your daft proclamation."

Geordie pushed the blade until blood streamed down the man's chin. "And swear on your mother's life you will never again set foot on Gordon lands."

"I swear, goddammit. Tell your bloody men to stand down." The man's eyes shifted. Akira trusted him no more than she'd trust a mouse not to swipe a morsel of cheese.

Lowering the sword, Geordie shook his head. "Clan Gordon will remain as they are until I secure your signature on a bit of parchment."

Akira watched while Geordie pulled writing materials from his saddle bags and used his horse's rump as a makeshift table. All the while, Oliver held his pistol to

Captain Weaver's head. The duke carried out the signing with expert efficiency—like a man born to lead—forcing the captain to sign with his wrists bound.

After the proclamation was signed and sealed, Geordie demanded the key to Akira's manacles. He allowed the dragoons to mount their horses and ride away without so much as a wee knife to spear their food. The duke even kept the pack mule with the soldiers' supplies.

It wasn't until the sound of hoofbeats disappeared that Geordie turned his attention to Akira.

He focused on her with the intensity of a man who knew what he wanted and would fight heaven and hell to achieve it. His eyes were dark, the hard line to his mouth set, and a tic twitched in his stubbled jaw. Watching him while he released her shackles, she'd seen him angry, but she'd never seen him this determined, his posture taking on unquestioned command.

A shudder coursed through her soul when he grasped her hand and pulled her into the wood, his limp hardly noticeable. Her mind raced. What would he do? Would he unleash his anger upon her? Her heart hammered a rapid rhythm. Oh, for the love of everything holy, she wanted to wrap him in her arms and tell him how much she loved him. But too many warring thoughts muddled her mind. She must hold fast to the reason she fled. She must hold fast to her values, no matter how much his rugged allure disarmed her.

His grip on her remained firm until they reached a trickling burn.

When he stopped, the intensity of his gaze grew even darker.

She absolutely had to make him understand. "I—"

He pulled her into a powerful, consuming embrace.

"My God, Akira, I never want to be so worried as long as I live."

Filled with a surge of relief, she flung her arms around him. His warm, solid presence infused her with strength. "I-I-I wasn't thinking when I left."

"You could have been killed."

"I ken that now." Tears welled in her eyes as she clung to him for dear life. "The captain was taking me to Inverness to try to force me to betray you." She shook her head against his chest. "But I would not. I could never ruin you. I would have marched up the gallows steps afore I told them anything."

His fingers kneaded her back, a wee tremor in his strong hands. "Och, you are such a brave lass. I believe you would take a shot to the heart to save any poor soul."

She rested her head against his chest, the thrum of his heart so soothing. If only she could listen to that reassuring beat for the rest of her days. "But I was so afraid."

He smoothed his big hand over her hair. "Of course you were. Anyone would have feared for their life with that festering maggot threatening them."

Squeezing her hands tighter around his sturdy form, Akira drew him even closer. "How did you find me?"

"I will always find you. You are in my soul." He cupped her cheek with his palm and lowered his lips to hers. Filled with urgency, his kiss grew demanding and greedy. Akira's body came alive. Her breasts pressing against his hard chest ached to feel his warmth, to remain forever cradled in his protective arms. Heat spread through her center, and she moved her hips forward, craving more touch, craving more of him.

His body responded in kind as his hardness bored

through layers of wool. "I want you more than I want the air I breathe."

She sighed deeply, closing her eyes and savoring him. "I wish it could be true."

"'Tis more truthful than anything that has ever slipped past my lips." He grasped her shoulders and gazed into her eyes. "Why did you leave me, lass?"

She blinked in rapid succession—she hated to utter it, but she must reveal the truth. She must lay her feelings before him and endure the consequences. "The duchess said you didn't love me—that you've had many mistresses and always tire of them."

He bared his teeth with a hissing grumble. "God's teeth, that woman has caused me a lifetime of consternation. You needn't worry, she will not bother you again."

"No?"

"She's under arrest in Aberdeen, and when she sails for Flanders, I pray she never returns to Scotland again." He wrapped Akira in his arms, his embrace protective and loving. "Come back to Huntly with me. I need you. And there could be no other. Ever."

Akira closed her eyes, her heart breaking. She needed Geordie as well, more than the food she ate and the water she drank. But first she must ask one more question—one she dreaded. "Return as your mistress?" she whispered, praying there was another way.

He sucked in a breath. "Och, ye ken I cannot remarry."

A hollow bubble spread throughout her chest. Did he not love her enough to seek out some other course of action, another possibility? He was a *duke*. Could he not have word with a priest or the queen? Or was their love truly not important enough to him? The words formed on her lips, though Akira closed her eyes and bolstered her courage before she spoke. "Lady Elizabeth called me a whore and she was right. If I agree to be your mistress, I would be your whore."

Despair filled his hazel eyes. "Nay. You would be the love of my life. And you would want for nothing."

With a shake of her head, Akira cast her gaze downward. "I'd be a woman you could cast aside at any moment when a younger, prettier face struck your fancy." Dear God, her heart tore with every word.

"What the devil?" His voice took on a tremor. "That blasted woman spoke to you for all of five minutes and managed to completely turn you against me?"

"Please try to understand. I ken you have a good heart, but you've admitted yourself that you've had mistresses." She released her trembling hands and took a step back. "What will happen to me and my family when you tire of me like you did the others?"

* * *

Geordie dropped his arms in disbelief. For the love of God, there he stood, a duke, offering a better life to a woman who lived in a one-room cottage with a dirt floor. Albeit he loved this woman, it was beyond him how she could stand her ground and refuse his generous offer.

Christ, he wanted to score his hands with his dirk, plunge into an icy loch, anything to prove the depth of his love. "This is different." He slammed his fist against his chest. "What I feel in my heart is different. How can I prove it to you?"

She crossed her arms, looking quite flummoxed—and far more kissable than she deserved to be at this moment.

"You want me to move into the dower house with my family? How will that appear to your children?"

"Jane and Alexander already love you—especially Jane."

She tapped her foot. "That is not my point. Will we not be setting a poor example for them?"

"Bloody hell, you do not understand the ways of the gentry." *How could she possibly?*

"Oh? I think I am growing to understand you more and more." Akira squared her shoulders and looked him in the eye. "What is marriage without love? No wonder Lady Elizabeth is a bitter shrew. How humiliating is it to endure a husband who is unfaithful? I would go mad given such circumstances."

Geordie blinked, his cheeks burning as if he'd been slapped.

Dropping her arms, Akira softened her gaze. "Take me home, and think on what I've said. If you can come up with a solution to ease my doubts, then we can talk again."

He gulped. *Christ, I should have had this woman behind Edinburgh Castle walls during the negotiations. She would have had every noble utterly confounded.*

She shook her finger under his nose, looking like a determined badger. "Do not misunderstand. I love you with my entire being, but I will not be played for a harlot."

Stunned, Geordie watched Akira march back to the camp holding her head high like a queen. Had he just been outdone by a slip of a lass?

And why couldn't she accept that it would take an act of God—or at least an application to the pope and another to wretched Queen Anne—for him to marry again? For Christ's sake, the queen would withhold her approval just to be an arse. Och, if Geordie were to announce he'd fallen in love with a horse-faced daughter of a baronet, the queen might be delighted—perhaps be influenced by the lass's father—but a Gypsy goddess who lived in a hovel?

No bloody chance.

He paced back and forth along the burn.

*Why is marriage so important? Isn't it enough that I love her more deeply than I've ever loved anything or anyone in my life?*

*I would recognize any bastard children for my own.*

*She would want for nothing.*

"Your Grace." Oliver hastened toward him. "The lass said we are riding to Dunkeld."

"Aye." Geordie threw up his hands. "No use wasting any more time lingering in these parts. With my luck, the captain will meet up with a full battalion of grenadiers and return to murder us."

"We should have killed him when we had the chance."

Geordie started back toward the camp. "Mayhap, but I reckon humiliating the bastard will be bitter enough. He's hungry for power, that one."

# *Chapter Twenty-Nine*

The delicious smell of roasting venison wafted through the campsite. Some of the men had hunted a deer. Geordie had sent Oliver and one of his sentinels to follow Captain Weaver to make sure there wouldn't be an ambush. After scouting a mile out from the perimeter of the campsite, Geordie was satisfied they were ready to settle in for the eve. And after having ridden through the previous night to intercept the dragoons, he was swaying on his feet. Nonetheless, no one could rest until the camp was secure.

He'd even ordered a pair of men to erect a makeshift tent for Akira from the canvas covering the pack mule's supplies. At least something finally went his way: Geordie found a cask of whisky in the bundle—nothing like a wee bit of liquid gold to raise his spirits and ensure a good night's sleep.

He'd also found a medicine kit, which appeared to please Akira more than Geordie's heroic rescue. She happily took the leather satchel, spreading salve and tying bandages on any Gordon clansman who showed her a wee cut. Finlay carried on about an injury he'd sustained sparring in the courtyard two weeks prior. The miserable sop hadn't complained a lick about it when he'd been cut, but now a bonnie lassie was issuing salve with a gentle hand, he bemoaned the pain like a wet-eared lad.

After filling his flask with whisky, Geordie reclined against his saddle across the fire from Akira's temporary hospital. Watching her grace, her friendly banter with the men, the glow in her cheeks, he sipped. The fiery liquid burned a path all the way down his gullet and sloshed in his empty stomach.

"When will the meat be ready?" he asked, his eyes continuing to watch her. Who wouldn't be enchanted by such a lass?

Patrick stopped turning the spit for a moment. "I reckon we can slice a few strips off the flank, Your Grace."

"Is there enough cooked for the lot of us?"

"Not yet. But soon."

Akira tucked a lock of hair behind her ear and examined one of Finlay's old battle wounds. Thank God it was on his elbow. The man was insufferable.

Geordie raised the flask to his lips again and drank. "Then we shall wait."

Within two ticks of his pocket watch, the spirit helped to dull the tension in his shoulders. Relaxing further, he continued his observation while Akira chatted with Finlay—honestly, the battle-scarred warrior did most of the talking, puffing his old chest like a molting pheasant. The heat above the fire made the air ripple. Geordie's eyelids grew heavy; he was hypnotized by her beauty and her raven tresses. The locks had grown even longer since they'd met, and wisps swayed, brushing against her shapely hips as she gestured with her hands.

Geordie rubbed his fingers together, imagining the softness of her buttocks. Aye, he could caress her as gently as her tresses were doing right this minute. A fluttering heat rose in his chest. His touch would stir a passion deep within her soul—a passion only he knew she possessed.

Such a thought made his heart race, while his cock lengthened beneath his sporran. Christ, he wanted her. Though his desire went far deeper than the flesh. Indeed, their connection ignited much more than carnal desires. He sipped again. Surely a divine power had brought them together—a power no man could wield. Who knew he was capable of loving someone as deeply as he loved her?

Losing Akira would cut him to the quick.

He drummed his fingers against the flask.

*How can I convince her to return to Huntly with me?*

"Hello the camp," Oliver hollered as he and the scout rode in and dismounted.

Geordie beckoned his lieutenant to his side and offered him the flask. "What did you find?"

"They're headed west—haven't met up with a single sympathetic soul." Oliver took a drink and wiped his mouth with the back of his hand. "Bloody oath, this is good spirit. Where'd you find it?"

"It seems the captain has a taste for our Scottish whisky." Geordie pointed. "The cask is over there. Help yourself."

After the meat was served, Oliver tossed his saddle beside the duke and took a seat. "Why are you not over there with the lass?"

Geordie scowled. Bloody Finlay had consumed all of

Akira's attention since they'd fashioned the spit, and now he sat beside her chewing on his meat like he was king of a dung pile. "She's been busy tending to the men's wee cuts and bruises."

"Och, I've a bruise on my arse she can apply some of that salve to," said Patrick on Geordie's left.

He smacked the buffoon with a jab of his elbow. "Shut your gob unless you want my fist in it the next time you flap your mouth."

The sentry rubbed his arm. "Apologies, Your Grace. I thought you'd laugh."

When it came to Akira, the only laughing he'd do was when she decided to return to Huntly. "Well, now you ken differently."

His breath caught when she glanced his way. The corner of his mouth ticked up, while his heart hammered in his chest. Christ, he'd almost waved.

She smiled and nodded, but that damned Finlay tugged her arm, rattling on about something inconsequential, his head swimming with spirit, no doubt.

Kenneth, the clan bard, cleared his throat. "Miss Akira, have you heard the tale of the smith and the fairies?"

She clapped her hands. "No, I cannot say I have."

"Och, 'tis a good yarn," said Finlay, rolling his hand through the air.

Kenneth looked to Geordie for a nod of approval, then, rubbing his hands, he turned his eyes skyward as he always did before launching into one of his fables. "Years ago, there lived in Glen Tanar a smithy by the name of MacEachern..."

Geordie reclined on his elbows and listened to the familiar tale. Akira smiled, enraptured with the story. She even laughed in all the appropriate places. And Finlay cackled like the bard was the funniest nincompoop in Scotland.

By the end of the story, Geordie had stopped listening. He sat forward, cracking his knuckles, deciding where to hit Finlay first. The jaw would do nicely—it would keep him from flapping his mouth. But then, the eye might be a better option. The ugly bastard would have to explain what happened to every passerby for the next fortnight.

When everyone applauded, the liberty-taker slung his arm around Akira's shoulders. "I could tell ye a tale that would tickle your toes, miss..."

His gut clamping into a lead ball, Geordie sprang to his feet and marched around the campfire, his fists clenched at his sides. "Remove your filthy paws from Miss Akira's shoulder this instant."

Wide-eyed, Finlay looked up and hiccupped. "Och, Your Grace, I was only having a wee bit o' fun with the lass."

"Please, m'lord." She batted those goddamn black eyelashes. "He's merely been friendly."

"Aye?" Geordie grabbed her hand and pulled her up. "A bit too friendly, I'd reckon."

He slid his arm around her waist and drew her tight to his side. "Hear me, men. The lady is under my protection, and no one will place so much as a finger upon her person. Am I understood?" Panning his gaze around the circle, he received a nod from every clansman. "Miss Akira has been attacked by outlaws and dragoons, and she is in a fragile state."

She arched her eyebrows at him. "Your Grace, I—"

"Come." He tugged her toward the tent. "'Tis time for everyone to turn in for the night. We've a long ride on the morrow."

Giving her shoulder a pat, he winked. "We'll be bedding down in here this eve. I've placed a pelt atop the moss—it should be a fair bit more comfortable than our sleeping arrangements when we traveled across the mountains."

"We, Your Grace?" She drew her fists beneath her chin as if the thought of lying beside him was distasteful.

*Perhaps I shouldn't have winked.*

He gestured inside. "Aye."

She inclined her lips toward his ear. "But wouldn't it be unseemly?"

"I beg your pardon?" he asked in a heated whisper. "That was never a problem afore."

Her eyes shifted to the Highlanders as she cupped her hand over her mouth. "Doesn't it look bad to the men?"

"Damnation, woman, I'm not going to raise your skirts," he said, loud enough to be heard by everyone. "Have you so easily forgotten there are outlaws and redcoats in these woods?"

She shuddered. "Do you think we'll be attacked? A-a retinue as large as this?"

"We're only twelve." He squinted with a stern eye. "Indeed, anything can happen and we haven't Huntly's walls to protect us."

"Aye," hollered Oliver, God bless him. "You'd best listen to the duke. He kens what he's on about."

When this was over, Geordie would need to find a suitable reward to recognize his lieutenant. He again gestured inside the tent. "After you, m'lady."

A ping of desire swirled through his loins when she bent down to climb inside, her shapely hips clearly outlined beneath her kirtle, presenting to him just the way he liked a woman.

He swiped his hand down his face and forced himself to think of her security. He pulled his dirk from its scabbard. And once she was settled, he slid beside her and rested the weapon near his head.

He lay on his back, his shoulder butted atop hers. The damned tent was narrower than he'd thought. "Are you comfortable?"

"'Tis a bit close. Perhaps if I roll to my side."

"Good idea." Geordie rolled with her. The only problem? He was holding his arm midair with no place to rest it.

*By the saints, I ken she cares for me.*

He lowered his arm across her body.

Without a complaint, Akira sighed and shifted her hips. Pillow-soft female buttocks nestled flush against his cock.

He sucked in a sharp breath.

"Are you all right?" she asked, her voice sweeter than golden honey pouring from a spigot.

"Aye," he growled, while a lock of her hair grew a mind of its own and tickled his nose. Good God, the scent of jasmine made his eyes roll back.

"I'm so tired. I didn't sleep at all last eve." Of course, her voice had to sound sultrier than sin.

"Nor did I. We rode all night to catch up to you."

She shifted again. "You didn't sleep at all?"

Geordie couldn't help but tighten his grip around her waist and burrow his cock between those insanely delectable buttocks. "Nay," he managed hoarsely.

She sighed. "Then we must sleep."

He was too goddamn hard for sleep. Geordie sighed and settled in for another long night.

* * *

Akira opened her eyes and a sleepy grin spread across her lips. Though she couldn't admit to it, having Geordie lying beside her, his body warming her back, his arm protectively draped across her waist, sent her to heaven. If only they could cuddle together beneath the tarpaulin all day, but the birds had begun to call and soon the camp would stir. Regardless, she intended to revel in her wee bit of heaven as long as she could.

Who knew when she'd be this close to Geordie again—if ever.

Did she love him to the depths of her soul?

*Aye, more than anything or anyone.*

But vines of doubt sprouted and curled through her mind. He said he cared for her, but how could she be certain his feelings ran as deep as hers?

How could she be certain he would be faithful? Her father wasn't faithful to her mother, nor was her stepfather. As a matter of fact, none of the men who'd been close to Akira had shown any propensity for fidelity. With such awful examples from her childhood, she had difficulty trusting any man, let alone a duke with a reputation for…

She groaned. She didn't want to think about Geordie's past or her future. Right now, in this moment, he was unquestionably hers. He'd been adorably jealous last eve when old Finlay showered her with attention.

Akira laced her fingers through Geordie's and drew them to her lips. Closing her eyes, she kissed knuckles and savored his spicy male scent, the powerful breadth of his hand in hers.

Was she being overly stubborn?

*Time will tell.*

They hadn't arrived in Dunkeld yet. There were still many miles to traverse, and God willing, the idleness should allow him time to think. Allow her time to think as well. He'd promised fidelity. But if she gave in to his offer, what then? Could she trust him?

She bit her bottom lip.

*What in life is a surety?*

# Chapter Thirty

The sun was dipping low in the western sky when the whitewashed buildings in the village of Dunkeld came into view. Gray smoke swirled from every chimney and hung over the town, waiting for the wind to come and whisk it away. Geordie tightened his fists around his reins, while unease heated the back of his neck. These were lands governed by the Marquis of Atholl, a man who, at the first sign of adversity, declared his support for Anne Stuart rather than her half brother, James Francis Edward Stuart. Geordie didn't trust Atholl—could never trust anyone who cast aside his allegiance for the true king and raised his pennant for a usurper.

Akira rode beside him, her back erect. She'd become a more assured horsewoman since their journey had started, but now Geordie sensed the lass was as tense as he.

"Where is your family's cottage?" he asked, his voice gruff.

She pointed toward the outskirts of town, where a

cloud of wood smoke hung lower. "The settlement yonder," she said, chewing her bottom lip. "Are you certain you want to ride there?"

*Och, she's embarrassed for certain.* "You need not worry about what I might or might not think. I intend to accompany you to your hearth and meet your family."

She nodded and looked away, while her shoulders fell.

Geordie glanced back at Oliver. "Take the men to the alehouse and tell them to lay low. No carousing with the locals—especially Atholl's men, ye ken?"

"Aye, Your Grace."

"And nothing stronger than ale. They're to keep to the shadows and await orders."

After leaving his men in the village square, Geordie followed Akira through a narrow close. The farther they traveled from the center of town, the shabbier things became. People sat outside crumbling hovels with nothing but rags draping from their shoulders. Putrid slops lined the gutters. Men with wooden legs and women with vacant expressions stared, their cheeks hollow as if they hadn't eaten a decent meal in years. Dirty children with no shoes clung to their parents' sides. Geordie even reckoned he spied lepers slinking through the filth, tatters hiding their rotting flesh.

*And bloody Atholl is allowing this poverty right under his nose.*

The smoke he'd seen from afar stung his eyes, while the stench of sewage cast an unpleasant pall. "How can you tolerate these conditions?" Geordie couldn't help but grumble.

Akira's shoulders dropped a bit further. She hadn't looked at him since Dunkeld came into sight.

Bloody hell, he could be an insensitive clod. But his

observation only strengthened his resolve to convince her to return to Huntly.

A bit farther on, the squalor opened to small farms with shabby cottages. Akira turned into the first drive. "Our shieling is at the back. The widow took us in after Ma's accident and allows us to stay in exchange for chores."

Geordie nodded—the bloody widow's cottage looked dilapidated itself. Akira led him round the back to a hovel in such disrepair it leaned as if the foundations would give way in a healthy wind. Grass sprouted from the thatched roof, the doorway covered by nothing but a blue woolen plaid—completely inadequate to protect them from winter snows. There were no windows. Black smoke seeped out the thatch at one end of the shack, which had no proper chimney.

Afraid he'd make a thoughtless remark, Geordie clenched his teeth. When Akira finally pulled her horse to a stop, he hopped down and helped her dismount.

She squeezed his arms, uncertainty written in those indigo eyes. "Perhaps I should go in first?"

"Whilst I mind the horses, m'lady?" he said with a hint of sarcasm, then shook his head. "Apologies. Do what you think is best."

Blushing the color of a beautiful rose, Akira gave him a pat. "I'll only be a moment."

A puff of smoke swirled out when Akira pulled aside the plaid to enter. The shrieks and screams that followed from within made Geordie laugh. 'Twas definitely for the best she went in first. It sounded as if twenty female voices all asked questions at once, and he couldn't decipher a one.

"Silence!" a mature woman's voice bellowed.

All yammering ceased.

"Thank you, Ma," Akira said. "Before I utter another word, I must tell you someone very important is waiting outside."

"Oooooh?" Ma's voice slid up the scale until it squeaked. "Who is this? Why didn't you say something straightaway?"

"I tried, Ma." Akira drew the woolen plaid to one side again, poked her head out with another billowing swirl of smoke, and beckoned Geordie inside.

Forced to duck beneath the lintel, he straightened, then plastered on a polite grin. The place looked like a cannonball had hit—hazy smoke and all. It was dimly lit, but he saw disarray everywhere he looked. Clumps of dried herbs hung from the rafters, piles of fabric, sewing, and God knew what else cluttered every available space. At least the cooking fire at one end was reasonably tidy, with a cast-iron pot suspended from the support beam. A griddle, stone grain grinder, and utensils were neatly stowed, hanging against the wall from blackened iron nails.

Four pairs of eyes stared at him without blinking. By their shocked expressions anyone would have thought the lassies had never seen a Highlander before.

Looking very officious, Akira gestured toward him. "This is His Grace, George Gordon, the Duke of Gordon."

He gave her a wink. The title sounded sultry and far less pompous when it rolled off her tongue.

One of the lassies dropped her jaw, her eyes growing wide as sovereigns, while everyone else bowed their heads and dipped into curtsies.

Akira's mother appeared about to swoon and wobbled on her crutch. Akira steadied the woman. "This is my ma, Laini." Then she nodded to the others. "Kynda is the youngest, then Scota and Annis." Annis was the one who'd gaped at him, and though beautiful, she tossed her hair and assumed a haughty expression as if she were as self-absorbed as Elizabeth. Aye, most highborn women behaved similarly toward him—shallow lust that as a younger man would have caught his attention.

*But no more.*

Turning his attention to Akira's mother, Geordie bowed. "Pleased to meet you at long last."

Laini regained her composure and blessed him with a warm smile, her brown eyes full of intelligence. But her smile didn't work on one side of her face, where a deep scar trailed from the corner of her mouth down her jaw. "Please, do come in." She flicked her wrist at her brood. "Lassies, make room at the table." Then she turned back to Geordie. "We were about to sit down for a bite of pottage. I hope you can join us."

"Ah." He shot a panicked look to Akira, who nodded vigorously. Again he bowed, deeper this time. "I would be delighted, thank you."

The questions started again, with each lass yapping louder than the last. Akira held up her hands. "Once the meal is served, I'll start at the beginning."

"You'll sit beside me, Your Grace," Laini said with a great deal of confidence. She settled herself on one end of the bench and patted the seat beside her. "Before anyone says another word, I want to know what the Duke of Gordon is doing accompanying my daughter to my home."

"He's the man who was shot in the leg with the musket ball," Akira explained.

"Ooooooo," everyone said at once.

As he climbed over the bench, Ma gave him a most pointed look-over. "You appear as if you've come through your injury quite well?"

"Aye." Geordie affixed his most endearing grin—one that always worked on his mother. "Thanks to Miss Akira, I'm fitter than a colt on a spring morn."

Laughing, Laini shook her finger. Now he was closer, he couldn't help but regard the scar. She'd received a vicious cut, though it didn't mar her beauty overmuch. There were streaks of gray in her dark hair, tied in a chignon at her nape. "Thank you for bringing my daughter home. I've no idea what we would have done once the coin was gone."

Akira took a seat opposite Geordie on the opposing bench. "Unfortunately, I lost the ten-shilling piece when the highwaymen attacked."

"Attacked?" Ma drew her hand over her heart. "What on earth...?"

"Believe me, those men will never harm another soul." Geordie's eyes flashed to Akira, and he dug in his sporran. "That reminds me. I found this on the trail when we were looking for you."

"What?" Ma asked.

Geordie placed the ten-shilling piece on the table.

Everyone gasped—even Akira. "Thank heavens."

"Can I hold it?" asked Kynda, snatching the coin and raising it up as if it were solid gold.

Akira caught Geordie's eye and mouthed "Thank you."

"Stow it in the jar straightaway," said Ma. "We cannot afford to lose that kind of coin. It will feed the lot of us for a year."

Good Lord, a ten-shilling piece was insignificant change to Geordie, but it would serve to support these poor lassies for that long? His entire life seemed like a lavish string of unending excesses.

Annis placed a ewer and five wooden cups on the table. "Watered wine," she said, batting her eyelashes.

"Scota, serve up the pottage." Ma reached for a cup, poured, and pushed the drink in front of Geordie. "Akira, you've been silent long enough, lass. Now tell us what you've been up to with this handsome duke."

She regarded him with a wary stare, but only for a moment. He let it pass. Now wasn't the time to disclose his hand.

He sat mesmerized while Akira launched into their story. She had a good memory and recounted things even he had forgotten. He'd never realized how well she articulated her words, especially for a lass who'd grown up in poverty. The candle in the center of the table cast a glow, making her face flicker with gold like an angel.

Ma tapped him with her elbow. There he sat, a duke, being tapped in the ribs by a woman who'd asserted herself as matron of the cottage. He didn't dare rebuke her. When he blinked, she arched her brows and gestured to the bowl of pottage sitting before him. He'd been so enthralled with the story, he hadn't taken much notice when Scota placed it on the table.

He picked up the wooden spoon and shoveled in a bite. Good God, the stuff was flavorless paste without a sprinkle of salt—or any other seasoning for that matter. He stirred the mush, searching for a bit of meat. There was none to be found.

Everyone else ate heartily, as if it were manna.

Akira rattled off most of their story, leaving out the intimate bits, of course. But Geordie knit his brows when she ended without telling them of his offer to move the family to Huntly. For crying out loud, that was the most important part.

Ma rested her spoon beside her empty bowl. "When must you return home, Your Grace?"

"A few days, I suppose." He looked to Akira for her response, but she didn't utter a word.

"Can you come back on the morrow?" Ma patted his hand. "With my daughter home and ten shillings in the pot, we can boil a chicken."

Geordie would do anything to return, but boiled chicken? For a celebration? "Perhaps you will permit me to take Miss Akira to the market on the morrow and allow me to supply the meal?"

Laini drew her hand to her chest. "Heavens, that isn't necessary."

"Aye, but I'd like to, very much. Think of it as a thank-you."

"Can I go, too, Ma?" asked Annis. "I want to purchase some cloth."

"No," Akira said. "I need to talk to the duke alone."

"Alone?" Ma asked, sounding alarmed.

"Heaven's stars, Akira. You've been alone with him for *ages*," Scota whined.

Ma held up her palm. "Akira may go to the market with His Grace as long as her sisters act as chaperones. I'll not have anyone in Dunkeld speaking ill of my daughter."

Geordie climbed off the bench and took Ma's hand in his palm. "Then it shall be so, and all of the lassies will select silk and ribbon for new gowns."

The shieling erupted with youthful squeals of delight and an abundance of clapping.

Ignoring Akira's sisters, he bent over Laini's hand and

plied it with a kiss, praying he'd done something that evening to earn favor with the mother of the woman he loved.

"My heavens!" Laini beamed, a blush spreading across her time-kissed cheeks. Akira had indeed inherited her beauty from this woman. "'Tis settled. All my lassies will attend market day on the morrow."

* * *

Of course, everyone had to see Geordie to his horse, and Akira was forced to bid him good-night with her sisters all flapping their mouths and drooling over the duke as if he were a prince—which he practically was. But to Akira, he was Geordie, the man who'd been seriously shot in the thigh, a man who had needed her help, a man who had endured a great deal of pain to see to her safety, and the only man with whom she had ever fallen in love.

Her heart twisted. *Love.* Why did she have to love him more than he loved her? How on earth could she say good-bye to him? Never see him again? She wanted to drop to her knees and weep.

Coming home was bittersweet. At least it was a good sign when, after he walked into the wee cottage, he didn't turn tail and gallop his stallion for Huntly. Hopefully she'd given him enough warning, though she didn't miss the shock written on his face when he stepped inside her shabby home. The clutter seemed worse than she remembered, but what did one expect from five females who shared a one-room shieling?

Thank heavens he'd been gracious to Ma. After he left, she spoke of nothing but how mannerly the duke was and that she'd never in her life met an earl, let alone a duke, and there he sat and ate pottage like he was a commoner.

Akira reckoned the fact he had managed to eat the bland gruel her mother served up owed to his good nature. She lay abed staring at the shadows until her sisters drifted off to sleep. She'd been waiting all evening to talk to Ma without her sisters' interruptions, especially Annis's. At sixteen, Annis could be the most meddlesome, most irritating person in all of Dunkeld.

When, finally, all the excited banter about Geordie's visit passed and only deep breathing filled the air in the box bed, Akira slipped her feet to the cool dirt floor, wrapped a plaid around her shoulders, and tiptoed to Ma's pallet. She held a twig to the fire, then lit the bedside candle with it. "Are you awake?"

"Mm." Ma patted the floor beside her. "I was wondering if you'd want to talk."

"Aye." Akira sat and tucked her legs under like she'd done so many times in that wee shieling. It used to be home, but now she'd been away for so long, experienced so much of the world, it didn't seem so homey anymore. It was cluttered and crowded, smoky and dirty.

Ma gripped Akira's hand between her palms. "You're in love with him, are you not?"

"How did you know?"

"The way you look at him with longing in your eyes. He looks at you the same as well."

Akira hid her face in her palms and shook her head. "I do not ken what to think anymore."

"Why?" Ma pursed her lips, with a furrow forming in her brow. "Do not tell me he's married. Merciful fairies, I should have known. Most great men are married by his age."

"He *was* married—the duchess divorced him and now she lives in a convent in Flanders."

The furrow grew deeper. "Divorce? How preposterous."

"Oh no, 'tis true. I even met the duchess, because she was at Huntly Castle when we arrived. She thought Alexander—I mean the duke's son—would have to assume the dukedom as heir because no one kent what had happened to His Grace."

"I see." Ma patted Akira's hand. "You've had quite an adventure. But I want to ken what is really troubling you, lass—you've been away with a duke of all people for sennights. And now you cannot sleep. My mind has run the gamut of horrors. Quickly, tell me now afore I have one of my spells."

Looking down, Akira sighed deeply. "'Tis too humiliating to utter."

"Has he violated you?" Ma hit her fist against her palm. "Why, I'll have the—"

"No." Akira pressed steepled fingers to her lips. "He did not violate me."

Ma closed her mouth and squinted. "There's something more. Something you're not telling me."

"It was innocent, Ma. He said he wanted to take care of me—of all of us—but I misunderstood."

"Did you?" Ma looked in Akira's eyes and gasped. "You did!"

Holy Moses, her mother could read her mind. She never could hide anything from her. She'd hoped to leave that part out.

*Curses.*

Now she had no choice but to bare her soul. "I thought when he said he wanted to take care of me he was proposing marriage." Tears stung Akira's eyes. "B-b-but he asked me to be his m-m-mistress." She again hid her face in her hands. Oh, the shame of her admission. Would Ma throw her out into the gutter? Would she take the switch to her back?

"No." The disappointment reflected in Ma's eyes hurt more than twenty lashings.

"He said he could not marry me, because the bishop and Queen Anne will not allow it. He offered for us to stay in the dower house in Huntly. And I will not lie, Ma. 'Tis the grandest house I've ever seen aside from Geordie's castle. 'Tis furnished in the French style with silk tapestries on the wall and more rooms than I could count. He said the lassies could learn to read and write and ride horses. We could live like royalty."

"But you refused him?"

Akira nodded, wiping her eyes. "I did."

Ma shook her fist, thudding it against her chest. "Blast that duke, taking advantage of my daughter. I kent I should have forced you to stay home that night when you rode off to save his miserable life."

Grasping her mother's hand, Akira held it over her heart. "But I ken he's a good man. He's shown me kindness in every way. I just... I just..."

"What is it, my sweeting?"

"I worry about ten years from now." She shook her head as a lump stuck in her throat. "He's admitted to having mistresses before. What if he grows weary of me?"

"Of you?" Ma's frown sank into the deeply etched lines at the corners of her mouth. "Then he's an even greater fool than I first thought."

"What should I do?"

Ma rubbed her fingers over the bauble she wore around

her neck—said it was a charm to help divine the future, though it was merely a shiny stone, passed down from her mother. "He's worried about the bishop's approval? He wants a Christian wedding?"

Akira looked puzzled. "Well, aye."

"This is grave news. I wish your father were here to confront the man." Ma reached under her pallet and pulled out a wee flask. "You do love him?"

"Aye, more than anything."

"Well, have a wee sip of this and ask the Gypsy fairies to provide an answer to your quandary."

"What is it?"

"A bit o' whisky—and a wee drop of belladonna to put you in a deep sleep." Ma winked. "'Tis potent and mustn't be used often."

Aware belladonna wasn't only potent but potentially deadly, Akira hesitated. "Is it safe?"

"Aye, but I use it only when deeply troubled. And whisky is dear, my sweeting."

"Very dear." Good gracious, Akira had never seen whisky in the cottage except when Uncle Bruno called. She sipped and handed the flask back to Ma.

"I reckon I'll need a sip as well if I'm to face a naughty duke come morning." Ma took quite a healthy swig.

Akira's stomach twisted like it was clamped in a smithy's vise. "You're not going to be unkind to him, are you?"

Ma shoved the cork back into the flask. "Of course not, but seeing as he's plowed a field where he has no liberties, 'tis within my rights to understand his intentions."

Akira's head swam—Ma's concoction was powerful medicine indeed, and how often did she imbibe such a remedy? Blinking, Akira forced herself to keep her wits about her for a bit longer. “Perhaps confronting the duke is not a good idea.”

Like a seasoned matron, Ma batted her hand through the air. “Never you mind. The fairies will work their magic. They always do.”

# Chapter Thirty-One

Geordie arrived at the shieling midmorning—a respectable hour for an excursion with four maids. Before he could knock on the doorjamb, Akira pulled aside the plaid. Smoke billowed into his face. Coughing, he waved his hand to clear it.

"Thank heavens you've arrived. The lassies are about to jump out of their skin, and Ma's ready to have one of her spells." She took his hand and drew him to one side, turning her lips to his ear. "And Ma wants a word."

He grinned—adoring Akira's overwrought expression. "Does she?"

"Aye, *alone*."

The lassies all filed out of the shieling with rapt grins on their faces. "Good morn, Your Grace," they all said at once.

Laini hobbled to the doorway. "Go on now and collect the matron's eggs whilst I have a word with the duke."

Blanching, Akira gave him a wee shake of her head. "Not to worry."

Geordie smiled and patted her shoulder. He'd never met a mother who could get the better of him. And being asked to have a word was a good sign.

With a resolute sigh, his rose grasped his shoulder and squeezed. "I wish you luck."

"Come here now, Your Grace, and stop dawdling."

He arched a single eyebrow at the woman. "I beg your pardon, madam, but I *never* dawdle."

"Aye, well, I reckon that's exactly what you're doing out there ogling my daughter. Come. I need a word."

He chuckled and bowed his head to his rose, then did Ma's bidding and stepped inside the shieling. "How can I serve you this fine morn, madam?"

"Your highborn manners are wasted on me, Your Grace," the older woman said in a rather brusque tone. She leaned on her crutch and frowned. "It seems my daughter has saved your hide more than once."

*An odd way to start a conversation, but no matter, I'll not admonish her—yet.* "Aye." Geordie nodded. "I am indebted to Miss Akira."

"Hmm." Laini squinted like she mightn't trust him. "She told me you asked her to be your *mistress*—to live in some fancy house up north. She said you invited me and the lassies as well."

Hell, the woman spat the word *mistress* as if it were as vile as the word *whore*. Regardless, Geordie faced her, keeping his face devoid of expression, though he moved his fists to his hips. "I did."

"Tell me, Duke of Gordon, do you love my daughter?"

That he could answer without hesitation. "More than anything."

"And you are divorced from your duchess?"

"Aye."

"I'm having difficulty understanding this." Pursing her lips, Laini shook her head, making the gold hoops in her ears wobble. "You freely admit to being in love with my daughter, yet you've invited her to be your *mistress* and not your wife."

Geordie dropped his gaze to his square-toed shoes. "'Tis complicated."

"I see nothing complicated about it. You are asking my daughter to compromise her values. Is this because she is of Romany descent? Do you see her as inferior because of her heritage?"

His hands slid down to his sides. "Lord, no. I see Akira as a gift from God. She is an angel in my eyes."

Laini hobbled a bit closer. "Then why do you refuse to marry her?"

"As I said, 'tis complicated. I must seek approval from the bishop in Aberdeen and then from Queen Anne. The first is rather a problem and the latter is nothing but futile. The queen will do anything to see to my unhappiness. I have been marked as a supporter of King James—and my marriage to a commoner..."

"Ah ha!" Laini shook her finger right under his nose. "You *do* see Akira as inferior."

Bloody hell, if the woman had been a man, he would have snatched that defiant finger and bent it back until it snapped. Instead, he cleared his throat and met her gaze with a stern stare of his own. "That is not what I said."

The woman jutted her face up toward his, puffing her chest. "But as I see it, you refuse to consider marriage because of her station in life. You haven't even asked if there might be an alternative right in front of your noble nose—an alternative provided by Akira's very own roots, her heritage, the customs she holds most dear."

His jaw twitched. "I'm listening."

Laini leaned both hands on her crutch. "Are you man enough to act, once I show you the way?"

Crossing his arms, he stood erect and looked down at the matron. What did she know about the politics of the gentry? And if she had a solution, why didn't she just spit it out? 'Twas time to gain the upper hand. "If you know how I can pledge eternal love to Akira, tell me now, for I grow tired of your cryptic banter, even if you are the mother of the woman I love."

Laini reached up and twisted his ear. "Do not be disrespectful of your elders, Your Grace. I do not care if you're a duke or a pauper. I am queen of this cottage. Apologize now, or I'll call the lassies inside right this minute and forbid Akira from ever seeing you again."

"Ow." Geordie bent with the tug of the woman's fingers. "Forgive me. I meant no disrespect."

"Good." Releasing his ear, she brushed her hand on her skirt. "Now listen here, ye young whelp, I *will* show you the way to eternal happiness, but first you must prove your merit to me afore I give my consent."

"Ah." Dumbfounded, Geordie regarded the crone, leaning on her crutch, eyeing him like she was the queen of the fairies. He swiped a hand across his mouth. He'd march through Hades to win Akira for good. He eyed the matron back. Ah hell, this scrap of a woman couldn't pose him much of a challenge. "Tell me what you wish and it shall be done. A host of new gowns? A ruby brooch?"

"No, ye joob." Laini gave him a firm whack on the shoulder. "You must prove your love for my daughter.

You must show me the depths of your devotion—and you'll nay do it with spreading your coin around like a squanderer."

"Very well." Geordie exhaled—proving his love ought not to be a problem. He'd already done so many times over. "And when can I expect your decision confirming the depth of my affection?"

"When I am satisfied—and only then." Laini flicked her wrist toward the door. "Now be gone with you and shower my bairns with your good fortune. But only this once."

* * *

Geordie held back and walked with Akira on his arm while her sisters skipped ahead, yammering excitedly.

"So?" she asked.

Geordie feigned ignorance. "Hmm?"

"Oh please, do not pretend you have no idea to what I am referring." She nudged him. "What did Ma say to you?"

He chuckled. At least Akira didn't have any idea how much he'd allowed her mother to confound him. "I must prove my love for you before she gives her consent."

Slowing her pace, she regarded him out of the corner of her eye. "Consent? For... um, being your *mistress*?" She whispered the word as if it were a curse.

Geordie rubbed his temple. "I'm not exactly certain."

"Oh." Akira didn't sound very excited about whatever Laini had up her sleeve, either.

To give his rose a bit of reassurance, he patted the lassie's hand. "She was rather cryptic about the happily-ever-after part."

"Now that sounds like Ma."

"Do you trust her?"

"For the most part, but when it comes to making decisions for my life, I'd rather she didn't meddle."

"It seems that problem is the same no matter what your birthright." Geordie eyed the stunning woman on his arm. "You obviously talked with her about us."

"Aye—to ask her opinion."

"I take it she wasn't enamored with my proposal?"

"Or lack thereof," Akira mumbled, looking away. "But she said that with a bit o' Gypsy magic she could fix everything."

"Said the same to me... except..."

"Aye?"

"Like I said, I must prove the depth of my love to your ma's satisfaction."

"Did she say how?"

"No."

Akira grazed her teeth over her bottom lip. "And I imagine she didn't tell you how she'd fix our—ah—wee problem."

"No." Geordie swirled his palm over Akira's hand. "But something tells me your Ma is sharper than the dirk in my scabbard."

"I can attest to that."

Geordie narrowed his eyes. "What is it that impresses her?"

"Not certain." Akira tapped a finger to her lips. "Hard work. A job well done. Honesty. Sincerity. Trustworthiness."

"Hmm, there's a lot to chew on there." He looked up. The lassies ran into a tailor's shop on High Street. "I think we'd best keep up with your sisters."

She beamed. "Och, they're ever so excited."

By the time they stepped inside, Kynda was unraveling a spool of ribbon and Scota and Annis were fingering bolts of fabric.

"I want a dress with lots of lace and ribbon," Kynda squealed, dancing in circles as if she had ahold of a maypole ribbon.

The shopkeeper snatched it from the wee lassie's hand. "Shoo, the lot of you. I'll not tolerate a bunch of tinkers fouling my wares."

Geordie stepped up, snatched the ribbon from the man's hand, and returned it to Kynda. "These young ladies are accompanying me this day. I bid them choose whatever they like. New gowns for all."

The tailor peered over his spectacles, observing Geordie from head to toe. "Oh? And who might you be, fouling my shop with a mob of ragged street urchins?"

Geordie leaned forward, eyeing the dimwitted hound. "If you must know, I am the Duke of Gordon and these respectable young ladies are under my protection." He gestured to his sporran. "Unless you would prefer not to earn my coin this day."

The man wiped a stream of sweat from his brow and bowed. "Forgive me, Your Grace. A-a-a shopkeeper cannot be too careful in these times. Tinkers and thieves will rob me of every last bit of lace."

Geordie fingered a corner of damask and sniffed with displeasure. "I sincerely doubt that."

The man led him to the settee. "Please, Your Grace, I will fashion gowns for these lassies so beautiful, all of Scotland will admire."

"You had better, else I will take my business elsewhere." Geordie turned and kissed Akira's hand. "The day is yours, *mo leannan*."

Resolving to spend the next few hours swarmed by females, he took a seat where he could watch out the window. The shop became more and more cluttered as bolts of cloth were pulled from their shelves, and the shopkeeper measured and jotted notes as fast as his miserable fingers would allow. Several times, passersby pushed through the shop door, took one look at the raven-haired lassies, stuck their noses in the air, and swiftly retreated.

Geordie couldn't care less. If only he'd had a Gypsy force behind him, the redcoats at Hoord Moor may have all run for their lives. Queen Anne would have taken her Danish husband and sailed back to Denmark a failure. Geordie's ire piqued a bit, however, when a pair of dragoons stopped at the window and peered inside. Slipping his fingers to the hilt of his dirk, he leaned forward and snarled.

Fortunately, they moved on, but Geordie grew restless. He'd told his men to lie low and stay out of trouble. Were the soldiers just curious, or were they prying? He patted his sporran. There was little to worry about with Captain Weaver's proclamation tucked inside.

By the time they were ready to leave, two more pairs of dragoons had scrutinized them through the window and Geordie had grown hungrier than a fox in midwinter. "I'll take you ladies for a meal at the inn."

"On market day they have lamb on a stick in the tent on the end," said Annis.

Scota clapped her hands. "Och aye, I love lamb on a stick, and we haven't had it since Uncle Bruno visited months and months ago."

Geordie reckoned he could eat fifty sticks, but if that's what the lassies wanted, he wasn't about to quarrel. The lot of them chatted like excited hens while they led him along the line of white market tents. Still uneasy, he shifted his gaze across the scene.

*Bloody hell, there are more redcoats than civilians.*

The hair at his nape stood on end as he looked around for Clan Gordon men. Fortunately, they'd paid heed to his bidding and were well out of sight.

Akira ordered their food and Geordie gave the merchant his coin, then cleaned off his stick with one bite. About to order another five, he shoved his hand in his sporran.

"Well, well, Gordon, I'm rather surprised to see you here."

Spinning around to see who dared to call him familiar, Geordie faced the Marquis of Atholl—dressed in blue silk and velvet and sporting a pretentious chestnut periwig.

*May as well make nice.*

"Why, Atholl, 'tis a pleasure to see you out and about this day."

"Truly? I am rather shocked to see you showing your face in Dunkeld." He rubbed his slender fingers down his doublet. "I'm told you're still supporting James the *Pretender*."

Geordie clenched his fists when the fobbing measle emphasized *Pretender*. A circle of dragoons surrounded them, but as a duke, he outranked them all. "Mind your station, sir."

John smirked. "You may outrank me, but you are on my lands. I do believe that evens the disparity."

"Mayhap, but I am here on personal business, nothing to do with politics."

"Truly? You, *Your Grace*?" the marquis said, disbelief in his voice. "I hear you are suspected of riding against

Queen Anne in the wee Hoord Moor uprising a month past."

"You are sorely mistaken." Something told Geordie not to reveal his entire hand as to the reason for his visit to Dunkeld. "My pennant did not fly, and I resent your inference, which is clearly intended to sully my reputation."

The marquis snorted and swiped his thumb across his nose. "Och, you're doing a fine enough job of discrediting yourself all on your own." He leaned in. "I hear the duchess left you and now you're keeping company with a gaggle of Gypsy tinkers."

Heat flared up the back of Geordie's neck, so hot it was all he could do not to slam his fist into that smug sneer. Bloody oath, if it weren't for the army of men surrounding him, John would be sporting a misaligned face.

Casting an apologetic glance to Akira, Geordie grasped the marquis by the shoulder and led him aside—not that there was anywhere to go where they could have a modicum of privacy. He pressed his lips to John's ear, keeping his voice low. "I'll not stand by whilst you sully the reputation of these hardworking young ladies."

"Is that so?" The marquis coughed out a laugh. "How easily you forget that not three years past you sat on the Privy Council beside me when we voted to rid Scotland of their kind."

"That was to drive out tinkers and thieves, not women and children who put in an honest day's labor." Geordie lowered his voice and glanced over his shoulder. Akira had her back to him, standing several paces away. "Scarcely able to feed themselves, they are."

"And what is your affinity for these urchins? Surely they are not the cause of your appearance in Dunkeld?"

Geordie stepped a bit farther behind the tent. "I met

the eldest when I was injured *several* months past. She provided expert healing services and I am repaying her kindness."

Akira gasped.

Damnation, she'd moved closer and stood only a few feet away. Turning, she beckoned to her sisters. "Come, 'tis time to go."

"Wait!" Geordie called after them.

The marquis grabbed his arm. "I ken your cousin William was one of the upstarts. And I reckon you were at Hoord Moor as well."

Geordie tore his arm away. "You are sorely mistaken. All of Britain has gone mad, pitting brother against brother and family against family. Besides, I have a proclamation from Captain Roderick Weaver declaring I was in Inverness at the time of the battle. I've already proved my innocence to him, and I bloody well do not need to prove a thing to the likes of you."

Without a backward glance, he hastened after Akira. Good God, if word of his thoughtless exchange with the marquis about "repaying a kindness" got to Laini without an explanation, Geordie might just lose Akira forever.

# Chapter Thirty-Two

Akira's eyes stung as she hurried back to the cottage. Her stomach churned, threatening to bring up the food she'd just eaten. Her entire world spun out of control.

*Damn, damn, damn*, she swore as she stomped away. *Telling the marquis he was merely repaying my kindness? If that doesn't prove he's embarrassed to be seen with me, I do not ken what will.*

The outcasts on the outskirts of town gaped as she rushed past them. Staring and laughing behind their hands, no doubt. Who proved to be the fool now?

If only she could break into a run and hide in a haystack for the rest of her life.

"Why are you walking so fast?" Scota asked from behind.

Akira waved her off. "I felt like I was suffocating back there."

"Why?" Annis hurried alongside. "You're the Duke of Gordon's mistress, and goodness, did you see how he took charge of the marquis?"

Stopping, Akira grabbed her sister's arm. "Where on earth did you arrive at the notion that I am Geordie—" She shook her head. "I mean the duke's mistress?"

Annis shrugged away. "There are no walls in our cottage and you only *thought* I was sleeping last eve."

Akira had never wanted to slap her sister so much in her life. "That conversation was meant for Ma's ears only."

"You're such a ninny." Jamming her hands into her hips, Annis looked angrier than a mob of attacking dragoons. "You would deprive the rest of us of a better life where we could learn to read and write and ride horses? You are so selfish!"

*Lord give me strength.*

Shocked to her toes, Akira clenched her fists as her lips stretched across her teeth. This was exactly why she'd wanted to speak to Ma alone. Annis always had the most maddening way of turning things around to make Akira appear like a joob. Aye, she'd thought of her sister's comfort, but Ma had brought them up with sound morals. Agreeing to be any man's mistress wasn't something she should take lightly. Besides, she'd always dreamed of marrying one day, of having her own cottage, raising a happy family.

Huntly was as foreign to her as living in another country where she didn't speak the language.

"I cannot believe I've just been told I'm selfish by the most self-absorbed lass in Dunkeld. Do you expect me to cast aside my values for fancy gowns and riding lessons? You may think all is well with such an arrangement, but what example does such behavior set for Scota and Kynda."

"Oh, now you're the duchess of the gutter, are you?"

Annis seethed. "What do you think will become of us when Ma passes, or the roof to the shieling finally falls in? Do you think we'll all find dukes and become mistresses? If we were so fortunate, it would be a far better life for each one of us." She pointed to a leper crouched in a doorway. "Will we have to take to the streets? End up violated by some filthy tinker?"

Akira clamped her mouth shut, glaring at her accursed sister. Merciful father, the lass actually made sense.

Annis shoved her arm. "Have you thought whom we might marry, or do you think life will always be as it is, eking a bit of coin from hours of labor, hoping it is enough to feed us for a sennight." She fluffed out her skirts. "I've one moth-eaten gown I've mended so many times I doubt a thread of original stitching remains."

"I ken, we—"

"Do you? Or are you just thinking of yourself?"

"Akira!" Holy Moses, if things weren't bad enough, Geordie was running straight toward them.

"Oh, 'tis just a mere duke chasing after my sister, who happens to be blind!" Annis turned to Scota and Kynda. "Come lassies, Akie is about to ruin our lives."

Akira shook her fist. "That is not my intention."

"Aye?" Annis started to move away. "Then prove you care about us as much as you care about yourself."

With no place to run, Akira crossed her arms and blinked back tears. Annis was entirely wrong. For the most part. Akira had been thinking about the lassies' future. She wanted to do the right thing, and now her head spun even faster than before.

Catching his breath, Geordie reached for her, but quickly drew his hands to his sides. "Dear God, why did you race away from me like that?"

So many warring thoughts clouded her mind, she didn't want to have this conversation right now. "I heard what you said." A tear leaked from her eye and dribbled down her cheek.

He spread his palms, his face looking like a wounded puppy. "I ken it sounded bad, but I was just trying to avoid an ugly situation."

"Och aye?" Something inside snapped. She'd had enough. For once in her life she would stand up for herself, regardless of the berating she'd just received from Annis. "You either love me or you do not. I've realized love is the foundation of my concern."

"I do love you."

"Enough to be seen in public with me? Enough to face the Marquis of Atholl and not be embarrassed because I am so lowborn?"

"Of course." His eyebrows drew together, etching a furrow between them. "I escorted you to market day for all of Dunkeld to see."

"Aye, but when you were confronted by a man who is nearly your peer, you said you were merely repaying my kindness." Akira turned and hid her face in her palms. Now she'd blurted out her innermost feelings, the emptiness in her chest spread so wide she feared she might burst. What a complete mess she'd made of her life. Why did loving a man have to prove so difficult?

"Forgive me." He placed his hand on her shoulder, making her back tense. "I will march straight to the marquis this minute and declare my love, if that will allay your fears."

She shook her head rapidly. "No, I do not expect you to do that."

"Please, *mo leannan*. I grew angry back there and

acted poorly. Please, come with me. We shall purchase a leg of lamb for your mother's fire. Allow me to make amends."

"No." Akira stepped away from his palm. "I need time to think. So much has happened. I was upset when I left Huntly, then I was abducted, and then you rescued me... a-and for that my love for you grew ever deeper—"

"See?" He reached for her hand, but Akira snatched it away.

Her head spun as she looked up at him. "I-I-I was out of sorts at Huntly. I felt like an urchin trying to push my way into a life of nobility. I felt false."

"If you did not feel welcome in my home, then it was my fault. I should have insisted Elizabeth leave as soon as we arrived." This time he pulled her into his embrace, squeezing so tight he gave her no chance to push away. "I need to prove to you that I am worthy. Please, do not allow today's foibles to mar your judgment."

Akira trembled with tears that insisted on pouring from her eyes. "A-and yet I'm the one who feels unworthy."

"Nay, lass." His voice turned to melted butter. "Your value exceeds that of any noble in Scotland."

Merciful father, what was she to think? She loved him so much. She loved her sisters, too, but there were so many things to consider and she hadn't had a moment to herself to set her thoughts straight. "Would you mind postponing our feast for a day? I've said it afore. I'm merely a simple lass, and in a very short amount of time, you've turned my world upside down."

"A day?" He inhaled deeply, his strength and ever-present warmth providing far too much succor. "I think I can live with that."

"Thank you." Heaven help her, she was powerless to resist him—practically powerless to think when in his arms.

"I'll see you home. A day—that will give me time to organize the grandest feast your mother has ever seen."

Akira looked to the heavens. "I assure you there's no need to be extravagant."

He offered his elbow. "I ken just what to do. Leave the preparations to me."

* * *

As Akira bumbled through her chores the next morning, her head ached like she'd been hit between the eyes. And from the sideways glances from her sisters, she had not a single ally in the cottage. Even Ma had been unusually quiet since they returned from market day.

Kynda came inside with an armload of firewood. She stomped across the floor and dropped it in a heap. "So, what is a mistress? And why does everyone keep whispering like you're trying to keep secrets from me?"

"That is not your concern," snapped Ma, looking up from her mending. "Stack the wood properly and then sweep up after yourself. Look at that, you've brought in a trail of rubbish."

Annis bent down to help—odd behavior for her. "A mistress is a lady who has found favor with a gentleman."

Kynda fetched the broom. "What does that mean?"

"She keeps him entertained," Annis continued. "Helps him plan balls and gatherings and all sorts of important things."

"Ah." Kynda swept the bits of bark into a pile. "That doesn't sound so bad."

"No, it doesn't," said Annis, throwing a heated look over her shoulder.

"That's enough." Ma tied a knot and pulled it taut with added vigor. "I do not want to hear another word."

Akira picked up the bucket. "I'm off to fetch some water for washing up."

"Can I come?" asked Kynda.

"No." Akira hastened outside, then broke into a run.

*What is wrong with me? I should be thinking about the welfare of my sisters. I ken Geordie loves me. If he grows tired of me once I'm older, I'll simply have to find my way. I can always work as a healer.*

Mayhap Annis was right for once in her life. Akira had been acting selfishly. Why shouldn't they all move to Huntly? Perhaps if Ma and the lassies were there, she'd not feel so out of sorts.

She stooped to fill the bucket, yet a weight still hung around her neck like a smithy's anvil. Regardless of her lofty values, her life was far from a fairy tale, and she had no recourse but to face her lot. Akira's dreams of finding a husband and helping him become prosperous were but the fanciful musings of a stupid girl. It was time to look at the positive side of Geordie's offer.

Once they moved to Huntly, there would be innumerable opportunities for her sisters. Mayhap Geordie's physician could help Ma, too.

"Well, well," said a sinister voice from behind. "And I thought you'd give me a bit more sport."

Ice slithered up her spine like a snake.

She didn't need to turn around to know who it was. Filling the bucket, Akira tried to keep her voice level. "I thought you were heading west."

"Hmm, a ruse to divert the duke's men from my

trail." His nasal reply sent chills down the outside of her arms.

Akira's eyes shifted, and she peered over her shoulder. Dear God, Captain Weaver was flanked by at least a dozen dragoons. She set the bucket on the bank. "You thought you'd need a whole retinue of men to capture me?"

He reached. "I—"

Akira sprang up and leapt across the burn. "Help! Ma! Help!"

"Dammit, after her!"

Running for dear life, Akira headed for the cottage, waving her arms and shouting for help at the top of her lungs.

Footsteps slapped the ground behind. "God damn you to hell!" the captain roared.

Sucking in sharp gasps of air, Akira pushed her legs harder. He grabbed her hair. Knocked off balance, she threw her hands out to break her fall as a shrill scream tore from her throat. Grunting with the jarring thud, Akira scrambled for her footing, but her feet tangled in her blasted skirts.

In the blink of an eye, the captain pinned her to the ground. "No one makes a fool out of me," he growled in her face. "And now you're mine."

He dragged her arms together, slapping cold iron manacles around her wrists.

She struggled beneath his weight. "I have done nothing."

"You can tell that to the Marquis of Atholl. I've had word with him to ensure he kens of all the duke's misdeeds."

"No. He's innocent. You wretched man. Have you nothing better to do than bully innocent people?"

Weaver laughed. "If you were innocent, I'd be chasing after some other Jacobite upstart."

The captain dragged Akira to her feet while her sisters hollered, running from the shieling.

"Stay back!" Akira cried. Merciful Father, she couldn't pull her family into this mess.

"Remove your filthy hands from my daughter!" Ma shouted from the doorway.

All the lassies stopped, held back by the dragoons. "What are you doing with my sister?" demanded Annis.

The captain snorted through his enormous nose. "She's been caught aiding Jacobite loyalists and will stand trial for her crimes."

"How can helping someone be a crime?" Scota asked. "My sister is the kindest person in all of Dunkeld."

"Aye," Kynda agreed, stamping her foot.

Akira eyed her sisters. "Go back home. Ma will ken what to do." She dared not utter Geordie's name for fear it might be used against her—and even worse, against him.

"Don't bother." The captain pulled her along as dragoons fell in step around them. "I aim to make an example of this tinker, and anyone who stands in my way will receive the same harsh measures."

Akira gulped. Queen Anne sat on her throne in London, leagues away from Dunkeld. What did it matter that Akira had helped a fallen Highlander?

*I've committed no crime.*

# Chapter Thirty-Three

Forcing himself to wait in his chamber at the inn, Geordie read the gazette. He had read the same paragraph over and over, and still he couldn't recall what it was about. Though anxious to return home, he needed to be patient. At least somewhat patient. If Akira needed time, he would allow her a day, mayhap two. This evening, however, he planned a gathering of all gatherings. Laini and her daughters would be overjoyed, for certain.

Geordie didn't intend to use Akira's family to influence her decision, but treating them with kindness couldn't hurt his cause. He was turning the page when a clamor in the passageway caught his attention.

Shrill voices and multiple footsteps clomped over the floorboards beyond his door.

"What the devil—?"

Casting aside the gazette, he strode across his chamber and pulled on the latch.

"Oh, thank heavens." Laini clutched her hand over her heart, leaning on her crutch and gasping as if she'd just run a mile.

Geordie took quick note of the faces staring at him, with Oliver behind the lot. "Where's Miss Akira?"

"The dragoons took her, Your Grace," said Annis, her voice shrill.

Scota clutched her fists beneath her chin and cringed. "They slapped a set of manacles on her like she was a murderer."

Ma wobbled as if she were about to swoon. "Said there would be a trial."

Geordie took Laini's elbow and ushered her to the chair. "What? Who dares to be so rash?"

Annis fanned her face with her hands. "The officer looked mean and evil."

"Captain Weaver, no doubt," said Oliver.

Geordie's gut twisted. "You said he was well on his way west."

Oliver shrugged. "He could have doubled back."

"Bloody hell, man. Why did you not stay on his trail?"

Of course, the soldier had no response.

Dragging his fingers through his hair, Geordie paced. "We must act quickly. I'll try to see her and I'll speak to the marquis. Mayhap I can set the record straight."

"If it comes to a battle, we're in trouble." Oliver spread his palms. "We only have twelve men."

"I bloody well ken how many men are in my retinue," Geordie snapped. "Send runners. One to Gordon lands and one to the MacDonells."

"What about Ewen Cameron?" Oliver asked. "His army is unsurpassed."

"No time," Geordie said. "Tell them to ride night and

day—change horses when needed. No sleeping until their message is delivered."

"Come straight to Dunkeld, Your Grace?"

"Nay. Tell them to skirt the village. We'll assemble in the wood at Cally Loch." He thrust his finger toward the door. "Go now—and haste ye back. You'll be accompanying me to Blair Castle."

After Oliver took his leave, Geordie placed his hand on Laini's shoulder. "You and your daughters are not safe at the cottage. I want you under Gordon protection."

"In the forest?" asked Kynda, her eyes wide.

"You'll remain here for the time being—at least until I've had a chance to assess exactly what we're up against." He looked each lass in the eye. "But I do not want a one of you stepping outdoors without a Gordon guard escorting you."

"Yes, Your Grace," said Annis, with a bit too much cheer considering her sister had just been arrested.

He shook his finger to ensure each lass listened well. "And you are not to leave the premises whilst I'm visiting the marquis."

Laini wrung her hands. "But I need to see my daughter."

"You must obey me on this." He clutched Akira's mother by the shoulders and met her gaze. "I swear to you I will see to her release, or the Marquis of Atholl will rue the day he allowed that contemptuous Captain Weaver to meddle in my affairs."

* * *

Geordie paced Blair Castle's enormous entrance hall trying not to jump out of his bloody skin while Oliver stood like a statue with his hands clasped behind his back.

"How dare the insolent cur make me wait?" He snatched his pocket watch and opened it. "We've been here nearly an hour."

A tall, slender lad strolled into the hall with his nose in a book.

Clearing his throat, Geordie regarded the lad while he replaced his watch. Dressed in a kilt of fine wool and a doublet of silk, his brown locks pulled back at the nape, he sported a particular aristocratic arch to his brow. A handsome lad, indeed.

With a start, the lad stopped and lowered his book. "F-forgive me, sir."

"You're addressing the Duke of Gordon, young sir," Oliver said with a growl.

The lad formed an O with his mouth as his eyes grew round. They were unusually expressive eyes, a penetrating shade of moss green. Remembering his manners, the lad bowed. "Forgive me, Your Grace. Lord Aiden Murray here. Sorry, I wasn't informed of your visit."

*John's son, no doubt.*

Geordie looked expectantly past the lad's shoulder. "I'm here to see your father."

"Right. Da was in the drawing room last I saw him." Lord Murray stepped closer, examining Geordie from head to toe while a perplexed expression made his eyebrows pinch together. "So...you are the Duke of Gordon—the Jacobite Da has spoken about?"

*Nothing like blurting out an accusation akin to blasphemy.*

Geordie affected a stern scowl. "Your father has been spreading rumors about me?"

"I do not think so." The lad drummed his fingers on his chin as if he regarded scowling dukes all the time.

"'Tis just I'm trying to understand our present state of affairs. I mean, why is it the Protestants fear popery? It makes no sense to me at all for Parliament in London to refuse to name"—the lad peered around him, then cupped a hand to his mouth and leaned very close—"James Francis Edward Stuart successor on the grounds he is being raised a Catholic." It seemed Aiden Murray might understand the sensitivity of such a topic—and he truly seemed curious.

Regardless, Geordie crossed his arms. He could not be played for a dupe. The marquis could very well be using his son to evoke a confession. "Many a man has asked the same," Geordie said, seeking middle ground and admitting to nothing.

"It seems to me that Queen Anne is completely unprepared to rule," Lord Murray continued in a whisper. "She hasn't been properly educated. Her only qualification over James is her religion."

Bloody oath, Geordie could carry on for a month regarding this very topic. "Have you posed these questions to your father?"

"Aye, but he only shouts and tells me my lot is to accept the edicts of the land and keep my nose clean."

Geordie laughed. "Perhaps that is good advice for a lad of—pray tell, what is your age?"

"Eighteen, Your Grace."

"You're quite tall. Are you the heir?" the duke asked, steering the conversation away from anything that would see him accused of treason.

"Second son."

Geordie held up a finger. "And second in line to inherit."

"Och, my brother is better suited to inherit than I."

Lord Murray rolled his eyes with a wry grin. "He doesn't ask so many questions."

Perhaps the lad's curiosity was genuine, though Geordie couldn't take a chance and humor him. Instead, he opted to encourage the lad to talk. "And what do you aspire to?"

Squaring his shoulders, Aiden stood even taller. "After university I aim to seek a posting in the Royal Scots Navy."

Geordie gave an appreciative nod. "A young man with an adventurous spirit, I see."

"What better way to see Christendom?"

"Aye, and mayhap you'll find the answers to your questions." Geordie would have liked to invite the lad to the inn at Dunkeld and buy him a tankard of ale, if it weren't for his paternity. Alas, some friendships could never be. Especially when standing under the roof of the most influential Whig in all of Scotland.

The lad bowed, but before he had a chance to excuse himself, the valet stepped into the hall. "Your Grace, the marquis will see you now."

"'Tis about time." Geordie beckoned to Oliver. "Come."

The valet held up his palm. "His Lordship asked to see only you."

"What? Does he think I'm planning to launch an attack in his drawing room?"

The man bowed. "This way, Your Grace."

Geordie cast a backward glance at his man-at-arms and held up his palm, telling him to stay put. At least he hadn't been asked to surrender his weapons.

"'Twas a pleasure meeting you, Your Grace," called Lord Murray.

"And you," Geordie said over his shoulder. "Perhaps we can share a dram of whisky should you ever pay a visit to Huntly Castle."

The valet ushered him into a drawing room that rivaled his own. "The Duke of Gordon, m'lord."

The insolent marquis sat in an overstuffed chair beside his hearth, wearing a tawny periwig and dressed to the nines, reading a missive as if he hadn't a care in the world.

*The smug bastard.*

Geordie didn't wait for him to rise. "Damnation, John, what the devil is going on under your very nose? Captain Weaver arrested Akira Ayres this morning and then forbade me to visit her. I swear you have pushed me to the brink. This is an unacceptable and preposterous state of affairs."

The marquis opened his snuff box, pinched a bit, shoved it up an inordinately large nostril, then sneezed into a goddamned lace kerchief. "Are you referring to the lass I found in your company at the market?"

"You ken very well to whom I am referring." Geordie strode straight up to the table. "What, exactly, are the charges?"

"Aiding a traitor." The man didn't even look up.

"But you yourself supported James—Jesus, man, you stood beside me when I held Edinburgh Castle." Throwing up his hands, Geordie paced. "The way you're behaving, you'd think Queen Anne has offered you a dukedom."

The marquis smirked, picking up his missive.

Geordie lunged forward and slapped the parchment from his hand. "That's it. You've been behind the miserable captain all along. What? Have you promised him a portion of *my* lands in return for *my* ruination?"

John studied his fingernails. "That's taking things a bit far. But I must say, the queen desires to rid the Highlands of all those who seek to dethrone her."

*I could wring the swine's neck right here and now.* "Right, so the childless woman on the throne wants to keep her arse in Kensington Palace? I fail to see where the queen's wishes have anything to do with the wee lassie."

Crossing his arms and his legs, John made a show of looking bored. Christ, he was as talented at the aloof noble act as Geordie himself—except he doubted the onion-eyed codpiece was acting.

The Marquis of Atholl frowned, as serious as a judge. "There are a litany of reasons why I agreed to Miss Ayres's arrest. First, my captain believed she helped you escape when you rode against the queen's men—after all, it was your flask found on the battlefield." John leaned forward and shook his finger. "It might smear my reputation to arrest you, since you hold in your possession a document signed by my captain declaring your innocence—though written under duress."

"You are wrong," Geordie fumed, certain that steam was blowing from his ears. "Akira has done nothing illegal, nothing traitorous, and I will attest to it before a magistrate if I must."

"Aye? But her name is Ayres." John smirked like a boor. "Does that not strike a chord with you, George? We've both suffered at the thieving hands of tinkers."

Geordie's gut clamped into a knot. This man was insufferable. "Can you let nothing go? We cleared Scotland of the thieves—of those who were our true enemies. Any who remain have molded into society. They're no more outlaws than I."

The marquis chuckled. "I see you make my point so well."

Now the cur had crossed the line. Sauntering forward, Geordie didn't stop until he stood toe to toe with the marquis, towering over the seated stuffed pheasant. But he wasn't about to start making threats—threats would only serve to show his hand. He wasn't about to let the bastard know how much he cared for Akira, either, because that would give the marquis more power than he deserved. "Come, John," he said in a low, pointed tone. "As one peer to another, I appeal to you to release Miss Ayres into my custody. I shall remove her and her kin to Huntly, where they will never bother you again."

"I wish it were that easy."

"But it is."

"I think not."

Geordie's jaw twitched. "Do you truly want Clan Gordon as your enemy?"

"Times are changing." The marquis sat back, making a show of panning his gaze up to Geordie's face, his eyes blacker than coal. "Anyway, 'tis not the lass I want. Confess to being a traitor and I will release her."

The duke's throat went dry.

*Dear God, this whole ruse is a plot to ruin me—the bastard is sitting there salivating. I'll wager he cannot wait to sink his claws into my lands.*

"Me? A traitor? Preposterous." Cracking his fingers, Geordie again imagined wrapping them around John's neck and squeezing the life out of the varlet.

John shrugged. "You held Edinburgh against King William."

"And you were there, you turncoat." Narrowing his

gaze, Geordie fought for self-control. Aye, he'd insure he walked out of Blair Castle to exact his revenge. "Must I remind you that after William marched on London, many of us were outraged—including you, my friend. We stood behind James the Second, our sovereign, God rest his soul. After all, he inherited the throne. And furthermore, I would not be here before you this day if I hadn't received a pardon."

"Ah yes, yet another pardon." Licking his lips, the marquis chuckled. "You're such a rogue, George."

Heat spiked up the back of Geordie's neck. "Do not toy with me."

"Very well." John waved a dismissive hand. "I'll give you a sennight to set your affairs in order. If you do not come forward and confess, then I will ensure the lass swings from the gallows."

"For what?" Geordie yelled, on the brink of losing control—something a duke would never do. "She's a goddamned healer, for Christ's sake."

"Aye, and she's woven her tendrils around your heart."

He scoffed—revealing the depth of his love would be a mortal mistake. No, no, he must plant the seed of doubt in the man's mind. "She helped me, and that is all."

"Aye? Well then, I'm sure a man like you wouldn't even consider saving a good-for-nothing's life by offering up his own."

"You have no idea what I would and wouldn't do. But I've learned one thing from meeting with you this day."

"And what is that, pray tell?"

Geordie's lips thinned. "You have no soul."

* * *

Akira curled in a corner of the dank pit with her arms wrapped around her shins, her head bent over her knees. She'd been there for hours with no food, no water, and not a word from another soul. After the captain pushed her into the hole in the pit prison of the tolbooth, muttering curses and threatening to ruin the Duke of Gordon, she'd been left with a twisted ankle and nothing but her wits to keep her sane.

The only light in the pit shone through the hole in the ceiling, which was covered by an iron grate. Across the chamber, water trickled, enough to cause a chill to hang in the air. She was cold and hungry, her entire body numb.

When she'd refused to bear witness against the duke, Captain Weaver had shown no mercy. "*We'll talk again after you've had a chance to commune with the rats.*"

She shuddered and raised her head enough to peer through the dim light. Something scampered—something dark.

*I hate rats.*

That miserable, hollow chasm stretched inside her chest again.

If the captain planned to kill her, she prayed for a swift death.

The scraping from the iron grate above made chills skitter up her spine. Someone shoved a rickety ladder through the gap.

Pushing to her feet, Akira kept her back against the wall while a pair of black boots stepped on the top rung. Bile churned in her stomach as she watched Captain Weaver climb down and place a torch on the wall.

Her gaze darted around the chamber. Slimy green algae lined the far wall, and a pile of rotted straw appeared to move.

When he faced her, the torchlight illuminated his form, his eyes but a shadow. She didn't need to see his face to know he was smiling, and then his chuckle confirmed it. "I offered you a chance at freedom once before, but it seems you value the duke's life more than your own."

Akira pursed her lips, crossing her arms. Aye, this pit might be hell on earth, but she would not betray Geordie.

He braced his hands on the wall, either side of her head. "But I no longer feel like being lenient."

Her chin ticked up. "Do what you like with me, I'll not speak ill of an innocent man."

"Hmm." He sniffed and rubbed her hair between his fingers. "I've spent a fair bit of time thinking about what I'd like to do with you. Tell me, has the duke sampled your wares?" The cur laughed. "Did he force you, or did you offer to spread your legs for him?"

"Stop this. You are vulgar." Akira focused on the ladder, just over his shoulder.

"Indeed, I find my vulgarity most entertaining, especially when faced with such tempting quarry."

A spike of vigor rushed through her blood as she ducked under his arm and sprinted for freedom.

"Argh!" Akira's head snapped back. She clapped her hands to her head as he practically tore her hair from her scalp. Worse, he snatched her into his steely arms, thrusting himself against her back. "You're mine. You cannot run from me."

Ice pulsed through her veins. The man was insane. "I'm no slave."

"Truly? You're my prisoner and I can do anything I please with you." He slid his hand to her breast and squeezed. Hard.

Struggling to free herself, she pushed against him,

only to be met with an unmoving chest. "Geor—th-the duke will chase you to the ends of the earth if you dare..." Dear Lord, she couldn't utter it.

The captain rubbed himself into her buttocks and licked her neck, his hand still groping like he was wringing out a sponge.

Holy Mother, the ice in Akira's blood turned to fire. She'd die before she allowed this cur to violate her—allowed him to touch her the way the blackguard at the alehouse had hurt Ma.

The captain pushed her against the wall, trapping her by holding his hand to her neck. Clothing rustled. She glanced over her shoulder.

Uncle Bruno's voice whispered in her head. *Break away toward the thumbs.*

Throwing her elbow, she hit the captain in the jaw as she whipped around, breaking the weakest part of his grip. In one fluid motion, her fingers wrapped around the hilt of his dagger and ripped it from its scabbard.

"Bitch!" Weaver howled and faced her with a snort. "You think you can take the likes of me with that wee dagger."

She swiped an X through the air. "Mayhap not, but I can certainly have a go at severing your ballocks."

His gaze hawkish, he slid back a step. "With you in my clutches, we have the traitor right where we want him." He smirked. "I didn't realize how much an urchin like you could mean to him until he betrayed himself on the road to Inverness."

Akira's heart fluttered, and then it sank right down to her toes when realization set in. "You're using me to blackmail him?"

"I wouldn't call it blackmail." Weaver licked his lips,

watching the knife as it shook in Akira's hand. "You see, if he admits to treason, his lands will be forfeit. And with my ties to the marquis, I reckon I'd like a piece of that—mayhap I'll even earn a barony."

She clamped her other hand over the knife and steadied it right in line with his loins. "You are disgusting."

"Who are you to talk? You're swiving a duke. In return for what? Fancy dresses? A suite of rooms? How are you any different from me?" He took a daring step forward.

Akira swiped the knife. "Stay back."

"Tell you what." He held out his palm. "Give the dagger to me, and I'll make you *my* mistress, and when they grant me lands and title you might even be kept in style."

"Not on your miserable life." She tightened her grip. "You signed a proclamation proving the Duke of Gordon's innocence. Why can you not leave us in peace? Surely there are real enemies out there for you to chase after and torture."

Akira backed up, hitting the stone wall.

"And yet you threaten me, brandishing a knife against one of Her Majesty's officers. You want to be tortured? Well, I have a notion to make you spend a week in the pillory for your treason."

He lunged from the side and grabbed her wrist.

Faster, Akira jabbed, the blade catching his forearm before he clamped hard and twisted.

She cried out as searing pain shot up her arm and the weapon dropped from her grip.

The captain snatched the knife from the ground, then clutched his wounded limb to his body. "You cut me, you bitch."

Akira bared her teeth. "I'd do it again."

Fast as a viper, he snatched her hair and pulled. "I'll

bend you to my will, and soon you'll be begging for me to give it to you."

Gritting her back molars, she twisted with the force of his savage tug. "You'll never break me."

He raised his palm.

Akira flinched.

"Captain, you've a caller," a voice shouted from above.

With one last yank of her hair, Weaver shoved her to the ground. "Until you grovel at my feet and worship me, I promise to make your life a living hell."

Akira covered her mouth and forced herself to hold back tears. Only after the ladder was pulled up and the grate slid back over her only window to freedom did she slump in a heap, despair numbing her entire body. Her head swam. How could that man be so evil when he was supposed to be defending the queen's people?

Akira muffled her cries in her hands until a voice resounded from above. A deep voice that lifted her heart and made it soar.

"If you touch her, I will see to your hanging myself," Geordie boomed.

"She'll pay for her crimes," the captain countered.

"The lass is innocent."

"The magistrate will determine that in due course."

"When this is over, I swear on my father's grave I will not be the one ruined."

Akira dropped to her knees and folded her hands. *Dear Jesus, help us.*

# Chapter Thirty-Four

Geordie hated waiting, and now days had passed, driving him to the brink of madness. He'd set up a makeshift command post, taking over the entire inn, barking orders because there was little else that could be done until his damned reinforcements arrived.

While he paced, Akira's sisters sat at a rickety table, playing a game of dice. With every clanking roll, Geordie wanted to swipe the wooden cubes from the board and throw them into the fire. Moreover, with every roll of the dice, the knots in his shoulders wound a bit tighter.

But telling them to find something else to do was out of the question. He needed to keep them nearby in case they had to make a quick escape. And he wasn't about to see another Ayres daughter fall into Captain Weaver's clutches.

Their mother had shut herself in a chamber above stairs and refused to come down. Geordie had never seen anyone so afraid to show her face in public, and he now understood how much gumption it had taken for Laini to leave the shieling and fetch him.

"I have news, Your Grace." Oliver pushed through the door. Thank God. He'd gone to rendezvous with the troops at Cally Loch yesterday.

"Damn it, man—" The lassies gasped at his curse, but Geordie ignored them. "Have out with it."

"Three hundred Gordons and a hundred MacDonells rode day and night. They've set up camp at the loch and are awaiting orders."

"Will there be another battle?" asked Annis.

Geordie frowned. "Let's just say I aim to alter some priorities."

A rumble like an army on the march resounded from the road. He looked to Oliver. "You told the men to stay out of sight?"

"Aye, even told them no fires."

Geordie hastened to the window. "Holy hellfire, what is it now?" The door burst open and a rather disheveled tinker strode inside, scowling and brandishing an ax like he was ready to start swinging. The crazed man wore orange-and-green striped breeches with a saffron shirt. His black hair spiked every which way—it looked like the mop hadn't seen a comb in a fortnight. Though his skin was olive and tanned, he had oddly piercing blue eyes. Geordie leaned in—the man's eyes looked just like Akira's.

"What is the meaning of this?" the character demanded in a most accusing tone, while townsfolk filed in behind him—not the well-dressed folk who lived in the nice houses near the square, but the ones dressed in rags with dirty faces. Some carried broom handles and rocks, as if they were ready for a fight.

Drawing his sword, Oliver stepped between them. "Who the hell are you?"

"Uncle Bruno?" Annis said.

"Brunooooooooooo!" Kynda ran to the crazed man and wrapped her arms around him.

Maintaining a distrustful gaze on Oliver and Geordie, Bruno pushed the lass behind him. "Are you holding these lassies against their will? Where is my sister? I went to her cottage to find the place empty, the fire pit cold." Peering over Oliver's shoulder, the man snarled. "Worse, these good folk tell me my niece is in the pit on account of the Duke of Gordon. And by your finery, I'd reckon that would be you."

"That's right," said a man brandishing a broomstick. "I saw His Grace with her—and they were arguing, too."

Geordie held out his hands. "You misunderstand. I'm trying to free Miss Akira, I—"

"Liar!" someone shouted from the rear.

"He's a Highlander of the worst sort," another hollered.

"Bruno!" Laini stood at the top of the stairs, grasping the banister with both hands. "The duke is helping us, you joob. Put the ax down afore you hurt yourself."

The ax lowered. "But these good folk—"

"—do not ken the whole story," Laini said as she remained in place, her arms shaking.

Bruno eyed Geordie. "What the devil...?"

"Would you care for a pint of ale, *my friend*?" He stressed the words *my friend*, hoping to cool off the man's misplaced ire. Careful not to take his eye off the varlet in case he decided to charge like a bull, Geordie gestured to a table. The last thing he needed at the moment was to deal with a pack of hostile townsfolk and their confused, wildly dressed leader.

Once Bruno and a number of other misguided people were seated with a tankard of ale in front of them, Oliver helped Laini down the stairs. Geordie stood beside her, keeping an eye on her brother while she filled them in on the truth.

His scowl set firmly in place, Bruno didn't seem convinced. "But the duke is still the reason why Akira's in the tolbooth."

"That's true," Geordie interjected for the first time, slamming his fist into his palm. "But I have a plan."

Everyone looked at him expectantly, including Oliver.

A lad pushed through the crowd, panting like he'd run a footrace. "They've locked her in the pillory!"

The hall rumbled as Bruno shoved his chair back and sprang to his feet. "I'll not stand for it."

"Nor will I." Geordie drew his dirk and held it high. "I've an entire army waiting to attack."

"Not in the square. You'll not win in the square. There are too many dragoons guarding the prison." The crease between Bruno's eyebrows eased, and he took on a crooked grin. "Now I'm the one with the plan."

Good God, he didn't have time to muck around. "You'd best talk fast."

Bruno gestured to the crowd. "We have an army in disguise right here."

Geordie regarded the soiled faces, most of them scowling. At him, no less. "You mean this lot of tinkers?"

"Aye. Gather round." Bruno grasped the back of his chair and leaned forward. "I'll take my men and cause a stir. Kynda—do you remember what I taught you about having tricky fingers?"

"I do." The wee lass slipped a dagger from Geordie's sock and he didn't feel a damned thing.

Geordie plucked the knife from the lass's fingers. "You taught this child to be a thief?"

"I taught her how to survive in the gutter." Bruno grasped Kynda by the shoulders and looked her in the eye. "We'll form a mob by the pillory—shout about how outraged we are, then when the pushing and shoving starts, you snatch the keys from the captain's belt. Can you do that?"

Laini lumbered to her feet. "You're asking my wee bairn to put her life in peril?"

"*Dordi, dordi*, sister," Bruno said, using some sort of Gypsy gibberish. "I swear nothing will happen to her."

Geordie didn't like it. He shoved his finger under the lassie's bullheaded uncle's nose. "If we're going to do this, once Kynda has the key, she must give it to me."

"Nay." Bruno shook his head. "Ye cannot be there, 'cause then they'll ken it is a trap."

"Dammit, man." Geordie stepped closer, towering over Akira's uncle. "I'll not stand in the shadows whilst you risk Akira's life and that of her sisters."

Bruno met the duke's glare with a scowl of his own. "But any man will ken 'tis you from a mile away."

Shifting his gaze down the man's ridiculous costume, Geordie snorted. "Not if I'm wearing a tinker's orange-striped breeches and a saffron shirt."

"Aye?" Bruno scratched the black stubble on his chin, shifting his gaze to one of his men. "I merely have to look at that bonny face to ken you're nobility."

"Nothing a bit of soot cannot fix." Geordie squared his shoulders and loomed over the man. "Just try to stop me."

"You have a set of cods—for a duke." Bruno lifted his

chin and crossed his arms. The man might think he had the upper hand, but his change in attitude showed his accord. "How many men do you have?"

Oliver held up his palms, with a cautious gesture toward the crowd. "More than you."

Geordie leaned closer to the man and whispered, "Three hundred."

"What about horses?"

"What do you need?"

Bruno grinned. "I reckon we might get along just fine, Your Grace."

* * *

Praying for a miracle, Akira waited with her head and wrists restrained in the wooden pillory. She'd seen it many times before—the hecklers always came and tormented the prisoners. They threw rotten food and all manner of vile rubbish at the poor souls, some of whom were guilty of nothing more than being unable to pay their taxes. She always feared one day she'd be accused of something and end up here, on display for public humiliation. No matter how much she tried to help people, no matter how much she tried to be honest and caring, there were always those who pointed the finger her way and accused her of some misdeed or being a Gypsy witch.

Footsteps stomped from up the road—as if the soldiers were marching. She could raise her head enough to see a hundred paces or so along High Street before the wooden board pushed into the back of her skull. Heaven give her strength—an entire line of townsfolk came into view, marching shoulder to shoulder, heading straight for the pillory platform. As far as she could see, angry faces were approaching, the men carrying broomsticks, picks, and shovels as if they aimed to bludgeon her to death.

Her throat constricted. Every nerve ending trembled. *Dear God, please let my death be swift.* She closed her eyes and steeled her mind for the pain to come.

"Free the lass!" a man shouted.

Akira's eyes flashed open.

The mob started to run, the roar almost deafening. In seconds, they surrounded her like a crowd hell-bent on murder.

She cringed as a man jumped onto the platform, pounding the handle of his shovel onto the floor. "This is an outrage!"

A bead of sweat trickled from Akira's forehead as she listened to the bellows of the mob. Rather than taunting her, their shouts demanded her release. They hollered out praise and support.

"She's a sweet lass!"

"She healed my ma!" That was Tommy MacCarran's voice.

She wanted to cry and laugh all at the same time. If only these good Samaritans could do something to free her head and arms. If only the townsfolk were judge and jury.

Out of the corner of her eye, she saw a man dressed like a tinker approach, his face black, as if he'd been cleaning a flue. Tingles skittered across the back of Akira's neck.

*Uncle Bruno? Nay. He's not that tall.*

The shouts grew louder and more people climbed atop the platform, blocking her view of the street.

"She helped to birth my wee bairn."

"Akira has never lifted a finger to harm a soul."

"Silence!" Captain Weaver shouted over the throng. "Disband immediately or I will command the musketeers to fire."

The cur stood in front of the magistrate's door, brandishing his flintlock pistol and flanked by three dragoons—the same three who'd laughed when they'd tied her wrists and taunted her, threatening to send her to the gallows in Inverness.

Kynda ran toward the captain, her black braids flapping behind her. "Release my sister!"

"No!" Akira screamed, fighting against the wood clamped around her neck and wrists. Her heart thundered in her ears. "Kynda, stop!" She twisted her head, searching for anyone who would listen. "Stop my sister! They'll hurt her!"

The wee lass paid no heed to Akira's shouts, now lost in the roar of the crowd. No one listened. No one noticed the child charging straight for the officer and swinging her fists.

Akira fought harder against her wooden snare. "Leave my sister be! She's done nothing wrong."

Captain Weaver reached for Kynda. The lass slipped from Akira's line of sight. Suddenly, someone smacked the officer with a bat, and he clapped a hand to his nose, blood gushing through his fingers, while the dragoons beside him thrust their bayonets into the crowd.

Weaver fired his pistol into the air with a deafening crack. "I'll kill—!"

The rumble of the crowd drowned out the captain's threat as they mobbed him, a big hand reaching in and taking his weapon.

Frantically trying to break free from her bonds, Akira

searched for Kynda in the melee. Everything was a blur in the mayhem of rioting villagers.

"Kynda!" she screamed at the top of her lungs.

Orange-and-green striped breeches blocked her line of sight.

"Easy, lass. I'll have you out of here before you can say a Hail Mary."

*Geordie!*

Dear blessed Jesus, Akira would recognize the deep bass of his voice anywhere.

And he was right. Metal scraped like a key in a padlock. The lock dropped and the wooden pillory arm released. She rubbed her wrists, taking a deep breath.

Geordie's face was hidden beneath a hood, but his grin was every bit the man she loved. He tugged her hand. "I have mounts waiting."

"Thank God you're here—my sister—" She started to run toward the mob, but Geordie swept her into his arms, taking her away. "No!" Akira thrashed. "I must find Kynda."

Geordie kept running. "She's safe."

Akira pointed. "But she was—"

"'Twas a ruse to steal the key." He sped toward two tethered horses. "Can you ride?"

"Are you mad? You used a wee ten-year-old?" She pounded a fist against his chest. "No. I refuse to flee until I ken what's happened to my sister!"

Geordie set Akira down beside a horse and grasped her shoulders, the intensity of his hazel eyes pinning her where she stood. "Listen to me, dammit. She's with your uncle."

"Bruno?"

"I'll explain later." He bent down to give her a leg-up.

After she mounted, he handed her the reins and patted her knee. "We must make haste. They'll be after us soon."

"After us? But what of Ma? What of my sisters?"

He climbed aboard his stallion and tugged the hood lower on his brow. "They're all safe, but we won't be unless we ride like hellfire."

# Chapter Thirty-Five

And ride they did. Since the first time they'd set out together, Akira had grown quite adept at handling her mount. Pushing their horses to a gallop, Geordie led her out the south side of the village, over the River Tay, then he cut north. Just as he'd done numerous times that day, he prayed their ruse would lead Weaver straight to Cally Loch.

If he erred…

Devil's spit, he couldn't think about it.

Every few steps, he glanced over his shoulder to ensure she was in his wake and to look for redcoats in pursuit. He hated running. He wanted to stand and fight, but saving Akira trumped his every deeply bred Gordon instinct. That's right, a man had to choose his game and then outsmart his enemy.

He raced his mount up a crag. The horse beneath him snorted with exertion, but upward he climbed.

At the summit, Geordie reined the horse to a stop right before Akira rode up beside him.

"Thank God." He pointed. "We're not being followed."

"We're safe?"

His heart squeezed when he regarded the worried furrow in her brow. He'd been agonizing over the plan ever since the damned tinker decided they could be mates. "For now."

"Where's Ma? My sisters?"

Geordie's jaw clamped—had he put too much faith in Akira's uncle, a man he barely knew? "We're meeting them at Glenshee in the mountains."

"What about Uncle Bruno?"

"Him, too." Geordie slid down from his horse.

Akira did the same, peering at him over the saddle. "He came to Dunkeld because I was in the tolbooth?"

"Actually, no." Geordie took Akira's reins and tied both mounts. "He was passing through with a band of minstrels and found the cottage empty."

She stepped closer, those sultry almond-shaped eyes growing hypnotic. "Ah. That sounds more like my uncle." God, she was beautiful... and strong. Any other woman would be a simpering mess after spending days in the bowels of a prison and suffering the humiliation of the pillory. He'd been so damned worried. But now she was free, and as she neared, her strength grew, making Geordie's heart swell.

He wanted to tell her how much she meant to him, how much he loved her, how she could grow old and gray and his love for her would remain boundless. He wanted to tell her he would give her anything she desired. He wanted to say he'd protect her kin, he'd find husbands for her sisters, he'd have his physician care for Laini, but his tongue twisted.

*Words are not enough.*

Grasping her waist, he tugged her into his body. Lord have mercy, his knees buckled. Soft breasts molded into his chest, breasts he'd come to adore and wanted to explore further. Her moan vibrated inside his mouth as he met her lips. Every fiber in his body craved her, needed her, wanted to hold her, caress her, care for her, and be inside her.

When she eased her hips forward, his body reacted with potent desire shooting through his blood. He could throw her down on the moss right there and take her before God Almighty. But they had so far to go, and daylight was fleeting.

He pulled away enough to suck in a deep breath. "We must ride," he said, sounding like an iron rasp.

Akira's breath blew warm between the laces of his saffron shirt. Her hips pushed into him a bit harder when she looked to the moss. "Must we?" Aye, there was no mistaking her meaning.

A low chuckle rumbled in his chest. "Now I ken I'm in heaven." Och aye, a lusty rogue like George Gordon needed no more invitation. It had been too damned long since she'd forbidden him to bed her. He rubbed his hips from side to side, ensuring she felt the hard column of his desire.

She matched his motion, her moan driving him to the edge of his sanity.

Together, they descended to the ground.

"You're certain all is well with my kin?" Akira asked breathlessly.

"Aye." Geordie covered her mouth and laid her in the soft moss, slowly tugging up her skirts. "I want you hard and fast, and we haven't much time."

"I can't wait, either." Her breath came quick and as

raspy as his while she fumbled to unlace his breeches with trembling fingers.

He started to help, but with one quick tug, she had the front open. Her lips parted and her breathing sped as she tugged the breeches down his thighs. The cool air swirling around his member only served to make the moment more sensual.

He lifted her skirts higher and higher, bare knees leading to bare thighs, and finally, the most delectable nest of black curls he'd ever imagined. The sight ripped through the remaining shreds of his defense and rendered him completely and totally at her mercy.

Lithe fingers wrapped around his manhood. "I want you to join with me and never part."

A bead of his seed seeped out the tip of his cock as he lowered himself and hovered at her entrance.

Waves of black hair sprawled around her, parted lips, half-closed eyes. By the saints, she was a goddess. "Please, Geordie. I cannot wait."

Taking in a ragged breath, he fulfilled her wish in every way. Working her, watching her, swirling inside her, he waited, his every thrust taking mountains of control, until her eyes rolled back and a cry of pleasure caught in her throat. At that moment the floodgates opened. Satan himself could not have prevented Geordie's deep thrusts. Over and over he drove into her like a wild man staking his claim. In all his life, all his exploits, he'd never felt so connected with another. He'd never joined with a woman and experienced a consuming need to possess her, protect her, devour her, and yet love her with his flesh and soul.

The woman quivering and panting beneath him had completely and utterly broken the rake, and now Akira owned him.

After they'd made earth-shattering love on the crag, Akira stood by as Geordie changed his clothes, wrapped Uncle Bruno's striped breeches and saffron shirt around a rock, and drowned them in a pond.

"Do you think they'll blame you for my rescue?" she asked.

Geordie watched the ripples of water spreading and finally fading from where he'd tossed the clothes. "Nay. I was never there."

He gave her a leg up and together they climbed into the mountains, farther and farther from civilization.

* * *

In the pandemonium, Captain Weaver's nose throbbed and hurt like a son of a bitch, while blood oozed from his nostrils and splattered his coat. But not even a smack to the face would stop him from murdering the bastard with the bat. He was the person with the little brat who stole his key.

Hiding his face with a hood, the tinker wore the most obnoxious pair of orange-and-green striped breeches he'd ever seen.

The whole goddamn town had turned against him. Thank God he'd kept the battalion on full alert. He'd thought it would be the crazed Duke of Gordon who would stage something stupid to free his wench. God on the cross, Roddy had never seen a man embarrass himself so much. George Gordon paraded around Dunkeld like a lovesick fool, and now, at the hour of crisis, the captain hadn't seen a trace of the oversized Highlander.

Yes, there had been a skirmish, but Roddy had taken control quickly. After Sentinel Muldoon fired his musket into the mob, they'd disbanded as fast as they'd appeared. The only problem was that his quarry had slipped away to waiting horses.

*They planned the whole thing.*

But they wouldn't get far.

Not this time.

His horses were fresh. He had a battalion of fifty men in his wake. Wealth was so close he could taste it. George Gordon had practically signed a confession the way he ran after his lowly waif. By God, the marquis would salivate when the headsman sliced his ax through the Duke of Gordon's neck.

"I have Gordon in my clutches," Roddy shouted with a hearty laugh.

"Where is the bastard?" asked Corporal Snow, waving the pistol over his head.

"The tinker in the saffron shirt will lead us straight into his lair for certain."

Roddy swiped the blood from his face. Now he'd catch the varlet and the wench. Forget the pillory, he was now within his rights to lead them all straight to the gallows—even the damned snot-nosed brat who stole his key.

The iron taste of blood incited his lust for lands and power. He'd be recognized for his valor. He'd earn a barony for certain. Build a manse on a lake near his home in York.

All along, he knew he could outlast the Duke of Gordon. It was but a matter of time before His Lordship did something rash. The hooded man leading the pack was no duke. Dressed in outlandish breeches and a yellow shirt that was easier to spot than a homing beacon, he had to be one of the tinker's kin.

But Roddy would recognize the woman anywhere, riding behind a tinker with her long black tresses whipping in the wind. The vixen must pay. He'd lain in his bed at night thinking of all the ways he'd have her. Yes, he'd punish the spawn of the devil. No black-haired woman with such beauty could be pure or holy. When he caught the wench, he'd show her the might behind his uniform, and nothing would stop him this time. He'd bend her to his will, make her scream. Yes, she would become his whore, and when he was through with her, he'd leave her in the gutter to rot with the lepers.

"I've got a shot!" Sentinel Grey hollered as his musket fired.

Roddy's heart hammered faster as he watched for one of the riders to fall, but they all disappeared over the crest of a hill.

"Onward!" the captain shouted. Bloody oath, the entire town would pay when this was over.

*I will tighten the curfew, and anyone caught out after hours will be hanged.*

"They're heading for Cally Loch," shouted Snow.

"Fan out," Roddy bellowed. "We have them cornered." He laughed to himself as visions of his grand manse played in his mind. He'd have a parlor and a library and a drawing room to rival the Marquis of Atholl's.

They crested the hill, and a barrage of musket fire flashed and cracked. Lines of Highland musketeers faced them.

"It's a trap!" shouted Grey.

An icy weight dropped to the pit of Roddy's gut.

Musket fire smacked his chest, knocking him from his mount. Before Roderick Weaver felt pain, his world went black.

# *Chapter Thirty-Six*

Well past dark, Akira rode alongside Geordie while they climbed higher and higher into the mountains, negotiating a trail with steep drop-offs and hairpin curves. They'd been riding for hours and her eyelids had grown heavy.

"Where are we?" she asked in a whisper, but her voice carried like a shout.

"Scotland's hidden route to the Highlands." Geordie sounded as tired as she felt.

"How many people ken about it?"

"Not many, else it would be no secret."

"Do you ken where we're heading?"

"Aye."

"Aaaand . . . ?"

"The Spittal of Glenshee—have you heard of it?"

"Nay."

"I thought not."

"What's there?"

Geordie pointed through the shadows. "If you look close enough you can see for yourself."

Akira peered through the moonlight. Sure enough, the horses started down a slope, heading into a wee glen with rows of tents surrounding an enormous bonfire. "Who are all those people?"

"An entire army." Geordie ran his reins through his fingers. "You and I took the most circuitous route, so I reckon we might be late for the gathering, but I'll wager you'll ken some of the folk."

Up this high, violet heather still kissed the hills, welcoming them together with a carpet of wildflowers. Side by side, they cantered all the way to the bonfire, while shouts and cheers rose from the countless people who surrounded them. Uncle Bruno, Ma, and Akira's sisters were the first faces she recognized. Astonishingly, Annis was standing arm in arm with Oliver. Akira thought to give her sister a good talking to, until Sir Coll grasped her horse's bridle.

The big redheaded chieftain grinned and offered his hand. "'Tis good to see you've learned how to handle your mount, Miss Akira."

She let him help her down. "As I recall, His Grace didn't give me much choice in the matter." She chuckled. "'Twas ride like hellfire or die."

"Och, I always say 'tis best to be baptized by fire. One has no choice but to be a fast learner." He greeted Geordie with an elbow-to-elbow handshake. "'Tis good to see your ruse worked, Your Grace. We were starting to worry."

"About me?" Geordie clapped the chieftain on the shoulder. "Nah. My part of the plan was sound. The question is, how did you fare on your end?"

"You question me?" Coll threw back his head with a deep belly laugh. "Next time I'll need a bigger challenge, old man."

"Old man? What are you, one and twenty?" Fire suddenly replaced the fatigue in his eyes. "I can best you any day, ye aging pup."

"Did you hear?" Annis squeezed in beside Coll and grasped Akira's hands. "We dressed like you and led the redcoats into a trap."

"You dressed like me?" Goodness, Akira had rarely seen her sister with such a broad grin.

"And I rode double with Lieutenant Oliver." She flashed a huge smile at Geordie's man-at-arms. "I couldn't believe we were riding so fast, and the redcoats even shot at us, but we got away—"

"Shot at you?" She grimaced at at Geordie.

"Akira! My sweeting!" Uncle Bruno pushed his way through the crowd and wrapped her in a smothering embrace. "You look so much bonnier without your head and wrists locked in the pillory."

"'Tis a lot more comfortable, too." She held Bruno at arm's length—goodness, he was dressed in orange-and-green striped breeches and a saffron shirt identical to those Geordie had been wearing. As a matter of fact, so were the minstrels behind him. "But where did you come from? You only ever visit at Yuletide."

"The minstrels and I were passing through—and we discovered your duke needed some help freeing you from the jail."

Moving her hands to her hips, Akira faced Geordie. "So you put Annis in danger? And what about Kynda stealing the key from Captain Weaver?"

The duke's face fell. He looked like a setter caught

being naughty. "Your uncle promised the lass would be safe every step of the way, else I would not have allowed it."

Bruno looked even guiltier—more like a deerhound with his tail tucked between his legs. "Och, you ken Annis was in no real danger. After Kynda pinched the key and gave it to His Grace, the townsfolk swarmed the captain so he couldn't see the pillory platform, then while the duke took you south, I caught the captain's eye and headed due north with Annis—while two of the duke's guardsmen took your ma, Scota, and Kynda straight up here."

Rolling her eyes, Akira drew her hand to her forehead. "Oh, my word. I'm glad I wasn't aware of all this at the time."

"We had a good head start," Bruno explained. "The dragoons had to fetch their horses, and ours were ready to ride."

"Och, that makes me feel much better." She rolled her eyes to Geordie. "How could you have allowed this?"

Mr. Aristocratic All-powerful Duke shrugged like a wee lad. "It was the best idea I'd heard since arriving in Dunkeld."

"And no one can prove a thing," added Sir Coll. "They cannot blame the duke because he was nowhere to be seen."

"The townsfolk came to me, outraged." Geordie slung his arm around Akira's shoulder. "They all wanted to help you."

"Me?"

He gave her a warm squeeze. "Aye. It seems you've healed many of them, and they haven't forgotten."

Dear Lord, so much ado just for her, and so many people gathered. Her gaze panned across the faces. "Where is Ma?"

Bruno motioned with his head. "By the fire with Scota and Kynda."

"I'm here." The crowd parted and Ma hobbled forward on her crutch, then pulled Akira into an embrace. "And I cannot tell you how happy I am to have you back in my arms, sweeting."

Closing her eyes, Akira breathed in the homey scent of Ma. "I cannot believe you let them do it. Weren't you afraid?"

"Aye, but we needed to stand together to save you." Ma pulled away and cupped her cheek, her brown eyes shining with happiness. "And His Lordship was right when he said this was the best plan."

Akira chewed her bottom lip. It all seemed so dreamlike, and everyone she loved was right there. Mayhap it was the shock of everything happening at once, but that old hollow feeling spread through her stomach again. "We cannot return to Dunkeld, can we?"

"Never," Geordie said. "And I'm not allowing you out of my sight ever again."

She nodded and looked to her toes. Being the duke's mistress had its merits, and her sisters would live such better lives. Moreover, Ma would live in comfort. And by her life, she loved the man standing beside her.

Ma swatted Geordie's arm. "Afore the whisky starts flowing, I need a word with you."

The duke gaped like he'd been affronted, though his mien quickly softened and he offered his elbow with a polite bow of his head. "M'lady."

* * *

Geordie didn't escort Laini far, given her limp. They stopped in the shadows between two tents and he gently patted her shoulder, his heart flitting with anticipation. "Please tell me I have proven the depth of my love for Akira."

She chuckled in a low, raspy voice. "Many a man would have given up, and you did not. You took charge, you met with the marquis, you tried every peaceful resolution available to you, and when that failed, you acted swiftly with all the power owed to you as a duke of the kingdom."

He stood a bit taller. The woman had been fairly free with her jibes. This string of compliments was a side of her Geordie hadn't seen before. "So tell me, where is this magical key to eternal happiness?"

She thumped him in the chest. "'Tis right there in your heart, m'lord."

Dear Lord, there was absolutely no doubt from whom Akira had inherited her gumption.

"You will marry my daughter in a Gypsy wedding. It will be binding in the eyes of God. She will be called your wife, and she will sleep in your bed and provide you with my grandchildren."

"A Gypsy wedding?"

"Aye—and my brother, Bruno, is the one to preside over it."

"Is such a thing legal?"

"I married in a Gypsy wedding and nary a soul questioned our nuptials."

Geordie grinned, his mind racing.

*What if the queen discovers I wedded the lass without her permission? What would she do to me? Try to annul it? Hardly. Ban me from court for a year? I'd be overjoyed.*

He peered at the woman standing across from him. "If a Gypsy wedding can be held without permission of the bishop or queen, then I imagine neither party's move to annul it would be binding?"

"You are right." Laini shook a knowing finger.

"There would be no applications, no list of invitations, no royal ball, nothing except family and Clan Gordon." A weight lifted from his shoulders. "It would be like ancient times, where the clan chief had all the say. To hell with the usurping queen in London. No one needs to ken I intend to wed my Gypsy rose."

Laini patted his cheek. "We'll do it here at Dun Shith—the Hill of the Fairies. The magic will bring your marriage good fortune."

"Then we'll wed on the morrow." Grinning wider than he had in months, Geordie picked up Laini and swung her round, her crutch clanking to the ground.

"Put me down, ye big brute."

"Oh no." He spun her twice more. "You've just made me the happiest man in the Highlands."

* * *

Akira wrung her hands while Geordie and Ma were absent for their secret exchange. Ma could be a mite domineering, and the duke probably wasn't accustomed to taking brazen remarks from an old Gypsy woman.

But a sigh of relief whistled through her lips when they returned grinning like they'd just pinched an apple tart from a street vendor.

Geordie strode straight up to her and grasped her hand. "I have something to say," he announced, loud enough for all to hear, though his gaze never left her face.

As the hum of the crowd died down, he dropped to his knee.

Gooseflesh rose across her skin, every nerve ending alive. She couldn't breathe.

"Miss Akira, you saved me from certain death. You rode into danger when you could have fled. You stood by my side only because you cared for a wounded man. You are a healer who puts others before yourself. In my eyes you are the most beautiful woman in all of Scotland both inside and out. I love you and will love only you forever."

A tear slid down her cheek and her lips trembled.

He smoothed his hand over hers. "I have no ring in my sporran, but I give you my word you shall have rings and jewels to your heart's delight. Please, please, please tell me that you will be my wife."

Her throat closed, while tears of happiness poured down her face. She nodded. "I will," she squeaked, as he pulled her into his strong arms and wrapped her in warmth. "How?"

"There will be a Gypsy wedding at the fairy standing stone on the morrow." Ma clapped her hands with a happy grin.

Akira gaped at her mother. All her life, the woman had spurned the old ways, telling her children they were Scottish born and nothing else mattered. Never in Akira's life would she have thought about marrying in secret and in a Gypsy ceremony. It was scandalous—and ever so delicious.

The crowd bellowed their approval. Coll poured the whisky while Bruno and his band of minstrels provided the music. Who needed an enormous hall when they had a fire and stars twinkling above and were surrounded by the people she loved and a carpet of purple, green, and violet? They celebrated well into the night, while Akira stayed glued to her man.

Until Ma intervened. "Come. You will sleep beside me tonight, my sweeting."

# Chapter Thirty-Seven

There had been no mirror in which to regard his image when Geordie dressed for his wedding day. But it didn't seem to matter as he stood atop Dun Shith at the standing stone of Scotland's ancestors, wearing a plaid, a velvet doublet atop a linen shirt and cravat, his hair pulled back and tied at the nape.

"Are you ready, Your Grace?" Bruno asked.

Butterflies swarmed in his stomach. "Aye."

Clasping his hands behind his back, Geordie watched down the hill, where a footpath wound through the trees, edged with grass so green it could have been part of a painting. Wildflowers danced along the trail, teasing him as if they knew he had more than a few wee butterflies flitting inside. He rocked up and down on his toes. Despite his momentary jitters, he'd been more certain about making this commitment than he'd been about anything in his life.

His wedding to Elizabeth had been filled with pomp—

an empty mockery. There had been the betrothal and announcements, balls, and petitions to King William. Geordie had never looked upon the union as anything but a duty. Elizabeth, too.

But he didn't want to think of that ever again.

Today he stood in the chilly morning air, on grass kissed by Scotland's dew, surrounded by clan and kin. Birds sang and wisps of cloud sailed above. He inhaled the crisp scent of the Highlands. Heather and wildflowers brought the scene alive, as if butterfly fairies actually floated amidst the crowd, touching every shoulder with magical droplets of happiness. This was how a wedding should be, a joining of two souls under God's creation without all the pageantry, without meddlesome in-laws and stuffy formalities dictating behaviors.

He drew in a deep breath of clean air just as Akira stepped from behind a tree.

His exhale stuttered and his heart swelled. Everything faded into a blur—the flowers, the grass, the guests, the fairies.

His bride was the most stunning creature he had ever seen. Her black locks were adorned with a wreath of late-blooming mountain heather. The rich violet brought out the vivid color of her indigo eyes. She wore her tresses unbound and they kissed her hips with her graceful gait as she walked toward him. She wore a simple blue kirtle, laced in the front, and to Geordie, it was the most flattering gown he'd ever laid eyes upon. In her hands she held a posy of violet heather and fern, its ribbons of lace flowing with the breeze. And most beautifully, on her face, she wore a radiant smile—the very smile with which he'd fallen in love.

When she stepped into the circle of stones, her eyes twinkled with the sunlight, and a piper began a Highland ballad as Geordie watched her grow nearer.

When, finally, she joined him, he took her soft fingers in his. "Good morn, *mo leannan*."

"Good morn." An adorable blush blossomed in her cheeks as the bagpipes faded with the gentle breeze.

"I've never seen a woman so lovely."

She gave him a wee wink. "And I've never seen a man so braw."

Bruno cleared his throat and held up a stole. "Give me your hands."

Akira's uncle bound their wrists together while Annis and Scota sprinkled fresh earth in a circle around them.

Akira's pulse beat a steady rhythm, warming Geordie's wrist as Bruno held his hand under their wrists and waited for the lassies to finish making their circle.

When they completed their task, Bruno addressed the bride and groom. "The circle has been cast. You are now standing upon sacred ground, encircled by Mother Earth in a ring that cannot be broken. Do you understand this?"

"Aye," they said together.

"The circle itself is an infinite thing. It is magical and never-ending. It will never change and yet will always be adaptable." Bruno swayed to and fro. So did Akira. When she nudged him, Geordie followed.

"Like the circle, love is infinite, with no boundaries and no restrictions. Whether light or dark, it flourishes and blooms. Love is. It cannot be forced. It knows no limits. It cannot be taken away. Your love is a gift you grant each other with reverence and honor."

Bruno tightened the stole around their wrists. "You must pledge to each other your sacred gift of love."

When Bruno nodded at Geordie, he took the cue. "I pledge my love to you alone."

Akira blessed him with a smile. "And I pledge my love to you. You are the only man I have ever or will ever love."

Bruno raised their joined hands above his head. "When two people come together because their souls have found mutual love, it is the most sacred gift of all. They are joined as man and wife in the eyes of the heavens—in the stars above and on the earth of our mothers. They are two souls coming together to form one single being, two hearts beating in perfect rhythm."

The brash Gypsy minstrel with his untamed hair unwrapped the stole with a cockeyed grin. "Congratulations. You are married."

Geordie's heart soared like stars.

Never in his life had he experienced such happiness.

Wrapping his woman in his arms, he dipped his chin and plied her with a real kiss. Not a kiss fit for a church ceremony, but a meaningful connection of lips. An act of sealing their bond—one that would never be severed.

* * *

Ever since she stepped from behind the tree and joined Geordie in the circle of matrimony, Akira had floated like a cloud. Everything seemed magical, as if she'd indeed been touched by the fairies. During the ceremony, standing in the circle of stones, she could have sworn they were floating. It wasn't until after Geordie kissed her that she'd realized her feet were planted on the ground.

And now, music swirled around them as people danced and made merry, eating venison and drinking MacDonell whisky.

Sitting beside her on a plaid, Geordie bit into a honeyed crisp, then held it to her lips. "Mm. Made this morn by the locals—try some."

When she nipped a bite, the pastry melted on her tongue. "Mm, it tastes sweet and buttery."

He held up a pewter tankard. "Sip."

The whisky tasted mellow with the crisp, but it still burned a bit going down. Akira wiped her mouth.

"Did you like it?" he asked.

"Very much." Right now nothing could spoil her merriment. How did this happen? She'd married a duke?

*No, not a duke, but a braw Highlander who will be mine forever.*

Oliver stopped by their plaid. "The horses are ready, Your Grace."

Akira knit her brows. "Horses?"

Geordie grinned like he did when he had a devilish scheme. "You don't expect to spend your wedding night in a tent, now do you?"

Her heart skipped a beat. Och aye, she loved it when his eyes flashed with a wee bit of mischief. "You have a plan?"

"I always have a plan."

And since the horses were saddled, it must mean they were traveling farther than a mile or two. She leaned closer. "But what of Ma and my sisters?"

Geordie affected a frown. "I didn't marry *them*."

She opened her mouth to protest, but he brushed her cheek with the back of his finger. "Not to worry, *mo leannan*. Oliver will ensure they meet us at Huntly." He winked. "But now we ride. I want to take advantage of what's left of daylight."

They slipped away quietly. Once they were mounted, Akira asked, "Where are we headed?"

He took a trail leading northwest. "My hunting lodge."

"You have property up here?"

"Aye, I have a great deal of property—some even the queen doesn't ken about."

They rode for an hour, maybe two. Akira lost track of the time. It didn't matter. She was with her man, her Highlander. Her family was safe and fed and warm. She had not a worry in the world.

When, finally, the path opened to a clearing, Geordie stopped his horse.

"Good heavens," Akira said, staring at a castle with turrets on two sides. "You call this a hunting lodge?"

"Aye, 'tis a bit rustic, but I thought you wouldn't mind—besides, it's better than a tent."

Inside, the fire was lit in the hall—in an immense fireplace higher than Akira's head. "Is there a watchman?"

Geordie tugged her hand. "Aye, but he will not be bothering us this eve. Come. I've a flagon of wine waiting in the lord's chamber."

Up the wheeled stairwell, Akira followed him, their footsteps resounding as if they were the only two people in the Highlands. He led her down a passageway, opened a door, and bowed. "M'lady."

She curtsied. "Your Grace."

He caught her hand and pulled her inside. "To me you will always be my only true duchess. You will never want for anything."

Melting into his arms, she closed her eyes and kissed him as he swept her off her feet and carried her to the hearth.

She unfastened the brooch at her neck and allowed her arisaid to drop to the floor. "The fire's warm." Hardly aware of her surroundings, she glanced back at the four-poster bed. Aye, that was all they needed for now.

He sucked in a sharp inhale as she tugged the laces on her kirtle. "I want to see you bare."

Akira's body shuddered. She wanted to be naked with this man, skin to skin. So many times when she'd lain abed at night, she'd ached to be with him, ached to join with him as God intended a man and a woman to share passion. She wanted to feel him wrap her in his arms and love her like she was the queen over all the fairies.

She stood very still while he removed layer after layer. As every piece of clothing dropped to the floor, the insides of her thighs quivered a bit more. The heat surging in her nether parts grew more intense, and the tips of her breasts became ever so sensitive, craving his lips upon them.

And after he swept her shift over her head, how erotic it felt to be completely naked and standing in front of Geordie while he was still clothed. She liked it when his lips parted with a gasp as he stood back and made love to her with his eyes.

But it wasn't enough.

She ran her hands down his hard stomach, feeling ripples of muscle beneath her fingertips. "Now you."

He grinned. "I'll give you a wee bit of help." Before she blinked, he slipped out of his doublet, unpinned his plaid at the shoulder, released his belt, and sent his kilt sailing to the floor. He reached for the hem of his shirt, but Akira stilled his hands.

Her hips swished as she stepped into him, every inch of her skin firing with desire. "I'll do it."

Very slowly she exposed him, tugging the shirt higher and higher until he had to help her pull it over his head. She stood back and regarded him—chiseled male perfection—as the firelight danced across his skin. She couldn't help but touch him, moving both hands over his velvety soft skin, swirling her fingers down the dark trail of hair running from his navel to the tight curls above his swollen manhood.

But she didn't touch it—not yet. Stepping a bit closer, she placed a finger in the center of his chest, her tongue slipping to the corner of her mouth. "This time I want to ravish *you*."

He growled—a low, feral moan that told her how much he liked her idea.

She moved her finger down, down until she met his navel, then swirled circles inside.

Again he let loose a rapturous moan—a sound that pulsed through her body as if he'd touched her between the legs. "You'll bring me undone if you keep teasing me like that."

Drawing out the moment, she slowly moved her finger lower and chuckled. "But that's what I want." Her voice came out deep and breathless.

When she wrapped her fingers around his manhood, his eyes rolled back and his knees flexed. "My God."

She could scarcely inhale as she smoothed her hand up and down. "Can I kiss it like you did to me?"

He shuddered as he gazed into her eyes. "If you'd like."

Licking her lips, Akira dropped her gaze. "Will I hurt it?"

He smiled. "Nay, you cannot hurt me with a kiss."

He backed to the bed and lay on his back. Akira slid beside him. Taking his enormous member in her hand, she pressed her lips to the tip. Geordie released a deep rumbling moan, his hips moving jolting reflexively. His reaction making her hotter, she timidly licked him.

"Aye, that's it, lass."

Emboldened by his encouragement, Akira opened her mouth wider and swirled her tongue around and around, up and down. His breathing grew labored, his moans more frequent, as he shuddered in concert with her licks.

Panting, Geordie tugged her up. "You want to ride me, woman?"

She gulped. "Aye."

"Then mount me like you would a horse."

Akira straddled him, her body completely afire, her womanhood clenching with need. Rocking her hips back, she rubbed her wetness along his length.

"You're so wet for me, I have to feel my cock inside you." Grasping her hips, Geordie moved so his member pushed against her, hard and thick. She wanted him to make love to her. And the more he panted, the hungrier she grew.

Needing friction, needing him deeper, she brazenly grabbed his shoulders and impaled herself on his erection.

His eyelids heavy, those hazel eyes full of lust, he looked like a god of passion. "Do. Not. Stop," he growled, commanding the tempo with his powerful fingers sinking into her buttocks as he plunged in and out.

Ripples of wild need quaked through her body. Her mind focused only on Geordie and his magnificence as, faster and faster, her hips rocked in a frenzied motion.

"I'm coming," he said, bucking into her and quaking against her.

With two more thrusts of her hips, the world burst into a maelstrom of raw passion. She arched her back and cried out, while shudders coursed through her body.

Then at once she dropped atop his chest, fully spent, fully satiated, fully loved.

Geordie smoothed his hand up her spine. “Was it good for you, wife?”

“Unbelievably wondrous,” she said, her insides still quivering.

“Ye ken the best part?” He captured her mouth with a wee kiss. “We can do it again and again. For a lifetime.”

# *Chapter Thirty-Eight*

Two days later, Geordie and Akira caught up with the Gordon retinue not far from Huntly. Ma, Scota, and Kynda rode in a wagon, while Annis rode a horse all by herself, taking up the rear alongside Oliver.

Akira smiled and waggled her eyebrows at her husband. "I think my sister is flirting with your man-at-arms."

Geordie glanced over his shoulder. "Mm hmm. Oliver is a good man."

"You approve, then?"

"Absolutely."

"Then I shall not worry."

An easy smile stretched Geordie's lips. "We shall ride into the courtyard first to greet Alexander and Jane, then we will take your family to the dower house."

Akira didn't have to see the castle in the distance to know it was in sight: The resumption of Geordie's commanding tenor indicated they were near. Mayhap he needed a wee adjustment so he'd be her Geordie even when at Huntly. "What if I think we should do it the other way around?"

He frowned. "But Alexander and Jane will ken we've arrived."

"That's not my point. What if I disagree?" She arched an eyebrow. "Will you take a moment to listen to my side?"

"As long as it is something that won't hurt my children's feelings, I'll listen to anything you have to say."

"Excellent." She smiled. "Then I think we should definitely stop by the courtyard and collect Alex and Jane afore proceeding to the dower house." She twisted her mouth. "Are you certain Lady Elizabeth will not be there?"

"That I can vouch for. I received a missive from Mr. Wallis before leaving Dunkeld, and she has returned to Flanders."

"Thank heavens." She clapped her hands. "I can barely wait to see Ma's face."

Geordie returned her grin with a devilish one of his own. "Me as well."

The stop in the courtyard didn't last long. Geordie didn't say anything to the children about the fact that they had a new stepmother, but the pair were delighted to see them and anxious to accompany the retinue to the dower house. Alex hopped up behind his father, Jane behind Akira.

The young lass wrapped her arms tight around Akira's waist. "I kent you'd come back."

"You did?"

"Aye, because Da loves you."

Akira looked to Geordie. "I think you should tell them."

"Tell us what?" asked Alexander. "Did you find a way to marry Miss Akira?"

Geordie snorted. "Where did you come up with a notion like that?"

The lad rolled his eyes. "Good God, I'm nearly twelve years of age, Da."

"Watch your mouth, son."

Akira covered her lips to hold in her laugh. Aye, she'd heard the duke use such a curse far too often.

"Well then, aye. *Lady* Akira is now your stepmother."

"I knew it!" Jane squeezed tighter. "You will be staying with us forever."

Arriving at the dower house, the entire retinue stopped. Akira and Jane dismounted and dashed to the wagon. Akira made the introductions all around, which seemed to take forever.

Jane grasped Kynda's hand. "Would you like to see the rooms abovestairs?"

The wee lass who'd stolen the key from the captain to set her sister free grinned like she'd just been kissed by the queen. "There's more?"

"Ever so much more. Come with me—we can go exploring." Jane tugged Kynda's hand and they disappeared into the manse with delighted squeals.

Geordie lifted Ma down from the wagon. Once she had her crutch ready, he offered his elbow. "Would you care to see your new home, m'lady?"

Ma blanched, her gaze shooting to Akira. "This?"

"Aye."

Geordie strengthened his grip as Ma swooned a bit. "Holy fairies, I think I need to pinch meself."

Alexander offered his elbow to Scota. "May I escort you inside?"

"Ah." The lass blushed, but she slowly took his arm. "My thanks."

"I'm practicing to be a duke," the lad said, puffing out his chest.

Scota grinned like it was Christmas morn. "I reckon you're doing a fine job of it, too, m'lord."

Akira watched, a smile playing on her lips.

*Goodness gracious, so many possibilities and they've all only just met.*

Uncle Bruno slapped Akira's backside as he followed the entourage into the house. "I kent you'd land a big fish." Then he leaned in and whispered, "You are the queen of the fairies."

* * *

When at last everyone was settled in the dower house and Laini had recovered from the shock of moving from a hovel with a dirt floor to a manse decorated in the latest French style, Geordie was able to spirit his bride away from all the excitement and steal a moment alone.

He pulled her into his immense castle foyer festooned with antlers, with displays of medieval weapons on the walls, and kissed her. "I've been wanting to do that all afternoon."

"I'm ever so glad you did." Rising up, she kissed him again. "Do you realize I've never been in your bedchamber afore?"

Geordie swept his Gypsy rose into his arms. "That is something I must rectify straightaway." She felt featherlight in his arms as he started up the stairwell. "Would you prefer to see the duchess's chamber or the duke's chamber first?"

Her lips twisted. "I kent you and—well, that other woman—were in discord, but isn't the duchess supposed to sleep beside the duke?"

"Mayhap not when the marriage is for lands and riches rather than for love." He chuckled, his gaze sweeping down to hers. He would never grow tired of looking into those deep blue eyes, made more prominent by Akira's black lashes. He liked that she wanted to stay with him. "But the duchess has her suite of rooms just as I do."

"Oh." She looked away, pursing her lips.

"Though I'd like it very much if you shared my chamber."

"You would?"

"Aye."

"Then what should we do with the duchess's chamber?" she asked.

"Whatever you wish. You must order new tapestries and new furniture and make it your own."

He thought that would make her happy, but a furrow formed in her brow.

Geordie stepped out into the passageway. "Is something troubling you?"

"It seems there is so much to learn. Last time I was here, I felt out of sorts—like I didn't belong."

"Believe me, you belong. You are the love of my life and I want you with me wherever I go."

"I worry the servants will laugh at me."

"If anyone dares, I will turn them out on their ear. I'll not tolerate anyone in my household who is disrespectful to you or your kin."

Her teeth grazed her bottom lip. "It's not going to be easy at first."

"I think you'll take to being duchess of Huntly like a queen bee to her hive."

"I hope you're right."

He kicked the door open and carried her across the threshold. "Our chamber, Your Grace."

Akira blinked, looking at him rather than the impressive suite. "That's the first time you've called me Your Grace."

He set her down and kissed her forehead. "Do you like it?"

"Not sure."

"Then I shall only refer to you thus when we are being very serious."

"Good." She grasped his hand and stepped further into the chamber, taking in everything. She stopped at the four-poster bed with its red silk canopy. "I do believe this is big enough."

"Are you jesting?" He chuckled. "That's the largest bed between Inverness and Aberdeen."

"'Tis a good thing," she said with a wicked sparkle in her eyes. "I think we need a bed this size for all the fun we'll be having."

His heart took flight and soared. "I've waited all my life to hear such words."

Akira squealed as Geordie swept her into his arms and tumbled onto their enormous bed. "Let the games begin, lady wife."

# *Author's Note*

Thank you for joining me for *The Highland Duke*! This story was incredibly fun to write. It's very loosely based on George Gordon, the first Duke of Gordon. I exercised a plethora of literary license when I discovered he was, in his day, considered a libertine and fop. Indeed, his wife and duchess, Elizabeth, divorced him and retired to a convent in Flanders.

Among other things, I adjusted the duke's age to fit with the timeline of the Lords of the Highlands series. The Duke of Gordon was a Jacobite, and in 1689 he held Edinburgh Castle against Protestant Conventionists. He gained favor with Queen Anne when he was recognized by her as a Knight of the Thistle, though the duke, being a true Gordon, couldn't stay out of trouble for long. In March 1708, he was arrested with several other lords for being implicated in the "Old Pretender's" failed Jacobite invasion. Fortunately, they were all released (this time) with no lands or titles forfeited.

But all fallen angels deserve a second chance, and I

saw it as my duty to provide His Grace the Duke of Gordon with a fresh affair in which he could exonerate himself and give his heart once and for all. Akira Ayres is a fictional character. Interestingly, in the late seventeenth century the Privy Council did vote to ban all Gypsies from Scotland. Many people of Romany blood either fled to England or melded into society, giving up their traveling "tinker" ways and settling into Scotland's burghs as Akira's family did.

The Battle of Hoord Moor is fictional, but Sir Coll of Keppoch is not, though I did alter his age by a few years. I also took literary license with his last name, changing it from MacDonald to MacDonell, because the hero in *The Valiant Highlander* was Donald MacDonald, and I felt it would be less confusing if I employed Coll's clan name of MacDonell. Besides, I do believe there might be a book for Sir Coll on the horizon.

I hope you'll join me for the next in the series, *The Highland Commander*, about Aiden Murray, the handsome young man with a cameo appearance in this book, who met with Geordie while he was awaiting an audience with the Marquis of Atholl (who became the Duke of Atholl).

Please see the next page for a preview of

# THE HIGHLAND COMMANDER

the second book in the Lords of the Highlands series.

Available in Summer 2017

# *Chapter One*

*31 December 1707*

After riding from the port of Stonehaven to Dunnottar Castle, First Lieutenant Aiden Murray stepped out of the coach and stretched. Dear Lord, it felt good to be off the ship.

"Bloody oath, 'tis so cold my cods are about to freeze." Second Lieutenant Tearlach MacBride must have received top marks in complaining at the university, for he never ceased to have something unpleasant to say.

"Then you'd best keep moving, else someone else will be plowing your wife's roses," said Captain Thomas Polwarth—God love the man, he could be counted on for a stern retort to any complaint.

Aiden had heard tales of the magnificence of Dunnottar, but even beneath the cover of darkness, the dramatic fortress dominating the expansive peninsula ahead left him awestruck. A steep path led down to the shore, and from there torches illuminated hundreds of steps climbing to the arched gateway, looking like something straight out of medieval folklore. On the wall walk above, sentries stood guard, their forms lit by braziers with flames leaping high on this chilly eve.

"This way." Aiden beckoned, leading the men down the steep path. "I'm starved."

"Have you been here afore, Your Lordship?" Aiden's superior officer, the captain, only used his formal address to be an arse.

"Never, sir."

"I would have thought the duke and the earl would have been best mates."

Aiden looked skyward with a shake of his head. "Not likely. My da's a Whig and the earl sides with the Tory party."

"Bloody Whigs," said MacPherson.

Aiden chose not to respond to that remark. Since the Act of Union one year past forced the merger of Scotland's navy with England's, he'd grown more sympathetic with the Tories as well. Though he'd rather not let his loyalties become common knowledge at the moment. He'd be the one to break the news to his father in due course.

As they started the steep climb up to the gates, the captain slipped and crashed into Aiden's back. "God's teeth, 'tis slicker than an icy deck."

Steadying Polwarth with his elbow, Aiden chuckled under his breath. Fit as a stag, he could sprint up the steep slope to the gate even with ice making the stone steps slippery. And it was all he could do to suppress his urge to run. Officers didn't race through castle gates like wee lads. But by the saints, he'd been aboard the *Royal Mary* for the past month without setting foot ashore. Bloody oath, he intended to kick up his heels this eve—swill ale, swing the lassies in a reel—mayhap he'd even find a bonny lass he fancied.

*Damn the cold.*

*Damn political posturing.*

*Damn the war.*

*And whilst I'm at it, damn the queen.*

This was Hogmanay—a pagan Scottish holiday—and he would enjoy the piss out of it for once in his miserable, highborn life.

Before he reached the gate, he stopped and regarded his companions, thirty paces behind and looking like a gaggle of old men. "Put on your bloody masks."

"What?" sniggered MacPherson. "Do you not want to hear your name boomed throughout the hall?"

MacBride laughed. "The right royal and very miserable..."

"Don't forget honorable," piped Captain Polwarth.

True, Aiden could tolerate a ribbing from his mates, but the captain? Good God, he was sunk.

"Aye, the miserable yet honorable Lord Aiden Murray," MacBride finished.

"Shut it." Aiden tied his mask in place just beneath his tricorn hat. The officers had received masks from groomsmen once they'd reached the shore—compliments of the earl, as were the coaches that had ferried them to the castle. "Last I checked, I was First Lieutenant Murray, division officer of the Watch."

Stepping beside him, Captain Polwarth clapped his shoulder. "Nay, tonight you're a courtier behind a mask, m'lord."

"A rogue," said MacBride.

MacPherson snorted. "A rake."

"I'm a bloody maker of merriment." Aiden gave Fraser a shove. "Give me a meal and a tankard of ale and I'll be in heaven."

"Not me. I'm looking for a woman to ignite my fire." MacPherson secured his long-beaked mask in place. At least Aiden didn't have to put up with a crook on his face that looked like a phallus.

MacBride pushed to the lead. "Ye ken what you need, Murray?"

Aiden followed beneath the sharp-spiked portcullis. "I ken I bloody well do not need you to tell me."

"Och aye?" MacBride snorted. "'Tis on account of you're too embarrassed."

"You're full of shite." Aiden threw his shoulders back and clenched his fists. He could best every one of them, and showing an iota of fear now would only serve to elicit a month of jibes in the officers' quarters—but he knew what was coming, and the twist in his gut merely increased his dread.

"I agree with MacBride." MacPherson jabbed him in the shoulder. "Young Aiden here needs to dip his wick."

"Ye miserable, ox-brained maggot." Aiden could have slammed his fist into the papier-mâché beak on the bastard's mask. They'd all guessed he was a virgin, though he'd *never* admitted it to a soul. How in God's name was he supposed to sample the offerings of the finer sex? He'd matriculated at the university at the age of seventeen, spent three years with his nose in volumes of books, and from there went straight into the Scots Navy, where he'd scarcely had a chance to step ashore. Aye, the whores in port always tempted him, rubbing their buxom breasts against his chest, but it only took one peek at a flesh ulcer to turn his gut inside out.

At the age of two and twenty, the last thing he needed was to contract the bloody pox.

Regardless, Aiden refused to allow MacPherson's remark to pass. Oh no. There wasn't a self-respecting sailor in all of Christendom who wasn't man enough to come back with a retort. "And whilst we're ashore, make certain you go shag your mother."

*Take that, ye bastard.*

Before the braggart could take a swing and start a brawl on the icy gateway steps, a yeoman stepped between them. "Welcome to the Royal Scots Navy."

Aiden shot a look to Captain Polwarth and grinned. "It seems news of the Act of Union hasn't reached this far north."

"Beg your pardon, sir," said the yeoman. "Only the *Royal Mary* and the *Caledonia* are moored in our harbor. Mark me, no bleeding English warships would be welcomed to a Hogmanay gathering at Dunnottar."

"I would think no less from the Earl Marischal," said the captain.

"Indeed." The yeoman gestured to the gatehouse. "Gentlemen, if you'll check your weapons, we shall escort you to the gallery forthwith."

Once inside the enormous fortress grounds, a sentry ushered Aiden and the officers past the old keep to the North Range, where stood the more modern buildings of the castle. Luck rained down upon them when he found the dining hall spread with platters piled with meats and slices of fine white bread to fill his gullet. Aiden continually ate like a glutton, yet never managed to put on an ounce of fat.

Tankard of ale in hand, he and Lieutenant Fraser MacPherson headed from the dining hall to the long gallery where the music had already grown jaunty. Though constantly at odds, Aiden always stepped ashore with the stout Highlander, the son of the MacPherson laird. They quarreled like brothers, though if Aiden had to choose anyone from the crew to watch his back, it would be Fraser MacPherson...or the captain.

Aiden jabbed his mate in the ribs. "Why did you choose a beaked mask? You look like a charlatan."

"Isn't that what a masquerade is about?" MacPherson's grin stretched under the ugly black nose. "Besides, the lassies like charlatans."

Aiden rather doubted such wisdom. "Do they now?"

"Aye, but you wouldn't ken anything about that, young pup."

"Two years my senior and you're so much wiser in the ways of the world, aye?" Pushing through the crowd toward a gathering of more masked gentlemen, Aiden took a healthy swallow of ale.

"Agreed." MacPherson slapped him on the back, making froth slop down Aiden's doublet.

He brushed away the mess. "Well then, why is it I outrank you?"

"That's easy. Your father's a duke."

Nothing like a cutting slight to make Aiden's gut clench—most every officer in the navy was a second son of a noble lord. "You ken as well as I my da has nothing to do with my rank." Holy Christ, how many times must he prove himself? Being the second son of a duke should have made his lot easier, but thus far his birthright had brought only a heavier burden. Aiden learned early on he had to be better skilled with a sword, have better aim with a musket, be wittier at the captain's table, and sing like a lark while doing it all.

"Jesus, I've died and have gone to heaven." MacPherson's jaw dropped like a simpleton's while he gaped at the dancers.

Aiden followed his friend's line of sight. With a quick inhale, he tightened his fist around his tankard's handle. The woman dancing a reel smiled as if a dozen torches formed an archway around her. She wore a shimmering blue gown, and her fair hair curled down the back of a slender neck, secured by a plume of feathers. Though a bejeweled mask hid part of her face, by the smile on her rosy lips Aiden could tell the lass was bonny—possibly the bonniest woman in—

MacPherson gave him a nudge. "I saw her first."

Aiden arched an eyebrow. "Stand down. That's an order." Being a senior officer did have its merits and before the braggart could make a move, Aiden strode straight to the line of dancers. He tapped the lady's partner on the shoulder. "Cutting in."

The man gave a haughty cough. "I beg your pardon? Have you officers forgotten your manners whilst at sea?"

"Forgive me, sir. I meant no impertinence, 'tis just that the ship sets sail at dawn and I haven't much time." Perhaps the rake in him had finally come to call. Aiden handed the man his tankard of ale, then stared directly at the lady, who stood aghast with her hands on her hips while the other dancers skipped in a circle. He bowed slowly and politely. The last thing he needed was to ruin his chances before he even kent the lassie's name. "Forgive me, m'lady. Have mercy on a young lieutenant. On the morrow I'll be back at sea for months on end, leagues away from civilization."

Gripping the tankard with white knuckles, the man didn't budge. "Do you approve, my dear?"

The beauty gave Aiden a look from head to toe. "Very well. After all, you told me to ensure the officers enjoy the merriment this eve."

Aiden sized up the man. Far older, he was nearly as tall and broad-shouldered, he wore finely tailored velvet and sported a periwig that had not a hair out of place. Recognizing nobility, Aiden again bowed. "I thank you, m'lord."

The lass resumed the reel, regarding Aiden with an enormous pair of blue eyes peeping through her mask—blues as hypnotizing as a shimmering crystal.

He quickly joined the men's line, thanking his mother for her interminable enforced hours of dreary dancing lessons.

"You're light on your feet for a sailor," she said as they moved together and joined elbows. Heavens, her voice sounded alluring like nothing he'd before heard.

"Thank you." A subtle grin played across his lips. "But my polish is nothing compared to your grace."

She actually laughed out loud—quite audacious for a lady. "It must be exciting to see exotic places."

A frigate, the *Royal Mary* mainly patrolled the waters of Scotland, and now England. Not exactly exotic. "Aye, but 'tisn't much fun when you're under cannon fire."

Those blues grew rounder beneath her mask. "Cannons?"

"Aye, we are at war, miss."

They parted as he took his place in the men's line and waited for the next couple to sashay through. Across the aisle, the dance partner seemed enlivened by their separation, smiling and clapping. Though poised like a queen, there was something about her that was more common. Possibly explained by the fact she actually looked like she was having a good time rather than donning aristocratic airs and pretending she but merely endured the dance.

The tune ended and Aiden dipped into a bow, but he knew the fun to be had this night was only just beginning.

Amy Jarecki is a descendant of an ancient Lowland clan and adores Scotland. Though she now resides in southwest Utah, she received her MBA from Heriot-Watt University in Edinburgh. Winning multiple writing awards, she found her niche in the genre of Scottish historical romance. Amy writes steamy edge-of-your-seat action adventures with rugged men and fascinating women who weave their paths through the brutal eras of centuries past. Amy loves hearing from her readers and can be contacted through her website at AmyJarecki.com.

*Fall in Love with Forever Romance*

**A SMALL-TOWN BRIDE**
**By Hope Ramsay**

Amy Lyndon is tired of being "the poor little rich girl" of Shenandoah Falls. In her prominent family, she's the *ordinary* one—no Ivy League education and no powerful career. But when her father tries to marry her off, she finally has to stand up for herself, despite the consequences. Cut off from the family fortune, her first challenge is to find a job. And she's vowed to never rely on another man ever again, no matter how hot or how handsome.

## *Fall in Love with Forever Romance*

**HOLDING FIRE**
**By April Hunt**

Alpha Security operative Trey Hanson is ready to settle down. When he meets a gorgeous blonde in a bar, and the connection between them is off the charts, he thinks he's finally found the one. But after their night together ends in a hail of gunfire and she disappears in the chaos, Trey's reasons for tracking her down are personal... until he learns she's his next assignment. Fans of Rebecca Zanetti and Julie Ann Walker will love the newest romantic suspense novel from April Hunt!

**THE HIGHLAND DUKE**
**By Amy Jarecki**

Fans of *Outlander* will love this sweeping Scottish epic from award-winning author Amy Jarecki. When Akira Ayres finds a brawny Scot with a musket ball in his thigh, the healer will do whatever it takes to save his life... even fleeing with him across the Highlands. Geordie knows if Akira discovers his true identity, both their lives will be jeopardized. The only way to protect the lass is to keep her by his side. But the longer he's with her, the harder it becomes to imagine letting her go...

*Fall in Love with Forever Romance*

**CRAZY FOR YOU**
**By Rachel Lacey**

Emma Rush can't remember a time when she didn't have a thing for Ryan Blake. The small town's resident bad boy is just so freakin' hot—with tattoos, a motorcycle, and enough rough-around-the-edges sexiness to melt all her self-control. Now that Emma's over being a "good girl," she needs a little help being naughty…and Ryan is the perfect place to start.